W9-BOY-286

THE THIN BLUE LINE

THE THIN BLUE LINE

CHRISTOPHER G. NUTTALL

The characters and events portrayed in this book are fictitious. Any similarity to real persons, living or dead, is coincidental and not intended by the author.

Text copyright © 2017 Christopher G. Nuttall
All rights reserved.
No part of this book may be reproduced, or stored in a retrieval system, or transmitted in any form or by any means, electronic, mechanical, photocopying, recording, or other-wise, without express written permission of the publisher.

ISBN-13: 9781544261683
ISBN-10: 1544261683

http://www.chrishanger.net
http://chrishanger.wordpress.com/
http://www.facebook.com/ChristopherGNuttall

All Comments Welcome!

HISTORIAN'S NOTE

The Thin Blue Line starts one standard month after *When The Bough Breaks*.

PROLOGUE

"It doesn't look very comfortable from up here, does it?"

Captain Kevin Vaughn – who was only a Captain by courtesy – turned and smiled at his sole crewmember. Cynthia was a bright young thing, a girl from a diehard Marine family who had insisted on becoming a spacer rather than a groundpounder like her father, brothers or cousins. He had to admire her resistance to peer pressure, even though he privately doubted that she would have survived the Slaughterhouse. It chewed up and broke an alarmingly high percentage of young recruits who made it through six months of Boot Camp.

"The Slaughterhouse isn't meant to be comfortable," he said, feeling his legs itch. It was psychometric, the shrinks had said; he'd lost his legs on an operation that had gone badly wrong and had to have them regrown in a tube. "It's meant to push its victims to the limits."

He sighed as he gazed down at the planet below. The Slaughterhouse was a confused patchwork of environments, each one possessing its own nasty surprises for unwary recruits, the result of a failed terraforming program. By now, keeping its environment as uncomfortable as possible required a full-time crew, who did everything from replace topsoil to introducing nasty critters from right across the Empire. The Slaughterhouse might break far too many of the recruits, but those who survived were the best damned soldiers in all of history.

"Everything is in working order," Cynthia assured him. "How long do we have to remain here again?"

Kevin shrugged. The Commandant's orders had been clear. *Polly* was to remain behind in orbit after the evacuation, watching and waiting, until something happened. Something had already happened, Kevin had thought rebelliously when he'd been given his orders, but he'd done as he was told. The empty planet below was living history, even if it was a part of history most of the Empire would prefer to forget. Watching it from high orbit was not a particularly unpleasant task.

"As long as we are ordered to do so," he said, patiently. Cynthia was young. She'd learn patience soon enough. "Besides, it does give us a chance to run all those checks we never managed to do before the state of emergency was declared."

He sighed, inwardly. The reports had been all too clear. Earth had been destroyed, her society ripped apart by social conflict, then smashed flat as pieces of debris fell from orbit and struck the surface with terrifying force. Kevin had no particular attachment to Earth – he'd been born on a planet hundreds of light years away – but it was still horrifying. Mother Earth might have been a poisoned, polluted mess, home to literally billions of civilians who did nothing but suck at the government's teat, yet she was still the homeworld of humanity, the planet that had birthed a hundred thousand colony worlds. To know she was gone was terrifying.

Something has been removed from our lives, he thought. He'd heard any number of rumours before the Commandant had ordered the Slaughterhouse closed down, with all of the staff and recruits moved to a secure – and secret – location. *And nothing will ever be the same.*

"I could bring you a cup of coffee, if you're busy wool-gathering," Cynthia said. "Or would you like to find something else for me to do?"

"Coffee would be nice," Kevin said. "And..."

He broke off as an alarm sounded. "Contact," he snapped. "Man your station!"

Cynthia obeyed, scrambling into her chair and bringing the sensor console online. *Polly* was really nothing more than a handful of passive sensors and stealth systems, mounted on a squashed drive unit that had been pared down to the bare minimum. Kevin had no illusions about what would happen if they were detected, even by something as small as a gunboat or a corvette. He and his ship would be blown out of space before they knew they were under attack.

"I have five contacts, all coming out of cloak," Cynthia snapped. "They must have realised there's no one here to greet them."

Kevin nodded, unsurprised. The Slaughterhouse was barely defended, compared to Earth or Terra Nova. No one in their right mind would consider attacking the Slaughterhouse when the reputation of the Marine Corps reached right across the galaxy. But Earth was gone and nothing would ever be quite the same. Who knew what was about to happen now?

"That wouldn't have been hard," Kevin said. They weren't in the best position for optimal observation, but they were close enough to separate individual targets. It helped that the newcomers weren't even trying to hide. "Give me a complete breakdown, if you can."

"Three destroyers," Cynthia said. "All *Falcone*-class, I think, but one of them has been heavily modified. The other two are light cruisers, probably *Peacock*-class. They appear to be standard specification, sir."

"From a self-defence force, then," Kevin said. That proved nothing. A number of star systems possessed semi-independent self-defence forces. The Grand Senate had regularly considered bills to disarm them, only to run into the threat of outright rebellion. "There aren't any *Peacocks* left in the Imperial Navy."

"Ship-spotter," Cynthia accused. On the display, the small flotilla moved into orbit, scanning aggressively. "What are they doing here?"

"Good question," Kevin said. "I have a feeling we're not going to like the answer."

The unknowns, whoever they were, were thorough. It was nearly forty minutes of constant scanning before they decided, apparently, that the planet was abandoned. Kevin wouldn't have taken that for granted, not with the Slaughterhouse; he'd seen entire army divisions carefully camouflaged against orbital observation. There were no shortage of places where the Marines could have hidden their personnel, if they'd remained on the planet. Planets were big, after all. Spacers had a nasty habit of forgetting just how difficult it could be to move from one place to another.

Particularly if there's an enemy force trying to stop you, Kevin thought, with grim amusement. *It can take days to move from one system to another, but it can take weeks to move a hundred kilometres if the enemy is willing to do whatever it takes to slow you down.*

Cynthia tapped his shoulder. "What are they doing?"

"I don't know," Kevin said, shortly. "I..."

An alarm sounded. "Missile separation," Cynthia said, swinging her chair back to her console. "Multiple missile separations...sir, they're firing on the planet!"

Kevin swore. The Slaughterhouse was living history. Hundreds of thousands, perhaps millions, of Marines had emerged from the Slaughterhouse to fight for the Empire. The structures on the surface contained histories and relics the rest of the Empire, even the military, had chosen to forget. And it was part of a tradition he'd embraced with all his heart, long ago. To be forced to watch it die...

"Airburst detonations," Cynthia said. "Sir...I don't understand."

"Radioactive poison," Kevin said. Planet-killing weapons were forbidden, full stop. Bombarding a planet was one thing, but actively rendering it uninhabitable...the entire galaxy would rise up in horror. "I..."

He gritted his teeth in bitter frustration as lethal radiation spread through the planet's atmosphere. Within days, there would be nothing left alive on the surface, unless it was *very* well protected. Even combat suits would be hard-pressed to shield their users against such levels of radiation. It would be years before radiation levels dropped to the point that anything could be recovered from the surface, then it would need intensive decontamination before it could be touched safely. He sought, frantically, for options, but found nothing.

There was nothing he could do but watch, helplessly, as the Slaughterhouse died.

CHAPTER

ONE

The law, as the old saying goes, is the true embodiment of society. One can tell a great deal about a society by what it chooses to forbid and what it chooses to permit – and, perhaps more importantly, how it handles crimes.

- Professor Leo Caesius, *The Decline of Law and Order and the Rise of Anarchy*

Earth was gone.

Marshall (Detective Inspector) Glen Cheal shook his head bitterly as the unmarked van made its way through Terra Nova's darkened streets. The sun was setting in the sky, the remaining shoppers hurrying home for fear of being caught outside after curfew. Everywhere he looked he could see the signs of decay and despair; closed shops, abandoned vehicles and armed guards everywhere. It wouldn't be long, he thought as they drove past a soup kitchen, before Terra Nova followed Earth into the fire.

He caught sight of his own reflection in the wing mirror and shivered. His brown hair was turning grey, his skin leathered and lined after too many stressful years as an Imperial Marshal. It was impossible to escape the feeling that he was old, old and tired. After Hazel had died, after his unborn daughter had died with her, part of him had just wanted to give up on life. Or maybe it was just a reflection of the lost Earth. What was humanity without its homeworld?

"Sandy's been volunteering at her local kitchen," Marshall (Detective) Isabel Freeman said, softly. "She says it's getting harder to find anything, even processed algae."

1

Glen nodded, unsurprised. The soup kitchens were the only places still feeding vast numbers of people who had been rendered suddenly destitute by the economic crash, when they'd discovered that all the money they'd invested in the imperial banking system had suddenly evaporated. But with funds drying up everywhere, it was getting harder to ship food from the farms and growth facilities into the cities. It would *definitely* not be long before the first food riots started, even without the Nihilists pouring fuel on the flames.

"Tell her to stay indoors in future," Glen said. He rather envied Isabel her skill at managing her work along with a personal life, but right now it just gave her hostages to fortune. His daughter would have been fifteen two days ago, if she had lived. "The shit is heading towards the fan."

He rubbed his eyes as they passed a school, now shuttered and dark. In his early years as a Marshal, he'd been called to deal with one riot or another on school grounds when the permissiveness of Imperial society finally led to its logical conclusion. Now, the children were either on the streets or cowering at home, mesmerised by the thought of the onrushing tidal wave of destruction. Earth was gone. There were no longer any certainties in the universe.

Isabel nodded. She was tough, Glen had to admit, certainly tougher than she looked. He'd been astonished when she'd been presented to him as a new graduate, one of the last before the Marshal Academy had been closed for the duration of the emergency. At the time, he'd looked her up and down and concluded she'd slept with one or more of the examiners. Now, he knew better. Isabel was tough enough to survive anything. And warm enough to join a group marriage and become a part of something greater than herself.

Something else greater than herself, Glen thought, tiredly. It was late; he would have preferred to go back to his apartment and sleep until his next shift was about to begin. But the tip-off had been urgent, urgent enough for him to forget the idea of going home and arrange for a raid without waiting for clearance. The Nihilists, God damn their black little souls, had a nasty habit of moving around at short notice before popping up to cause chaos.

The handful of people on the streets faded away completely as they drove into the tangled network of warehouses surrounding the nearest spaceport. Most of the warehouses were completely empty, he knew from the reports. Anyone with access to a starship had boarded it and set out for somewhere safer, somewhere isolated from the coming storm. He didn't blame them, any more than he blamed the endless lines of civilians waiting to book starship tickets, or even taking short hops to asteroid settlements. Terra Nova, Earth's oldest colony world, was less densely populated than Earth – than Earth had been, he reminded himself sharply – but it couldn't support itself indefinitely. Law and order were teetering on the brink of falling into absolute chaos.

"I hope your informant was right, Glen," Isabel said quietly, as they reached the RV point and parked the van. "The boss isn't going to be very happy if this is a fuck-up."

"There's no point in taking chances," Glen said. The tip-off had been too good to ignore – and besides, part of him would be grateful if he *was* suspended or fired. He could have left the star system with a clear conscience. "And besides, if we'd waited for approval from our superiors, someone might have tipped off the bastards."

He gritted his teeth as he checked his pistol, then carefully stashed it beneath his trench coat and opened the door. It was an open secret that criminal gangs had made connections to senior officers within the Civil Guard, paying them for everything from advance warnings of any raids to military-grade supplies. And the criminals often had their own links with the Nihilists. The terrorists wouldn't give a damn about crime, regarding it as yet another manifestation of the hopelessness of existence, but they'd be happy to trade with the crime lords. If someone had advance notice of an attack, they could use it to hide something while the law enforcement forces were distracted.

Outside, the air smelt faintly of oil and burning hydrocarbons. Glen glanced around, spotted the other vehicle some distance from the target warehouse, then made a hand signal inviting Isabel to join him outside the van. Surprisingly, the Civil Guardsmen had actually managed to be discrete when they moved their SWAT team into position. Normally, there was nothing so conspicuous as a Civil Guard force trying to hide. Glen smiled to himself, then led the way to the other vehicle. Inside, it was a mobile command and control centre.

"Marshal Cheal," a tough-looking man said. "I'm Major Daniel Dempsey, local CO."

"Pleased to meet you," Glen said. "Status report?"

He allowed himself a moment of hope. Dempsey looked surprisingly competent for a Civil Guard officer and, more reassuringly, he was wearing nothing more than a basic uniform. The only trace of vanity was a hint that the uniform was tight enough to show off his muscles. Compared to the lines of fruit salad many officers wore, Glen was quite prepared to excuse it.

"Stealth drones reveal the existence of a low-power scrambler field within the warehouse," Dempsey said, tapping the console. "Passive scans have turned up nothing. Marshal, but the mere presence of a scrambler field is justifiable cause for a raid."

Glen nodded, shortly. A scrambler field would make it impossible to slip nanotech bugs inside the warehouse – and, unsurprisingly, civilian ownership was thoroughly illegal. The citizens of the Empire had nothing to fear as long as the Empire was allowed to spy on them at will, Glen had been told. But he'd also been a Marshal long enough to know just how easy it was to take something innocent, something that certainly shouldn't be a criminal offense, and use it as evidence to get someone condemned.

And merely using the field suggests they have something to hide, he thought. *But are they really terrorists...or just smugglers trying to get their goods off-planet?*

"I will be sending in two teams," Dempsey said. "And I *will* assume tactical command."

"I want prisoners," Glen said. "Tell your men to stun without hesitation, Major. The Nihilists are rarely taken alive."

"And one of them might trigger a bomb," Dempsey agreed. He picked up a helmet, then placed it on his head. "I would prefer it if you two remained here while we carried out the operation..."

Glen made a face. The Civil Guardsmen had made a good showing so far, but the real test would begin when the raid started. He wanted to be on the spot, yet he knew he hadn't trained beside the Civil Guardsmen. It was quite possible he'd be shot by accident if he inserted himself into the scene before the bullets stopped flying. The Civil Guardsmen were low on enthusiasm and even lower on training.

"Very well," he said. He took one of the chairs and began studying the views from microscopic cameras inserted around the warehouse. If everything had gone according to plan, the Nihilists had no idea a SWAT team had surrounded them and taken up positions to launch a raid. "Good luck."

Isabel elbowed him as soon as Dempsey had made his way out of the command vehicle. "You don't want to take command for yourself?"

"He's the guy on the spot," Glen said. In theory, Imperial Marshals had supreme authority to take the lead on any investigation, if they felt like it. But, in practice, it was normally better to let the locals handle it unless there was strong evidence the locals were likely to screw up, deliberately or otherwise. "And his men know him."

He settled back in his chair and forced himself to watch as the display updated, rapidly. The team had done a good job of surveying their environment, he noted, as well as obtaining the warehouse's plans from the rental authority. There was only one way into the warehouse, a large pair of double doors on the north side of the building. But, as the Nihilists would almost certainly have the entrance rigged to blow if the wrong people came through, Major Dempsey intended to assault from the rear and blow his way through the walls. Glen rather doubted there was any better options, given the short time they had to mount the raid. God alone knew when the Nihilists would try to move to another location.

And we could try to grab them when they moved, he thought. *But that would be too risky.*

"They're moving," Isabel said. "Team One is assaulting the wall; Team Two is moving to seal the doors."

Glen took a breath as explosive charges blew holes in the walls. Moments later, armoured troopers ran forward, spraying stun bursts ahead of them. It ran the risk of stunning their own people, Glen knew, but it was the quickest way to clear the building. The prisoners would be moved to the cells, where they could be searched and then woken safely. They would have no opportunity to present a threat to their enemies.

He swore as he heard the sound of gunfire echoing out from the warehouse. Caught by surprise or not, the Nihilists had clearly been prepared – and ready to fight back. He wondered, absently, if someone had tipped them off despite the speed the raid had been organised, then decided it wasn't likely. The Nihilists were mad, but they weren't stupid. If they'd expected the raid, they would have rigged the warehouse to blow or cleared out before the shit hit the fan. They had to know that not everyone was as fanatically committed to destroying everything, purely for the sake of destruction, as their leadership.

"Two men down," Isabel said. "One more injured, but still fighting."

Glen ground his teeth, helplessly. He *hated* the waiting, hated having to watch helplessly as other men fought and died. If he'd had a choice, he would have taken a weapon himself and gone into the building, rather than watch the Guardsmen die. But all he could do was wait...

The sound of shooting grew louder. Pushing his thoughts aside, Glen reached for his terminal and began to type out an emergency update. The shooting would attract attention, even now. No one in their right mind wanted to run the risk of one group of Civil Guardsmen turning up to engage another group of Civil Guardsmen. Besides, he had to explain himself to his superiors when they demanded answers. He'd lost quite a bit the moment they opened fire.

"Take the com, tell them to send reinforcements, forensic teams and ambulances," Glen ordered, as the shooting finally came to an end. One way or another, he was definitely committed now. He would have to pray that the raid had been a success or that his boss was feeling merciful. "I'll be out there on the spot."

He jumped out of the command vehicle and strode towards the warehouse, stripping off his trenchcoat to reveal a glowing yellow jacket. No one liked them, particularly the Marshals who had seen military service before making the jump to law enforcement, because they attracted attention, but the risk of being shot by one of his own snipers was far too high without some clear means of identification. He paused long enough to allow the snipers to eyeball him, then walked towards the hole in the wall. Dempsey met him as he reached the gap into the warehouse.

"It's a mess, sir," Dempsey said. "Four of my men are dead, two more badly injured."

Glen made a face as the Civil Guardsmen carried their dead comrades out of the building and laid them, as respectfully as possible, on the roadside. The two wounded were escorted out next, their wounds already being tended by their fellows. In the distance, Glen could hear the sound of sirens as the emergency services converged on the warehouse. He sighed, then followed Dempsey into the building. Inside, it was definitely a mess.

There were hundreds of shipping pallets everywhere, some already broken open and spilling their contents on the ground. One of them was crammed with rifles, a knock-off of a design that was older than the Empire itself, another held SAM missile launchers, although there didn't seem to be any missiles. *That* was odd, Glen noted, as he walked deeper into the building. Normally, the missile launchers were single-use fire and forget weapons. But their mere presence boded ill for the future.

"There are over a hundred crates in the warehouse," Dempsey said, as several dead bodies were carried past them and out into the open air. "If they're all crammed with weapons..."

"We might have had a serious problem," Glen finished. Terra Nova was, in theory, a gun-free zone. In practice, the planet was awash with illegal weapons, mostly bought or stolen from the Civil Guard. But the stockpile before him was enough for a major war and it had all been in the hands of the Nihilists. What had they intended to do with it? "Where did they get them from?"

"This is a transhipment warehouse," Dempsey said, dryly. "Someone must have shipped the weapons in from out-system, then smuggled them past the security guards."

Glen shook his head in disbelief. Every year, more and more security precautions were added to sweep everything and everyone heading down to the surface. Every year, more and more visitors were irritated or outraged by body-scans and even close-contact searches. Every year, the number of tourists visiting Terra Nova declined still further, damaging the planet's economy...and yet, the Nihilists were able to smuggle hundreds, perhaps thousands, of dangerous weapons though security without setting off any alarms.

But we caught them, he told himself. There was no way his boss could refuse to say the raid wasn't justified, not now. *We caught the bastards before they could start distributing the weapons.*

He turned to look at Dempsey. "How many did we take alive?"

"None, so far," Dempsey said. He didn't seem flustered by Glen's accusing look. It was far from uncommon for terrorists who had killed policemen or Civil Guardsmen not to make it to the station after being taken into custody. "They all had suicide implants, sir. They died moments after they were stunned."

"Make sure the place is secured, then have the forensic team go through every last inch of the building," Glen ordered. "I want every one of them identified, I want to know just who let them through security and why..."

"If we have the manpower," Dempsey cut him off. "Will your boss authorise such an effort?"

Glen swore. With the threat of food riots, nearly every law-enforcement official on the planet had been diverted to patrolling the cities. Even the backroom experts who made the service work had been forced to remember their basic training as they donned armour and set out to try to make the streets a little safer. It was a recipe for disaster, everyone knew, but there was no alternative. They just didn't have the manpower to flood the streets with officers, let alone Civil Guardsmen.

His terminal bleeped, loudly. It was Isabel's ringtone. "Excuse me," he said, removing the terminal from his belt. "Glen here."

"Glen, I just got called by the boss," Isabel said. "She's sending a team of experts over here, but she wants you to report back to the station at once. I think you're in the shit."

"Come back this evening...tomorrow morning and dig me out," Glen said. He wasn't surprised. The raid had been a great success, but he would still have to answer a great many hard questions. "And bring coffee."

"Will do," Isabel said. "What would you like me to write on your gravestone before I dig you up and put you back to work?"

Glen laughed, tiredly. "Something witty," he said. "Take over here; let me know if we took anyone captive. We need answers from them."

He stepped back out of the warehouse and walked over towards the line of vehicles screeching to a halt. One of them would take him back to the station, probably far too quickly for his peace of mind. He needed coffee and a rest, not a lecture from the boss.

But an Imperial Marshal's work was never done.

CHAPTER
TWO

The definition of crime is, of course, part of society. Throughout history, there have been no shortage of acts that we would unhesitatingly deem as criminal, yet were not considered crimes at the time.

- Professor Leo Caesius, *The Decline of Law
and Order and the Rise of Anarchy*

Belinda closed her eyes. When she opened them, she saw the city.

It was an ugly sight. Dozens of gray cookie-cutter houses, each one completely unremarkable, completely indistinguishable from the others. There was nothing to separate each of them from their partners, no trace at all of individuality. Whoever had designed this suburb, she decided as she started to walk, had no intention of allowing human sentimentality to affect their design work. There were no shops, no schools...nothing, but endless rows of houses...

...And there were no traces of any living beings, none at all.

Alarm bells rang in her mind as she started to run. The mission was simple enough, which meant, in her experience, that there was a nasty sting in the tail. All she had to do was get from one end of the city to the other, without allowing anything to impede her path. She'd run countless such missions before, when she'd been nothing more than a Marine Rifleman, but then she'd been surrounded by the rest of the company. Now, she was alone.

Her enhanced senses, such as they were, probed the darkness as she ran faster, keeping to the shadows as best as she could. If someone was setting an ambush ahead of her, she was reasonably sure she could hear them lying in wait before they realised she was there, unless they knew what she was. Or they were just being paranoid. Even the most enhanced humanoids known to exist couldn't hear something if it wasn't making a sound, even breathing. Belinda had set enough ambushes in her time to know how the ambushers were thinking. They'd try to lure her into a killing zone and do whatever it took to stop her.

She darted down an alleyway, then out into the next street, ducking into the shadows long enough to scan for anything out of place. The soulless buildings seemed to mock her, casting dark shadows that were almost completely shrouded, even to her enhanced senses. She hesitated, then ran onwards, trying to keep the sound of her footsteps to the bare minimum. And yet, she knew she was making noise, too much noise. If someone was lying in wait...

I should have asked for more time, she thought, as she entered another alleyway and jumped over a set of garbage cans. *Enough time to run around the city, rather than through the buildings...*

A sound caught her attention and she froze, listening carefully. It sounded like someone was crying, very softly, and trying not to be heard. Belinda turned, using her enhanced senses to triangulate the source of the sound, then crept forward. It was coming from a nearby alleyway...

It's a trap, part of her mind yammered. The rest of her told that part of her mind to shut up. She couldn't leave someone in pain, all alone in the dark, not if she wanted to live up to the Marine ideal. And besides, she knew – all too well – what it was like to be alone. She peered into the alleyway and frowned as she saw the girl lying on the ground, her arms and legs akimbo. Belinda's eyes narrowed as she moved closer. She'd seen too many horrors wrought by mankind on its fellows, but this was odd. There had been no sign that anyone lived within the city...

A sudden motion flickered behind her. Belinda ducked instinctively as something flashed overhead, through where her head had been seconds ago, then swung around to see a gangbanger standing there. She didn't hesitate. Before he could take another swing at her, she lashed out herself and slammed a punch into his chest. She felt his bones breaking under the impact, but he staggered forward, his arms flailing rapidly. Belinda darted back, then watched dispassionately as he fell to the ground. And then she sensed the others shimmering into view.

Personal cloaks? She thought, surprised. *Where did a bunch of gangsters get their hands on personnel cloaking devices?*

There was no time to consider the mystery, not when she was surrounded by at least five gangsters. None of them seemed to be carrying projectile weapons, which surprised her, but they all moved as if they had some degree of martial arts training. Belinda considered trying to negotiate, then dismissed the thought impatiently. Falling into their hands would be a fate worse than death, even if they merely took her captive and traded her to their backers for additional weapons and supplies. And besides, she had no intention of surrendering – ever.

The first gangbanger lunged forward. Belinda triggered her enhancements, then leapt up and over his head. He didn't seem surprised as she landed behind him and started to run, rather than stopping to fight. Instead, he barked a command and three of his men started to follow her, back out onto the street. Belinda ran faster, calling on her enhancements, then swore mentally as she realised they were keeping up with her. It should have been impossible...

And then one of them threw himself forward and slammed into her back.

Belinda fell, twisting around to land on her back and bring her legs up to kick out at her captor. Her boot caught him in the head, which snapped backwards with a satisfying cracking sound. There was no time to be pleased with her success. Belinda jumped back to her feet as the other gangsters advanced towards her, their hands suddenly sprouting a mixture of knives, clubs and steel bars. Belinda smiled, feeling truly alive for the first time in far too long, then allowed them to close before she started to fight with enhanced strength and determination. Two of the gangsters fell before her fists, then the leader slammed *something* into her back. There was a sudden shock that send her falling to her knees, as if she'd been struck with an weakened stun beam.

A neural whip, the analytical part of her mind pointed out. *You've had your nerves jangled...*

She gritted her teeth and started to force herself to her feet, but it was too late. One of the gangbangers caught her arms and yanked her back to the ground, while two more caught her legs and wrenched them apart. Belinda struggled, feeling panic bubbling at the corner of her mind, as the leader produced a sharp knife and went to work on her trousers. He wasn't fool enough to have his men let her loose, she realised numbly. It was clear he had a good idea of just who and what she was. And then she felt cold air on her exposed skin...

"Lie still," the gangbanger ordered, as he started to undo his trousers. "This will be..."

"End program," another voice said.

Belinda cursed under her breath as the droids holding her went limp, then looked up. Major General Jeremy Damiani, Commandant of the Terran Marine Corps, was standing to one side, looking disapproving. His bulldog-like face was twisted into a scowl that left her feeling as though she'd disappointed him, which she probably had. At the peak of her prowess, before the Fall of Earth, she could have cut her way through any number of gangbangers without a second thought. But a great deal had changed since then.

"Well," the Commandant said. "I've never seen anyone almost *raped* by the simulators before."

"No, sir," Belinda said. She stumbled to her feet, ignoring the remains of her trousers as they fell off her legs. Dignity wasn't something permitted to Pathfinder Marines. She'd carried out missions buck naked, once upon a time. Maybe she would again, one day. If she managed to recover from the Fall of Earth. "I wanted to test myself."

"You set the simulator to extreme levels," the Commandant said. "I believe the medical corpsmen will want a few words with you."

Belinda shrugged, refusing to show any of the bitter despondency that threatened to overwhelm her as she turned and started towards the hatch. Her emotions had once been tightly controlled, but no longer. She'd lost count of just how many times she'd found herself in tears since Earth had died, since Prince Roland had been sent to the Safehouse. It was almost a relief that he was no longer with her, even though she missed him more than she cared to admit. At least he wouldn't have to see how far she'd fallen from the dispassionate Marine he'd met on Earth.

The Commandant cleared his throat. Loudly.

"You were badly injured on Earth," he said, following her through the hatch. "I don't expect you to regain your health so quickly."

"I was always an overachiever," Belinda said. She started to strip off her uniform jacket, boots and panties, heedless of his presence. The *Chesty Puller's* simulator had left her sweaty and uncomfortable. It had really been too real for comfort. "And I will not surrender to despair."

"Good," the Commandant said. His tone was artfully flat, so carefully controlled she knew it had to be an act. "But you are also pushing yourself too hard."

"I don't think so," Belinda said. "The medics have always erred on the side of caution."

She finished undressing, then stood naked in front of the mirror. Physically, she looked normal; a blonde-haired young woman with a heart-shaped face and a body that was healthy and fit without seeming unnaturally muscular. Her long blonde hair alone would have made it hard for anyone to believe she was a Marine, not when almost every Marine in the Corps shaved their hair to keep it from getting in their way. But Pathfinders had always been allowed a certain level of latitude, particularly when they were operating undercover. They couldn't afford to *look* like Marines...

But her blue eyes were haunted and her skin was unnaturally pale...

"The medics are trying to keep you alive," the Commandant said. "We don't want to lose you because you pushed yourself too hard."

"I have to *know*," Belinda said. Giving up wasn't in her nature. Her family had seen to that a long time before she'd ever heard of the Terran Marine Corps. But, at the same time, she'd never been so weepy and upset over nothing before. It was hard to escape the sense that something was badly wrong with her mind. "Earth is gone. Is there any point in further struggle?"

"The human race lives on," the Commandant said. There was something in his voice that caught her attention. "Although not for much longer, perhaps."

Belinda looked up, surprised. "Sir?"

"Someone attacked the Slaughterhouse," the Commandant informed her. "The entire planet is dead."

Belinda recoiled in horror – and disbelief. The Slaughterhouse was more than just another badly-terraformed planet, she knew. It was the heart and soul of the Terran Marine Corps, the place where Marines were created, sent out to fight on behalf of the Empire and laid to rest when they died. If, the cynical side of her mind reminded her, there was enough of their bodies left to be buried. The Corps would do everything in its power to recover bodies, even trading with the enemy if necessary, but it sometimes wasn't possible to bring the dead home and lay them to rest properly.

It couldn't be gone. Centuries of tradition, of iron discipline and loyalty to the ideal of Empire, couldn't be gone. But she knew the Commandant wouldn't lie to her.

"Shit," she said, finally.

"Yes," the Commandant agreed.

Belinda looked down at her unmarked hands. She'd seen them bleeding and broken on the Slaughterhouse, when she'd forced herself to go on and on until she'd found herself unable to even *think* about quitting. Others had taken far worse injuries and kept going, daring the universe to try to stop them. And even those who had failed the final hurdle had found a home with the Corps. The Corps couldn't function without the auxiliaries in the background, the men and women who were still devoted to the Corps, even if they couldn't wear the Rifleman's Tab. It was hard to escape the impression that the Slaughterhouse was irreplaceable.

She looked up at the Commandant, feeling cold anger blossoming to life within her breast and turning to rage.

"Who did it?"

"We don't know," the Commandant said. "There's no shortage of suspects."

Belinda nodded, ruefully. The Grand Senate had feared the Marines, knowing the Corps couldn't be controlled as easily as the Imperial Army and Navy. They'd done their level best to weaken the Corps long before the Fall of Earth and, she had to admit, they'd done a very good job. And then there were the countless secessionists, terrorists and other rebel factions that had good reason to want to cripple or destroy the Marine Corps. The Nihilists, in particular, would seek to take advantage of the chaos caused by the Fall of Earth.

She took a breath. "Survivors?"

"The planet was evacuated as soon as I sent word of the Fall of Earth," the Commandant said, shortly. "Everyone on the planet was moved to escape ships and transported to the Safehouse, which is in another system entirely. The only people left in the system were a handful of observation staff, watching from a safe distance. They could do nothing as the planet was rendered uninhabitable."

Belinda swore. "Uninhabitable?"

"They used planet-scaled enhanced radiation weapons," the Commandant said. "It will be hundreds of years, perhaps longer, before the planet can be considered habitable once again."

"If ever," Belinda said. The Slaughterhouse had started its existence as a terraforming mistake, after all. Whatever polity replaced the Empire, if any such polity came into existence, would have to invest vast resources in restoring the planet. "What about the records? And the Crypt?"

"We have copies of the former," the Commandant said. "The latter...is lost to us, for now."

Belinda gritted her teeth in bitter rage. She'd spent time at the Crypt, when she'd been a recruit, learning about the Marines who had given their lives in service to the Empire. She'd wondered, at the time, if there was anything she could learn from men and women who had died in the course of their duties, and it had taken her some time to realise that *was* the lesson, that there were people who had made the ultimate sacrifice for the Corps. They hadn't fought for the Empire, in the end, but for their buddies, for the Marines on either side of them when they'd gone to war. And now their legacy was lost forever.

"Fuck," she said, finally. She wanted to hit something. But there was nothing to hit. "Just...fuck!"

"Quite," the Commandant agreed.

He looked her up and down, his gaze contemplative rather than unpleasant. "I may have a mission for you," he said. "It isn't one I am comfortable assigning to you. Quite frankly" – his voice hardened – "you are in no state to do anything, beyond slowly recuperating to the point you can be assigned to a line company or redirected to the auxiliaries. Under the circumstances, we would even accept your resignation."

Belinda eyed him, fighting down a surge of hope within her heart. "I can do it, sir," she said, quickly. "Whatever you want me to do..."

The Commandant met her eyes. "Last time I assigned you to a mission, I told you that I had doubts," he said. "Do you remember?"

"Yes, sir," Belinda said. "I remember."

She winced in memory. She'd been the lone survivor of an operation that had gone badly wrong from the start, thanks to Admiral Valentine and his cronies. The medics had told her she was suffering from Survivor's Guilt and had urged her to take a long rest. Instead, she'd been given a mission that should have been a milk run. And it had almost killed her.

And it did kill eighty billion people on Earth, a voice reminded her. *You watched helplessly as the planet died.*

"This time, I have more doubts," the Commandant said. "If I had another Pathfinder available, I would send him instead and keep you here, where you can recover safely. But I don't and so I have to rely on you. If you feel you cannot complete the mission, after I brief you, I expect you to tell me so."

"Yes, sir," Belinda said, already knowing she wouldn't. She didn't know how to quit – or how to rest. "What do you want me to do?"

"Get dressed, then report to Briefing Room A," the Commandant said. "I'll brief you there."

He paused. "And you might want to consider writing a new will afterwards," he added. "I do worry about you."

Belinda kept her face expressionless with an effort. The Commandant wouldn't normally have expressed concern about any of his Marines. For him to do so, openly, suggested that he felt he had good reason to worry, over and beyond the normal call of duty. Her medical records were sealed, but she'd had a look at them once her neural link had been repaired, allowing her to hack into the computer networks. She'd come far too close to death on Earth, they'd stated, and she would never be a fully-functional

Pathfinder again. There was no way to replace some of her burned-out implants without risking brain damage.

Or more brain damage, she thought. She hadn't told anyone she sometimes heard the voices of her dead teammates. Perhaps the Commandant *did* have good reason to worry. *But I won't give up now.*

Sighing, she reached for her uniform as he walked out of the hatch, leaving her alone. She'd get dressed, then hear the briefing. But she already knew she wouldn't refuse the mission, even if it was certain death. She just didn't know any other way to live.

CHAPTER
THREE

One particularly shocking example might be 'bride rape.' Put simply, courting in those unenlightened times consisted of a man snatching the woman from her male relatives, then carting her off somewhere and having sex with her (presumably against her will). Once deflowered, the woman would be considered married and everything would be settled.

- Professor Leo Caesius, *The Decline of Law and Order and the Rise of Anarchy*

"They're waiting for you in the conference room," Sergeant Chou said, as Glen strode through the heavy blast doors that separated the public parts of the Marshal Station from the private sections. "I thought you'd need this first."

He shoved a plastic mug towards Glen, who took it absently and took a swig. The coffee was strong enough to wake the dead, blended with a unique cocktail of drugs intended to keep Imperial Marshals and Police Officers awake and functional for several additional hours. It wasn't something Glen cared to use, but he suspected he had no choice. The inquest into his decision to launch a raid without consulting his superiors would need him at the top of his game.

"The Boss wanted to give you some more time, but she was overruled," Chou added, as he escorted Glen through the waiting room. A number of civilians, some in handcuffs, looked up at them as they passed, their faces bleak with misery. The really dangerous suspects would be held in the cells and only brought up when it was their turn to face the desk officers. "General Ramsey insisted, you see."

Glen sighed. General Ramsey was the Civil Guard CO for the entire planet, a man on such a rarefied level that he normally wouldn't have anything to do with Glen – or even his immediate superior. But using the Civil Guard's assets to mount a raid had clearly been reported up the chain and their commander was not happy. Four of his men were dead and two more were badly injured. Heads were likely to roll.

"I see," he said, feeling a sudden burst of energy as the cocktail did its work. "Shall we go into the lion's den?"

The conference room was guarded by a pair of armed Civil Guardsmen, who scowled at Glen and waved scanners over his body before grudgingly allowing him to enter the compartment. Glen kept his thoughts off his face – there was no reason for General Ramsey to bring bodyguards into the station with him – and forced himself to remain calm. Inside, General Ramsey, Marshall (Superintendent) Patty McMahon and two people he didn't know were waiting for him. He saluted, then took the chair positioned in front of the table.

"Marshal Cheal," General Ramsey said. He was a heavyset man, his muscles slowly turning to fat, with red hair and a beard that was largely against regulations. "We have called you here to demand answers. Why – exactly – did you launch a raid without requesting permission from your superiors?"

Glen met his eyes, evenly. "The tip-off we received suggested that time was not on our side," he said, reaching for his terminal. "I was led to believe that the stored weapons would be moved at any moment, which would make it difficult to track them further, particularly once they were distributed. Therefore, sir, I decided that an immediate raid was the best possible solution."

The General scowled at him. "You put a lot of faith on your source, Marshal?"

"This source, General, has been hidden within the Nihilists for several years," Patty McMahon said. She gave Glen an encouraging smile. "We had no reason to doubt his word."

"We still don't," Glen said. He had no idea what game General Ramsey was playing – Glen had done nothing outside his authority and they both knew it – but he was too tired for any form of verbal sparring. "The raid netted hundreds of weapons, General, including some rather more dangerous than simple projectile weapons. In the wrong hands I believe they could have been used to put together a serious challenge to the military."

"I doubt it," the General snorted. "We still control the high orbitals, don't we?"

"You would have had to fire on our own cities, causing massive civilian casualties," Patty said. Her voice was very droll. "I think the evidence suggests that Marshal Cheal acted in the best traditions of the Imperial Marshals."

"The fact remains that we should have been consulted," General Ramsey said. His piggish eyes fixed on Glen. "I shouldn't have to remind you, Marshal, that we are in dangerously uncharted waters. The merest spark could set off a bloodbath. This should have been put before the Emergency Council."

Glen took a breath. "And how many people would have known something was up before we even had a chance to launch a raid?"

"The Emergency Council is above suspicion," General Ramsey snapped.

"Are all their aides above suspicion?" Glen countered. "Their advisers? Their speechwriters? Their mistresses? The more people who knew, the greater the chance that something would have leaked out onto the datanets. And one of them could easily be a Nihilist operative."

The General snorted again, but didn't argue.

"I believed that speed was our only hope of capturing the terrorists and seizing their weapons," Glen said, pressing his advantage. "And we successfully captured a vast amount of weapons that could do real damage in the wrong hands."

"I still have to write letters to the families of those who died on the operation," the General said. "And I would like to tell them something about how their loved ones died."

If you are actually going to write the letters, Glen thought, sardonically. It was Major Dempsey who would have the task, if any of the dead had friends or family outside the Civil Guard. There were some guardsmen who lived up to the propaganda, but too many others were nothing more than thugs in uniform. *And why are you even holding this meeting?*

"They did their duty," Patty said. She gave the General an understanding smile. "I think you have good reason to be proud of your men."

The General tossed her a sharp look, then looked back at Glen. "You will answer a barrage of questions from the staff," he said. "And then I would suggest a few days on leave."

Glen opened his mouth to protest, but Patty got there first.

"I believe that would be wise," she said, standing. "Glen, you're with me."

She led the way out of the chamber and down the corridor towards her office. Glen wanted to demand answers, but he forced himself to keep his mouth shut until they were safely inside her chamber, which was swept for bugs on a daily basis. Competition between the various law enforcement agencies had always been intense, even before Earth had died and waves of chaos had started to spread across the Core Worlds. Now...there were times when Glen found himself seriously considering trying to get on one of the colony ships that were still departing Terra Nova. A world on the Rim would be safer than anywhere else.

"You did well today," she said, as soon as the door was shut. "Don't let Brian Ramsey tell you any differently."

"I won't," Glen said. Patty had always been a good boss to her Marshals, standing up for them when necessary. "But why was he so determined to demand answers so fast?"

"Someone managed to get a report off to higher authority," Patty said. She sat down behind her desk and motioned for Glen to take the chair facing her. "The General was caught by surprise and ended up looking incompetent in front of the Governor. And so he came here to look as though he was Doing Something. Politics."

"Politics," Glen repeated, treating the word as though it was the vilest of obscenities. "And you let him do it?"

"I had no choice," Patty said. She shook her head, sadly. "The Civil Guard has been agitating to take over the Imperial Marshals for years,

Glen, and now, with Earth gone, some of them think they have a chance to make it work. And our superiors are gone."

Glen winced. The Civil Guard had offices on each and every planet with a population large enough to support a Civil Guard force. They tended to develop local allegiances fairly quickly, no matter how often their superior officers were rotated in and out to break up the corrupt networks that seemed to spring up in their wake. Either they found themselves more concerned with the planet than the Empire, which happened when the planet's local government was paying the bills, or they became the enforcers of the local rulers.

But the Marshals had always been an interstellar force, intended to serve the interests of the Grand Senate and the Emperor, right across the Empire. It hadn't made them popular, Glen knew, even with the general public. There was so much corruption in the Empire's law enforcement systems that the Marshals were tainted with the same brush, even though they had a better record of dealing with corruption than any of the other agencies. And now Earth was gone. The Civil Guard on Terra Nova had their chance to take over the Marshals for themselves.

"I see," he said, tiredly. "Did I make a mistake?"

"I think not," Patty said. She rubbed her tired eyes with her hands. "I am so *sick* of all the damn politics, Glen."

She sighed. "Go see the debriefing officers," she said. "Get everything recorded, then go home and snatch a few hours of sleep. I'll try and do something about the suspension, because you damn well don't deserve it, but I think Brian will insist you go through with it to salvage something of his pride. The man can be quite petty on occasion."

Glen took a breath. "We still don't know how they got those weapons down to the surface," he objected. "And we have to find out where they were going..."

Patty held up a hand. "You have a partner, who is perfectly competent, and dozens of supporting officers who will do the legwork," she said. "The case won't be lost because you took a few days off work."

"I suppose," Glen said, sourly. He *hated* leaving an investigation in someone else's hands, even Isabel's. For one thing, it had been his decision to launch an immediate raid. It had been the right choice – he would have believed it was the right choice even if they'd found nothing, but an empty warehouse – and he should bear the blame for anything that went wrong. "You'll keep me informed?"

"Of course," Patty said. She pointed at the door. "Go."

Glen obeyed. He liked Patty, even though she'd spent much of the last five years playing politics rather than running investigations, arresting suspects and everything else the Imperial Marshals were expected to do. But politics, he knew, were important, even though most of the politicians he'd met had been self-indulgent assholes. Patty had a harder task now that Earth was gone, taking with it the Marshal Headquarters and her direct superiors. It was easy to believe, no matter how hard he tried to think otherwise, that the Marshals on Terra Nova were completely alone.

How long would it take, he asked himself, *to establish contact with other Marshals?*

As promised, the debriefing officers were waiting for him in their compartments, ready to hear his story from his own lips. Glen had always hated sitting down with them – it took time away from everything else, from policing the streets to following up leads – but it was a vital part of police work. There were entire *armies* of lawyers ready to represent anyone who had the money to hire them and, given half a chance, they could destroy a case if there was the slightest hint of misconduct. Glen had lost count of how many major villains had been allowed to return to the streets after their lawyers had gone to work, even though the cases against them had been largely solid. The smaller fry had been sent to jail, or simply deported to colonies along the Rim, but it hadn't mattered. Their masters had simply hired new footsoldiers and gone back to work.

"And that's a wrap," Officer Reynolds said, when Glen had finally finished. "Thank you!"

"Just don't leak it," Glen advised, tiredly. The cocktail of drugs was starting to wear off, leaving him with a pounding headache and a sense that it was time he headed to bed. "And make sure everything remains sealed."

"We know our jobs," Officer Reynolds assured him. "The file will be added to the evidence locker, sealed from all tampering."

Glen shrugged. Marshals were selected for incorruptibility, but their support staff was sometimes a different matter. They weren't paid very well and they tended to get the shit duties, which bred either desperation or resentment. And, as much as he hated to admit it, there were a few Marshals who had gone off the rails in a big way. One of them had been running a criminal network through an entire CityBlock on Earth when he'd finally been discovered and sentenced to permanent exile. And two more had been responsible for the largest slavery ring to be uncovered for years. No, he knew better than to assume that everyone was honest, utterly without a price. Given the right incentive, anyone might break and join the dark side.

He turned and walked back through the network of unmarked corridors – anyone who had a right to be there knew the way without having to refer to maps – and entered the common room in search of coffee and a place to lay his head. It wasn't quite going home, as Patty had ordered, but a few hours of sleep before he made his way back to his apartment seemed a very good idea. But Sergeant Chou intercepted him before he could lie down on one of the beds and close his eyes.

"The Boss wants to see you," he said. "Now."

Glen blinked in surprise. "Did she say why?"

"No," Chou said. "But she did say it was important."

Glen sighed and made his way back to Patty's office. Inside, Patty was seated at her desk, reading through a stack of paperwork. Glen felt a flicker of sympathy and tapped on the door, alerting her to his presence. She looked up, then nodded towards the chair and turned back to her paperwork. Glen sat down, fighting the urge to close his eyes. He had no idea if anyone had dozed off in Patty's office before, but he didn't want to be the first. She would be far from pleased.

"There's been a development," Patty said. "We found something unusual in the warehouse."

We, Glen thought, nastily. Patty wasn't normally given to stealing credit from her subordinates...although, to be fair, she wasn't given to hanging them out to dry either. She did look after her subordinates, after all. No one could get to them without going through her first.

"We found enough weapons to fight a minor war," Glen said. Terra Nova was brutally hoplophobic, with the private possession of weapons completely banned. The Nihilists would be able to do real damage before the military responded with crushing firepower, which would cause as many civilian casualties as the terrorists themselves. "Define unusual."

"We found a young girl," Patty said. "Around thirteen years old, according to the medics, and seemingly a prisoner."

Glen winced. The Nihilists had absolutely no regard for social norms, but it wasn't like them to hold young children prisoner. They merely wanted to kill as many people as possible before they were killed themselves. Indeed, given that they believed that death freed them from a pointless existence, it was rare for them to take prisoners. Their insane creed urged them to kill prisoners, rather than try to use them as hostages. The fact they'd kept a prisoner...it didn't look good. He didn't want to *think* about what kind of abuse might have been heaped on her before she'd been freed.

"There was no signs of abuse, as far as we can tell," Patty said, as if she'd been reading his thoughts. "But there was no time to do more than a basic scan."

"I see," Glen said. He met his superior's eyes. "I thought I was suspended."

There was a flash of annoyance in Patty's eyes. "I'd like you to take the girl with you," she said. "Someone needs to look after her – and make sure she doesn't go anywhere once she recovers from the shock of being held captive."

Glen blinked. "I'm not a bloody nursemaid..."

"Right now," Patty snapped, effortlessly overriding him, "the poor girl is in custody. We can't hold her here indefinitely. By law, if we can't make other arrangements, she would have to go to Kiddie Hall" – juvenile detention – "or the Civil Guard. Given her age and relative health, you know what would happen to her there."

"I know," Glen said, sourly. "She'd be sold to the highest bidder."

The thought was bitterly unpleasant. Prisoners – particularly young and fertile women – were in high demand along the Rim. They had no rights, after all, and couldn't complain if they were sold into servitude as mail order brides...if they were lucky. There were brothels for the unfortunate ones, places where horny miners or contract workers could slake their lusts outside working hours. He'd shut down several himself, during his first assignment out on the Rim, but he knew others would have already sprung up to replace them.

He sighed. The last thing he wanted was a child underfoot, particularly one the same age as his daughter, if she had lived. But he couldn't leave her in custody either.

"You're the only Marshal with an apartment to himself," Patty added. "Anyone else would have to explain her presence to their partner. It could be awkward."

"Yes, it could," Glen agreed. He was too tired to argue further. "I'll take her."

"Good," Patty said. "You'll find her in the waiting room."

CHAPTER

FOUR

This is horrifying, of course, to modern readers. But to the locals of that time, the woman's opinion was largely irrelevant. Indeed, when a woman saw a man she liked, she often had to resort to allowing herself to be kidnapped and raped, in the hopes everything would fall the way she wanted it. The concept of allowing men and women to meet on friendly terms would have been alien to them.

- Professor Leo Caesius, The Decline of Law and Order and the Rise of Anarchy

It felt like years since Belinda had entered a briefing compartment on a starship. None of her Pathfinder missions had required a full brief; she'd taken her orders from her superior in the team, rather than the overall commander on the ground. And, as a Marine Rifleman, she'd spent most of her time on the ground, rather than in space. Her unit had never been deployed onboard a battleship.

But then, she thought, as she took her seat, *they were removing the Marines from the ships long before the shit hit the fan on Earth.*

"The current situation is dire," the Commandant said, shortly. "Right now, the Core Worlds are teetering on the brink of anarchy. The interstellar economy has crashed along with Earth, the various military and political officers are considering independent action and it won't be long before one or more of them makes a grab for outright power. And when they do, Belinda, we will have an all-out civil war on our hands."

Belinda nodded. She'd met enough politicians – and senior military officers – to know that most of them put their careers first and foremost. Given the sudden disappearance of Earth, and the Grand Senate, they'd certainly consider trying to take supreme power for themselves – and the sooner, the better. The ties that bound the Empire together were snapping, one by one. It wouldn't be long before the full effects of the economic shockwave were felt right across the Empire. And who knew what would happen then?

"We've already seen some major riots on various planets," the Commandant continued, darkly. "Normally, the riots have specific grievances – or are organised by one political faction or another. This time, the riots appear to be largely spontaneous, directed against the remaining elements of the power structure. I imagine they will get worse as the news heads out beyond the Core Worlds."

"And planets start rebelling against corporate authority," Belinda said. She'd seen enough planets that had tried to rebel to know that hundreds of millions of colonists bitterly resented the corporations that milked their worlds for all they were worth. Most of their rebellions had been brutally put down. Now, without Earth or a unified military command, the next wave of rebellions might just succeed. "And what will that do to the economy?"

The Commandant laughed, harshly. "There isn't an economy any longer," he said. "It will take years, perhaps, to build something new. Right now, I suspect that a number of planets are planning to simply seize the Earth-held property in their systems. They'll have to become part of the local economy."

Belinda considered the implications as best as she could. The Empire had done its best to ensure that each and every Earth-like world was capable of feeding its population, but it hadn't tried to ensure an equable distribution of factories, orbital industrial nodes or cloudscoops. There would be a colossal shortage of fuel for everything from starships to planet-side fusion plants, spare parts would suddenly become rarer than gold and anyone who had control over *any* production plant would suddenly be in a position to dictate terms to everyone who didn't. The Empire's collapse would lead straight to civil war.

And how could anyone, even the Marines, hope to stop it?

"Are you intending to present Roland to them as the next Emperor?" She asked. "I don't think he'd want the job."

"Even if he did, I doubt it would be enough to stop the collapse," the Commandant pointed out, dryly. "Legally, he might be the Emperor; practically, he controls nothing, not even his own life. At best, one of the warlords would use him as a puppet; at worst, he'd be killed out of hand by whoever got their hands on him first."

"Then what can we do?" Belinda asked. She had never despaired in her life, but thinking about the sheer scale of the coming disaster – the disaster that was already upon them, no matter how much they might wish to deny it – was terrifying. It was almost completely beyond her comprehension. "We're staring at a war that will make the Unification Wars look like a genteel disagreement."

"That is unfortunately true," the Commandant said. He took a breath. "We are not the only ones to realise this, Belinda. Governor Theodore Onge has also recognised the problem."

Belinda's eyes narrowed. "Is he related to Grand Senator Onge?"

"They're related, yes," the Commandant said. "It would probably not be politic for you to tell the Governor that you killed his family's patriarch."

"Oh," Belinda said. "And would it be politic for me to tell him that his...patriarch did more than anyone else to start the crisis that led to disaster on Earth?"

"Probably not," the Commandant said. He tapped a switch and a holographic starchart appeared in front of them. Tiny icons beside each star marked the location of military, industrial and political nodes. An alarming number seemed to be marked STATUS UNKNOWN. "The Governor has been spending the last two weeks trying to organise a conference of the surviving civil and military authorities within the Core Worlds."

"A conference," Belinda repeated.

"A conference," the Commandant said. "I believe he intends to convince them that they can gain more by sharing their resources and dividing up the bounty than by fighting. It may not be a laudable goal, from our point of view, but it might prevent further chaos for a number of years."

Belinda had her doubts. Trust was something in short supply in the highest ranks of the Empire, not without reason. There was no way an Imperial Governor would risk exposing his back so overtly, not when one of his rivals might take it as an opportunity to stick a knife in him. And even if Onge was being honest – and everything Belinda had seen and heard about that family suggested they were incapable of seeing anything, but opportunity for themselves – there was no guarantee that all of the other governors and military leaders would act in good faith. Indeed, Belinda would bet half her salary that at least five of them would be plotting ways to turn the conference into a bloodbath.

"It seems absurd," she said. "Do you really think it can work?"

"I think we have no alternative," the Commandant admitted. For a moment, he suddenly seemed very old. "If the Core Worlds start fighting amongst themselves, Belinda, we can say goodbye to any hope of restoring humanity's unity."

Belinda studied him for a long moment. "Would that be a bad thing?"

"Explain," the Commandant ordered, a sharp edge in his voice.

"The Empire, in the name of unity, stifled development," Belinda said. "And it provoked hatred across a third of the galaxy. If the Empire were to vanish, sir, would it not be better for the rest of the human race?"

She sighed. The Empire was supposed to unite humanity – and, if that were the case, why were there so many rebellions against the Empire? She'd lost count of planets that had had uprisings, from tiny affairs that were quickly squashed to outright rebellions that consumed vital resources and invariably cost more to crush than was gained in the aftermath of war. And then there were the countless resistance groups that sprung up, sharing information and thoughts on how to make the next uprising far more costly for the Imperials...

"The problem, Belinda, is that every war we have fought over the last thousand years has been relatively restrained," the Commandant pointed out. "If the Empire vanishes completely, we will see warfare on a previously unknown scale. There will be planetary bombardments, mass slaughter of civilians and far worse. Billions upon billions will die, either in the wars themselves or as the remains of the infrastructure breaks down. The conference may be our only hope of salvaging something from the wreckage."

He sighed. "I understand your feelings," he admitted. "But we have no choice."

"Yes, sir," Belinda said. "What do you want me to do?"

"The Conference is due to be held on Terra Nova, three weeks from today," the Commandant said. He sounded irked, unsurprisingly. Travel times between star systems were far too slow for any form of centralised decision-making. The Empire had never quite learned that lesson, which partly explained why so many minor riots had become major rebellions by the time the military hastened to pour water on the flames. "I want you to go there and...do your best to ensure the conference takes place – and succeeds."

Belinda winced. She was used to vague orders – standard practice in the Marines was to give someone an objective, then let them get on with it – but the Commandant wasn't being even remotely specific. What did he actually want her to do?

"I've attempted to convince the Governor to accept a Marine Security Team, but he refused," the Commandant explained. "I want you to go in under cover, make your way to the conference location and then do whatever you have to do to keep it secure."

"I see," Belinda said. She didn't. "Will you be attending the conference?"

"I was told that my presence would be a distraction," the Commandant said. "And the Governor might well be right."

"If they're taking precautions," Belinda said slowly, "I may not be able to get anywhere near the conference."

"Which will prove they're on the ball," the Commandant said. He looked up at her. "I have never liked issuing instructions that were so incomplete, Belinda. And there is very little I can tell you about the situation on the ground – or even the security precautions the Governor is taking to safeguard his brainchild. All I can do is send you in and pray for a miracle."

"Yes, sir," Belinda said. "Why me?"

"Because you're used to fitting in," the Commandant said. "If I had another Pathfinder on hand, you would remain in the medical bay until you were fit to return to duty. As it is, I have no choice, but to use you. You're the only person qualified for the mission."

And the only expendable person, Belinda thought, without rage or hatred. A single Pathfinder cost millions of credits to train and equip with their implants; even if the Commandant had had another to hand, he would have good reason to consider ordering Belinda to go anyway. She was damaged goods. *But what does it matter?*

The Commandant met her eyes. "Do you have any doubts about your ability to complete this mission?"

No, because the mission is so vague I don't really know what I'll have to do, Belinda thought.

"No, sir," she said, out loud. "If worst comes to worst, I'll improvise."

"It worked last time," the Commandant said. He reached out and clapped her on the shoulder. "Good luck, Operative."

"Thank you, sir," Belinda said. She felt a strange queasy excitement, a sensation she hadn't felt since her first combat mission. It had long since become routine to go to war and place herself in dreadful danger. But now...she felt excited and nervous, determined to prove herself and yet terrified of screwing up.

And there's one definite advantage to going in alone, her thoughts reminded her. *There's no one else to be put at risk by your failures.*

She was still mulling over her thoughts when she was shown into Major Quincy's cabin. The Marine Intelligence officer nodded to her, then reached for a terminal and clicked a switch, activating a holographic display. This time, instead of a star chart, it showed a biography.

"We went backwards and forwards on what kind of cover to give you," Quincy said, cheerfully. He had a zest for life that Belinda had once shared, before the disastrous mission on Earth. "It was deemed inappropriate for you to have anything linking you to the Corps, not when it might earn you more attention than you might wish. Instead, we decided to give you a very loose profile, but one with military ties."

He tapped a switch. "Lieutenant Belinda Lawson," he said. "Native to New Washington, but joined the Imperial Army instead of the local self-defence force. You spent seven years as a military policewoman, then you had an...accident and retired, choosing to seek employment on tramp freighters rather than returning home. One of our covert operations starships will drop you off on Terra Nova, adding to your cover story."

Belinda frowned as she took the datapad and read the cover story. It was as complete as it was likely to be, without inserting details directly into local databases. Sending an inquiry to New Washington would probably raise red flags, but it was unlikely anyone would dig that far into her cover. If they did, she'd have to leave the planet before they zeroed in on her and started asking awkward questions.

"There should be a copy of the Imperial Army's records on Terra Nova," she said, slowly. "What happens if they check these records against my cover story?"

"That's the beauty of it," Quincy assured her. "The...details of your accident are classified, so the records won't be copied to Terra Nova. They were on Earth when the planet died, so they can ask questions all they like and...well, there will be no answers. Unless they hire a medium, I suppose."

"Very funny," Belinda said, crossly. "And what sort of accident am I supposed to have had?"

"I was going to suggest that you claimed to have been molested or raped by someone with powerful connections," Quincy said. "It would explain why the records are sealed – we can probably add a record hinting that you received a colossal payoff for keeping your mouth shut."

Belinda grimaced. It was vanishingly rare for female marines to be sexually harassed, certainly not by their male comrades. The men knew that the women had been through the same Slaughterhouse as themselves, without any allowances made for their gender. But it was far from uncommon for female soldiers outside the Marines to be harassed, not least because the Imperial Army *did* reduce the training program for them. And rapes were not unknown. The Civil Guard had no female soldiers at all.

"It will do," she said. On Greenway, her homeworld, there had been one way of dealing with rapists. The bastards were shot – and if the would-be victim shot him herself, before he could knock her down, she would receive a medal for improving the human gene pool. But it wasn't a standard of justice known in the Core Worlds, where defending oneself could lead to criminal charges. "I don't suppose you could add something about me defending myself?"

"Not really," Quincy said. "It would attract attention."

"Then leave it as it is," Belinda said. She sighed. "What can you give me to take down to the surface?"

"You have a gun permit issued by the Spacer's Guild," Quincy said. "We have quite a number of blank permits, so it's only a matter of adding your name and ID number into the blanks and tagging it to the weapon. I doubt you'll be allowed to bring it down to the surface, but they'd be more surprised if you didn't have one. But we can't give you any overt weapons."

Belinda nodded, unsurprised. It wouldn't be a problem. No matter the law, there was no shortage of illicit weapons in the Core Worlds. A few days on the surface, with access to local records, and she would be able to obtain any number of weapons. The trick would be doing it without being detected or identified.

And besides, she still had some of her implanted weapons. It would be enough to give her an advantage if the shit hit the fan.

"We can give you several different kinds of money, as would be expected of a spacer," Quincy continued. "The problem, however, is that they may be worth less than nothing on Terra Nova. I suspect the value of the Imperial Credit is still plummeting and...bearer bonds from a different world may be useless if there is no overall backer of debts. I've taken the liberty, therefore, of giving you copies of some of the latest music and entertainment flicks from several different worlds. You may be able to trade unsecured copies for cash. I've also given you some rare metal chips, but they may take them off you when you pass through customs."

"Understood," Belinda said. If worst came to worst, she could break into an unsecured apartment and rob it, or even pick up a man for a night. She'd done both before, during her first missions as a Pathfinder. It wasn't something she cared to do, but it was part of her job if necessary. "What other equipment can you give me?"

"A modified multitool, for a start," Quincy said. He held up the pencil-like device and demonstrated one of its hidden functions. "You can use this as more than just a lockpick, with a little effort. And it passes for a standard multitool unless someone takes it completely to pieces."

Belinda leaned forward, interested. She loved her rifle, even if she hadn't carried it since Han, but she enjoyed hearing about spy technology.

It never failed to amuse her, particularly when Quincy demonstrated how a sex toy could become a useful tool with a little manipulation.

She was almost disappointed when the call came for her to board her starship and leave the *Chesty Puller* far behind.

CHAPTER
FIVE

This may make more sense when you realise that a woman's virginity was vitally important to the locals. The parentage of her children could not be called into question. Even if it became clear within a few months that she was not with child, she could never give up her virginity again.

- Professor Leo Caesius, *The Decline of Law and Order and the Rise of Anarchy*

The waiting room had, if anything, grown fuller since Glen had entered the station and made his way to the conference room. Dozens of men and a relative handful of women sat on the hard chairs, some watched carefully by the security staff. Quite a few of them looked dangerous, which suggested the holding cells were already full. Glen sighed, remembering a handful of riots that had started in the waiting rooms, then started to look for the girl. She wasn't hard to spot.

He felt a flicker of rage as soon as he realised how she'd been treated. She was tiny, very obviously not a threat to a grown man, yet someone had cuffed her hands behind her back and shackled her legs together, before sitting her down on a hard metal chair. It was nothing more than an attempt to make it clear how helpless she was, that her fate was completely in the hands of her captors. Glen knew, all too well, that the Civil Guard considered it standard procedure. Helpless captives were safe captives.

Up close, it was clear she was alarmingly thin, so slight she barely came up to his shoulders. Her face was thin and pinched, her long brown hair was tied in a single ponytail that hung down over her shoulder and past her breasts. Her eyes were bleak and hopeless, suggesting depression and tiredness. Glen looked at her and felt nothing, but pity. She was very definitely not a suspect who needed to be chained up to prevent movement.

Damn you, he thought, looking towards the security staff. Procedures were procedures and no one, it seemed, had seen fit to apply some common sense. He wished he was surprised, but it was a common problem in the Empire. Someone could avoid punishment, even after a complete disaster, if they could prove they had followed procedures and stuck firmly to the letter of regulations. The morality of keeping a young girl in chains took second place to keeping one's job. But then, it wasn't really a surprise. These days, being unemployed meant the kiss of death.

He stopped in front of the girl and knelt down to face her. "Hi," he said. "My name is Glen, Glen Cheal. What's yours?"

"Helen," the girl said. Her voice was accented, suggesting she hadn't been born on Terra Nova. "I..."

She shuddered, her wrists flexing against the cuffs. Glen winced in sympathy, realising that she was on the edge of shock. Being a prisoner couldn't have been much fun, even if she hadn't been abused by her captors. And then she'd moved from one prison to another. Hell, it was quite possible the Civil Guardsmen who'd captured her had taken advantage of the situation to cop a feel. Glen considered making a full report and demanding satisfaction, but he knew it would be futile. The Civil Guardsmen regarded molesting captives as one of the perks of their underpaid job.

"It's alright," Glen said, patting her shoulder. She flinched away from his touch. "I have to take you out of here, really."

"They said I had to stay here and wear these," Helen said. She kicked her legs, rattling the chains. "And they told me I wouldn't be going anywhere."

Glen listened, but couldn't place her accent. There was something oddly formal about it, suggesting that Helen had grown up largely isolated from planetary society. Given her pale skin, he was fairly sure she'd lived on a spaceship rather than a planet, which might explain her build as well. It was quite possible that she'd been exposed to a low-gravity environment from a very early age, which would have left marks on her body even if she'd had treatments to prevent muscular decay. She'd just have to be given proper treatment before she went anywhere else.

"I think they were lying to you," Glen said. He winked at her. "And since my boss outranks their boss, what she says goes."

He reached into his belt and produced a handcuff key, which he pressed against her cuffs. They clicked free, allowing her to start rubbing her hands. Glen cursed under his breath when he saw the bruises – the cuffs had really been on too tight – then released her legs as well. It was against regulations, but if he couldn't catch Helen if she started to run he'd be well advised to hand in his resignation on the spot. And besides, where would she go?

"Come on," he said, holding out a hand to help her to her feet. "You need to go somewhere else."

Helen ignored his hand, but rose slowly to her feet under her own power. "They said I was a flight risk," she said, stumbling over the unfamiliar words. "Why...?"

"Well, I'll leave your hands free if you promise not to try to run," Glen said, turning to escort her down the corridor. "There's always someone who wants to show how badass he is by slapping cuffs on everyone in sight. I think they're compensating for something."

Helen giggled.

Glen smiled, then led the way through a pair of metal doors, into the examination chamber. A harassed-looking medic glanced up at him, then gave Helen a sharp look. Glen motioned for Helen to stand in front of the scanner, then turned to face the medic. The medic – her nametag read LAURA - looked as tired as Glen felt.

"I don't have time to do anything more than a basic examination," she said. "I've got thirty prisoners to process before the end of the day."

"That's fine," Glen said. He looked over at Helen. "Do as the nice medic says, will you?"

Helen said nothing as the medic poked and prodded at her, then took her fingerprints and ran them against the planetary database. Glen wasn't too surprised when the scan came back negative; in theory, every civilian on Terra Nova was supposed to be listed, but in practice there were plenty of people who had escaped the registration program. Helen's blood didn't produce any matches either, although there were definite traces of genetic modification, suggesting that she *did* come from a spaceship. It looked as though she'd been starved too badly for the modifications to do their work.

"She's underweight, probably hasn't been fed properly, and in mild shock," Laura said. "Be nice to her. I'd write a prescription for her wrists, but it would be quicker if I gave her the ointment now. There's no guarantee you'd be able to find it outside the station."

Glen nodded. There were shortages of everything now, from medicines to spare parts and weapons systems. The average citizen was entitled to free prescriptions, in theory, but the Marshals had busted a dozen criminal rings involved in producing fake medicines that, at best, would have been completely useless. At worst, they would have killed their victims or crippled them for life. Only the very rich or the well-connected could hope to find what they needed at once, rather than queuing for hours and taking their chances.

"Make sure you give her plenty of food too," Laura added. "She really needs supplements as well as proper meals, but I don't have any on hand. I'll put a request in through the system and you should get them within the next two weeks. No promises, though."

"I understand," Glen said.

Laura checked Helen's wrists again, then found her a small bottle of ointment. Glen took it – one of the security officers would probably object to a prisoner carrying anything through the station – stowed it in his pocket and motioned for Helen to follow him. She obeyed, walking beside him as they made their way through the corridors. Oddly, he noted that she didn't show any real interest in her surroundings. The last time he'd escorted a group of students through the station, they'd asked questions about everything until he'd been on the verge of tossing them all into the drunk tank for the night.

Maybe it's just an act, he reminded himself, *and she's just biding her time until she can make a break for it.*

He sighed, inwardly, as he pushed open the doors to the canteen. It was half-full, with officers and guardsmen sitting at various metal tables and stuffing their faces with half-edible food from the cooking staff, all of whom acted as though they'd been dragged out of the nearest mental asylum and chained to the stoves until they produced enough food to keep the officers fed. Glen pointed Helen towards a two-person table in the corner, then walked over to the counter and inspected the choices. As always, the food looked unpleasant to the eye, although it was plentiful. The Marshals joked that prisoners in the cells were fed better than their captors. There were times when Glen was sure it wasn't a joke.

"Two plates of chips and beans," he said, when the cook condescended to glower at him. It wasn't a healthy dinner for either of them, but it was hard for the cooks to turn it into foul-tasting sludge. "And two bottles of water."

"I suppose you'll be wanting extra chips," the cook grumbled, as he served the first portion and reached for the second plate. "For the girl, that is."

"Of course," Glen said. He pressed his ID badge against the scanner, then rolled his eyes as it deducted the price of the meal from his account. The Marshals were supposed to have their bed and board provided by the service – it helped keep them free from corruption – but it had long since been cancelled by the endless budget cuts. If Glen hadn't been paid a considerable sum in compensation after his wife had died, he would never have been able to afford his own apartment. "She would appreciate it."

"She'd probably also appreciate some hot chocolate," the cook said. "But we don't serve that here."

Glen glowered at him, then carried the tray over to where Helen was sitting, staring at nothing. He'd half-expected complaints about the food – the chips were stringy, while the beans looked as though they'd passed through the digestive system of a cow – but Helen merely started to eat without comment. It was another piece of evidence, he decided, that she was used to living in space. The spacers tended to eat algae-based ration bars and reprocessed foodstuffs rather than anything planet-dwellers would consider edible food. And they tended to rewire their stomachs to make eating it easier for them.

He felt his head swim, briefly, as the food interacted with the remainder of the drugs in his system. The tiredness faded, but he knew from bitter experience that it wouldn't be gone forever. He needed to get home and lie down before he collapsed completely, which meant taken Helen home with him and putting her in the guest bedroom. The food tasted as appalling as he'd expected, but at least it was edible. He looked up and saw her looking back at him, her pale eyes nervous. She had no idea, he reminded himself, what to expect from him.

"We'll go somewhere you can sleep," he said, as reassuringly as possible. The dammed guardsmen who'd taken her into custody had a lot to answer for. She probably thought he intended to take advantage of her as soon as they were alone. "You won't have to worry about answering questions for the moment."

Helen lowered her eyes, then opened her bottle of water and took a long swig. Glen did the same – the water tasted flat, as if it had been run through the purifier a few times before being bottled – and then replaced the lid and stowed the bottle on his belt. He knew, all too well, that they might be caught in a traffic jam when they drove back to his apartment and they might need the water then.

"We'll go back now," he said, standing. "Do you need to go potty first?"

"I'm not a child," Helen said, crossly. "I can go to the toilet on my own."

Glen concealed his amusement, then showed her to the nearest toilet and waited outside for her to finish. Standard procedure insisted that no prisoner was to go to the toilet alone, but he had no intention of forcing her to go with him in the room or finding a female officer to stay with her. He'd never liked sharing a toilet, even during basic training. But he was starting to worry when she finally came out of the room, having washed her face and remodelled her hair as well as using the facilities. He nodded to her, then escorted her through the sealed doors that led out into the enclosed car park. His service-issued car was parked at the far end of the giant compartment.

"You should use an aircar," Helen said, as he opened the door for her. The rear was configured for prisoners, but he didn't see the point in chaining her to the seat. "I think that would get you home quicker."

"The Air Traffic Control system was taken down a day or so after we heard the news from Earth," Glen said, as he started the engine. "Besides,

I never trusted the system. We were having countless accidents each day even before the Nihilists went to work."

He drove out and onto the darkened streets. There were no non-official cars on the roads, but there were far too many vehicles that had been branded as official after the curfew had been placed over the entire planet. He noticed a handful of troop transporters making their way through the streets, carrying soldiers to replace the guards on the central government buildings and other places of importance. The curfew would have been difficult to enforce over the city, but the Governor had imposed it on the entire planet. There just weren't enough men to hold the curfew in place, let alone arrest everyone who might break it for one reason or another. Glen had a dark suspicion that the Civil Guard had been making quite a bit of money from catching curfew-breakers, then letting them go in exchange for cash. But nothing had been proven.

"The stars look odd from down here," Helen said, suddenly. "They're twinkling!"

"That's the atmosphere distorting the light," Glen explained. He glanced upwards, briefly, then returned his attention to the ongoing journey. "The stars that appear to be moving faster are spacecraft and space stations. I believe the bigger ones are the giant battlestations protecting the planet."

"And making life harder for spacers," Helen said. "Daddy always says the crews require much bigger bribes than anyone else."

"That sounds about right," Glen said. He briefly considered probing at her, to see what she might tell him, but decided she probably didn't trust him enough yet. "Everyone tends to have a price."

He turned the car and drove down into the underground garage, then parked near the elevator. His apartment was midway up the giant skyscraper, behind the finest security system available to civilians. It wasn't a reassuring thought. He knew just how easy it would be for a determined attacker to make his way through the security screens and break into the apartment blocks. The only real defence was a solid – and firmly non-regulation – lock on the door.

Helen yawned, loudly, as they entered the elevator and rode up to the apartment floor. Glen encouraged her out, then pressed his fingertips against a scanner, opening the door that led into the main corridor. There was no one there, which didn't surprise him. The inhabitants of the floor kept themselves to themselves, most of the time. Earth's habit of obsessively ignoring what everyone else was doing had translated nicely to Terra Nova, even if it was annoying to a police officer. Few people could be considered reliable witnesses when paying no attention was considered a virtue.

He opened the door to his apartment and motioned for Helen to get inside. She looked a little disappointed at the bare walls – the only decoration was a picture of his dead wife – but Glen found it hard to care. Instead, he showed her the bathroom and told her to have a wash while he sorted out the guest bedroom. Isabel had slept there on more than one occasion, which was why he kept the room ready for guests at a moment's notice. He uncovered the bed, placed one of the bottles of water on the bedside table and checked to make sure there was nothing dangerous in the room. His personal weapons were stored in a safe – they should be inaccessible to anyone, but him – yet he knew that almost anything could become a weapon.

Helen eyed him nervously as she came out of the shower, wrapping a towel around her body. Glen carefully averted his eyes, making a mental note to go shopping if she was staying with him for longer than a couple of days, then pointed to the guest bedroom. Helen scurried inside and ducked under the covers. Glen found her his spare dressing gown – it was the only thing he had she could wear – then told her to get a good night's sleep. Closing the door behind him, he turned and walked back to his bedroom. He was so tired that he didn't bother to undress, or do more than stow his pistol in the safe before he lay down on the bed and closed his eyes. Sleep came almost at once.

And then, what felt like moments later, he heard screaming.

CHAPTER

SIX

Bride rape is far from the only act that is now criminal. It was not uncommon for children to be beaten at school – this is now considered child abuse. It was not uncommon for workers to be forced to slave for hours for tiny sums of money – we now have minimum wage laws to prevent exploitation. It was not uncommon for factories to be dangerously unsafe places, with workers killed or injured on the job – we now have laws in place to protect workers from unscrupulous employers.

- Professor Leo Caesius, *The Decline of Law and Order and the Rise of Anarchy*

Glen was on his feet at once, one hand reaching for his gun before he realised that the screaming was coming from his guest bedroom. He turned on the light, then opened the door into the hallway and stepped out into the hall. The noise was definitely coming from his guest bedroom. He hesitated, then opened the door, unsure quite what to expect when his eyes adjusted to the gloom. Helen was lying in the bed, thrashing helplessly in the grip of a nightmare. Glen cursed, then stepped forward and sat down next to her. She promptly hit out at him.

"It's alright," Glen said, taking her in his arms. Helen shuddered against him, her body dripping with sweat, then fell still. "You're safe now."

He held her gently as she started to cry, cursing his own inexperience with children and teenagers. If his daughter had lived...he pushed the thought aside angrily, then wiped the tears from her face with a pocket handkerchief. Helen looked surprised at his touch, then wrapped the dressing gown around herself tightly. Glen slowly started to release her, only to have her grab hold and cling to him for all she was worth. It was clear that she'd had more than *just* a nightmare. The aftermath of a traumatic experience could be just as bad, in many ways, as going through the experience itself.

"It's going to be all right," Glen promised her. He sighed, wondering if he was telling the truth. At some point, he would have to interrogate her about precisely what she was doing in that warehouse – and just where she'd come from, in the first place. Patty might not consider the girl to be a criminal, but she would want answers. And then...who knew where Helen might end up? "It will be fine."

He rose to his feet, then helped her stand up and walk into the kitchen. It was a smaller room than she might have expected, but Glen took most of his meals at the station, even if it did unpleasant things to his digestive system. Helen sat at the table as Glen poured them both hot milk, then stirred chocolate powder into her mug. She took the mug and wrapped her hands around it, but didn't try to drink. It was clear she was still caught in the aftermath of the nightmare.

Glen sat down facing her and took a sip of his own milk. "Do you want to talk about it?"

Helen looked up at him, her eyes haunted. "You wouldn't understand," she said. "You're a grown-up."

"I was a child too once," Glen said, giving her a sly smile. He was pretty sure, now, that Helen had been the only child on her ship. It didn't narrow the field as much as he would have liked, but at least it was a start. He made a mental note to start querying the Orbital Traffic Control service in the morning, then turned his attention back to her. "And you really should have seen my nightmares."

"It wasn't a nightmare," Helen said. "They felt *real*."

"Nightmares always do," Glen said. The day after they'd started basic training, he'd had nightmares about being on the wrong side of the law. Being shut up in a cell for training was bad enough, he'd decided; he hated to think about what it must be like to be locked up for real. "And then you wake up and start wondering what is real and what isn't."

Helen nodded, very slowly. "I was dreaming that they were cutting me open," she said, softly. "Their knives were digging into my very soul. And then there was nothing left of me. And then..."

She took a sip of her hot chocolate, then looked up at him. "Is that normal?"

"I used to dream of worse," Glen said. Dreams could be significant, he knew, but they could also be randomised nonsense. He'd watched entertainment flicks as a child, only to dream about them in later years. "Having nightmares after a traumatic experience isn't really uncommon."

He smiled at her, trying to be reassuring. "I find that talking about it can help," he added, softly. "Do you want to talk about it?"

"I don't know," Helen said. "They said..."

She broke off, her face twisting into a bitter grimace. "They said they'd kill my parents," she added, after a moment. "But they're already dead, aren't they?"

"The people in the warehouse are dead," Glen said. He was privately surprised that Helen had survived. The Nihilists had never been reluctant to kill children, let alone teenagers, in the past. They wanted to kill as many people as possible before they died themselves. "And we can try and help your parents, if you help us to find them."

Helen eyed him, trying to keep her face blank. Glen could read her, though; she simply didn't have any real experience in trying to lie to a law enforcement officer. She'd probably been taught not to trust officers, or anyone connected to the Empire's authorities, something that wasn't entirely uncommon for spacers. Independent spacers, in particular, dreaded attracting official attention, with good reason. Helen's parents wouldn't want to risk being charged with negligence on flimsy evidence and having their daughter taken away.

Glen cursed, inwardly. It was hard enough to enforce the law without the vast majority of the Empire's population regarding the bureaucrats – and the police officers who enforced their will – as implacable enemies. And it was impossible to placate the bureaucrats. They were happy to do whatever it took to ensure that everyone toed the line, or upheld standards that simply didn't apply to everyone. Spacers, in particular, often ensured that their children had a better – or a more practical – education than planet-born children. But the bureaucrats regarded trying to keep children out of the educational system as a form of defiance, one to be stamped on as quickly as possible.

"I don't know what's happened to your parents," he said, carefully. "But if they're in trouble, they won't be found unless you help us to find them."

Helen looked down at the table, obviously torn between the desire to keep her mouth shut and her fear for her parents' safety. Glen watched, hoping the Civil Guard never got it into their head that Helen could be a valuable source. They were authorised to use everything from starving a suspect to outright torture to extract information, if they felt the need. And Glen knew he couldn't protect Helen from them, not if they had good cause to suggest that he wasn't doing his job. They'd insist that Helen be turned over to them and Patty would be unable to object.

But all he could do was wait and see what she said.

"My parents command a freighter," Helen said, finally. "They were talking about going out beyond the Rim, now their contract with the shipping firm has expired. And then they took a contract to ship items to Terra Nova."

Glen frowned. The weapons?

"We had to take some staff onboard too," Helen said. "I don't think they liked me very much, because they kept glowering at me whenever they saw my face. But then they insisted I went down to the planet with them and they kept me in the warehouse and..."

She started to cry. Glen silently filled in the gaps as he stood and walked around to give her what comfort he could. Helen's parents had picked up the weapons, probably from one of the less-controlled worlds on the edge of the Core Worlds, and transported them to Terra Nova, accompanied by a team of Nihilist commandos. And then, to make sure that her parents kept their mouths firmly shut, the Nihilists had taken Helen as a hostage and transported her down to the planet. Somehow, Glen rather doubted she would have remained alive for long after the Nihilists had finished with her. Helen's value as a hostage had been shrinking rapidly ever since the weapons had been moved to the surface.

But it still didn't explain how they'd managed to get the weapons down without being detected.

Someone must have been slipped a very considerable bribe, Glen thought, although he knew the answer had to be more complex. He doubted there were more than a handful of officers on the orbital towers or spaceports who could have made sure the weapons slipped through without being inspected. *Or did they manage to subvert an entire team of inspectors?*

He sighed, then put the thought aside. The investigators would have to do the legwork, tracing the weapons back through the system until they uncovered the people responsible for letting them through the security screening and down to the planet. And then they could be interrogated thoroughly until they spilled their secrets, one by one. But it was unlikely they knew very much. They probably had gambling debts or other weaknesses the Nihilists had used to subvert them.

"You're not to blame," he said, looking back at Helen. "You didn't know what they were going to do."

Helen met his eyes. "So why am I here?"

"Because there is nowhere else for you to go," Glen said. He took a long breath. "We can't leave you in the cells or hand you over to the Civil Guard. If you have to stay here more than a week or so, we can probably find you a foster family..."

"On the surface?" Helen asked. Her face twisted in disgust. "I'd rather die."

"I understand," Glen said.

He did, although he didn't want to say why out loud. Most children on Terra Nova were insufferable brats who, if they were half as smart as they thought they were, would be rated as super-geniuses who could devise the next generation of phase drives or starship weapons systems. Most of them would spend fifteen years of their lives in the educational system, then graduate...and discover they were utterly unsuited to any form of proper employment. It was no surprise to him that they tended to either fall back on the Basic Living Stipend, and spend their time turning out the next generation of useless civilians, or turn to crime. What else could they do with their lives?

And Helen wouldn't have fitted in at any of the local schools. As someone from a spacer background, she would be too smart, too independent-minded, for her teachers. She'd be held back, then probably marked down as a trouble-maker before she finished her first week in a planetary school. And she would probably be bullied, or worse. Glen wouldn't have dreamed of sending his children to a public school. He knew them too well.

But it was harder and harder to find a private school that was actually affordable...

"I want my parents," Helen said. Tears appeared at the corner of her eyes. "I want to go back to the ship and forget everything. I want..."

"I know," Glen said. He helped her to her feet, then half-carried her back to the bedroom. "I don't know what will happen to you, but I will do my best to ensure you don't have to stay on the planet."

Helen looked up at him as he placed her on the bed. "Promise?"

"I promise," Glen said. "Now...do you want something to help you sleep?"

"No, thank you," Helen said. "But please stay here for a while."

Glen hesitated, then sat down beside the bed and turned off the light. "I'll be here," he said, as she pulled the covers over her head. "You go to sleep."

He thought, rapidly, as she tried to go to sleep. What *would* happen to her? If her parents were tried and convicted of shipping illegal weapons to a planet where weapons were banned, they'd be lucky not to be transported to a penal world and dumped there without any way to escape. Their daughter would either be taken into care – which would mean a foster family, eventually – or exiled herself, sold to a planetary development corporation as an involuntary colonist. Neither one would end well for Helen, unless she was very lucky. Few of the indents had decent lives, even on well-developed colony worlds. They were always called upon to do the shit work.

Or have as many babies as possible, Glen thought, bitterly.

He felt an odd surge of protectiveness that surprised him. It wouldn't be impossible for him to apply for her guardianship himself, although it was unlikely the Child Support Services would give her to him without a fight. They'd think that an Imperial Marshal wouldn't make a good father, even though he made a good salary and had an apartment of his own in a reputable part of town. He had no wife, after all, despite the fact that children and teenagers were expected to spend at least fourteen hours a day at school, then afterschool care.

You're being silly, he told himself, as he heard the sound of snores from under the sheets. *You don't know the girl, not really. You just feel protective because you saw her treated like a suspect by the Civil Guard. Patty won't go to bat for you if you want to take her into your home – and even if she did, would Helen want you if she blamed you for what happened to her parents?*

He stood, as quietly as he could, and crept out of the room, leaving the door half-open behind him. There was little point in going back to sleep, so he found his terminal and sat down in the kitchen, then accessed the private government communications network. The forensic teams had worked throughout the night, struggling to pull as much evidence as they could from the warehouse before they were redirected to yet another crime scene. Despite their haste, they had done a fairly good job. Most of the dead Nihilists had been identified, much to his surprise. But the Nihilists had probably classed the warehouse staff as more expendable than usual.

All former students, he thought, as he scanned the files. That wasn't a surprise. The students had spent years in education, gaining their degrees, only to discover that they were worthless pieces of paper. The Nihilists had plenty of experience in spotting people who might join their crusade and kill as many people as possible, everyone from the sexually-frustrated to the emotionally deprived who thought nothing of going out with a bang. *But why were they at the warehouse in the first place?*

The handful of unidentified bodies were more interesting. They'd been killed by the Civil Guard, according to the brief autopsies, but they'd also been carrying suicide implants that had flashed their brains to ash, as well as destroying the implants themselves. *That* was odd, for the Nihilists, suggesting their leadership had been more interested in protecting their secrets than normal. Who had the unidentified men *been*?

They're probably trained men, Glen thought. The reports made it clear that they had been at the peak of physical fitness, something unusual for the Nihilists. Another oddity to add to a series of odd points that didn't quite make sense. *Were they mercenaries to train the terrorists in using their weapons or were they just there to safeguard the consignment?*

He shook his head. The investigators would be heading to the homes and families of the identified Nihilists already, hoping to use them to track down their contacts. Glen knew the families had to be investigated, but he had a feeling that they would be useless. The Nihilists weren't known for urging their members to keep their families informed, not when the families might have other ideas. Instead, it was far more likely that the families would either be abandoned or quietly killed. The Nihilists were a jealous faction. Besides, killing one's own family ensured that one had nowhere to go.

Bastards, he thought.

He poured himself a mug of coffee, then settled back to start pulling information from the datanet. Hardly anything moved on Terra Nova without leaving an electronic trail, although spotting the *correct* trail could be quite difficult. Glen would normally have left the task to the data-crunchers on the support staff, but if he was technically suspended from duty he might as well have a look and see if anything jumped out at him. The person who had rented out the warehouse, for example, might have left an electronic trail for the investigators to follow. Or Helen's parents might have left a trail of their own.

Should have asked her for the name of the ship, his thoughts mocked him. *Some investigator you are.*

He shook his head, then buried himself in the data, only surfacing when it became clear that he was overloading his mind. To relax, he forced himself to access the local news instead, although it was far from relaxing. The news was heavily censored – the Governor had slapped strict controls on the media as soon as the Fall of Earth had been confirmed – but what little had gone through was a constant liturgy of horror. Terra Nova was slowly breaking down into anarchy...

...And all hell was on the verge of breaking loose.

And you're stuck on the planet's surface, he thought, coldly. *It might be time to leave.*

CHAPTER

SEVEN

And there are also acts that are now considered permissible where they were once forbidden. In the past, homosexual sex was often forbidden – and sometimes punished by death. Now, homosexuality is recognised as yet another kind of sexuality, no more or less deviant than heterosexuality.

- Professor Leo Caesius, *The Decline of Law and Order and the Rise of Anarchy*

"We're crossing the Phase Limit now," Captain Rogers said. "I thought you might want to be on the bridge."

Belinda nodded, then sat upright and swung her legs over the side of the bed. The flight to Terra Nova hadn't taken more than a day – the *Happy Wanderer* had a stardrive that was practically military-grade – giving her barely enough time to sleep and read through the endless series of updates from Marine Intelligence. She'd never visited Terra Nova – the files stated that no Marines were currently based there – but the briefings didn't paint a pretty picture. Terra Nova was threatening to go the same way as Earth.

Officially, Terra Nova had been humanity's first major settlement outside the Solar System, back when the Phase Drive had been first developed. It's development had been oddly-patterned, for reasons that the files didn't state, but by the time of the Unification Wars it had become one of the most heavily-populated colony worlds and a firm supporter of the First Emperor and his bid to unify the human race. Or, she noted cynically, the history books *claimed* it had been a firm supporter. It was astonishing how easily history could be rewritten to suit the victors.

She stood and made her way out of the cabin and up into the bridge. *Happy Wanderer* was a small freighter, with a five-man crew, all Marine Auxiliaries. On the face of it, she'd been told, there was nothing to set her apart from the thousands of other independent freighters in the galaxy, apart from her drive. And even *that* was explained, if inspectors bothered to demand answers. Standard procedure was to pay little attention to starships unless they intended to offload cargo or take it onboard.

And even if they do, she thought, as she stepped through the hatch, *manifests and papers can be faked.*

The bridge was dreadfully cramped, somewhat to her surprise. She found a chair and sat down, watching the main display as *Happy Wanderer* made her way into the system, heading directly towards Terra Nova. The system was heavily industrialised, with cloudscoops supplying a network of industrial plants second only to Earth's, but even her inexperienced eye recognised that the number of starships and spacecraft making their way through the system had fallen sharply, practically overnight. The cluster of warships orbiting Terra Nova itself looked isolated, while the Naval Base seemed half-empty. Or maybe she was just imagining it. She'd never set eyes on the system before the Fall of Earth.

"The traffic has definitely fallen sharply," Captain Rogers confirmed. "They might have started heading out to greener pastures."

Belinda couldn't have faulted the starship crews for wanting to run, even though their absence was damaging what remained of the galactic economy. The Core Worlds were on the brink of anarchy, with suddenly-independent governors and admirals considering private bids for power. It was no place to try to make a living when one's ship might be snatched without warning by a private navy and pressed into government service. Hell, it was quite possible that *Happy Wanderer* wouldn't be permitted to leave Terra Nova.

"We won't be going too far," he added, "but we won't have the ability to intervene openly."

"I understand," Belinda said. She would be on her own. If there were any retired Marines down on the surface, they weren't registered with the Corps. But she rather doubted there would be any, not when military veterans were poorly regarded in the Core Worlds. They tended to prefer heading out to the Rim, where their training and experience brought high salaries and genuinely satisfying work. "Just stay within communications range and I'll call you if I need you."

Hours passed slowly as the starship made its way into orbit and headed towards the nearest orbital tower. Belinda spent the time silently analysing the reports from the sensors and accessing news broadcasts from the planet itself. Most of them were so bland she *knew* they were censored, but what little slipped through the censors was alarming. Terra Nova was definitely on the verge of social collapse. The planet might not be *quite* as vulnerable as Earth – there was no planet-wide network of megacities and cityblocks – yet it was definitely at risk. And there were twenty billion people on the planet's surface...

"We've been offered a dozen charters already," Captain Rogers said, when she commented on that. "I think everyone with a lick of sense is trying to get the hell off the surface before the shit hits the fan."

Belinda shrugged. The entire Imperial Navy, at the height of its strength, would be hard-pressed to evacuate an entire planet in less than a decade. Terra Nova had far too many civilians for any uplift, even if they could be relied upon to cooperate without panicking or demanding that they were left alone on the planet's surface. The vast majority of the planet's population were doomed, unless their Governor actually *did* manage to save part of the Empire. Belinda distrusted the Onge Family through bitter experience, but the Commandant had been right. There was no other option.

"Just keep telling them that you're already chartered," she said. The last thing she needed was to have the *Happy Wanderer* sent off to a different star system. "And remind them that you won't be staying long enough to take up a new charter."

She returned to her quarters to collect her gear as the freighter slowed, then docked at the orbital tower with a faint bump. Belinda smiled to herself, knowing that the mission was about to begin, then glanced at herself in the mirror. The shipsuit clung to her curves in all the right places, leaving little to the imagination even though she was completely covered below the neck. It would suffice, she was sure, to distract attention from her. She checked her belt one final time, feeling naked without her pistol, then started the walk back through the ship to the personnel airlock. Captain Rogers was waiting for her there.

"Good luck," he said.

"Thank you," Belinda answered.

Captain Rogers saluted her, despite his sloppy uniform and generally unmilitary appearance, then opened the hatch for her. Belinda stepped through and took a breath, tasting the unique smell of Terra Nova as the hatch closed behind her. She couldn't help thinking that it smelled of fear.

"Please proceed to security gate five," an automated voice said. "Please be advised that objects on the list of forbidden contraband will be confiscated without warning or compensation if found in your baggage. Possession of any such items may also result in criminal charges, with a maximum penalty of permanent indenture or exile."

Belinda snorted and made her way down the stairs and into the security compartment. Like Earth's orbital towers, the security gates were set below the docking ports, but above the elevators that would take passengers and crew down to the surface. The complex was surprisingly deserted, at least of passengers. There were more armed security guards, fingering their weapons noticeably, than there were people passing through the gates. It was unlikely, she decided, as she removed her bag from her shoulder and placed it into the scanner, that anyone could slip any weapons through the barricade. But then, she wasn't planning to try.

The security guard studied her, his eyes hidden behind sunshades. Belinda didn't – quite – roll her eyes. The trick of hiding one's eyes to make oneself more intimidating was an old one, probably predating the human race's first fumbling steps into interstellar space. She surrendered her ID papers upon request, then settled back to watch how carefully he went through them. The documents should pass any level of inspection, she was sure, but she would learn a great deal by just how *thoroughly* they were inspected. It was barely five minutes before he looked up at her again.

"You're not staying on your starship?"

"No, sir," Belinda said, trying to look irritated at the question. It was the normal response, even though the question was actually surprisingly reasonable. What sort of idiot would *want* to go down to the planet's surface when chaos was threatening to sweep over the entire world? "I'm taking a few days leave and trying to look up a few of my old comrades."

"You might find that difficult," the guard observed. "Anyone with any valid military experience is being conscripted into the SDF. You might find yourself co-opted too."

"I'll take that chance," Belinda said. Was he actually trying to do her a favour? Or merely urge her to return to the ship instead of forcing him to process her paperwork? "It's been far too long since I've seen them."

The guard passed her the folder of documents, then smiled. "You have permission to spend up to four weeks on the planetary surface," he said. His voice became bored as he rattled off a well-practiced speech. "Should you wish to remain longer, without employment, you will have to apply to immigration officers down below. If you take up any form of employment, bear in mind that you will become liable for planetary tax as well as imperial tax. You will not be permitted to access any form of public funds and any attempt to do so will be considered a criminal offence. Do you understand me?"

"Yes, sir," Belinda said.

"Good," the guard said. "Money?"

"I have enough," Belinda said, shortly. She didn't want to show what she'd brought, if it could be avoided. They might start slapping extra charges on her if they thought she could pay. "And I will return to the ship long before I run out of cash."

"Glad to hear it," the guard said. He waved a hand towards the scanner. "If you'll step into the unit..."

Belinda made a face, as any passenger would, as she stepped into the scanner. Warning messages popped up in front of her eyes as the scanner went to work, her implants hastily accessing the control processors and feeding back false responses. The system wasn't advanced enough to detect some of her implanted weaponry, she noted, but it would certainly detect her other enhancements. And if they had a reason to think she merited further investigation, they would definitely discover her true nature. *That* would be inconvenient.

She glanced over towards the guard and saw him staring down at the display, a faint leer on his face. He was studying the curves of her body, she realised, rather than her innards. It was annoying, but it was a relief. She just hoped he didn't plan a strip-search as well, even though it would be technically legal. The last time she'd undergone the dreaded Conduct After Capture course, she'd been stripped and then poked and prodded in places she hadn't known she'd had. It wasn't an experience she cared to repeat.

"You seem to be clean," the guard said, finally. He waved for her to step out of the scanner. "Follow the red line down to the elevator, Miss Lawson. The next one departs in thirty minutes."

Belinda thanked him, then took her bag and walked down the corridor, uneasily aware of his eyes following her until she turned the corner. She'd expected the inspection – it was standard procedure whenever someone wanted to pass through security and go down to a planet – but she couldn't help feeling slightly defiled. Once, she knew, she would have taken it in stride, endured whatever she had to endure to get close to her target. Now, she felt...uneasy, or worse.

Mary O'Donnell would be shocked, she thought morbidly, remembering a legend among the Pathfinders. She'd endured far worse than a brief grope to get close to *her* target – and then she'd killed him and ripped his gang apart from the inside. They'd never known what sort of viper was crawling closer and closer to them until it was far too late. *Look how far you've fallen.*

She forced the thought aside as she stepped through the sealed hatch and into the elevator cabin. Unlike the shipboard elevators, it was large enough to pass as a lounge, complete with comfortable chairs, a small bar and a large viewscreen showing the outside universe. It was also almost completely deserted, apart from a handful of spacers and businessmen who eyed her carefully, then looked away when they decided she was harmless. One of the businessmen rose to his feet as she stepped up to the bar and made his way towards her, his eyes following the curve of her bottom. Belinda sighed and braced herself for a chat-up line she *knew* would be awful.

"Let me buy that for you," he said. He gave her a smile that was probably meant to be seductive, but looked rather like he was too pleased with himself to care about her feelings. "I can afford it."

"I'm sure you can," Belinda said. She was tempted to hit him – in her experience, businessmen were rarely interesting – but resisted the temptation. Instead, she took a measure of sadistic delight in ordering the most expensive drink on the menu and signalling the bartender to prepare it before her unwanted admirer had even managed to check the price. "I'm sure this drink will get you whatever you want."

The businessman smiled at her. No doubt he felt the same way.

"I've just signed a contract to produce material for a massive expansion of our shipbuilding program," he said, as they sat down at a table. He sat too close to her, although not close enough she could legitimately call foul. Somewhat to her disappointment, he hadn't blinked at the steep price tag for her drink. Instead, he'd bought the entire bottle. "Would you care to join me for a celebration?"

"It could be done," Belinda said, with the private thought that if he kept gulping expensive liquor like it was water he wouldn't have any money left soon enough. "But what sort of contract have you signed?"

The businessman – his name turned out to be Thomas Augustus – was quite happy to chat, a trait made more pronounced by his rapid descent into intoxication. Belinda sipped her drink and listened, carefully, as he boasted of his successes, starting with his ownership of a private manufacturing concern. Most of his boasting seemed to be nothing more than empty bragging, but – reading between the lines – Belinda started to realise that Augustus might own an industrial node that had no connections to anyone outside the Terra Nova System. It was, as strange as it might seem, the easiest one to repurpose for local purposes. The contact code he'd given her certainly indicated that he was a wealthy and well-connected man.

She made a mental note to look into it as Augustus sagged against her, then collapsed into a drunken stupor. Belinda briefly considered placing him in an embarrassing position, then thought better of it and arranged his body so he was lying on the seat instead. Once he was comfortable, she leaned backwards and closed her eyes, then started to use her implants to access the planetary database. It was a disappointing experience. The datanet was heavily censored, with all of the interesting files behind heavy protections she couldn't break without careful preparations. And she certainly couldn't risk attempting to do so while she was on an elevator. It would be far too easy for counter-hackers to trace the attempt back to her.

Augustus didn't wake up for hours, almost until the elevator had finally reached the ground station. He looked too woozy to do anything, but go home and sleep, so Belinda left him a copy of her contact code and walked out of the elevator before he could say a word. The security on the ground-side was noticeably thinner than it was in orbit, but she couldn't help noticing that there were hundreds of armed guards and soldiers on the streets. It looked as though the Governor was trying to make a show of force, using the appearance of strength to try to keep the civilians under control. But how quickly, Belinda asked herself, could he regroup his forces if the shit hit the fan?

And, she wondered, *does he even have anything left in reserve?*

She pushed the thought aside as she strode through the complex and found a datanet terminal, already keyed to show the addresses and booking details for the most expensive hotels in Landing City. Belinda rolled her eyes, then opened the selection criteria and altered it to ensure that it showed *all* the hotels, then searched for one that was reasonably cheap and yet moderately private. There seemed to be a shortage of hotel space, as far as she could tell; in the end, she had to pick one that looked suspiciously cheap. Shaking her head, she stood up and walked over to the taxi rack, firing queries into the local datanet as she walked. There would be time to decide her next move once she'd settled into her apartment and accessed the local situation.

The hotel, according to the map, wasn't *that* far from the orbital tower. She considered, briefly, walking, then dismissed the thought. There was too great a chance of being mugged and, while she was confident she could beat any muggers on the streets, it would be far too revealing. The alternative would be to surrender the bag, along with her tools. *That* would be far too inconvenient to be tolerated.

Sighing, she climbed into the first taxi and paid the driver, then settled back to watch as the taxi powered its way out of the orbital tower. If nothing else, she knew, she could spend the time studying the people on the streets. And then, she told herself firmly, she could decide what to do next.

CHAPTER
EIGHT

In sum, there is no ironclad rule of law enforced by an outside force. Humans, fallible humans, are forced to devise their own laws, their own codes of conduct.

- Professor Leo Caesius, *The Decline of Law and Order and the Rise of Anarchy*

"Who is that person?"

Glen looked up. He had been so engrossed in his work that he hadn't heard Helen rising from her bed and sneaking out into the hallway. She was looking at the viewer, which he'd left on, but muted. The screen would flash a red light if the regular news was interrupted by an emergency bulletin.

"That's the Governor," Glen said, as he waved Helen to a seat. He knew he sounded irritated and he didn't quite care. "He's making yet another broadcast asking people to remain calm and have faith in the government."

Helen looked down at the table. "And do they?"

"Not really," Glen said. He shrugged, then rose to his feet. "I think the Governor would be better off keeping the broadcasts for when he knows something genuinely new."

He walked around the table, found a large packet of cereal and placed it in front of Helen. A quick check of the food preserver revealed that he was almost out of milk, as well as juice and pre-prepared meals. He hadn't really bothered to cook for himself since his wife had died, knowing that she would have done a far better job. The mere act of putting a meal together reminded him more of her than he cared to admit. But if Helen was going to be his guest for the next few days, he couldn't really feed her nothing more than packaged algae bars and water.

"Pour yourself some of that, then add milk," he said, as he passed her a bowl. "We'll have to do some shopping today, I'm afraid."

"Oh," Helen said. "I don't have any money."

"Don't worry about it," Glen said, with the private thought that even having money might not be enough to buy more than the basics. The government had started trying to ration food, which might have worked if the black market hadn't been so active before the Fall of Earth. Right now, it was the only truly effective part of the economy, largely because it existed outside the control of the bureaucrats. But it also drained the planet's resources.

"I *should* worry about it," Helen said. She looked up at him, mournfully. "How should I pay for all this?"

"You don't have to worry about it," Glen reassured her, fighting down the impulse to tousle her hair. "I have enough saved to pay for your care and feeding for a few months. You won't have to repay it in future."

Helen didn't look happy, but she stopped arguing and poured herself some breakfast. Glen wasn't too surprised by her reluctance to accept charity, let alone a debt she didn't want to assume. It proved, in a way, that she had grown up on a trader ship. A child born on Terra Nova would be much less hesitant about accepting free food, or even something with a deferred payment scheme. The students who joined the Nihilists had so much debt that they couldn't hope to pay it off, no matter how hard they worked. It was part of the reason the economy had snarled up long before the Fall of Earth.

And if everyone owes money, he thought sourly, *how long will it be before we're all slaves?*

The thought was a worrying one. There was no such thing as debt relief in the Empire – unless, of course, there was a very real possibility that someone could pay their debts in the non-too-distant future. In theory, anyone who fell into debt could be forced to repay it in any manner the lending corporation chose. Hell, it was how some of the mining colonies kept their workers in bondage, through manipulating the prices until the miners were loaded with so much debt they could never hope to escape. And who knew what would happen if someone tried to enslave the entire population of Terra Nova?

He pushed the thought aside, then reached for a bowl of his own and took a large helping of cereal. Helen ate slowly, savouring the unfamiliar taste; Glen watched, with some amusement, as she took a second helping for herself. He'd definitely have to purchase more food if she stayed with him for more than a day or two, he told himself, despite the bureaucratic hassles. And she would start putting on more weight if she ate properly, given the genetic engineering worked into her DNA. A shortage of food hadn't been very good for her.

But when is it ever? He asked himself, as he finished his breakfast and placed the bowl in the sink. Helen eyed it with some puzzlement, clearly expecting the sink to start cleaning the dirty washing automatically, as it would on a starship. Glen smiled, then started to wash the bowl, before taking hers and washing it too.

"Get your clothes on," he said. Helen's shirt and trousers hadn't been washed, he knew, but there was nothing else for her to wear. He'd thrown out his wife's clothes after her death, unable to handle looking at them without her. "We'll go get you something more to wear."

He checked his message buffer – there was nothing, apart from a handful of low-priority updates – and then dressed himself. When he was finished, Helen was already waiting at the door, looking oddly nervous. It took him a moment to realise that she was probably agoraphobic to some degree, like most children who were born on starships. They had no real conception of the sheer size of a planet and found the open skies and landscapes terrifying. But then, planet-dwellers had the same feelings about being cooped up on starships for the rest of their lives.

"Don't worry," he said, as he opened the door. "The world won't kill you."

Helen tossed him an odd look as she walked outside, then waited for him to lock the door before leading the way down to the elevator. Glen briefly considered several separate choices of shopping mall, then decided to take her to the mall closest to his apartment block. It wasn't the largest in the city, let alone on the planet, but it should suffice for the basic essentials – and, as it was inside a giant building, should be less of a problem for Helen. Or so he hoped.

Helen blinked as they reached the lobby and walked out towards the underpass. "We're not taking the car?"

"It's only a few metres away," Glen said. "There's no point."

The air smelt vaguely unpleasant as he stepped through the door, a whiff of burning that bothered him more than he cared to admit. A dozen armed guards, wearing bright green uniforms, eyed them carefully as they walked into the sunlight, then ignored the newcomers completely. Their uniforms, Glen knew, marked them as private security guards, rather than any police or military officials. They tended to be poorly trained and alarmingly trigger-happy, even on Terra Nova. But then, the companies that hired them could afford to pay the fines for unauthorised discharge and cover up any unfortunate accidents. And anyone who happened to be hurt by accident would find it impossible to seek any recourse.

Helen clung to his hand as they made their way through the underpass, trying to ignore the dozens of homeless people leaning against the walls, trying to sleep or beg for money. Glen remembered watching helplessly as people were evicted from their homes, after losing their jobs, and told to sleep on the streets. Or die. Every day, bodies were found lying where they'd fallen, having died of exposure or starvation or simply giving up and sitting down to die. The social network that should have helped them had failed completely.

"You don't see people like that on space stations," Helen murmured. "Why are they here?"

"Space stations can afford to feed everyone, even if it's just algae," Glen muttered back. It was rare for anyone to actually *starve* on a space station, though they might wish to starve rather than force more tasteless ration bars down their throats. "Here, it's not so easy to keep people fed."

"It's awful," Helen said, out loud.

Glen nodded in agreement as they reached the entrance to the mall. The door remained firmly closed until he pressed his credit chip against the scanner, confirming that he could afford to buy something. The Civil

Guard had arrested too many people sneaking into the mall in hopes of shoplifting or pick-pocketing; now, the only way to enter was to prove that one could afford to pay. Glen had a feeling the security measures wouldn't last for long, not when there were more and more desperate people on the streets. There had already been rioting and looting at some of the smaller shopping districts.

They passed through the doors, then headed for the clothing stores. Glen had always hated shopping for clothes, so it was a relief to turn Helen over to one of the shopping assistants, with orders to purchase a basic wardrobe suitable for a young girl. Once Helen was chatting happily to the assistant, Glen walked down to the food stores and winced when he realised that prices had gone upwards, again. He took a cart, picked up everything he and Helen would need for several weeks, then pushed it back towards the counter. The till-keeper eyed the small pile of food with some concern.

"You don't have a need for half of this," he said, once he'd run Glen's ID through the datanet. "Some of it should be returned..."

Glen ground his teeth. A person's shopping was carefully monitored, either to supervise their health or to watch for anyone purchasing more food and supplies than they should have needed. It had never failed to annoy him; hell, as a junior officer, he'd been called out to hundreds of fights when someone had objected to being told they weren't being allowed to purchase something they thought they needed. And to think there wasn't anything *dangerous* in what he'd chosen.

"I have a need for it," he snapped, angrily. His patience failed completely and he produced his Marshal ID from his pocket. "I suggest you hit the override and process the purchases."

The till-keeper looked dubious. "I should ask my supervisor..."

"I think you can make a decision for yourself," Glen snarled, although he knew the till-keeper would be blamed for anything that went wrong. There were times when he felt that half the Empire's problems stemmed from a simple lack of willingness to make decisions. But when it was safer to pass the buck up the chain to higher authority, few people could be expected to put their necks on the block. "Or would you like to explain to *my* superiors why you are delaying my shopping trip?"

He watched, unsurprised, as the till-keeper hastily scanned the purchases, then dropped them into small plastic bags. There'd probably be a notation made in the system that he'd purchased more than he should have needed, he knew, and there would probably be someone sent out to ask a few pointed questions. It was incredible, he thought, as he paid for his purchases. The Empire was strangling itself to death with red tape and a bureaucratic attitude that assumed *everyone* had to be guilty of something. But there was no point in trying to fight. Civilians without connections were helpless against the full weight of the bureaucrats.

"I'll send back the trolley later," he said, once everything was bagged up. "And *thank you.*"

The till-keeper said nothing as Glen took his trolley and pushed it away, back down to the clothes store. He heard someone arguing with the security guards in the distance, and briefly wondered if he should intervene, then realised there was no need as the guards led a pair of tough-looking young men out of the store. They'd probably be pushed in front of a judge's assistant, then sentenced to involuntary colonisation within a day, he knew. It was unlikely they'd ever have a chance to contact their parents before they were banished from their homeworld forever.

They might be the lucky ones, he thought. *Terra Nova might not remain very civilised for much longer.*

Helen was waiting for him at the entrance to the clothing store, looking overwhelmed. Her assistant waved to Glen, then showed him a dozen separate outfits and pieces of underwear, several too frilly for Glen's peace of mind. He vetoed two of the outfits – he wouldn't have willingly allowed any girl to wear something that barely covered her private parts, even if she had been old enough to live on her own – and shook his head at a third. Helen looked oddly relieved, but the shop assistant looked furious. Glen wondered, absently, if she or her managers had an arrangement with the company that manufactured the outfits.

"She has a human right to wear what she likes," the assistant said. "And this will suit her..."

"If she happened to be working in the red light district," Glen snapped, placing the rejected outfits on the desk. "I wouldn't have *any* daughter of mine wearing these pieces of overpriced crap *anywhere.*"

The assistant looked as if she wanted to argue further, but clearly thought better of it. Glen wondered what she was thinking, then decided it didn't matter. Maybe she could make a complaint against him – it was a common tactic for kids who had parents who were unwilling to let them run rampant – but it wouldn't get her very far. Helen wasn't Glen's daughter, after all, and he had no obligation to do *anything* for her.

"Wrap the remainder up, then charge them to my card," he said. He turned to face Helen as the assistant leapt to obey. "Did you chose several practical outfits?"

"You saw them," Helen said. She pointed to two outfits that resembled loose shipsuits. "I can wear those anywhere."

"But they'll look so basic, so *cheap*," the assistant said. "She has to look fashionable."

"No, she doesn't," Glen said. He didn't follow fashion, but there was something wrong about a society that thought young girls should walk around nearly naked. Besides, Helen wouldn't be going outside his apartment, at least until Patty made a final decision about her future. She certainly wouldn't be going to any clubs or schools – and besides, she didn't know anyone on Terra Nova besides Glen himself. "Now, bag them up and we can go back home."

As soon as they were out of the shop, Helen gave him a sudden hug.

"She just kept insisting I take more and more," she said, softly. "I thought you were going to be mad. My parents would have been furious if I'd brought so much back to the ship."

"I wouldn't blame them," Glen said. He looked down at the bags, then smiled. "She's paid a commission for every outfit she sells, I think. Don't let her bully you into buying anything you don't want."

Helen looked upset. "But she kept saying I would *have* to wear stuff if I didn't want to look like an outsider."

Glen winced. It was perfectly true that wearing the wrong clothes could mark someone as an outcast, certainly in the more unpleasant schools on Terra Nova. He'd arrested too many kids trying to steal clothes their parents couldn't or wouldn't buy for them, just because they were bullied if they didn't wear the right clothes. But when they did, their clothes were often stolen by the school bullies. It just wasn't fair.

"I think you should always ask yourself *why* you're being told something," he said, dryly. "I think she wanted you to buy as much as possible, so she would hardly try to talk you out of buying lots of crap."

Helen giggled.

On impulse, Glen took her to the nearest entertainment shop, found her a datachip and allowed her to purchase a number of movies and flicks for her to watch while he was at work. Helen seemed more interested in movies meant for older teens, he noted, rather than anything intended specifically for children...although there were times when the lines were hard to determine. As an afterthought, he bought her a few days worth of access to the online gaming network, then added a handful of educational programs. There had been no time to assess just where she was, academically, but he was pretty sure she'd be ahead of planet-side students in the same age group.

"Thank you," Helen said, when they were done. "But how will I ever repay you?"

"Don't worry about it," Glen said, again. He could ask Patty for compensation, if he kept receipts and submitted them to her, or he could simply pay himself. "It's not as if I have much else to spend money on, these days."

He took her to a small eatery and bought her a buffet lunch, then watched with some amusement as she tasted everything on the menu. Glen had never been really impressed with buffets – they were often heavily flavoured to disguise the fact the cooks used very poor meat – but Helen seemed to like it. And she ate enough to ensure she would start to recover from her imprisonment.

"We'd better go home," he said, once she'd stuffed herself. "And you can watch your new shows, if you like."

"Thank you," Helen said, rising. "And what will you do?"

"My work is never done," Glen said. Actually, he'd reached the limits of what he could do without returning to the office. All he could do now was watch the progress of the investigation from a distance and make suggestions. "Or I could watch with you."

"Please," Helen said.

After a moment, Glen nodded.

CHAPTER

NINE

This is not an easy task. Many of the examples I outlined above consist of flawed humanity responding to problems they faced at the time, which then became enshrined in law. The legal hatred of homosexuality might well date from a time when breeders were of vital importance and, thus, homosexuality could not be tolerated.

- Professor Leo Caesius, *The Decline of Law and Order and the Rise of Anarchy*

"This is your room," the hotel bellhop said. "I trust it is to your liking?"

Belinda peered past him into the small room. It was simpler than she'd expected, with a large bed, a small table and a small washroom, complete with shower and wash basin. The room wasn't really big enough for more than one or two people, but she'd had worse. She'd had to share a barracks with nine men back when she'd been a Rifleman, years ago. Compared to that, the hotel room was almost luxurious.

"It is satisfactory," she said, flatly. She turned to look at the bellhop, absently noting how he tried hard not to look at her chest. "Do you offer room service?"

"The menu is in the desk," the bellhop said. He gave her a smile that was probably intended to be seductive, but he wasn't old enough to pull it off. "My name is James, My Lady. If you need anything, don't hesitate to call me."

Belinda smiled back, then strode into the room and placed her bag on the desk. She'd once spent a week working in a hotel along the Rim and it was astonishing what some guests asked for – and got, if they paid enough money. James might just get lucky with an older female guest, if she wanted some company for the night. His superiors would turn a blind eye as long as his duties were completed to their satisfaction. But she knew he wouldn't be getting lucky with her.

"Thank you," she said, instead. "And goodbye."

He closed the door, which clicked to indicate it was locked. Belinda wasn't impressed. If she couldn't pick the lock with a hairpin, or a standard terminal rigged to serve as a hacker system, she would be very disappointed in herself. The door wasn't *meant* to be completely secure, anyway. All it was meant to do was deter thieves who had slipped past the guards on the ground floor and made their way up to the guestrooms.

She opened her bag, then carefully checked the room for bugs. There were two, an audio pickup hidden within the light over her back and a visual pickup in the doorframe, ready to record pictures of her undressing. She wasn't unduly surprised; these days, there was no real expectation of privacy anywhere, unless one paid enough money to guarantee it. The recordings could be accessed by local law enforcement, if they requested them, or anyone else, if they supplied a sufficient bribe. She studied the location of the bug for a long moment, then carefully plotted out ways to block its vision if necessary. For the moment, she would just have to endure knowing that the hotel staff could peek in on her whenever they felt like it.

Idiots, she thought, as she unpacked her bag, then lay down on the bed. A quick check revealed that the hotel was using a very basic datanet monitoring system, intended to record everything the guests did online. There was no warning notice barring them from any particular parts of the datanet, she noted, which struck her as ominous. It seemed the hotel either didn't care to make legal warnings or threats...or that the staff were watching for opportunities to blackmail their guests, later. Somehow, she wasn't too surprised.

She opened her implants and activated a handful of hacking programs designed by the finest WebHeads in the Marine Corps. The hotel's system barely even spluttered as she inserted her commands into the system, then took over, ordering it to ignore everything she did through the network. A handful of minor changes would make it harder for anyone to zero in on her particular access, although she knew there were limits to how far she could go without being caught. It wouldn't be hard for investigators to deduce the use of a neural link and a simple scan of her brain would reveal the link – and much more besides.

Closing her eyes, she drew on the vast tidal wave of data and started to try to search for additional pieces of information. But there was very little, beyond censored news bulletins and reassuring broadcasts from the government that didn't seem very reassuring at all. There was no barrier to accessing the entertainment networks – pop-ups in her head invited her to download the latest pornographic videos, or view endless bland crap from Earth before the Fall – but there was very little hard data on the datanet. Even the omnipresent datanet forums seemed to have been closed down.

They're trying to make it harder for panic to spread, she thought. It *was* standard procedure if the shit was threatening to hit the fan, but she couldn't help thinking that it was a mistake. Rumours would spread faster than anyone realised, rumours which would be impossible to counter before they had already reached far too many people. *But the people can still talk face-to-face, spreading the word from person to person.*

She poked through the datanet, looking for the links she knew had to exist, the links that would allow her to access the government's datanet. But, no matter how she tried, she couldn't break into the network through her implants. The system looked to have been altered to the point where standard access codes, even hacker tools, wouldn't work properly. It was an impressive achievement, she had to admit, but it was also worrying. What was the government trying to hide?

Opening her eyes, she undressed and climbed into the shower, careful to keep the links to the datanet open. If she couldn't get into the government's files, she could pull more out of the civilian datanet than they might have realised, including the names and details of government officials. But there were just too many for her to process properly, she realised, numbly. The Governor seemed to be assembling his own private army. Everyone with military experience was being called up to serve at the Governor's pleasure. Was it a sensible precaution in the face of chaos, she asked herself, or a sign of something more sinister?

And there was nothing on the planned conference at all.

Belinda finished washing herself, then strode back into the main room, disconnecting the links. There was no point in trying to hack the system further, not now. She would need to be in close proximity to a government-owned node without access codes of her own, she suspected, and she'd have to *find* a node first. It would be tricky, unless she got very lucky; she knew, all too well, that most such nodes were concealed within military bases. But there were other ways to get access to government codes.

She dressed – a shirt that was just tight enough to draw attention to her breasts and a skirt that hung down to her knees – and then picked up the information brochure the hotel had supplied for its guests. One page detailed all the various pubs and nightclubs around the centre of Landing City, including one that largely catered to government employees having a drink after a hard day at work. Belinda rather doubted they knew what a hard day really was – she'd spent weeks on campaign before she'd submitted her name for Pathfinder Selection – but it hardly mattered. The pub would be a good place to start trolling for potential sources.

Picking up a small handbag, she carefully noted where she'd left everything and then walked out the door, taking care to lock it behind her. It was possible that *someone* would search her bags while she was out, although she had nothing to hide. She walked down to the elevator, then rode down to the ground floor and made her way out onto the streets, aware of eyes following her as she left the building. She'd dressed, after all, to attract attention.

Night was slowly falling over Landing City as she walked towards the pub, but despite the threat of the imminent curfew people were thronging around, eating, drinking and trying to enjoy themselves. And yet, Belinda could sense a tension in the air that reminded her of countless worlds about to undergo a massive social upheaval. The population wouldn't be partying so hard if they hadn't been trying to convince themselves that everything was normal. Most of the younger people – including some barely entering their teens – had eyes that revealed their desperation. They knew, even if they didn't want to admit it to themselves, that their time was running out.

She sucked in her breath as she saw the pub. It was larger than she'd expected, with hundreds of men and women inside, drinking beer and chatting to their friends and workmates. They had the same attitude as the people outside, she noted, but there was a nastier edge to it, one that worried her more than she cared to admit. These people were prepared to be nasty because they still had jobs, yet they were also unwillingly aware that they could lose their jobs very quickly. The world had turned upside down.

Switching her audio-discrimination programs into primary mode, she scanned the crowds for a likely target. Seduction had been one of the classes for Pathfinders – it wasn't part of the normal Slaughterhouse training – but it had also been largely intuitive. There were men who would think it was normal to have a beautiful woman chatting them up and men who would find it instantly suspicious. The trick, she'd been taught, was deducing the method most likely to work for one's prey and using it ruthlessly. It was only five minutes before she spotted a suitable candidate sitting at the edge of the room.

A wallflower, she thought, as she made her way towards him without being obvious about it. He was in his early thirties, if she guessed right, but he had a haggard expression on his face that made him look older. It was obvious he wanted to join in the conversation, in the mindless drinking and women-chasing his peers engaged in after work, but it was also clear that he simply didn't have the nerve. Belinda concealed her amusement as she sat down facing him. Unless she was completely wrong, this was going to be easy.

"I don't like the crowds here," she said, by way of introduction. "How about yourself?"

"I don't like them either," he said. He looked up at her, allowing her to see his face clearly. It would have been handsome if he'd taken proper care of himself. "But..."

He looked back down at the table, trying to avoid staring at Belinda's chest. She could practically read his thoughts; lust, a desire for her, and yet a fear that she would reject him in a manner so crushing that it would destroy whatever was left of his pride. Such a man feared humiliation because he'd been humiliated so often. Belinda had a feeling that he wouldn't advance in the Civil Service, if only because he couldn't make the connections his fellows could by chatting to their superiors. But at least he wouldn't be kissing their buttocks in public.

"My name is Benny," Belinda said. It was close to her real name without being too close for comfort. Her target wouldn't have any clear memories of her after she was done, but there was no point in taking chances. "I'm new here."

"Welcome to Terra Nova," the man said. "My name is Julius. Julius Stevenson."

Belinda smiled at him, then ran his name and face through the datanet, wondering what it would turn up. Moments later, she had her answer. Julius Stevenson was listed as a low-level Civil Service official, a data-entry officer. He was a suitable target for a first attempt at gaining government-issue codes, she decided. At the very least, he might be able to tell her who to target next.

She chatted about nothing for long moments, wondering absently when he would find the nerve to buy her a drink. It was nearly ten minutes before Julius offered, so quietly that it was clear that he expected rejection. Belinda smiled, accepted the offer, then kept chatting to him as he drank several more glasses in quick succession. She had a feeling he was nerving himself up to ask her if she wanted to go somewhere more private.

"This place is getting too loud," Julius said, as someone turned on a jukebox and heavy metal music started to play. "Do you want to go elsewhere?"

"Yes, please," Belinda said. She took his hand, noting with some amusement that he was swaying slightly on his feet. This was not a man who drank heavily, she deduced, from how quickly the alcohol had affected him. Her presence had affected him more than he'd realised. "I'd like to go elsewhere."

His nerves clearly grew worse the further they moved from the pub. Belinda, feeling an odd moment of sympathy, made it easier for him by kissing him as soon as they were alone, then smiled inwardly as he tried to kiss her back. He was either out of practice, part of her mind noted, or he had never been *in* practice. Moments later, his hand was groping her bottom through the skirt. Belinda pushed herself against him, then pulled back. He made no attempt to keep her close to him.

"Not here," she said. "How close is your apartment?"

Julius's apartment turned out to be a single-room compartment in a towering block that looked like a smaller version of Earth's city-blocks. Belinda allowed him to lead her inside, his hands roaming her body as though he had never touched a woman before, then pushed her fingertips against the back of his neck. The hidden injector didn't even hiss as it shot a light sedative into his body, sending him staggering to his knees. He was out before his body hit the ground. Belinda picked him up effortlessly, then carried him to his bed and laid him out on the sheets. There was a grin on his sleeping face that seemed remarkably out of place.

She smiled back, then started to search the apartment for anything useful. Julius, like most civil servants, had kept copies of all of his personal documents, stashing them in a hidden safe behind a painting on the wall. Belinda snorted to herself – hiding a safe behind a painting was so old that it was the first place anyone would look – then started to work on the combination lock. It clicked open within seconds, allowing her to open the metal hatch and bring out the paperwork. A glance at each page, using her implants, allowed her to record what she saw for later study. And then she found the access datachip.

"Twit," she said, out loud. Julius would be in deep trouble if his superior found out just how easily she'd stolen his access codes. "You're lucky I'm going to blur your memory."

She used her implants to access the chip, then copied the codes over into her neural link. It was easy enough to test them, although she was careful not to try to actually hack into the sections outside Julius's authorisations. *That* would have to wait until later, once she'd parsed out enough of the system to be fairly sure she could hack into it without immediate repercussions. If she had been designing the system, she would have made sure it was capable of tracking any access, even if it seemed to have the right codes. Hell, she would have ensured the system was inaccessible outside heavily guarded and secure locations.

Julius moaned in his sleep. Belinda looked up from where she was carefully replacing everything where she'd found it, then frowned. She knew what she had to do, now; she had to inject him with something to blur his memories, then walk away and leave him alone. His imagination would give him an encounter that had ended well for both of them. She'd seen it done before. And yet...part of her didn't want to simply walk away. She felt a strange pity for Julius, someone so out of place and yet trying to do his job.

And someone who will be blamed for giving me the codes if I'm caught, Belinda thought, as she rose to her feet. *He won't have a chance.*

She looked down at him, torn between two conflicting emotions. The cold dispassion she'd been taught to embrace told her to drug him, then go; the other feelings she'd felt welling up inside her said otherwise. She could have stayed with him, reassured him that she was real, even made love to him. But she knew she couldn't risk it. Julius wouldn't be content with a one-night stand, not really. He'd want to see her again and again until he saw through her cover or she had to do something more drastic to cover her tracks.

"I'm sorry," she muttered, as she pressed her fingertips against him for the second time. His body twitched against hers, then subsided. "But I don't have a choice."

Julius moaned, again. Belinda watched him fall into deeper slumber, then kissed his forehead and turned to walk out the door, feeling oddly unclean. She'd done worse than drug someone for information before, ever since she'd become a Pathfinder. But why did she feel remorse now?

You're not quite a Pathfinder any longer, a voice said, *and you're no longer stable. How long will it be before you go completely mad – and rogue?*

"Shut up, Doug," she growled, as she closed the door behind her. "You're dead."

CHAPTER

TEN

Furthermore, prejudice will have its say when laws are written. There are no shortages of past legal structures that denied women equal rights to men (or vice versa), gave rights to parents denied to their children or made judgements based on such oddities as skin colour or age.

- Professor Leo Caesius, *The Decline of Law and Order and the Rise of Anarchy*

"You know, you should get yourself a head-com," Patty said, as soon as Glen answered the call. "You'd be woken in a flash."

"I always thought they were sinister," Glen said. He glanced at his watch, then swore under his breath. It was five o'clock in the morning, an hour before curfew was due to be lifted. "And I didn't want *more* voices in my head."

"How very reassuring," Patty said. His boss snorted, rudely. She'd called him out of the blue, which meant trouble. Unlike some of his superiors in the past, she'd *been* a Marshal and understood the value of a good night's sleep for her men. "I'm afraid your suspension has been suspended. I need you back at the station."

"Wonderful," Glen said, dryly. He would have been more enthusiastic if he hadn't been woken far too early in the morning. Spending time watching movies with Helen had been curiously enjoyable, to the point they'd both stayed up too late. "And my charge?"

"Leave her in your apartment," Patty said. "Does she have enough sense to stay there?"

"I think so," Glen said. He hastily ran through a mental checklist of everything that would have to be locked away, out of reach. "I can lock the door, if necessary, but if there was a fire..."

"Take the risk," Patty said. "Unless you'd like to bring her to the station for the day?"

"I think that would bring bad memories back to her," Glen admitted. "She's told me a few things, but I've been reluctant to press her too far."

"Then leave her at your apartment," Patty ordered. "I'm sending Isabel to pick you up, so I'll expect the both of you here in sixty minutes."

The connection broke. Glen swore to himself, then climbed out of bed and hastily jumped into the shower. The cold water snapped him awake, but he still felt too tired for comfort as he returned to his room and dressed, then pulled his pistol and terminal onto his belt. He'd made enough notes from what Helen had said over the last couple of days to help push the investigation forward, if he had time. He had a feeling that Patty wouldn't have called him back into work, risking the wrath of the Civil Guard, if she hadn't thought she needed him. It didn't bode well.

As soon as he was ready, he tapped on Helen's door and waited for her to call out. He opened the door and smiled at her, noting that she was wearing the new nightgown he'd purchased her. She looked adorable and terrifyingly young, far too young for the outfits she'd been offered at the shop. The surge of protectiveness he felt at the thought was terrifyingly strong. He'd only known Helen for a couple of days and he was already prepared to walk through fire for her.

"I have to go into work," he said, when she was awake. "Stay in the apartment, ok? Don't try to leave."

Helen nodded, wordlessly. Glen gave her a reassuring smile, then walked out of her room. Helen wouldn't be bored – she had flicks and games and even the educational programs – but he knew how tempted he would have been to explore the apartment block on his own, once his parents had gone out for the day. He hoped she wouldn't try the door, no matter what else she did. She might not respond well to being locked in like a prisoner.

Which she is, a voice at the back of his head reminded him. *To all intents and purposes, she is a prisoner. And you have no idea what will happen to her in the future.*

His wristcom buzzed. Pushing the disturbing thought aside, he stepped through the door, checked the lock, then took the elevator down to the garage. Isabel had already parked the cruiser near the elevator doors, blatantly ignoring the signs ordering guests not to park anywhere near the spaces reserved for the wealthiest residents. Glen doubted anyone would complain, not when they saw the cruiser. The Marshals might be a shadow of the force they'd been in the glory days of the Empire, but they could still cause trouble for anyone who got in their way.

"I hear you've become a dad," Isabel said, as he clambered into the cruiser and closed the door. "Congratulations."

"Thank you," Glen said, sourly. "What progress has been made on the investigation?"

"We spoke to the families of the dead terrorists," Isabel said, as she guided the cruiser back onto the exit ramp. "None of them knew a thing, of course. They're shocked and outraged that *anyone* could believe their little darlings capable of such a shitty act. It won't be long before they start calling for an independent investigation."

Glen nodded, ruefully. It was unlikely the families would get anywhere, but there were always ambitious populist politicians who might take their grief and turn it into a weapon for their campaigns. He couldn't blame the families for wanting to think the best of the dead, yet it was hard to give anyone the benefit of the doubt when he'd seen the aftermath of too many Nihilist attacks.

"They all fit the standard patterns," Isabel added. "Had poor grades and big debts – a couple actually had debts to loan sharks as well as the standard loan companies. I've had teams going through their possessions, but unless we get very lucky we won't find any leads there. The data-crunching might turn up a more promising angle of attack."

"True," Glen agreed. The electronic trails of the dead terrorists would converge, he was sure, if they'd been fool enough to leave a trail. And where they'd been together, they might well have been planning their operations. "What else did they have in common?"

"They took a number of classes," Isabel said. "The only one they had in common was Ethical Treatment of Minority Communities."

Glen snorted in amused disbelief. He had never been opposed to allowing people to find their own ways to live, no matter how crazy they sounded to his ears, but he had never believed that such independent communities were exempt from the law. If a religion happened to demand something from its believers that was against Imperial Law, that religion couldn't be used as a shield for the believers to hide behind. It wasn't an attitude that was shared by idealistic students, who thought that minorities were picked on simply for being minorities. They never seemed to realise that some minorities included a number of very unpleasant human beings.

"That class is probably worth investigating," he said, instead. "Do we have anything on the staff?"

"A few minor citations for being public nuisances," Isabel said. She turned the cruiser, then headed into the underground garage below the station. "One of them was arrested at a demonstration twenty years ago and managed to parley it into a successful academic career. I think she was actually accused of plagiarising at some point, but it was settled in-house, with no need for police involvement."

"Lucky for us," Glen muttered. The various law enforcement agencies had quite enough problems without trying to tackle academic plagiarism as well. "What's got the boss so steamed up?"

"There have been attacks," Isabel said, as she parked the cruiser. "But you'll hear about them at the briefing."

The station didn't seem any less busy, Glen discovered, although it was the early hours of the morning. Crime never slept, he had been told when he joined the service, and the Marshals couldn't really sleep either. He yawned openly as he followed Isabel into the briefing room, then poured himself a mug of black coffee and took a seat at the front of the rows. Behind him, a number of other Marshals and Civil Guard personnel filled the remaining seats. Glen drank his coffee and waited, impatiently, for Patty to appear. It was nearly ten minutes before she hurried in and took her place in front of the podium.

"I'm sorry for the delay," she said. "I had an urgent call from the Governor's Office and it turned out to be someone complaining about the paperclip allocation. Again."

Glen joined in the polite chuckles, although he knew it might not have been a joke. It wouldn't be the first time someone with more power than sense had demanded answers on an utterly pointless topic. Did it really matter, he asked himself, just how many paperclips had been used over the past couple of weeks? The world wouldn't come to an end if each paperclip wasn't accounted for, would it?

"At least they're not asking about arrest statistics," Marshal Brant called, from the back row. "*That* would be awkward."

"How true," Patty agreed. "And that's enough of that, you lot."

Definitely, Glen thought. Arrest statistics might seem a good idea for monitoring how well the law enforcement agencies were performing, but they didn't tell the complete story. How many crimes were prevented through aggressive patrolling? There was no way to know, so some of the departments had been arresting more people in the hopes of boosting their ratings. It had worked, to some extent, but it hadn't been particularly *just*.

"Right," Patty said, slapping the podium for attention. "Those of you who have been sleeping the sleep of the terminally lazy won't have heard that there were a series of minor attacks on planetary infrastructure last night. We assume" – she nodded towards Glen – "that the weapons and explosives in the captured warehouse were intended to make the attacks more unpleasant than they actually were. As it was, we've lost a handful of power transfer nodes and a couple of datanet routers, but the other attacks did minimal damage."

Marshal Cho lifted her hand. "These attacks were coordinated?"

"It would seem so," Patty said. "However, the attacks were also largely ineffective."

Glen felt his eyes narrowing in suspicion. The best time to disrupt a terrorist attack was before it had actually begun, but once the terrorists were committed. It made securing evidence and convictions a great deal easier. However, there hadn't been any warning before the targets had come under attack – and the attacks had largely been useless. The handful of destroyed targets hardly made up for revealing the existence of a terrorist network capable of carrying out attacks on such a scale.

Isabel put his thoughts into words. "They seem to have screwed up beyond the bounds of probability, boss," she said. "And yet it seems too big an attack to be a diversion."

"It does," Patty agreed. "They might have been intending to use those attacks to divert us from other possible targets, but nothing else has materialised."

"They might have thought the warehouse terrorists were also going to go into the fray," Glen offered. "The rest of their cells might not have picked up a stand-down order."

"It's possible," Patty agreed. She took a breath. "I should note that we didn't manage to take any survivors from the attacks. That's par for the course, I know, but it's still a problem. We have to track down the command network before they do something more dangerous."

Glen nodded. He wasn't the only one.

"The Civil Guard has secured the targeted sites," Patty told them. "I'm dividing you between the various targets; I want you to investigate, find out what happened and see if you can locate anything that leads back to their base. It is of the utmost importance that we shut this band of terrorists down before they manage to get their act together and do something worse."

She glared around the room, threateningly. "So far, the general public hasn't realised how close we came to disaster last night," she added. "The Governor wants it to stay that way, so anyone who leaks will be skinned alive and then fed to the pigs. And I am not joking."

There was a long pause. "Glen, remain behind," she added. "The rest of you, collect your assignments from the desk and get on with them. And good luck."

Glen waited until the room was empty – he knew from experience that Isabel would wait for him – and then stood up.

"Patty?"

"I need you to continue looking into the warehouse," Patty said. "I've been ordered – *ordered* – to redirect all available manpower to the latest terrorist attacks, but I'm not expecting to find much. The attacks were somewhat amateurish, quite pathetic compared to the usual bloody slaughters. They may have been expending useless assets to try to force us to abandon the warehouse investigation."

Glen looked down at the scruffy floor. "Just me?"

"You'll be the prime investigator," Patty confirmed. "You can call on the support staff, as usual, but I need every available Marshal out on the streets. Try not to fuck up."

"I'll do my best," Glen said. He shook his head in disbelief. An entire investigation in one pair of hands! He hadn't heard of anything like it outside bad fiction and worse flicks. "And what about Helen?"

"Keep her under your wing, for now," Patty said. She reached out and touched his shoulder. "I know it won't be easy, Glen, but I have utmost confidence in you."

Glen nodded, knowing there was no point in protesting. Patty literally *couldn't* give him any support. But even with the clues he'd gleaned from Helen, handling everything on his own would be an absolute nightmare.

"You can tell the bureaucrats that I have her when they start whining about purchasing too much food," he said, instead. "Do you know what's going to happen to her?"

"It depends," Patty said. She shook her head. "Once we have the full story, Glen, we can start making some proper decisions."

She frowned, then smiled at him. "Are you starting to like her?"

"Yes," Glen admitted.

"It's always easier to like kids who aren't actually yours," Patty said. "But remember, she may not be a suspect, yet she is definitely involved."

Glen had always supposed it was the other way round, but he kept that thought to himself.

"Good luck," Patty added. "And bring me something I can show the Governor when he comes knocking – again."

Glen saluted, then walked out of the briefing room. Isabel was waiting outside, as he'd expected, reading her terminal with an expression of disbelief. She gave him a sharp look as he closed the door, then motioned for him to walk with her towards the garage.

"She wants me to go to the Southside Power Distribution Centre," she said, dryly. "And I'm not the only one going out alone."

"Call for support if you need it," Glen urged. "But I'm stuck here until I turn up a lead."

He filled her in, quickly. "Sounds tough," she said, when he'd finished. "But the best of luck to you."

Glen sighed, then bade her farewell and walked back to his cubicle. His computer was already online, just waiting for his access codes. He poured himself a new cup of coffee, then sat down and started inputting the data from Helen into the growing matrix. Added to the legwork Isabel and the support crews had already done, it painted a worrying picture. The warehouse had been hired by a local shipping firm, which had largely taken over a chunk of the spaceport after gaining approval for purchasing shares in the installation. Reading between the lines, Glen suspected that someone had been paid a considerable bribe to make it happen. But it had also allowed the weapons crates to be unloaded and shipped to the warehouse without an inspection.

The Humming Bee was Helen's ship, he mused. It had entered orbit a week before the warehouse had been raided, then left orbit two days later, after transhipping a considerable amount of cargo to the surface. There was no mention of Helen or her parents – a quick check revealed that Helen hadn't passed through immigration, either on the orbital tower or any of the spaceports. Glen rather suspected that she'd been sedated, then loaded into one of the crates and transported down without passing through any security screening. Even now, there was still so much cargo being transhipped that it would be difficult to inspect it all.

He scowled down at the display, then rose to his feet. The shipping firm needed to be investigated, at the very least. They'd cleared the consignment, after all, which meant they were either dupes or actively involved with the terrorists. He suspected the former, if only because crashing shuttles could have done real damage and the Nihilists, so far, hadn't shown any signs of possessing shuttles.

As soon as he'd donned his coat, he knocked on Patty's door.

"I'm going to visit the shipping firm," he said, and outlined his reasoning. "If I don't check in within the hour, feel free to send the SWAT team."

"Don't even joke about it," Patty said. "Right now, the SWAT team is on the other side of the city, watching a gang clash that might turn into outright warfare. They can't be called out for anything other than a major disaster."

Glen nodded. "We should just squash the gangs," he said. "Why don't we kick the shit out of them and send the survivors to a penal world?"

"They have connections," Patty said. She looked down at the table, then up at Glen. The frustration in her voice was almost palatable. "Wouldn't it be wonderful if we didn't have to deal with corrupt officials all the time?"

"Yes," Glen agreed, "it would. But what can we do about it? Even if we took the bastards into custody, they'd be out within hours."

"True," Patty said. She sighed, then returned her attention to her paperwork. "Good luck with the shipping firm. Don't fuck up."

CHAPTER
ELEVEN

And then there are the lawyers. As the old saying has it...there are two sides to every problem, until the lawyers become involved. At that point, there will become a thousand sides – and all of them will appear to be correct.

- Professor Leo Caesius, *The Decline of Law and Order and the Rise of Anarchy*

Belinda did as she was expected to do as soon as she returned to the hotel and ordered room service, then tipped the steward and urged him out of the door. The steak tasted surprisingly good, although the meat was definitely vat-grown rather than natural. Belinda munched her way through the steak and chips, then had another shower and lay down on the bed. To watching eyes, she appeared to be sleeping. Instead, she was using the access codes she'd stolen to slip into the governmental network.

It was, as she'd expected, a multi-tier system. One general set of briefing notes and alerts for everyone with access codes, then various subsections that would require specific access permissions to enter. It was typical, she noted, as she immersed herself in the tidal waves of data spreading through the network. The civil servants worked hard to ensure they knew more than the common citizens, even to the point of ensuring that emergency warnings went to them first. If the shit really did hit the fan, she noted, the civil servants would be well-placed to grab their families and flee the cities before the general exodus began.

If they can get through the barricades, she thought, sardonically. It wasn't obvious to the untrained eye, but one glance at the police and military deployments had shown her that they were intended to keep much of the population firmly in place. She'd seen similar deployments on worlds hit by disasters, yet she doubted that the Governor had enough strength to keep the lid on indefinitely. Panicking civilians could be dangerous, if they formed a mob, and pose a threat even to armoured soldiers.

The first set of alerts referred to attacks that had taken place over the night, while she'd been seducing Julius and stealing his access codes. None of the attacks had been reported publically, she discovered, although it might be just a matter of the Governor's staff trying to decide what spin to put on the attacks before they told the world. But she took a long look at the targeted locations and felt her blood run cold. None of the attacks had been dramatically successful, nothing like some of the more dangerous terrorist assaults on Earth or the other Core Worlds, but collectively they added up to a dangerous picture. The terrorists had been targeting the infrastructure that kept the planet's cities alive.

Just like Earth, she thought, recalling the final nightmarish days of humanity's homeworld. One by one, pieces of infrastructure – sorely abused and barely maintained over the last few centuries – had started to fail, setting off a domino effect that had eventually triggered riots and fighting on the surface of Earth. And then the government had collapsed, civil war had broken out and hundreds of asteroids had fallen from the skies. If there was anyone left alive on Earth, they were almost certain to die in the next few months. It was highly unlikely they would receive any help from the remainder of the Empire.

But not quite, she added, a moment later. *These attacks seem remarkably half-hearted.*

The pattern was clear when she pulled back and *looked* at the records. On one hand, the attacks had been mounted with an alarming level of skill, competence and stealth. The terrorists had got into position to mount their attacks without being detected and, in most cases, had managed to break contact before reinforcements arrived. Belinda had a low opinion of the Civil Guard – she didn't know any Marines who thought highly of the overpaid and undertrained bastards – but even they should have been able to capture or kill their attackers. And yet, on the other hand, only a handful of the attacks could be deemed successful, as if the terrorists hadn't expected success. They certainly hadn't made any plans to exploit their success. All they'd really succeeded in doing was alerting the security forces that they were facing a new and dangerous foe.

Check the observed end result, she reminded herself. *And determine if that wasn't meant to happen all along.*

Belinda sighed, thoughtfully. One thing civilians never grasped was that some operations were doomed from the start – and others had failed through no fault of the soldiers involved in launching them. The civilians always assumed that someone must be to blame and demanded that heads roll for the failure. It was quite possible that the terrorists had simply blundered, or assumed that the security forces would do a better job of fighting back than they'd actually done. But it was also possible that what had happened might be what had been *meant* to happen.

Assuming that is the case, she thought slowly, *why?*

She went through it, step by step. The attacks had done nothing more than illustrate the vulnerability of parts of the planet's infrastructure. Indeed, reading between the lines, she had a feeling that whoever had planned the attacks had studied the fate of Earth and tailored their own attack plans to match. But all they'd managed to do was alert the security forces and get additional manpower deployed to cover everything from water purification plants to food processing centres and power stations. It would make it much harder to launch such attacks in future.

And that meant...what?

A trick, she thought, coldly. *Another Eudemon Station.*

She'd been in Basic Training at the time, but she still remembered the story. A military governor had intended to declare independence, yet he hadn't had the ships and men to defend his worlds against the Imperial Navy when it finally responded to the rebellion. He'd set out to create a perception of a threat, ensuring that additional reinforcements were sent to his system, which he'd then tried to subvert and use to secure his territory. His plan had come alarmingly close to success, Belinda recalled, and it *would* have succeeded if someone hadn't parsed out the records and realised that half of the reported attacks were fakes. But someone else might be trying to make the plan work.

The Governor, she told herself. *Who else would benefit from creating a false state of emergency?*

It was a tempting thought. She knew the Onge's Family's reputation. Grand Senator Stephen Onge had been intending to take supreme power for himself, in the twilight days of Old Earth. He'd once been the richest man in the Empire, controlling a vast patronage network that had reached from the lower decks of the Imperial Navy to the rarefied heights of the Imperial Civil Service. But all of his wealth hadn't been enough to save him from Belinda, she recalled, remembering how the Grand Senator had tried to capture Roland and use him as a scapegoat – or puppet. She'd killed him moments before she'd collapsed and almost died.

But his relative might be taking over the family business, Belinda thought. Governor Theodore Onge might well have dreams of supreme power for himself, even if he *was* trying to organise a conference to save what remained of the Empire. *And yet he already controls Terra Nova. Why would he need to launch terrorist attacks in his own cities?*

She shook her head, then started to chew her way through the data. Terra Nova, unfortunately, *did* have a major Nihilist threat, with a number of bloody slaughters reported in the last month alone. Her investigations led to another set of reports, one identifying a warehouse where the terrorists had been storing weapons in preparation for...what? More brutal attacks or something worse? There had been enough weapons in the warehouse, one slightly hysterical commenter had claimed, to take over the government. Belinda was experienced enough to doubt it was possible, although the Nihilists might well have tried...

It would certainly cause a slaughter, she thought, *but they'd get better results if they concentrated on the planet's infrastructure.*

Once, the Nihilists *had* managed to take over a medium-sized planetary population. They'd managed, somehow, to worm their way into a more rational insurgency movement and take over, then seize supreme power after overthrowing the local government. And then, before the Imperial Navy had responded, they'd slaughtered over a million people directly and far more in the ensuing civil war, when saner factions had tried to take back power. But the Nihilists hadn't cared. All they'd wanted to do was kill people to prove the hopelessness of life. It was impossible to conceive of how many people would die on Terra Nova if they managed to take over.

The files on precisely *what* had been captured were stored behind a firewall, she discovered with some irritation. She poked and prodded at the database, then decided she would need to either obtain more access codes or take the time necessary to crack through the security barriers. The longer she tried, she knew, the greater the chance of being detected, yet she had a feeling that anyone with access codes would be more careful than poor Julius.

Bitch, she told herself. *What you did to him was far from fair.*

Life isn't fair, Pug's voice mocked her. *You should know that, sweetheart.*

"Shut up," Belinda muttered, and sat upright. "Shit!"

Belinda rubbed her face, tiredly. She hoped she wasn't being observed – or, if she was, her unseen watcher had assumed she'd woken from a nightmare. One of the other reports she'd seen on the datanet had stated that planetary prescriptions for tranquilisers, antidepressants and other drugs had skyrocketed over the last month, after the Fall of Earth had been confirmed. The drugs had always been freely available – a drugged population was a docile population – but even the civil service thought the new trend was alarming. For once, Belinda had to agree. A drugged population wouldn't be able to react to any sudden change in their status.

She glanced at the clock and muttered another curse as she realised it was eight o'clock in the morning and that she hadn't slept a wink all night. Duty was definitely a harsh mistress, but she'd once gone several weeks without sleep, relying on her implants to cleanse her body of fatigue poisons. Now, she'd barely been awake for – she had to check her implants to be sure – forty-eight hours. And she wanted to go back to bed and sleep for the rest of the day.

Still better than human norms, Doug's voice said. Her former commander sounded pleasantly amused in her head. *You should be proud of yourself.*

Belinda grabbed a towel, then walked out of the room and marched down towards the swimming pool. It wasn't anything like as big as the swimming pool on the *Chesty Puller*, nor did it have the various modifications designed to make life interesting for Marines practicing swimming against waves or strong currents. Belinda had always been a strong swimmer, but even she had struggled with the water phase of Boot Camp. It always surprised and depressed her just how many recruits washed out, sometimes literally, when they discovered what they were expected to do.

The hotel had provided free swimwear, carefully branded with the hotel's name. Belinda pulled on a swimsuit, discovering to her amusement that the swimwear was barely modest, then dived into the pool and swam as hard as she could. As she had hoped, the cold water woke her up, but the pool was nowhere near large enough for her to swim properly. She made a mental note to look up other swimming pools in the city – there was bound to be a number large enough to suit her – then cursed herself under her breath. The mission was to make sure the conference went ahead, not to waste time enjoying herself.

You really need some leave, Pug's voice said. *The Commandant wouldn't begrudge you a few months holiday before you went back to duty.*

Belinda shook her head, feeling water running through her hair as she reached the end of the pool and swam back towards the far side. She didn't want to go on holiday, even if it was possible, but she was damned if she knew how much good she'd be to the Corps. There was no way she could fit into another Pathfinder unit, nor could she really go back to the infantry and serve as a Rifleman. She'd simply lost too many habits in her quest to be the best Pathfinder she could possibly be.

It wasn't your fault, Doug said. *You can't be blamed for our deaths.*

Belinda reached the edge of the pool and stopped, blinking away tears. She had never really come to terms with her team's death on Han, let alone her guilt for being the only survivor of the brief, but savage engagement. And it had all been for nothing. Han had been nothing more than a brushfire war compared to the chaos that had swept over Earth... and, she knew, would be coming in the future. As news of Earth's fall spread through the galaxy, countless independence movements would take heart, while ambitious military officers would start sharpening their swords...

"Darling," an elderly voice said. "Are you all right?"

Belinda looked up. An old woman, easily old enough to be her grandmother, was standing by the edge of the pool, looking down at Belinda. Her face was kind and open, without any attempt to hide her feelings or her deeper character. She was old enough, Belinda realised, not to care what happened to her.

"I'm fine," Belinda said. "It's just been a long day."

She looked past the elderly woman and saw an equally old man, following his wife with worshipful eyes. They were still very much in love, she saw, despite their age. Something tore at her heart as she wondered, suddenly, if anyone would ever look at her like that. And then she cursed herself under her breath for such sentiments. She couldn't imagine settling down with anyone.

"My daughter was just the same," the elderly woman said, as she lowered herself into the pool. "She would always stay out all night and never listened to me when I told her to concentrate on her studies. And when she was upset, she would never tell me about it."

"My mother always listened," Belinda said. The thought bothered her more than she cared to admit. What had *happened* to Greenway, now the interstellar economy had come to a crashing halt? Would she ever see her parents again? "I could tell her everything."

The woman smiled at her. "And where is she now?"

"A long way away," Belinda said. She looked up as the elderly man joined his wife in the water, then sat up and pulled herself out of the pool. "Thank you for your time."

"My name is Clarissa, Clarissa Woodpecker," the woman said. She reached up and squeezed Belinda's hand, then smiled at her. "If you need to talk, you can just find me in my apartment."

"Thank you," Belinda said, surprised. On Greenway, everyone knew everyone else. It was rare to *not* have someone to talk to, if she'd needed to talk. But in the Core Worlds, it was vanishingly rare to have someone just open themselves up and offer to serve as a listening ear if necessary. She was almost tempted to join Clarissa and talk. But what could she tell the elderly woman? "If I have time, I will."

She watched, for a long moment, as the elderly couple swam together, then walked away, feeling uncomfortably like a voyeur. They were still very much in love – Clarissa's husband hadn't snuck glances at her, despite the revealing swimwear – and she didn't want to disturb them. People like them were what the Marine Corps existed to defend. Shaking her head, she dried herself in the changing room and then headed back to her apartment. There was no shortage of data to study...

All work and no play makes Belinda a dull girl, Pug said.

I dread to imagine what Doug would have done to someone stupid enough to goof off on active service, Belinda thought back. Rumour had it that the MPs hadn't found all the body parts of a young operative who'd done just that, although it was probably exaggerated. *And where would I go to play here?*

She stopped as a thought occurred to her. Thomas Augustus had bragged of his connections – and he'd given her a business card. She could call him, ask him for a date and pump him for information, perhaps even additional access codes of his own. It wasn't a pleasant thought, but she had far fewer qualms about using him and then discarding him than she'd had about Julius. And besides, Pug's ghost was right. She needed to do more than stay in her hotel room and drown in torrents of information.

That's right, girl, Pug said. *You go show him how it's done.*

Belinda smiled. Pug had been legendary for chasing everything on legs; male, female and anything in-between. She knew precisely how *he* would have tried to gather information – and he might well have succeeded, too. And so had she.

Walking back to her room, she opened the hotel datanet terminal and typed out a quick message, then opened her implants and started to probe through the network once again. This time, she looked specifically at the Governor's military deployments and his ongoing recruitment effort...

...And swore, under her breath, as a very disturbing pattern began to emerge. It wasn't clear, from the official reports, but as she started to cross-check the files the pattern simply leapt out at her.

He's building an army, she thought, *and rounding up everyone he can. But why?*

CHAPTER

TWELVE

Consider, for example, the precise issue of when a child becomes legally adult, legally able to have sex. If we set it at sixteen, we will face the problem of children becoming sexually mature before reaching legal age and, driven by hormones, having sex with one another.

- Professor Leo Caesius, *The Decline of Law and Order and the Rise of Anarchy*

The Vestries Shipping Firm was based well away from the spaceport, somewhat to Glen's amusement. It was understandable – the firm owned hundreds of warehouses as well as storage space in the orbital towers and transhipment stations in orbit – but it still amused him enough to make him smile as he walked in the door. If *he'd* been running the firm, he would have preferred to keep everything under his control.

But then, that would be impossible, he thought. He'd spent enough time unpicking the firm's publically-declared properties that it had become clear they owned more than could fit into the spaceport or an industrial estate. *And besides, they own a dozen smaller companies too, just to create the illusion of competition.*

He strode up to the desk, ignoring the handful of armed guards, and smiled down at the young girl on the desk. If he was any judge, she was an intern, paid minimum wage in exchange for looking pretty and acting as a shield between her employers and the outside world. She couldn't really be more than five or six years older than Helen. Glen held out his ID card and saw her eyes widen, then glance towards a communications panel half-hidden under the desk.

"Call your manager," Glen said. "I need to speak to him."

The girl hesitated, then reached for the panel and tapped a button. There was a long pause, then the far door sprung open, revealing an older man wearing a suit that didn't – quite – manage to hide the bulge of his chest. Glen suspected it was a statement, either that the man didn't care about his appearance or that he was wealthy enough not to have to care, but he didn't have time to worry about it. And besides, he didn't really care.

"I am Marshal Cheal," he said, mentally comparing the man's face to the files he'd accessed on the shipping firm. "Director Doyle?"

"Yes, Marshal," the man said. "Ivan Doyle."

"Then we can go into your office," Glen said, before the man could object or start threatening him with lawyers. "We need information from you."

"Our files are sealed," Ivan said. "It would require a court order..."

Glen reached for the sheet of paper he'd taken from the station and passed it to Doyle. It was a blanket warrant for information, signed by the Governor himself after the warehouse had been located and raided. There were lawyers who would probably try to argue that it wasn't legal, but Glen had a feeling they wouldn't get very far. The Governor had considerable powers to handle terrorism, including detaining suspects without trial and seizing records if necessary. Besides, even if they *did* win the case, it would be enough to blacklist them with the Governor and the military, which would utterly destroy their business.

Doyle read it carefully, word by word. "I will have to consult with my lawyers..."

"And you can, afterwards," Glen said, firmly. "I don't have time for you to try to hide records while your lawyers stall."

He looked around the office, resisting the temptation to make a snide remark. Patty's office was bare, apart from a handful of photographs and awards. Doyle's office was large, decorated in a fashion that suggested the occupant had money to burn and crammed with various artworks, several of which had to be copies. Glen wasn't sure if the whole design was meant to demonstrate Doyle's taste, or lack thereof, but he wouldn't have trusted anyone who crammed so much fancy decor into his office. It reeked of someone trying to pretend that he was more important than he actually was.

Ivan caved, as Glen had expected. "What can we do for you?"

"You rented out Warehouse #117," Glen said. "I imagine you know it's been raided?"

"Yes," Doyle said, flatly. The reports had stated that the firm had attempted to demand answers, but for once they'd been unable to learn anything from the Civil Guard. "And we need it reopened..."

"That may not happen for quite some time," Glen said, cutting him off. It was always a mistake to let someone like Doyle think he was in charge. "I require access to *all* the documentation from the rental, *everything*. You will have it sent to this office and I will go through it, now."

Doyle looked reluctant – Glen wondered, absently, what a search of his office would reveal – and then started to bark orders to a team of secretaries. They were all achingly young, Glen noted, wearing uniforms that left very little to the imagination. Ivan didn't seem to care about their opinions, Glen decided, or their feelings. Given how hard it was to get a job now, the secretaries probably had no choice, but to put up with his lecherous feelings as long as he wanted to favour them with his attentions. And some of them might well have thought they had no choice, but to go further.

He sat down in front of Doyle's personal terminal and opened the display, then started to read through the documents one by one. Doyle stood in front of him, pacing backwards and forwards as if he were too nervous to leave Glen alone in his office, which was a worrying sign. But then, Glen would have been nervous if Internal Affairs had started investigating his terminal too. There was nothing so innocent that a suitably motivated investigator couldn't turn into a damning piece of evidence.

There was less than he'd expected, although there were some interesting tips. Warehouse #117 had been rented by a transhipment firm, claiming that their cargo was merely being stored on the ground and would be returned to orbit when they chartered their next freighter. It was believable, Glen had to admit; storage fees for orbital space were far higher than fees for warehouses on the ground, and if the material was marked for transhipment it would attract less attention from the customs officers. Hell, if the warehouse was secure, they might not pay any attention at all. There was so much freight being moved from orbit to the surface for local distribution that they might not have time to check out Warehouse #117. And a few bribes would definitely ensure that anyone who *was* interested lost interest shortly afterwards.

"You didn't check out their company," Glen said, looking up at Doyle. "Why not?"

"Ah...that was an operational decision," Doyle said. He didn't know *precisely* what had been found in the warehouse, Glen was sure, but he knew it had to be bad. Passing the buck was standard procedure for any middle-ranking corporate executive. Given time, the intern on the desk would wind up with the blame and would be summarily fired. "And they paid up front."

"So they did," Glen said. He checked the manifest, then frowned. "You didn't think there was something odd about them paying for *four months* storage?"

"That's not uncommon," Doyle objected. "We have some long-term storage sites that are prepaid for up to a year..."

"But how many of them," Glen asked, "are transhipment warehouses?"

He snorted. "It seems a little uneconomical," he added, darkly. "Or did they want to make sure the warehouse was never inspected?"

"We don't inspect our warehouses unless the bills are left unpaid," Doyle said. "Our customers value their privacy."

"So it would seem," Glen said. He looked back at the manifest. "I think by now you've realised the warehouse wasn't storing farming equipment for new colonies."

Doyle made a face, but said nothing.

"You rented out the warehouse to terrorists," Glen added. "I need all the contact details they gave you, now."

"They'll be in the files," Doyle said. He walked around his desk, then pointed to the tab. "That's what they gave us."

Glen frowned as he scanned the file. It didn't take more than a casual sweep to realise that the transhipment company simply didn't exist. Hell, the Nihilists hadn't been very careful about constructing their bogus identity. A quick call to the Department of Commerce would have revealed that it was nothing more than a fake. The handful of testimonials on their datanet site were so bland they *had* to be fake. And the address they'd been given was nothing more than an office *anyone* could rent, in the heart of the city. Glen would investigate, of course, but he would be very surprised if he found more than an abandoned office complex.

"I want you to make sure you didn't rent any other warehouses to the same people," Glen ordered. He plugged a datachip into the terminal and made a copy of each of the files. It was unlikely they'd be able to learn anything else from the files, but the WebHeads would go through them anyway. There *was* a datanet presence, after all, and it might just lead them to the terrorist support network. "Go. Now."

"I'm sure they wouldn't have dared," Doyle protested. "Marshal, I..."

"Go," Glen snapped.

He waited until Doyle had retreated, then keyed a hasty command into the terminal. Marshal-issue datachips had much more storage space than civilian models and, combined with hacking software, could copy the entire contents of a terminal within seconds. It felt like hours before the datachip bleeped once, revealing that it had completed its task. Glen let out a sigh of relief, then pocketed the chip. There would be time to investigate Ivan Doyle's role in the whole affair later.

"There weren't any other contracts," Doyle said, as he stepped back into his office. His eyes were very nervous, suggesting he had something to hide. "But we have quite a few warehouses reserved for long-term storage."

"Then give me those files too," Glen said. "In fact, I think you should tighten up your procedures. Check out everyone who asks to purchase warehouse space and see if they're actually legitimate."

"But that would dissuade others from using our services," Doyle protested. "And..."

He broke off. "Sharon Wright was the booking agent," he added. "She's in the building, if you wish to speak to her."

"Please," Glen said. There would be time to check out the other applications for long-term storage later. "Show her into your office, then leave us."

Doyle flushed, but obeyed. Glen took advantage of his absence to scan the office for bugs, a brief scan which revealed next to nothing. Doyle, it seemed, didn't want to be recorded at his desk, something Glen had to admit was understandable. There were cameras in the station, he knew, but they were meant to cover the security staff's asses if a prisoner got rowdy, rather than spying on the marshals. Although Glen had sometimes wondered if Patty watched her subordinates through the cameras...

He broke off that chain of thought as the door opened, revealing a tall woman with long brown hair and a grim-faced expression of defiance. There was no way to be sure, but Glen had a feeling that Doyle had told her she would be the scapegoat if the company was threatened with legal sanctions for allowing terrorists to use their facilities. The look in the woman's eyes – a mixture of tiredness and despair – certainly fitted. She was old enough to be blacklisted for life if she were fired without notice.

"Take a seat," Glen said. He waved for Doyle to leave the room, then sat down facing her. "Miss Wright..."

"Please call me Sharon," Sharon said. Her voice was Earth-accented, the curious mumble that afflicted much of the planet. It meant nothing – Earth had produced most of the entertainment flicks that were distributed through the galaxy – but it was interesting. "I prefer not to be called by my mother's name."

"I understand," Glen said. He paused, then silently clicked on his recorder. "You're not under arrest, but I have to warn you that your cooperation – or lack of it – will be taken into account during the investigation and charges may be filed against you if it turns out that you have concealed information that later became important. Do you understand me?"

Sharon nodded, but said nothing.

"I need a verbal answer," Glen said. "Do you understand me?"

"Yes, sir," Sharon said.

Glen smiled. "Good," he said. "I understand you were responsible for renting out Warehouse #117?"

"I was responsible for showing the renters how to access the building and set up the facilities," Sharon said, quickly. "I wasn't responsible for renting it out to them in the first place."

"Noted," Glen said. He sighed, inwardly. Doyle had *definitely* hinted Sharon was going to take the blame. "What happened when you met them?"

Sharon took a breath. Glen understood; it was the age-old problem when interviewing witnesses and potential suspects. Even the most cooperative witnesses had problems recalling what the interviewers needed to hear, even without false memories and the understandable desire to please the listeners getting in the way. Sharon had had no reason to pay close attention to the renters, so she hadn't – and now she was being forced to recall every last detail from hazy memory.

"There were four of them," she said, finally. "I thought they were all young men, although one of them might have been a woman. The only one who spoke was the leader, who insisted on asking a number of questions about the air conditioning and other systems before signing the lease and making the first payment to the company's credit account. I didn't see the questions as particularly unusual, sir. Everyone asks how to manage the facilities before they take over the building."

Glen nodded, then pulled his terminal from his belt and opened it to show the faces of the dead men. "Do you recognise any of them?"

"That's the leader," Sharon said, after paging through five faces. "I don't recognise any of the others."

"I see," Glen said. The leader had been one of the mystery men, which meant...what? Assuming Sharon was correct, there were at least three others running around on Terra Nova and probably more. They'd always known the Nihilists had an interstellar presence, but the reports had definitely suggested the strangers were ex-military personnel. "Did they ask you anything in particular?"

"They talked about renting a shuttle," Sharon said. "We don't get that request very often, because most of the stuff we store in those warehouses comes from the planetary surface. I had to tell them that the shuttles were fully booked up for the week."

"Probably for the best," Glen said. He briefly considered inviting Sharon to the station for a full interrogation, then decided against it. Instead, he leaned forward. Women were often more observant than men, he'd been told. And sometimes they saw more than they realised. "Did you see anything else you want to mention?"

Sharon hesitated. "I'm not sure if it's worth mentioning," she said. "I could be wrong."

"I won't hold it against you," Glen said. "What did you see?"

"They seemed very comfortable with each other," Sharon said, finally. "Perhaps a little *too* comfortable. I had the impression they were homosexuals, but two of them were definitely staring at my butt when they thought I wasn't looking. Maybe they were bisexuals."

Glen kept his face expressionless. She might be right, but he could think of another explanation for their appearance. A trained commando team, one that had worked together for years, might be equally comfortable with one another. And they wouldn't be hesitant about admiring a pretty girl either. The suspicion that a rogue team was *precisely* what they had on their hands was too strong to be ignored.

If they're actually rogue, he thought. *Who might have sent them to Terra Nova?*

"I'll keep it in mind," he said. He reached into his pocket and produced a contact card, which he passed to her. "If you think of anything else, anything at all, feel free to contact me at once. Until then, keep what we talked about to yourself."

"They'll want answers," Sharon said, jerking a hand towards the wall. "And what do I tell them?"

"That the whole affair is classified," Glen said, rising to his feet. There would be time to go through the files he'd borrowed – stolen – later. "You won't have to worry about losing your job."

Sharon looked doubtful. Glen didn't blame her. It was illegal to dismiss someone because they'd been called to the colours, let alone interrogated by the Imperial Marshals. But Doyle could probably find another reason to dismiss her, if he tried. Glen sighed, then made a mental note to have a short talk with Doyle afterwards. The whole affair couldn't be left in the past until Glen and his superiors confirmed that there were no suspicions levelled at the shipping firm. He could delay clearing them for as long as he chose.

And how, he asked himself as he rose, *does that make you any different from all the others who exploit their positions?*

He watched Sharon leave the room, then had a long heart-to-heart with Doyle. The man seemed somewhat relieved, leaving Glen convinced he had a guilty conscience about *something.* But there was no time to follow up on it, not now. He checked his watch, then walked out to the car and climbed behind the wheel. There was just enough time to go home to check on Helen before driving to the office the terrorists had hired. It was unlikely they'd left any clues behind, but he had to check. And then he could start going through the remaining files from Doyle. Who knew what else the man had been doing?

But only if it's a major crime, he reminded himself. *You don't have time to waste.*

CHAPTER
THIRTEEN

Legally, the older one in the partnership will be guilty of statutory rape (an act that is always criminal because the victim is assumed to be incapable of granting consent) and thus can be charged with child molestation. But if one person is sixteen and the other fifteen, with both parties having raging hormones, is that actually a criminal act? Many readers would, I suspect, argue no. It is not a criminal act.

- Professor Leo Caesius, *The Decline of Law and Order and the Rise of Anarchy*

"I was surprised to hear from you again," Thomas Augustus said.

Belinda gave him a charming smile. *She* was surprised he'd answered her message so promptly, inviting her to dinner at the largest revolving restaurant in Landing City. Indeed, she'd barely had time to catch a few hours of sleep before his personal car arrived to transport her to the restaurant. Clearly, she'd made a much greater impression on him than she'd thought.

Or he's embarrassed about falling over in a drunken stupor, she thought, privately. *I'm surprised he even wants to look at me after embarrassing himself so thoroughly.*

"You left your code with me," Belinda said. "And I don't know many other people in Landing City."

"Well, I'm glad you did," Augustus said. He stood and waved a hand towards the window, indicating the towering skyscrapers outside. "What do you make of our fine city?"

Belinda had several answers for that, but most of them would be far from helpful. "Old," she said, after a moment. "Living history."

"That's true," Augustus said. "The other cities on this planet might be alarmingly like Earth, but Landing City is spread out for miles. Government House" – he pointed to a block of lights in the distance – "hasn't really changed since the planet gained self-government. It's a piece of living history too."

Belinda nodded. She had no idea what building on Earth had served as the model, but she had to admit the towering white edifice was very impressive. And, compared to some of the skyscrapers, it looked tiny. The building would be very hard to defend if an insurgent force took control of some of the surrounding buildings and used them to pour fire into the heart of Government House.

She looked around the room as Augustus sat down. The restaurant was very impressive, although there was a creaking sense of age that reminded her of some of the Imperial Navy's older battleships. There were gold and silver artworks everywhere, while the waiters were dressed up to the nines, with snooty expressions they directed towards every guest who didn't have at least a million credits in the bank. Even reserving a table in advance, according to the datanet, cost a thousand credits. Belinda was morbidly impressed that Augustus had been able to organise one on such short notice.

"But enough of that," Augustus said. He smiled at her, then picked up the menu. "Order whatever you want, my dear. My treat."

And then you plan to lure me into bed, Belinda thought, sardonically. But she wasn't too surprised. *If you knew what I was would you still want to go to bed with me?*

She pushed the thought aside as she opened the menu. The prices were literally staggering, even something as simple as fish and chips cost over a hundred credits. A quick scan of the wine list revealed some bottles that were unique, so rare she had a feeling that they were literally impossible to price. She was mildly surprised they hadn't been scooped up by a collector and stored in a high-security vault.

"Eat whatever you want," Augustus said. "I'm paying."

Belinda lifted the menu to hide her smile. On Greenway, her first date had cost her boyfriend – she couldn't remember his name, only that he'd been one of the few to match her sharpshooting skills – a handful of credits. They'd packed a picnic and taken it into the mountains to eat, well away from anyone else. She rather doubted that the richest man on her homeworld could have afforded to eat with Augustus. But he seemed confident.

"I've never eaten anything like this before," she said, instead. "What should I try?"

"The Chef's Special is always unique," Augustus said. "Or, if you want something *really* fancy, you could try the fish. They cook it in a special sauce, then serve it with vegetables – all naturally-grown, of course. None of that vat-grown muck here!"

"I'll try the Special," Belinda said. She placed the menu to one side and looked up at him. "I always wondered why they don't make vat-food taste better."

Augustus, as she had expected, launched into a long explanation. Belinda already knew most of it – the Empire didn't want people to become *dependent* on vat-food, let alone processed algae – but Augustus had a few private thoughts of his own. There might be an obligation to look after the less fortunate, yet there was no comparable requirement to let the poor think they had a right to eat nice food. It wasn't an uncommon attitude, but it caused Belinda a pang of guilt. There was no need to spit on people who had no hope of climbing out of the poverty trap.

"I provide jobs for thousands of people who want to better themselves," Augustus concluded, as the waiter arrived. "They can buy whatever they want with my wages."

"I'm sure they can," Belinda said. "What do you do for a living?"

Augustus snorted. "I own an industrial node," he said. "Didn't I tell you that?"

Belinda nodded. Augustus started to talk rapidly, outlining his work and how he planned to expand the node without the crushing presence of the Empire's bureaucracy. The Governor himself, apparently, had agreed to relax taxation and regulation in exchange for some unspecified service, something that Augustus remained tight-lipped about. Belinda listened, sometimes asking questions, as Augustus bragged. Reluctantly, she had to admit that if half of his bragging was accurate, he had good reason to be pleased with himself. In an age where the Grand Senate had drained innovation and inventiveness to the bare minimum, he'd built himself a private industrial empire that would be in a good position to take advantage of the Fall of Earth.

"But that's enough about me," Augustus said, leaning forward slightly. "Tell me about yourself?"

"I was a soldier, then a spacer," Belinda said, activating one of her implants to ensure she kept her cover story straight. Most civilians wouldn't recognise discrepancies when she talked about the military, but there was no point in taking chances. "I ended up leaving the service after...an incident and started travelling instead."

"I always wanted to travel," Augustus said. He shook his head wistfully. "What was the most remarkable sight you ever saw?"

The Slaughterhouse, Belinda thought. But it wasn't something she could say out loud.

"I saw the Silver Strand on New Paris," she said, instead. She *had* seen it, once upon a time, when her unit had passed through the system. "It was spectacular when the sun rose above the horizon and the space elevator began to glow."

"It must have been remarkable," Augustus agreed. "What else did you see?"

"There was the Hanging Gardens of Babylon," Belinda said, recalling a planet on the edge of the Core Worlds. There had been a nasty insurgency there, but it had been in its closing stages when her unit had been deployed and they'd found themselves doing nothing more than mop-up duties. "They claimed to have plants from every world in the Empire in their gardens."

"I can't imagine you liking a garden," Augustus said. "You always seem so...untamed."

Belinda found herself flushing. "The gardens were nice," she said, defensively. "And surprisingly peaceful."

She paused. "Why don't you go travelling?"

"I don't dare take my eyes off my business," Augustus said. "I have no one I can trust to take over, really."

Belinda lifted her eyebrows. "You don't trust your children?"

"They're brats," Augustus said, tiredly. "My eldest daughter blows through her allowance within the first day of the month, while my son and younger daughters refused to study anything useful at university. And to think they wanted to go to Imperial University on Earth!"

"That would have been bad," Belinda said, remembering the student uprisings in the last days of Earth. They'd ended badly for everyone involved. "They aren't interested in following in your footsteps?"

"They're only interested in money," Augustus said. "Gabrielle would spend everything I built up in a few months, if I let her, while the other three want to give it all away to various social justice parties. Where did I go wrong?"

"You made their lives too easy," Belinda said, quietly.

"I know," Augustus said. "But was it wrong of me to want them to have a good life?"

Belinda considered it. Her father had always remarked that suffering built character, but he'd also never had the money to spoil his children rotten. She'd grown up on a farm, helping her parents feed the animals and tend to the crops from a very early age. And she'd often had to hunt to keep her family fed. *And* she'd never been allowed to make allowances for her behaviour.

"I think you have to strike a balance between teaching them the value of hard work and deliberately depriving them," she said, finally. "Getting too much too easy just makes them accustomed to getting whatever they want, when they want it. And if they never develop the ability to work hard as children, they will find it very hard to learn as adults."

"I wish my wife had thought like that," Augustus said. "She always spoilt the children rotten."

He must have an open relationship, Doug said. *That's not uncommon among the very rich.*

Belinda shrugged, wishing she could erase the voices from her head. "You probably need to take a heir if you find your natural-born children unsatisfactory," she said, dryly. "Or send them off to reform camp. Or the Marines."

Augustus snorted. "What did the Marines ever do to deserve them?"

The waiters reappeared before Belinda could think of an answer, carrying two large silver trays of food. Belinda eyed the stew in front of her with some concern, realising that it was easily large enough to feed several people at once. She wouldn't have any difficulty eating the stew, thanks to her implants, but a more normal person would have struggled.

How the rich live, Pug muttered, in her head. *And to think this is all fiddling as the planet starts to burn.*

Belinda ignored him. Instead, following Augustus's lead, she started to tuck into her stew, silently blessing her trainers for the etiquette lessons. Augustus seemed to watch her with a strange level of interest, both lustful and – at the same time – more curious than anything else. Belinda puzzled over it for a long moment, then dismissed the thought as the first explosion of taste hit her tongue. The stew was an astonishing mix of meats and various spices and other flavours.

"The chef is rightly proud of his work," Augustus said, as he carved his way through a colossal steak. It was so large that Belinda couldn't help wondering if it had really come from a live animal or if someone had grown it in a vat, perhaps with proper treatment to make it taste natural. "I always have something different when I come here and it's always something good."

Belinda nodded, chewing her food. "The news is curiously bland," she said, when she finished swallowing. "Is there something I'm missing?"

"The Governor has the news censored," Augustus said, darkly. "I have to pay extra just to access the standard uncensored datastreams. The general public cannot be allowed to know about the problems we're having right now."

Belinda leaned forward, showing interest. "Problems?"

"I don't have any ties to Earth," Augustus said. "Problem is – just about everyone else in the space industry does, or *did*. No one knows what's going to happen to their industrial plants, so hundreds of trained workers are being laid off and I can't snap them all up for myself. Those men represent a reserve we cannot afford to lose, but everyone is dragging their feet on recognising that Earth is gone and doing something with the remaining industries in the system."

Belinda made a show of looking confused. "Can't they be passed to the heirs?"

"It's impossible to tell who the heirs actually *are*," Augustus pointed out. He took another bite of his steak, then gestured vaguely with the fork. "The corporations that owned a good two-thirds of the planet's industrial might were based on Earth, where most of their CEOs lived and worked. They tended to assign managers to handle their affairs here, but those managers didn't really own shares in the industries."

"That makes sense," Belinda said, slowly. "The stock exchanges were based on Earth."

"Precisely," Augustus said. "Now, if *I* were in charge, I would put the whole question of ownership to one side and just concentrate on restarting production. Sure, we'd be short of quite a few essential pieces of equipment, but we could fill those holes with a little effort and then start replacing what we lost over the last month. But, right now, there are too many interested parties to permit the Governor to take control and restart production. I'm trying to handle orders from so many people that I can't hope to fill them all."

"Ouch," Belinda said.

"And, to add insult to injury, no one really knows how much money is worth any longer," Augustus added. "Everything ran through the Imperial Central Bank on Earth. Now the bank is gone and the value of the credit is falling through the floor. Interstellar trade is doomed unless we can re-establish some idea of what money is worth from star system to star system. And if trade dies, the remains of the Empire dies with it."

Belinda looked down at her stew. "They didn't seem to question the price of this meal," she said. "Or is that different?"

"Anything local can be backed by locally-owned industries," Augustus said. "But anything interstellar..."

He paused. "Are you all right for money, right now?"

"For the moment," Belinda assured him. She had no idea if Augustus was being kind or if he was trying to find a way to control her, but it hardly mattered. "I'm not planning to stay indefinitely."

"I saw your file," Augustus said. "I could easily find a job for you."

Belinda had to smile. "Do you always make job offers to women you meet on the orbital tower?"

"Only the ones who might offer something to my company," Augustus said, sardonically. "And you might. We need more security experts right now."

"Because of the potential for riots?" Belinda asked. "Or is there another reason?"

"Both," Augustus said. He finished his steak and pushed it to one side. "You do realise there's a good chance you will be conscripted?"

"I know," Belinda said. She wasn't a native, but the Governor didn't seem to care. His growing army was trying to round up as many people with military experience as it could, including off-worlders. Hell, the whole *concept* of off-worlders being mistrusted was new to the Core Worlds. Once, the populations would have been largely interchangeable. "But I don't plan to stay here."

"I think the penalties for desertion will be rather high," Augustus said, dryly. "You need to be careful."

"I will," Belinda said. "But I've always preferred being a free agent or a starship crewperson, rather than one employee among millions."

She gave him a coy smile, then changed the subject before he could ask an awkward question. "And what were you planning to do for the rest of the evening?"

"It would depend on what you want to do," Augustus said. He took a breath. "But I would like to start by apologising for my behaviour on the orbital tower. I can endure space, but not the orbital tower's elevator."

"You're forgiven," Belinda said. She watched coolly as the waiters cleared away the table, then offered the dessert menus. "Would you like to dance on the lower floor?"

Augustus smiled. "Why not?"

Belinda felt another odd burst of guilt as he held out a hand, then led her to the stairs leading down to the lower levels. The Augustus she'd met on the orbital tower's elevator had been a drunken fool, but this one was something more sympathetic. Somehow, she didn't *want* to seduce him, then steal his access codes. Or worse. And yet, what else could she do?

"It's been years since I danced," Augustus said, as they reached the dance floor. A handful of couples were already moving across the floor, swinging to the beat of the tune. There didn't seem to be any real steps, merely moving up to the windows and back again. "Come on..."

"Attention," a sharp voice said. The musicians stopped playing and looked around in confusion. "This is a security warning. All guests are warned that there is a security emergency on the streets. This building will now go into lockdown; I say again, this building will now go into lockdown."

Belinda stepped over to the window and peered down to the streets below. The normal eye couldn't have seen more than a blur, but her enhanced eyes had no difficulty in picking out the signs of a budding riot. Crowds were gathering in the twilight, scattering the handful of security guards on the streets. It would take time, given how badly the police and military were scattered, to handle the growing crisis.

Augustus caught her arm. "What's going on?"

"I don't know," Belinda lied. She could make her way out, she suspected, but she would have to leave Augustus and the other guests behind. Somehow, that seemed unthinkable. "I guess we'll just have to wait and see."

CHAPTER

FOURTEEN

But if we determine that it is not a criminal act, we open the floodgates for claims that a relationship between a 15 year old and a 40 year old would also not be a criminal act. The law deals in absolutes and precedents and is incapable, quite often, of recognising the subtle points of a situation.

- Professor Leo Caesius, *The Decline of Law and Order and the Rise of Anarchy*

"So," Helen said. "How was your day?"

"Tedious," Glen said. He'd gone to the office the Nihilists had rented, but – as he'd expected – they'd cleared out months ago. "And yours?"

Helen gave him a shy smile. "I worked my way through the puzzle chip," she said. "Most of them were simple."

Glen had to smile. He'd purchased puzzles and educational games intended for someone two or three years older than Helen...and she considered them *simple*? But then, she *had* grown up on a starship, where puzzle-solving was often a matter of life and death. And she hadn't been held back by the rest of her class, as she would have been if she'd grown up on the ground.

The thought caused him a pang. If she stayed with him – and part of him *wanted* her to stay with him – she would have to go to school. Homeschooling was illegal, even if he'd had the time and ability to educate her himself, and she'd find herself badly isolated in a normal school. Quite apart from her origins, she'd be smarter and more adaptable than the rest of her classmates. She wouldn't have a comfortable time of it.

"I can find you a more advanced one," he said, although he wasn't sure where to look. There weren't *that* many levels above the one she'd completed. "What would you like to do this evening?"

"Watch a flick," Helen said, after a moment. "I was saving them for when you came home."

"Something mindless," Glen said, dryly. "I've had to use my brain all day and it deserves a rest."

Helen giggled.

He sent her to choose the flick she wanted to watch, then stepped into the kitchen and started to cook. It had been a long time since he'd cooked for more than one person and he wasn't quite sure of the quantities of food he should use, but he was parsing it out step by step. And he could simply reheat anything they didn't eat when it was cooked. By the time he'd started to heat up chicken and pasta, Helen had returned, carrying two datachips in her hand. Glen glanced at the titles and rolled his eyes.

"*Hero Cop* and *Law Enforcer*?" He asked. "Don't you have something more entertaining?"

Helen looked surprised. "What's wrong with these?"

Glen snorted as he reached for plates. "They were written by someone who knows nothing about police work," he said. "There are so many mistakes in them that...that it explains why we get so many idiots signing up for training. They think we're like Hero Cop with his Lantern Jaw of Justice."

Helen looked down at the table. "I always liked action movies," she confessed. "My mother used to think it was weird, but my dad had a vast collection and we would watch our way through them, one by one. They'd never let me watch anything fantastical."

"I'm not surprised," Glen commented. Fantastical movies were often anti-science as well as utterly unrelated to any form of reality. They were popular in the Core Worlds, but rather less so along the Rim. Besides, the basic background plot was always the same. The elders know better than the younglings and should never be questioned. "But I never got to watch cop shows when I was a child. They were too violent."

Helen smirked. "Worse than some of the sex flicks I'm not supposed to have watched?"

Her face shadowed. "My father had a collection of those too," she added. "My mother caught me watching one a year ago and went mental."

"You're too young to watch," Glen said, as he started to ladle out the food. "It causes too many problems down on a planetary surface."

Helen frowned. "It does?"

Glen nodded. The Empire's entertainment producers might have been deprived of the chance to produce anything with a plot, so they'd been forced to compensate with sex. Their latest flicks showed everything from couples enjoying an intensely sexual relationship to orgies involving multiple couples or every form of depraved sexuality under the sun. Glen wouldn't have cared if they'd been aimed at adults, but far too many of them were aimed at children who didn't understand the dangers of indulging in such acts. It helped keep the masses quiet, he knew, yet the price was far too high. How many of the problems the Marshals had to deal with among teenagers stemmed from watching endless streams of pornography?

It might not be so dangerous in space, he thought, although he didn't blame Helen's mother for being furious. *In space, the difference between fantasy and reality is harder to forget.*

He passed Helen her plate of food, then sat down to eat his own. It tasted blander than he'd expected – normally, he would have added more spices and sauces to give it some kick – but it hardly mattered. After a hard day at work, all he really wanted to do was cram more fuel into his body and then go to sleep. But staying up to watch a flick with Helen sounded good too.

"The chicken tastes odd," Helen said. "Is that normal?"

Glen took a bite, rolling the piece of meat around his mouth. "I think so," he said. "It's just the preservatives they force into the meat."

Helen gave him an odd look. "Preservatives?"

"People sue over everything," Glen said. "If someone bought a piece of rotten meat, they'd sue. So the shopping malls inject preservatives into the meat to ensure it lasts longer and no one gets hurt eating it. And if it doesn't taste as good as it should...well, it's for the good of society."

"And to ensure they can keep the meat on the shelves longer," Helen added.

Glen smiled. "How cynical," he said. "But yeah, you're right. They've been known to keep pieces of heavily-preserved meat on the shelves for weeks, then remove it just before the meat reaches its expiry date."

Helen looked at the piece of meat on the end of her fork. "But don't people sue over the taste?"

"Probably," Glen said. He sighed. Half of his time as a rookie had been spent dealing with safety precautions forced on society by endless lawsuits. It had been nightmarish because the vast majority of decent citizens couldn't afford to keep up with the regulations. "If there's a chance to make money from a lawsuit, Helen, someone will take it. And leave everyone else to clear up the mess."

He finished his meal, then dropped the plate in the sink. Helen had insisted that she be allowed to do the washing up in the daytime, rather than leaving it for Glen to do later. Glen had argued, but not too hard. Helen needed to do *something* to feel that she was earning her place in his home, if only to keep her from becoming an over-entitled kid like too many of the little bastards who ended up in holding cells. It spoke well of her parents, he decided as he poured himself a mug of tea, that they'd trained her to do a portion of the work as soon as she could walk. There were too many children on Terra Nova who never learned the basic life skills until they moved into an apartment of their own and discovered just how hard it was to manage a household.

And some of them never learn at all, he thought, morbidly.

Helen led the way into the sitting room and inserted the chip into the viewscreen, then sat back on the floor as the endless series of warnings against piracy popped up on the screen. Glen rolled his eyes – nothing, not even the most advanced encryption available to commercial interests, had been able to prevent electronic piracy – and poured himself a drink as the warnings scrolled on. No one, as far as he knew, paid any attention to them. They were just annoying, as were the series of trailers that followed. And if there had been a way to switch past them, he suspected, there would be fewer pirate copies on the streets.

"These trailers are all the same," Helen complained, as Glen sat down on the sofa behind her. "Why don't they come up with anything different?"

Glen smiled as yet another fire-breathing dragon flew across the screen. "Because they're not allowed to have a decent plot," he said. "It's easier to indulge in ridiculous special effects and gut-wrenching violence than try to get a story idea through the censors. Everything has to be as clichéd as possible."

Helen turned to look back at him. "Why?"

"Don't want the masses getting ideas," Glen grunted. "You couldn't have a resistance movement on a colony world that actually had a *point*. That might start people thinking."

He sighed. It hadn't been *that* long since he'd watched Colony Wars CXI – a remake of a remake – where a colony world had revolted against Earth. The leader of the revolt had been a sadistic coward, so fearful that it was hard to see how he'd ever worked up the nerve to revolt, while his behaviour had been so reprehensible that only utter depravity explained why his followers hadn't revolted against *him*. And he'd made a point of gloating, as often as possible, about how he was starving Earth. The whole flick had been nothing more than an exercise in poorly-disguised propaganda.

And they glossed over how he was finally removed from power, if not the execution, he thought, wryly. *Can't have the military seen in a good light now, can we?*

Helen looked doubtful. "People actually believe everything they see?"

Glen shrugged. The average citizen of Terra Nova – and Earth, before the Fall – lived in a single tiny apartment and rarely saw anything of the world outside, let alone the rest of the universe. They never questioned what they were told by their teachers, let alone the flicks that were supposed to be grounded firmly in reality. The smart ones saw the tiny discrepancies and eventually worked out the truth – and then applied to join colony missions leaving the Core Worlds far behind. By now, after centuries of the smarter ones weeding themselves out of the population, he had a private suspicion that most of Terra Nova's population couldn't tie their own shoes without government assistance.

"Mostly," he said. The screen brightened as loud music began to play. "Sit back and watch, if you still want to see it."

He had to fight the urge to throw something at the screen as Hero Cop went to work, or to provide commentary on the many boneheaded mistakes made by the producers. Hero Cop wouldn't have lasted five minutes as a Marshal before he was summarily sacked – or fired out of an airlock – for gross incompetence. Patty would have gone ballistic if any of her subordinates had acted in such a manner, Glen was sure. She'd certainly never hesitated to chew them out whenever they made a mistake.

And none of us are quite so loathsome, he thought. *And we certainly don't flirt with suspects.*

"He's handsome," Helen said. "But he's also as thick as a brick."

Glen had to smile. Hero Cop was tall, blonde and built like a bodybuilder. The uniforms he wore were designed to show off his muscles, rather than provide either protection or identification. His female colleagues wore uniforms that were barely there, not even covering their nipples. Glen considered, briefly, sending such a uniform to Isabel, then dismissed the thought when he realised she'd castrate him if she ever worked out who'd sent her such a useless gift. She wouldn't see the funny side, not when she had to work extra hard to earn respect from the Civil Guard and citizens on the street.

But the uniforms were a minor complaint compared to just how unprofessional Hero Cop actually was. He flirted with suspects, allowed himself to be distracted every five minutes by a pair of breasts and scattered evidence randomly over crime scenes. Any half-witted defence lawyer could take advantage of Hero Cop's carelessness to get the suspect off, even if he was as guilty as sin. And then there was the scene where he boned his partner in the back of a police van...

"I hope you don't do that," Helen said. "Or do you?"

"No," Glen said, shortly. Once, a Civil Guardsman *had* been caught having sex in the back of a prison van with a suspect, but he'd never heard of a Marshal being so careless. Or stupid, given how easy it was for a desperate suspect to take advantage of a moment of stupidity. "And having sex with one's partner is grossly unprofessional."

"My parents were partners," Helen objected. "They worked together..."

"That's different," Glen said. From what he'd heard, many spacer families were closely related, trading husbands and wives from time to time to keep the gene pool as wide as possible. "Isabel and I can't afford any emotional entanglement."

Helen looked oddly downcast. "I'm sorry," she said. "You deserve someone in your life."

Glen shrugged. "Most of the women I meet are suspects," he said. "It's hard to date someone when you're taking them into the station for one reason or another."

He sighed. It was an open secret among the Marshals that a pretty girl, arrested by the Civil Guard, could get out of trouble by offering herself to them. Glen had no idea how many girls had escaped jail because they'd made the trade, although he had to admit that the thought of having sex with a guardsman was horrific, perhaps a punishment in its own right. And besides, most of the girls couldn't have looked forward to anything other than being transported off-world as indentured colonists. They might have thought it was worth the trade.

"And don't forget it," Hero Cop announced, as he strode into battle. "The good guys always win."

Glen rolled his eyes as the shooting commenced. In real life, Hero Cop would have been riddled with so many bullets that there wouldn't have been anything left of him, apart from blood on the ground. But in the flick, he walked through a hail of bullets without being touched, then drew his pistol and started shooting back. Over a hundred shots later – the pistol hadn't been reloaded once – the shooting came to an end. Glen made a face as the camera panned over the dead bodies, the men having their faces blown away while the women were still beautiful, even in death. Gunshot wounds weren't like *that*! Hero Cop stepped forward, snapped off a couple more one-liners as the girl he'd rescued started to remove what remained of her clothing, and then the flick mercifully came to an end.

Helen frowned as she removed the datachip. "Where did that girl come from?"

"I don't think it matters," Glen said. If there was a plot, beyond 'Hero Cop fucks, shoots and fucks again' he couldn't see it. There was no link between the various scenes, as far as he could determine, nor was there any reason for the girl to be at the shootout at the end. A little imagination would have provided the answers, if the filmmakers had bothered to think about it. Perhaps the girl had been a hostage who'd been saved by Hero Cop...

He shook his head. "But they couldn't shoot a realistic cop movie anyway."

"Why not?" Helen asked. "It might be fun."

"It would be boring," Glen said. He could see why shootouts were considered exciting, but much of a Marshal's life consisted of gathering evidence, interrogating suspects and presenting his findings to court. Hero Cop hadn't bothered with forensic evidence, his interrogation technique would get him whatever he wanted to hear rather than the truth and he didn't seem to give a damn about proving the case afterwards. "And nothing like the movie. I wouldn't even know where to begin picking it apart."

"No sex with your partner," Helen suggested.

Glen snorted. That wasn't the worst of it, he knew. The complete disregard for forensic evidence was bad enough, but the treatment of suspects was worse. Beating people up at random didn't tend to produce hard evidence and defence lawyers could use it to suggest that their clients had lied out of self-preservation. And then there had been the detailed torture scene, where Hero Cop had beaten a half-naked woman bloody for information. The mere inclusion of the scene said more about the producers than about real life on the streets.

He shuddered in disgust. Two years ago, he'd arrested a conspiracy theorist who'd claimed that the prevalence of violence – particularly sexual violence – was a plot to manipulate the population into reducing itself. Glen hadn't thought much of it at the time, but now he tended to wonder of the theorist had had a point. It was difficult to be sure, as the figures were suppressed, yet he had a feeling that sexual violence had been on the rise for quite some time.

But then, most people feel helpless, he thought. *Taking it out on their partner seems the only way to cope.*

"No excuse," he said, out loud.

Helen stood. "Pardon?"

"Just woolgathering," Glen said. He glanced at his watch. "Bedtime, I think."

Helen nodded and walked to the bathroom to brush her teeth. She'd slept better since her first night, but she still had nightmares from time to time. Glen had found himself comforting her more than he cared to admit...

His wristcom bleeped. "Glen," Isabel's voice snapped," get your ass down to the station now. Priority One."

Glen swore. "Understood," he said. Priority One meant drop everything and do as you were told, without argument. Helen would have to sleep in the apartment alone. "I'm on my way."

FIFTEEN

Nor is that the only issue lawyers can raise. What justifies, for example, a murderous assault? The lawyers will find a justification that every sensible person will consider absurd, yet will find immensely difficult to dispute.

- Professor Leo Caesius, *The Decline of Law and Order and the Rise of Anarchy*

The station never really slept, Glen knew from long hours on the late shift as a rookie, but it was true that activity tended to slow down during the night. Prisoners were still booked, of course, yet they would be held in the cells until morning before they were properly processed and given a chance to call a lawyer or their families. If nothing else, the curfew had helped ensure that most people stayed off the streets overnight.

But the station was brightly lit as Isabel and he strode inside, hundreds of officers and guardsmen running around carrying weapons and equipment. Glen felt his blood run cold as he glanced from face to face, seeing a mixture of concern and grim resolve in experienced officers and outright fear on the faces of the rookies. Isabel caught his arm before he could start asking questions and pulled him into the briefing room. A number of officers were already there, looking puzzled and alarmed. It was rare for anyone to be summoned outside working hours unless the shit had already hit the fan.

"There's no time for formality," Patty said, shortly. She was wearing a suit of body armour and carrying her helmet under her arm. "There's a budding riot in the central district, one that is already out of control. We are to stop it before it causes real damage."

Glen cursed under his breath. Beside him, Isabel shuddered. No Marshal liked riots, not when the crowds were too maddened to realise that they were hopelessly outgunned – or, for that matter, when there were agent provocateurs in the mass, stirring up trouble. A great many people were about to be hurt and not all of them would be civilians. He'd seen police officers and guardsmen killed by mobs before, brought down and trampled to death before their comrades could intervene. It was a horrific way to go.

A large map of the central district appeared on the projector. "The crowds seem to have largely gathered in the shopping district," Patty continued. "So far, there's no real threat to Government House, but we're evacuating the Governor and his staff already, before the rioters see fit to take out their anger on the legitimate government. The eyes on the ground tell us that the rioters are concentrating on shopping malls, smashing windows and looting the hell out of the buildings. We have to stop them."

Glen sighed, inwardly. The central district was more than just the home of the Governor and his family. The shops there were among the most expensive in the Empire. No one was allowed to so much as look in the window if they didn't have at least a million credits in their bank account. And the apartments nearby were occupied by some of the richest citizens on Terra Nova. Their security staffs had to be burning up the airwaves with demands that someone – anyone – intervene before the rioters realise that Terra Nova's filthy rich were at their mercy. The law enforcement forces would be sent into the chaos before they could formulate a proper plan.

We couldn't let them burn themselves out either, he thought, as Patty started handing out assignments. *They'd do far too much damage.*

"Grab your riot gear," Patty concluded. "And watch your backs out there."

Glen nodded, then followed Isabel down to the equipment store. Normally, even a senior Marshal had to fill out reams of paperwork to take *anything* from the store, no matter how urgently it was required.

Now, someone had cuffed the procurement officer to the wall and slapped a mouth guard over his face, making it impossible for him to object as the store was raided for riot control gear. Glen concealed a smile – the officer wasn't a Marshal, merely a paper-pusher – and found a set of body-armour and protective gear in his size. Beside him, Isabel pulled her armour over her uniform and motioned for him to hastily don his own.

"It's always too hot," Glen muttered, as he pulled the protective gear over his head. He knew better than to trust it completely, no matter what the manufacturers said. Equipment had failed before, always at the worst possible times. "Make sure you take extra stunners and neural whips. We don't want to have to rearm ourselves in the midst of a fight."

He turned and checked her straps, then allowed her to check his before he pulled the helmet over his head. The helmets were designed to be intimidating, hiding all traces of individuality behind a black mask that rendered him indistinguishable from everyone else in the police line. Normally, the numbers on the armour would be noted, but there was no time, not when the richest citizens on the planet were demanding action. He removed the helmet, then strode over to the equipment racks and took a neural whip, a stunner and a large number of zip-ties. Beside him, Isabel did the same, hanging them on her belt. They would be needed if the shit *really* got out of control.

"Take your shield," he ordered, finally. He picked up the piece of transparent – and almost indestructible – plastic and held it up in front of his face. It never failed to surprise him just how light it was, for something that was so resistant to attack. "And let's go."

Outside, the armoured vans were already waiting for the officers, their engines rumbling impatiently. Glen led the way into the cramped rear compartment, resting his helmet in his lap, and forced himself to breathe normally as the vehicle rumbled into life. Beside him, the other officers did the same, listening to reports from the spotters as the riot moved further and further out of control. People were swarming in from the outskirts of the city, despite emergency broadcasts and a swift closure of the public transport system. Clearly, despite the need for swift movement around the city, leaving the tubes open had been a mistake.

This isn't one person breaking curfew, Glen thought, as he started matching the reports to street locations. *This is hundreds of thousands, perhaps millions.*

He thought, suddenly, of Hero Cop and had to fight down a very undignified giggle. No doubt, if called upon to suppress a riot, Hero Cop would just flex his muscles and the rioters would all run for their lives. It didn't work like that in the real world, he knew all too well. There would be a hardcore of rioters who would want to fight, a number who were trapped by the press of the mob and couldn't escape...and others who, hopefully, would make their retreat as soon as they realised the forces of law and order had arrived. Glen silently prayed that most of the rioters would run, even though it meant they would almost certainly escape arrest. It would reduce the coming bloodshed...

And this could be a diversion, Glen thought, feeling his blood running cold. They'd expected major riots ever since the Fall of Earth, but this was the first one to materialise, just when the Marshals had started to wonder if the prediction was wrong. *Someone else could be taking advantage of our distraction to do something. But what?*

He shook his head as the vehicle rattled to a halt. There was no longer any time for anything, but doing his duty.

"Helmets on," a voice ordered. A dull clang rang through the vehicle as something – a stone, perhaps – bounced off the armour. "Log into the secure network and prepare to deploy, as per orders."

Glen braced himself, then pulled his helmet over his head. The HUD lit up at once, drawing on the live feed from hundreds of security monitors – far fewer than there should have been, he noted – and datastreams from his fellow officers. Piece by piece, the riot was being surrounded, with only one avenue of escape left open. It wasn't how Glen would have preferred to handle it, but he had the feeling that Patty hadn't been given much choice. The upper classes wouldn't just want the rioters dispersed, they'd want them punished.

The doors banged open, revealing a scene from hell. Glen saw hundreds of people running in all directions, some carrying obviously-looted goods, as the officers deployed out of the van. The noise of people shouting and screaming, of windows being smashed and vehicles destroyed, was growing louder. He gritted his teeth and followed the others out of the vehicle, forming a line. Beyond, towards the centre of town, the real mass of rioters were waiting.

He thought, briefly, of Helen. And then he went to work.

————

"But I'm telling you that you have to arrange a pickup," a woman was pleading. "My husband is the Special Assistant to the Secretary of Health and the Environment and he would be most displeased if something happened to me."

Belinda had to smile at the waiter's barely-controlled exasperation. "The flight paths over the city have been closed down," he said, somehow managing to sound patient. "We can only wait for the law enforcement forces to clear the streets before we lift the lockdown."

"But my husband is *important*," the woman wailed. "I..."

"She's deluded," Augustus murmured in Belinda's ear. "Her husband wouldn't have his job if he didn't have a close relative on the Governor's Council. He gets paid bribes to stay at home and do nothing, even keeping his workers from doing anything. It's all he's good for."

Belinda nodded. The panicky woman wasn't the only customer on the verge of coming apart, but she was certainly the loudest. And definitely the most obnoxious. She might have been pretty, twenty years and much less makeup ago, yet right now she was just irritating. A few more minutes, Belinda decided, and she might just give into the temptation to sedate the woman, even though it would be far too revealing. Perhaps she should just bang her on the head.

She strode away from the door before temptation could overwhelm her and walked over to the windows, peering down into the darkened streets. Several vehicles had caught fire as the rioters crashed through the district, while a handful of shops were already aflame. The Hullmetal that had been used to make them was indestructible, at least by rioters, but the remaining stockpiles of clothes and other expensive goods would burn well. Belinda had no expensive tastes – it had never been part of her life, before or after joining the Marines – but she felt a flicker of regret at so much destruction. Businesses would be ruined, people would be unemployed and the local economy would take more damage.

"I can't see anything," Augustus complained. "What are they *doing*?"

"They're doing what people always do when there's trouble and rioting," Belinda said. Her cover story included a few riots. "They will smash a few things, kill or maim a few people and then disperse before the law arrives. Or they will try to fight the law. Or us."

She thought, rapidly, about her options if the mob managed to break into the building and find their way up to the dance floor. Avoiding them would be easy, if she was on her own, but it would be far too revealing if she used her augmented abilities to protect others. And yet, what else could she do? She no longer had the dispassion that had once allowed her to watch horrors without intervening, no matter how much she might have wished to do something.

You watched unmoved as a woman was beaten to death for talking back, Pug reminded her, nastily. *Why are you so moved now?*

I was not unmoved, Belinda thought back, angrily. *I was simply doing my duty.*

But it was a weak excuse. Han had been a brutal violent planet, on the verge of boiling over into a mad slaughter for years before the shit finally hit the fan. She'd been there long enough to see horror after horror, from wives killed for defying their husbands to a father killed for trying to stand in his son's way. The Slaughterhouse had been brutal, but it was focused brutality, aimed at preparing her for her work. Han...had just been a bloody nightmare.

"Don't worry," Augustus said. "The forces of law and order will get here soon."

Belinda nodded, trying to ignore the howls of laughter in her head. *She* was more dangerous than everyone else in the building put together, even in her reduced state, and yet he was trying to reassure *her*. But she appreciated the thought, even though she knew it was nonsense. If the rioters were too deeply embedded, or armed and prepared for confrontation, it might be hours before the law enforcement forces finally managed to disperse them. And it was quite possible that they would break into the building before the police arrived.

A dull tremor ran through the building. Belinda looked up, alarmed. The restaurant had been built to very strict standards, back in the days before a large bribe could get even a dangerously-unsafe building cleared for habitation. But if it was shaking now...she clicked through her implants, searching for any alert messages, but heard nothing apart from the standard emergency message. The law enforcement agencies hadn't managed to shut down the communications network yet.

Sloppy, she thought, as the building shook again. *Very sloppy.*

"Ah, we have a breach in the lower levels," a voice said, over the loudspeaker. "If you could all make your way up to the highest levels..."

Augustus caught Belinda's arm. "Come on," he said. "We don't want to be caught here."

Belinda nodded, thinking hard. "Shut down the elevators," she called over to the waiter, who was being badgered by another man with more importance than common sense. "And seal the staircase, completely."

"The system isn't designed to shut down," the waiter said, clearly glad of the interruption. "It's a sealed unit, My Lady. It doesn't even shut down if there's a fire."

Belinda resisted – barely – the temptation to snap at him, or slap him as hard as she could.

"Then call the elevators to this floor and put something in to keep the doors from closing," she ordered, when she was sure she could talk evenly. Honestly! It was so *obvious*! But she had a feeling that no one had drilled the staff in emergency procedures for years, not when it was easier to bribe safety inspectors than meet their requirements. "The idea is to keep the rioters downstairs from using them."

"Good thinking," Augustus muttered, as he pulled her up the stairs to the next level. "What else do you have in mind?"

"Lock and barricade the doors," Belinda said, shortly. She had her doubts about any of the rich idiots being able to put up a fight, but there were few other options. "And, if you have a terminal, start writing your will."

She turned and walked to the bar, inspecting the selection of alcoholic drinks. It was possible, assuming that the building *had* stuck with basic safety procedures, that the stairwells were intended to serve as fireproof shelters as well as a way of getting down to the streets when the elevators weren't working. And alcohol could be used to start a fire...

"Too dangerous," the waiter said, when she mentioned the possibility. "We don't want to burn the building to the ground."

Belinda sighed, then quietly collected several bottles anyway, just in case. The only other option was blocking the stairwell, which would be difficult now that almost everyone had moved to the uppermost levels. Silently, she cursed the designers for not leaving the staff a way out, even though she knew it was unfair. Any emergency escape chutes would lead down to the riot, where they would be torn apart if they were caught trying to escape. And the only other hope was to be picked up by an aircraft.

She turned and looked out over the city. One building had already caught fire, despite the design, the flames spreading too quickly to be entirely natural. She checked the location against the map she'd downloaded and stored in her implants and swore under her breath as she realised it was a government office, one responsible for enforcing countless hated and unnecessary regulations. There were too many horror stories about just how far the bureaucrats had slipped out of control for her to doubt that the building had been targeted deliberately. Hell, when the general population heard of the building's destruction, they'd probably consider the rioters heroes.

If they don't already, she thought, coldly. It had always puzzled her that the rioters, the rebels, were regarded as heroes while those who struggled to maintain law and order were spat on in the streets. But if the general population felt helpless against all-powerful bureaucrats, it might explain why they loved the rebels. And yet...what did the rebels intend to create to replace the government? Revolutions were called revolutions, the old joke ran, because they went round and round.

"You don't need to worry," Augustus said. He slipped his hand into hers and squeezed it, tightly. "We will survive."

"Thank you," Belinda said. He meant well. She knew he meant well, even though she also knew how absurd his words were. "But you don't have to worry about me."

She sighed as she saw helicopters appearing over the city, beaming light down towards the rioters. The forces of law and order had finally arrived...

...But she knew it was already too late to stop the rioters from causing havoc – and, perhaps, from unbalancing the government. And who knew what would happen then?

CHAPTER
SIXTEEN

This is, in short, the origin of the phrase "the law is an ass."

- Professor Leo Caesius, The Decline of Law
and Order and the Rise of Anarchy

Glen braced himself as the rioters surged forward, feeling a sick sense of fear in his lower chest. The rioters hadn't been cowed by the sudden appearance of the law enforcement forces as he'd hoped; if anything, it had given them new heart. Alerts flashed up in front of his eyes and he swore, silently. Someone was using civilian communications devices to coordinate the riot and direct fighters towards the police lines.

"We need to shut down the communications network," he said, as he lifted his shield. The line formed a barrier, locking their shields together into an unbreakable wall. "They're using it against us."

"The civilians are balking," Patty said, from where she was trying to coordinate the law enforcement agencies. "There's a shitload of money tied up in keeping the network active."

And that isn't a coincidence, Glen thought. *I'll bet my life that someone organised it deliberately.*

The line wavered as the rioters slammed into it, pressing against the transparent shields with all the force they could muster. Glen saw men and women, most of them only a few years older than Helen, staring at the police lines with utter hatred as they shoved at the shields, then started to throw projectiles over the barricade. Most of them were rocks and pieces of debris, but some were makeshift Molotov Cocktails and even a couple of improvised explosive devises. Glen's lips quirked at the fresh evidence that the bureaucrats who were responsible for ensuring that no one bought enough material to be dangerous were asleep at the switch, then he pushed the thought aside. There would be time for recriminations later.

"Use gas," he ordered, as the line shuddered. The first wave of rioters were in very real peril of being crushed by the second and third waves, as irresistible force met immovable objects with them caught in the middle. "Put them all to sleep."

He watched, grimly, as gas grenades arced over the barricade and started to spew out gas, but half of the rioters produced masks and pulled them over their faces before they could breathe in any of the gas. Glen swore under his breath – the manufacturers had flatly refused to make the gas effective if it touched a person's skin – and then winced in pain as a number of rioters fell to the ground. They'd be trampled by their fellows before the police could rescue them, he noted in horror. His decision had made the whole riot much worse.

"Hold the line," he ordered, bitterly. Stunners would be usable, but they'd just make a bad situation worse. "And prepare the neural whips."

The crowd seemed quieter now the masks were on, but no less determined to break through the lines. Glen drew his whip, activated it, then barked a single command. The shields were yanked back, allowing him and the second line to start lashing out at the crowd. Shrieks of pain echoed through the street, sending the rioters at the rear stumbling backwards, then running for their lives. Others lost their masks and fell, knocked out by the gas. Glen watched in relief and concern as the rioter mass collapsed, then started to flee. The Marshals advanced carefully, leaving the sleeping bodies on the ground. There was no time to tend to them now.

Glen had never visited the central shopping district outside working hours. It was simply too expensive for him, a monument to the vanities of wealth and power. The shops were wonders of design, constructed in a dozen different styles, all intended to showcase just how wealthy the owners were – and just how wealthy a person had to be to shop there regularly. There were no prices on any of the goods, he'd seen. If a person had to ask the price, they couldn't afford it.

Now, it had become a nightmare. Every window within reach – and a few that shouldn't have been reachable – had been smashed. Secure doors had been torn off their hinges, allowing the rioters and looters to break into the building and start taking whatever they wanted. A handful of vehicles burned merrily, adding smoke and fumes to the confusion. And hundreds of young men and women ran everywhere, carrying whatever they could away from the riot.

"Warn them," Glen ordered, as the Marshals spread out. In the distance, he could hear the sound of more fighting as another mass of rioters met a Civil Guard force. Red icons flashed up in his helmet display, noting facilities. "And stun them if they offer any resistance."

Isabel tapped her helmet. Her voice, when she spoke, was crude and masculine, without any traces of emotion.

"PUT DOWN THE STOLEN PROPERTY AND SIT DOWN ON THE GROUND, THEN PLACE YOUR HANDS ON YOUR HEADS," she ordered. "OFFICERS WILL BE ALONG TO TAKE YOU INTO CUSTODY. DO NOT ATTEMPT TO RESIST."

Glen lifted his stunner. Several of the looters obeyed, their bodies trembling as they realised that they'd stayed too long and now they were caught, others tried to run. The Marshals stunned them in the back and watched as their bodies hit the ground, then moved on and into the first set of shops. Glen vaguely recalled that it had once sold a tiny number of handbags, each one worth more than an entire CityBlock. Now, the handbags were gone, the shop was wrecked and completely deserted...no, he could hear someone snivelling in the far corner, trying desperately not to be heard. He motioned for Isabel to cover him as he peered through the shadows, eventually spying a young couple, one of them clutching a stolen handbag as if it were a life preserver.

"Get over here," he snapped, as they stared at him in horror. Part of him guessed that they'd seen the riot as the first chance of real excitement they were likely to have, after a long and boring life in the cityblocks. The rest of him didn't care. He unhooked a pair of zip-ties from his belt, then secured their hands behind their backs. "You'll wait here until we come back to pick you up."

"But..." the boy started to stammer. "I..."

"Quiet," Glen ordered. He was in no mood for excuses, not now. "Stay here. We will be back."

They searched the rest of the store quickly and efficiently, finding nothing apart from a dead body that looked to have been beaten to death. Glen made a note of the body's location for the datanet – it was very much a third-order priority right now – and then pressed on, leaving the two arrested teens behind. Outside, the riot was slowly dying away as more and more Civil Guardsmen appeared, brandishing weapons as if they were ready to use them at a moment's notice. Glen nodded to their leader, then led Isabel into the next store. This one had also been looted badly, but there were no rioters within the building. Glen was relieved, more than he cared to admit, as they moved back out of the building and sealed it. He was too tired to arrest people safely, not now.

"The riot seems to have been dispersed," Patty said, over the communications network. "Keep a sharp eye out for people who might have been organising the riot – I want them held separately and stunned until the techs can have a look at them. I don't want to risk losing them to suicide before they can be interrogated."

Glen nodded. If someone had deliberately organised the riot, capturing the organisers might be the first step towards rounding up and destroying the entire network. It might be a Nihilist plan, he considered, but it didn't seem too likely. The body count was surprisingly low for their normal plans.

"Understood," he said. "What about the remaining prisoners?"

"We're currently securing the sporting area," Patty said. "We'll march them there once the building is secure and turn it into a temporary detainment zone. After that...we'll see."

"Most of them are young idiots," Isabel said, as Patty broke the connection. "Just like my kids."

"Yeah," Glen agreed. He signalled to the Civil Guard officers, then looked back at his partner. "And their lives will be ruined after this crazy stunt."

Slowly, the stunned or sleeping rioters were cuffed, then left to sleep it off by the side of the road. The ones who had remained awake were marched into the centre of the road, then left to sit there under guard while the security forces searched the shops over and over again. A handful started to object, demanding to see lawyers or call their parents, until the dead bodies were dumped next to them. Glen noted, with some amusement, that the implicit threat was better than shouting for convincing idiots to be quiet.

"We've recovered over five hundred bodies," one of the dispatchers said. "And ninety-seven rioters have been injured so badly as to require immediate medical attention."

Glen winced. He had no sympathy for the rioters, but it was unlikely they would get any medical attention very quickly. There were only a handful of clinics in the central district and they were all primed for rich customers, not rioters from the cityblocks. And the less said about the medical clinics in the cityblocks the better. The doctors there, through bad training and worse equipment, were often more murderous than an entire legion of Civil Guardsmen armed to the teeth.

"Get them somewhere secure," he ordered. A quick check revealed that medical corpsmen had arrived, but were busy tending to the wounds of various law enforcement officers, not the rioters. "And then find one of the local clinics and order it opened up for treatment."

"Aye, sir," a voice said.

Glen walked back towards the rows of prisoners, shaking his head at their stupidity. What had they expected when they'd decided to defy the curfew and start a riot? The smarter ones had engaged in some quick looting, then vanished back into the shadows, leaving the slower ones to take the blame. They looked pitiful, sitting on the ground with their hands bound; hell, some of them were even crying. But it wouldn't get them any mercy from the judges.

His wristcom buzzed. "We've secured the Talbot Arena for the men and the Hastings Arena for the women," Patty said. Somehow, she didn't sound very tired. "Glen, I want you to hand the men over to the Civil Guard, then escort the women to the Hastings Arena yourself."

Glen smiled, despite his exhaustion. "Just me?"

"Take a squad of Marshals with you," Patty said. She sounded irked at his sarcastic question, while Isabel smiled wryly. "I just don't want them in Civil Guard hands."

"I know," Glen said. Most of the female prisoners were in their teens or early twenties – and hopelessly vulnerable, now the fight had been knocked out of them. The Civil Guard wouldn't hesitate to take advantage of the prisoners, not when the prisoners would probably be sent to a holding pen prior to involuntary deportation to a new colony world. They'd never see Terra Nova again. "I'll take care of it."

He closed the channel, then started to issue orders. The prisoners were helped to their feet one by one, patted down and then lined up for the march. Some of them complained, but most of them were quiet and submissive, keeping their legs tightly pressed together. Glen rolled his eyes – what sort of idiots didn't bother to wear proper clothes if they knew they were going into a riot? – and then dismissed the thought. As soon as all the prisoners had been patted down, they started to march through the city to the Arena.

"The media is out in force," Isabel warned, as they passed through the security cordon. "They're going to have their faces splashed over the datanet."

"Keep your helmet on," Glen advised. "We can't do anything for the girls."

Isabel was right, he realised; the media *was* out in force. Hundreds of reporters, photographers and others were standing just beyond the line, filming the prisoners as they were marched through the streets. Glen wondered, vaguely, if there was a law against public humiliation, then decided it didn't matter. The prisoners would be lucky if they had a chance to make a phone call to their families before they were herded into a holding pen. He kept a sharp eye on the prisoners as the reporters jostled at them, preparing himself to intervene if necessary. But the reporters didn't press close enough for him to have to act.

He heard a low moan run through the prisoners as they saw the Arena finally come into view, the leaders of the march somehow guessing that it was their destination. Given what sort of entertainments were hosted there, Glen didn't blame the prisoners for their sudden despair; they probably thought they were going to be thrown to the lions or sent to fight the gladiators with their bare hands. The Arenas were sickening places, in his opinion. For every young man who became a star, there were thousands who died before even passing through the first round or two.

A security officer, wearing a bright green uniform, met him as they approached the ramp. "We've set up the main chamber as a makeshift cell," he said, in a tone that grated on Glen's tired mind, "but we don't have any facilities for them. They'll have to make do with the animal showers and..."

He paused, significantly. "We could sell the footage..."

Glen punched him in the face, sending the officer stumbling to the ground. He'd known, of course, that the arena staff *did* make money by selling footage – particularly of the stars in their private moments – but it wasn't something he was going to tolerate. There might be a disturbing brand of pornography set in prisons – slightly more realistic than Hero Cop – yet everyone who took part in it were actors and actresses. He wasn't about to allow unsuspecting girls, even prisoners, to be recorded without their permission.

And some of the girls were no older than Helen.

"Get up," he snapped. "You will treat them with the maximum dignity compatible with the safety of your subordinates. Do you understand me?"

"Yes," the man stammered, staggering to his feet. "I do. I..."

Glen glowered at him. Clearly, he was too tired to make a proper impression. The man should have been out like a light.

"Good," he snapped. "I'll inspect the security arrangements once we have the girls settled in."

The interior of the Arena was large enough to play four football games at once, the ground coated with sand to soak up the blood after the contests were finished. Glen checked the walls and decided they were impossible to climb without special equipment, then peeked into the animal pens. They smelt funny, but they were clean and had enough room for the girls to shower, if necessary. And they probably would need a shower. One section had been turned into a toilet, which would suffice long enough for better arrangements to be made.

"The complex is secure," Marshal Davis said, appearing from a side door. "They don't seem to like the thought of fans getting into the arena, so it's really just a matter of reversing the thinking and keeping the girls on the *inside*."

Glen shrugged. The Arena's collection of animals included – *had* included – hundreds of samples of man-eating wildlife from across the universe. As important as the Arena was when it came to distracting the population, it was still vital to ensure that civilians weren't accidentally eaten by the monsters, or the lawsuits and bad publicity would ruin the Arena and its owners. The security officer he'd knocked down hadn't been impressive, but he wouldn't have to be if the Arena was as secure as it was supposed to be.

"Get some clippers up here, then free their hands," Glen ordered. "They'll be here for at least twenty-four hours, I think. Probably longer."

"Probably," Davis agreed, as Isabel came back to join them. "I heard the Governor was considering establishing a new detention centre on the outskirts of the city."

Glen wasn't too surprised. It would take days, perhaps weeks, to process all the prisoners, then decide their ultimate fate. Particularly, of course, if one or more of them could be convinced to explain just what had happened before the riot began. Had they all been moved into position beforehand or had it been spontaneous and they'd been caught up in the general excitement? Most of them – he cast a glance towards the prisoners, who were sitting on the sand and looking downcast – had probably been unaware of what was about to happen until it was too late. They'd probably be eager to talk.

"Make sure they're protected," he ordered, instead. "They don't deserve to be abused."

"They deserve a flogging," Isabel said, tartly. She yawned, suddenly. "Getting us out of bed like this."

Davis snorted. "Go ask the boss for extra pay?"

"And get stuck with all the shit jobs for the next few weeks," Isabel said. She shook her head. "No, there's no extra pay for anyone. And probably no sleep tonight too."

"There are rooms in the Arena," Davis said. "You can probably use one, if you ask."

"I'll see," Isabel said. "Glen?"

"I need to check on Helen," Glen said. He cursed, inwardly. Would Helen have slept peacefully, or had a nightmare, or stayed awake to watch the news? "But it can wait until relief arrives."

"It might be a while," Davis said. "I heard this wasn't the only riot, Glen. There were riots in a dozen cities. We're badly overstretched and its only going to get worse."

"Shit," Glen said.

No one bothered to disagree.

CHAPTER
SEVENTEEN

It also destroys respect for the law – and for those who enforce it. When the law-keepers are seen as enemies, when the law is a tool of powerful interests rather than society as a whole, the end cannot be far away.

- Professor Leo Caesius, *The Decline of Law and Order and the Rise of Anarchy*

"The security forces have secured the lower levels," the waiter said, suddenly. "This building is secure."

"It's about time," a loud and overweight man proclaimed. "This whole affair has been just disgraceful!"

Belinda ignored him, choosing instead to peer down into the streets, far below. Hundreds of Civil Guardsmen were moving around, shoving bound prisoners into lines and searching them roughly. It reminded her of some of the early battles on Han, when it had been impossible to tell the difference between friends and enemies...and the occupation force had ended up largely converting the former into the latter. Some of the prisoners looked to have been beaten too, unsurprisingly. The Civil Guard wasn't trained to handle riots without considerable levels of violence.

"I shall be complaining to the Governor about this," the man thundered. "I will..."

"Be quiet," another man said. "The Governor won't want to be bothered with you."

The waiter spoke before the argument could properly begin. "The security forces have established a cordon at the main entrance," he said.

"You will all have to pass through the security sweep, then take taxies to your homes. Please proceed to the elevators in an orderly manner."

Augustus caught Belinda's arm as the room slowly emptied. "I'm sorry about tonight," he murmured, as they walked towards the elevators. "I meant it to end better."

"It's not a problem," Belinda assured him. "None of this was your fault."

She mulled it over as they entered the elevator, which started to sink down towards the ground floor. Whose fault *was* it? Unless she was very much mistaken, the riot had been planned in advance, given when and where it had appeared. And that meant...that someone thought they could benefit from the chaos? A criminal faction, perhaps, or someone with darker ambitions? And what, if anything, did it have to do with the conference?

Augustus had hinted, once or twice, at doing something for the Governor. The conference? It was quite possible, Belinda considered. Augustus was clearly competent – a far cry from the drunk she'd met on the orbital tower – and if the Governor intended to build up a power base of his own, someone like Augustus would be invaluable. But she couldn't ask him without revealing that she knew too much, information that would not normally be available to a visiting tourist. She hadn't even found a *hint* about the conference on the planetary datanet.

The elevator shook as it reached the bottommost floor, then opened the doors. Outside, Belinda saw a line of uniformed Civil Guardsmen, all of them looked nervous. It was a worrying sight, given the way they were fingering loaded weapons, but she understood how they felt. Riots were never safely predictable; rioters might be cowed as soon as the security forces arrived or they might turn on the newcomers and attack them with terrifying force. And the people they were meant to process, right now, were among the planet's elite. A single complaint would be enough to ruin a career and a whole family.

If they have families, part of her mind noted. The thought of a Civil Guardsman going home to a wife and children seemed a little absurd. Marines rarely married when on active service, but they had the excuse of being moved around the galaxy like pieces on a chessboard. The Civil

Guardsmen were generally stationed on one planet, yet their idea of courtship was everyone else's idea of rape. Or maybe she was just being unpleasant for the sake of being unpleasant.

"Please form an orderly line," a senior officer – Belinda couldn't help noticing that he wore no nametag – ordered. "We'll process you as quickly as possible."

Surprisingly, no one complained. Or perhaps it wasn't surprising, Belinda decided; the hundreds of armed men were hellishly intimidating. So were the sounds from outside, the moaning and crying from the wounded or prisoners. She ran through her audio discrimination programs and decided that there were at least thirty wounded on the streets outside, all in need of help that might not come. Terra Nova wasn't as overpopulated as Earth, she knew, but the ratio of doctors to patients was still terrifyingly low.

One by one, the guests passed through the security check. Belinda watched carefully, nervous about the prospect of a deep-body scan, but it seemed to be nothing more than an ID check and a handful of questions. That was a relief, she told herself; a deep scan would reveal her implants, if the masking systems failed to work properly. A couple of thickset men were given a more thorough search – they were bodyguards, she suspected, and probably had some enhancements of their own – but they were let through the system afterwards. And then she watched grimly as Augustus passed through the check. It was astonishing how the guards moved from being suspicious to practically genuflecting as soon as they realised who he was.

"Please step forward," one of the guards ordered, once Augustus had passed through. "And place your ID chip in the reader."

Belinda activated her masking systems, then obeyed. Her sensors reported a light scan for concealed weapons, which wouldn't go deep enough to locate her implants, and nothing else. Like the scanners on the orbital tower, it would reveal the shape of her body, practically stripping her naked, but it wouldn't reveal anything sensitive. But then, she reminded herself, even a full strip and cavity search would reveal nothing. They'd have to cut her open to reveal and remove her implanted weapons.

"You're a long way from your hotel," the guard observed. "Why did you come here?"

"I was on a date," Belinda said, nodding to Augustus. She cursed herself under her breath, annoyed. Every so often, the Civil Guard revealed a surprising amount of competence. Her address on Terra Nova was well away from the central district, so they needed to understand why she'd been there in the middle of a riot. "We met on the orbital tower."

The guard looked disbelieving. "Really?"

"Yes, really," Belinda said, trying to sound haughty. A hint of weakness might prove disastrous. If he tried to take her into custody, she would have to leave it the same night and go underground. *That* would make her task much harder. "You can ask him, of course."

"We were dating, true," Augustus said, when asked. "And she was here for hours before the chaos started."

"That will be checked," the guard grunted, but he waved Belinda through without further questioning. He clearly didn't want to make an enemy of Augustus. "Your contact code has been noted. If you are called upon for questioning, you will need to report to the nearest police station as soon as possible."

"Asshole," Augustus muttered, as they stepped out onto the street. "You want me to have words with his superiors?"

"No, thank you," Belinda said. She shrugged. "I've been in his place, vetting people who might be innocent bystanders or who might be responsible for the trouble. It's never an easy job."

"I suppose it isn't," Augustus said. He looked up and down the street. "And to think this was such a peaceful place, once. My daughter used to love it."

Belinda followed his gaze. The shopping district had been wrecked. Hundreds of windows had been shattered, a number of burned-out vehicles lay smoking on the side of the road and dozens of prisoners sat in the middle of the streets, their hands bound behind their backs. She had a feeling that most of the prisoners had gotten in over their heads, but a handful eyed her coldly and calculatingly, suggesting that they might have helped coordinate the riot. It wasn't her job to report them to the Civil Guard, but she made a note of their faces anyway, recording their details in her implants. She could check them against the planetary records later.

"I've seen worse," she said. She shuddered at the memory. There had been a market on Penang, where shoppers could find and haggle over everything from food to brightly-coloured traditional clothing. And then one of the many factions had detonated a bomb in the midst of the crowds. The carnage had been unbelievable. "And this might be just the beginning."

She briefly considered going back to her hotel, then dismissed the thought as Augustus led the way through the security cordon and hailed a taxi. The driver looked astonished when he saw Augustus's ID, but happily opened the door and allowed them both to climb inside. Augustus issued orders, then sat back and stared out of the tinted windows as the vehicle hummed to life and headed away from the chaos, towards the wealthy residential zone.

"It looks almost as if nothing has happened," he mused, once they were a kilometre or two from the security cordon. "Is that normal too?"

"Yeah," Belinda said. She stared out the window too. The streets were dark, and largely deserted. She'd downloaded the patrol patterns for the Civil Guard from the datanet, but she had a feeling that those patterns had been completely disrupted by the riot. Even the Civil Guard wouldn't have maintained their normal patterns when confronted with all-out chaos. "But you need to be careful."

Augustus shrugged, then cleared his throat. "I...um...I think it would be best if you stayed the night in my apartment," he said. He sounded oddly embarrassed, like a schoolboy tying to ask out a girl for the first time. "I won't ask you to share my bed."

Belinda heard howls of laughter in her mind. She ignored them as best as she could.

"Thank you," she said, instead. There was no point in telling him that she could look after herself. Besides, slipping back to her hotel would be difficult and she would have to trick the security systems into thinking she'd always been there. "I'd be happy to stay with you for the night."

Augustus squeezed her hand lightly, then settled back in his seat as the taxi passed through a security gate, then came to a halt. The door opened moments later, revealing a large garage with a handful of high-class vehicles sitting under the lights. Showing off, Belinda noted, as Augustus paid the taxi driver and followed her out of the car. The apartment block was tiny, compared to the cityblocks of Earth – and staggeringly expensive. Augustus had a bigger home in the countryside, but this was where he worked. It was very close to Government House.

Which is probably why the rent is so high, she told herself, as her implants pinged the local network. It was largely secure, with some firewalls that were definitely a cut or two above what civilians were normally allowed to possess. But then, a large enough bribe could get anything in the Empire. *The people who live here are close to the Governor.*

"There are fifty floors to this building," Augustus said, as he led the way to the elevator and pressed his hand against a scanner. Belinda's skin tingled as a security sweep checked their identities, before the door hissed open. "I rent two of them."

Belinda gave him a surprised look. "You don't own them?"

Augustus snorted. "The people who own these apartments wouldn't sell if you offered them an entire planet in exchange," he said, snidely. The elevator started to move, so gently that Belinda barely sensed the motion. "There's too much to gain from having the richest and most powerful people in the system renting their apartments."

"Political access," Belinda said.

"Precisely," Augustus said. He sighed. "It's not how wealthy you are, really, so much as who you can influence. And the people living here have *plenty* of influence."

The elevator doors opened, revealing a large apartment several times the size of Belinda's first home. It fairly *glowed* with elegance, from carefully-chosen artworks to pieces of furniture that complemented the overall design. And yet, it was lacking something, something that Belinda found impossible to define. It wasn't somewhere she would choose to live.

It's not a home, she thought, sourly. *It's chosen more for status than comfort.*

"Daddy," a voice called. "Bill wouldn't let me go clubbing! And who's this?"

Belinda looked up, just in time to see a young girl enter the lobby. She was too beautiful to be real, with an utterly flawless face, blonde hair and bright blue eyes. Augustus had probably paid through the nose to ensure his daughter had the best possible start in life, including a beautiful face, but he'd definitely made her life too easy. His daughter reminded Belinda of Roland, in many ways.

Roland grew up, she thought, recalling the last time she'd seen the former prince. *Maybe this girl can grow up too.*

"This is Belinda," Augustus said. "Belinda, this is my daughter Violet."

Violet eyed Belinda with unconcealed disdain. "Your latest slut?"

Belinda blinked in surprise. It still shocked her, even after nearly fifteen years away from her homeworld, just how little respect the children of the Core Worlds showed to their parents, let alone their teachers and the security forces. There was a reason, she suspected, why most of the Marines came from the outer worlds. *They* grew up in environments where failing to learn from their elders could prove fatal – and where parents were less reluctant to discipline their children.

"My friend," Augustus said, tartly. "And Bill was quite right to keep you inside. There was a riot."

"Bill should be sacked," Violet snapped. "He blocked my access to the datanet!"

"Probably for the best," Augustus said. He gave Belinda an apologetic glance. "Can you take a seat in the living room? I'll be along in a few minutes."

Belinda nodded, then followed his pointing finger and walked into the living room. It was as tasteful as the rest of the apartment, but the effect was spoiled by a number of pieces of clothing scattered everywhere and a large viewscreen, which was displaying scenes from the riot. Belinda was surprised the Governor hadn't managed to clamp down on the news yet – the local datanet hadn't been deactivated until the riot was well underway – but it hardly mattered. She sat down on the sofa and sighed, inwardly, as she heard Violet ranting and raving about Bill. Whoever the man was, she decided, he had the patience of a saint.

Poor bastard, Pug said. *Did I ever tell you I used to be bodyguard to a famous movie star?*

No, Belinda thought. *And I wouldn't believe a word of it.*

They're always brats, Pug said. *Even if they weren't brats when they started, they become brats soon enough. It's the fame, you see. It drives them crazy.*

Belinda shrugged, then reached for the remote and started to flick through channels. Most of them were showing horrific scenes, almost competing to see who could show the worst pictures from the riot, but a couple were providing genuine analysis. She listened, carefully, as one of the talking heads informed the world that there had been riots in a dozen cities, including two within a giant CityBlock. The death toll was over several thousand and rising steeply. She would be surprised if it wasn't over a hundred thousand by the time the night finally came to an end.

And if there was more than one riot, she thought, *someone almost certainly planned for them to happen.*

She glanced up as Augustus entered the room. "I'm sorry for my daughter's behaviour," he said, as he sat down next to her. "She is a persistent trial. I don't know what to do with her."

Belinda smiled. "Find someone willing to take her in and bring her up properly," she said, darkly. "A strict mother figure would probably be good for her."

Augustus gave her a sharp look. "Would you be interested?"

"I think my strict upbringing would probably break her," Belinda said. She had a sudden vision of Violet, her head shaved to her scalp, standing in line with the other recruits at Boot Camp and snickered, inwardly. "You would probably do better finding someone kinder, but firm."

"My father expected me to work," Augustus said. "He was a hard man and I thought I was being kind to Violet by not demanding so much from her. But..."

Belinda shrugged. "It's never easy to find the proper balance between being strict and indulgent," she said. "I sometimes think that my parents made mistakes because their parents made mistakes – or did things my parents thought were mistakes."

"And you went into the military," Augustus said. "Maybe I should enrol her in military school."

"I wouldn't bother," Belinda said. "She'd get too much special treatment."

She paused. "Send her to work on a farm," she offered. "Have her responsible for the care and feeding of some of the animals. But make sure her work is carefully supervised at first, just in case."

Augustus nodded, then changed the subject. "I meant to give you a better evening," he said, softly. "I'm sorry."

"Not your fault," Belinda said. She yawned, suddenly. "And we can go somewhere else, later."

"I'll show you to your room," Augustus said. "And I won't disturb you in the morning."

You could take him to bed, Pug said. *He's interested in you and it's been years since you got laid.*

Shut up, Belinda thought back.

"Thank you," she said, out loud. She rose to her feet, then kissed Augustus on the cheek. "I will have to go back to the hotel in the morning, though."

"Don't worry about it," Augustus said, as he stood. "You can order whatever you like from the desk downstairs. And I'll have Bill give you access to the datanet too."

Yep, Pug said. *Definitely interested in you.*

Belinda sighed inwardly, then ignored the little voice.

CHAPTER
EIGHTEEN

It will come as no surprise to the enlightened reader that the Empire's attempts to enforce a unified code of law and order – otherwise known as Imperial Law – over thousands of planets was an outright failure. The Empire was simply too large for a 'one size fits all' approach.

- Professor Leo Caesius, *The Decline of Law and Order and the Rise of Anarchy*

Glen started awake as he heard someone opening his door. He sat upright, one hand reaching for the pistol he normally kept stashed behind his bed, then cursed himself as he realised that Helen was entering the room. Her pale face seemed to grow even paler as he stared at her, blearily, then relaxed.

"I brought you coffee," she said, holding out a mug. "What time did you get back last night?"

"Late," Glen grunted, taking the mug and sniffing it. He had to smile when he realised just how much powder she'd put in the drink. The coffee was too strong for anyone, but a police officer or a soldier. "Around five o'clock in the morning."

He reached for his wristcom and glanced at the time. It was just after ten in the morning, which meant he'd had around five hours of sleep. He was surprised Patty hadn't called to demand to know where he was, but after so many hours of overtime his boss would understand if he needed to sleep it off. She'd actually been a marshal on active duty before she'd been promoted, unlike so many others. And she knew how the job ground down her subordinates.

"I hope the coffee is all right," Helen said, sitting at the foot of his bed. "It wasn't easy to work out how much powder I should give you."

Glen took a long sip, then smiled. "I think you got it about right, for me," he said. "But don't make it so strong for anyone else."

Helen gave him a shy smile. "Thank you," she said. "I used to make coffee for my father, back when we were on the ship. And mum…"

She broke off, looking down at the floor. Glen sighed and reached out to pat her shoulder, wishing he could offer her more comfort. There was no way to know what had happened to her parents since they'd left orbit, but it was unlikely it would end well. If the Nihilists had kept Helen as a hostage, he knew, they'd probably intended to force her parents to do something else for them. And it might just get them killed…or dumped on a penal world for the rest of their lives. What would happen to Helen then?

"I'm sure you'll see them again," he said, unconvincingly. "And then…"

He shook his head. "I need to shower," he said, instead. "Can you get your own breakfast?"

"You have a microwave," Helen said. "I could cook you packaged bacon and eggs."

"Just get yours," Glen urged. "I need to shower and then…"

He sighed. Too much coffee the night before hadn't done wonders for his condition either, he had to admit. His stomach hurt, suggesting he really needed to go to the toilet and then throw up in the sink. He pulled himself out of bed and staggered into the washroom, then stuck his head under the showerhead. The cold water snapped him awake, but left him feeling dizzy. Undressing, he dropped his uniform in the laundry basket and showered properly, then pulled on a dressing gown. He felt a little better after the wash.

Helen looked up at him, concerned, as he stepped into the kitchen. "I can do you eggs…"

"No, thank you," Glen said. His stomach rebelled at the mere thought of anything to do with eggs. "Just pass me some cereal. I'll eat that and then see how I feel."

He clicked on the viewscreen as Helen passed him a bowl of wheat cereal. A talking head – rumour had it that she was nothing more than a computer-generated persona, because her breasts seemed far too large and shapely to be natural – was pontificating about the riot, intermingled with images of advancing security officers and rioters on the streets. They weren't showing any pictures of the aftermath, Glen noted, or anything that might make people feel sorry for the arrested morons. The whole display seemed designed to convince the general population that the rioters deserved everything they got.

And some of them do, he thought. He glanced down at his bowl as the spoon scraped ceramic and discovered he'd consumed the cereal without actually tasting it. *But what about the ones who just got caught up in the excitement?*

Helen leaned forward. "What are we going to do today?"

"I'll probably have to go into work," Glen said, reaching for his terminal and accessing his inbox. "You'll have to stay here. I can give you download codes for more flicks, if you like."

"Thank you," Helen said, "but can I get more games instead?"

Glen smiled. "Why not?"

He paused. "You could go to the exercise centre too," he added. "There's a small swimming pool there, if you don't mind sharing."

"Sure," Helen said. She paused. "But I don't know how to swim."

"Oh," Glen said. He opened his inbox and swore when he saw just how many priority messages had popped up overnight. "Maybe you'd better leave that until I can come with you."

He skimmed through the messages, deleting a handful that were clearly spam. Just why the datanet's limiters allowed so many spam messages through the filters had always puzzled him, particularly as he'd never purchased anything from a spam email message. Maybe the corporations had managed to convince the government that sending spam was covered under freedom of speech – or, more likely, they'd paid out huge bribes. After all, if political parties that questioned the validity of the Empire's claim to power were denied the right to spread the word, why were spammers allowed to annoy people freely?

"I have to go into work," he said, sourly. Patty had called a meeting for senior marshals at twelve o'clock. Isabel was already at the station, helping with prisoner processing. "I'll try to be back as soon as possible."

"I'll be fine," Helen assured him. "There's enough to do here."

Glen sighed as he walked back into his room to change into a fresh uniform. Helen didn't seem to be lonely, which wasn't too surprising if she'd grown up on a starship with no one apart from her parents for company, but it still seemed odd for her not to have friends. But then, who could he introduce her to in the apartment block? He didn't really know his neighbours – they kept their distance from him, because they knew he was a marshal – and the handful he did know had no children. It was possible, he supposed, that he could ask the staff which couples had children Helen's age, but that would cause other problems. They might try to report him to someone.

And so there is no trust, he thought, bitterly. *And people cross the road just to avoid seeing something that might come back to bite them, later.*

He dressed, then checked his weapons and terminal before waving goodbye to Helen and walking down the corridor to the elevator. For once, he could hear the sound of people chatting in the distance, rather than the normal almost supernatural quiet of the building. But then, most people would be staying at home today, after the riot. The economic damage from the riot itself might be manageable, he considered, but what about the long-term effects of most of the population staying home from work? It might be disastrous.

The streets were largely deserted, he discovered, as he walked down towards the station. A dozen light patrols of guardsmen, a handful of clean-up crews...and very little else. Half of the shops were closed and shuttered; the remainder were open, but empty, save for staff members who eyed him with open nervousness. It was obvious that they had stowed makeshift weapons in places where they could be easily accessed, if necessary. But it was against the law.

Glen sighed, shaking his head. There were times when he felt it would be a great deal easier to protect the population if the laws against self-defence weren't so strong. As simple as it sounded, leaving the job of protecting the people to the police and security forces, it was much harder in practice. Even a far larger police force couldn't protect everyone. A handful of dead or critically wounded would-be muggers or rapists might be more of a deterrent than the threat of years in prison. It could hardly make matters *worse*. Nine out of ten rapists were never caught, no matter what happened. And the Civil Guard barely gave a damn.

The station was heavily guarded, he noted as he strode in through the doors and submitted himself to the security scanner. As always, there were a handful of prisoners in the entry room, but they were cuffed and shackled to the wall, while the guards eyed them with undisguised concern. Glen gave them the once-over, decided they were looters who hadn't realised that the time for looting was definitely over, then walked past them and through the second set of security gates. Inside, he was quickly directed to the main briefing room.

"Glen," Isabel called, as he entered the chamber. "Get over here!"

She elbowed him as soon as he sat down. "You left me with a mess," she added, in a tone that suggested she was plotting revenge. "Do you know how many girls were added to the bag in the Arena?"

Glen shook his head. There had been an update in his terminal, but he hadn't had time to read it. He'd planned to catch up while waiting for Patty to begin the briefing.

His partner snorted. "Try nearly a thousand," she said. "And I hear tell that it's worse in the male section. Gavin was saying that he's responsible for over a thousand prisoners, most of whom are stupid or desperate. It's not good."

"I suppose not," Glen agreed. "And what about the other cities?"

"Lots of riots," Isabel said. "And lots more prisoners. I don't think we've ever arrested so many people in one day, ever. Fucked if I know how we're going to cope with them all."

She sighed. "And you know what happened this morning? A little piece of shit from a colony agency came round and offered to make me wealthy for life if I signed every girl in the Arena over to him."

"Shit," Glen said. "And what did you say to the bastard?"

"Bugger off," Isabel said. "I was tired. I'd have arrested him too, but he'd be out within a day and back trying to round up new servants for his colonists."

Glen nodded, then looked up as Patty entered the room and the low buzz of conversation slowly came to an end. He blinked in surprise and concern as he realised she was late, that it was seven minutes since the announced time for the meeting. Patty wasn't one of the asshole pointy-haired bosses who insisted on keeping everyone waiting, just to show how important she was. If she was late, he knew, it was serious.

"For those of you who haven't been paying attention to your briefing notes, we had more than one riot last night," Patty said, without preamble. She sounded tired and cranky. "There were twenty-one riots in total, scattered over seventeen cities. It looked as though there were going to be another three, but the crowds dispersed before they could get worked up into outright violence and defiance of the law. These were not random riots."

Glen couldn't disagree. So many riots in the same short space of time, without a clear provocation, could only mean that someone had planned and organised them – and done so without the various security forces getting any sniff of it beforehand. He thought, sourly, of just how much money was wasted on informers, for nothing. Or, perhaps, the informers had informed and their handlers hadn't passed the warning on to the people at the sharp end. It wouldn't be the first time someone had decided the marshals didn't need to know what was coming their way.

"The death toll, so far, is around ten thousand people, of which roughly five hundred belonged to the security forces," Patty continued. "The riots in Telomere City alone claimed two hundred, when the barricades failed and the Civil Guardsmen were crushed to death by the crowds. This is Terra Nova's bloodiest day since the early...hiccups...with planetary unification. I don't think I need to tell you that the Governor is most displeased."

No, Glen thought. *That goes without saying.*

"We also have around four hundred thousand prisoners in custody," Patty told them. "As local jailhouses were utterly unprepared for such a large influx of prisoners, they have been stored in stadiums and other makeshift prisons. Conditions are far from good and we've had to detail extra security forces just to keep them under control. Processing such a vast influx of prisoners will take far too long and determining their final fate will take longer still."

"Send them to a hellworld," someone called from the back row.

"The transport facilities for so many prisoners or indentured colonists don't exist," Patty said, with a glower that promised shit duty for the speaker. "More to the point, our arrests probably include quite a few of the people actually *responsible* for the riots, but we don't know it. The only way to find the people responsible is to interrogate the prisoners, one by one, and put together a comprehensive list of just who was arrested and why. This will not be easy."

Glen couldn't disagree. Even a very basic interview would take time – and doing it again and again, for over four hundred thousand people, would take weeks, if not months. They would all have to be fed and watered in that time, while their parents started hiring lawyers and causing trouble for the security forces. Most of them would have to be released quickly if they weren't going to be charged, then walked in front of a judge. The consequences of holding them without trial would be far too dangerous.

Patty sighed. "The Governor has decided to declare outright martial law," she said. "Troops from the Imperial Army will assist us and the Civil Guard in maintaining order. Furthermore, anyone arrested in the riots or successive events will be held under the terms of the Emergency Powers Act. They can be held indefinitely, without charge, as long as they are not deported or otherwise faced with severe penalties."

Such as execution, Glen thought.

He considered it, quickly. By law, only the Grand Senate could invoke the Emergency Powers Act – and the Grand Senate was gone. Could the Governor assert the Act on his own, without reference to superior authority? A lawyer could certainly argue that the mere act of invoking the Emergency Powers Act was illegal. The thought of using it sent chills down his spine, just because of the vast possibilities for abuse inherent in the law. And yet, the law was not a suicide pact. If they needed the authority of the Emergency Powers Act...

Fuck it, he thought, bitterly.

"The Imperial Army's Engineers have already begun construction of a number of containment centres for the rioters," Patty informed them. "Once the camps are ready, we will proceed with transferring, registering and housing the suspects currently held in the Arenas. You will have full authority to use lie detectors and truth drugs, if you feel them necessary, to interrogate the prisoners."

She cleared her throat. "In addition, the Governor is calling up everyone with police or military experience who hasn't already been called to the colours," she added. "They will be added to our forces in the hopes of strengthening our presence on the streets. I don't think I have to warn you to keep an eye on them. Some of them will be poorly trained, others will have left the service for very good reasons...they could be disasters waiting to happen. If you think one of them should be sacked or arrested you have my full permission to do so."

Glen blanched. The idea of adding newcomers, no matter their experience, to their ranks was horrifying. If nothing else, there would be no time to train together, let alone to learn their strengths and weaknesses. And the prospect for abuse was dangerously high. It was bad enough that they had to supervise the prisoners, just to keep them separate from the Civil Guard...this, he knew, could easily be worse.

"It will not be an easy few days," Patty admitted. "But I expect you to do your duty."

Marshal Singh stuck up a hand. "What about our other investigations?"

"Placed on hold," Patty said. "I need all manpower diverted to handling the rioters and hopefully keeping another riot from taking place. Everything else needs to go on the backburner."

Glen frowned. It was a mistake, he suspected, to stop hunting for the Nihilists. He couldn't escape the feeling that the riots were just a cover for something else...but he couldn't fault Patty for following orders from the Governor. Besides, she was right. Keeping another riot from taking place was definitely a priority.

And you don't know where to look for the Nihilists, a voice at the back of his head nagged him. *Every lead you looked at went dead.*

"You have your assignments in your inboxes," Patty concluded. "Good luck, all of you."

She turned and marched out of the room. Glen watched her go, then looked down at his terminal. The orders were blinking up already.

"Prisoner transfer," he said.

"Snap," Isabel said. "They *really* want to keep the Civil Guard away from the prisoners, don't they?"

"Yeah," Glen said. He stood. "Let's go before all the good vans are taken."

CHAPTER
NINETEEN

This shouldn't have been surprising. There were hundreds of different races, religions and creeds in the Empire. The basic Imperial Law had to be adapted to fit local circumstances, particularly on worlds that were – in theory – allowed to determine their own internal political and legal structures.

- Professor Leo Caesius, *The Decline of Law and Order and the Rise of Anarchy*

For the first time in years, since her completion of the dreaded Conduct After Capture course, Belinda woke up without knowing precisely where she was. The bedroom was large and luxurious, bright light was shining in through the window and there was a small tray of tea and coffee sitting by the windowsill. She had to replay her memories from the previous night to recall that she was in Augustus's apartment, where she'd gone to bed...

And slept like a corpse, Pug said, in her mind. *And alone too, mores the pity.*

Belinda sat upright, feeling grimy in the remains of her outfit from the previous day, and glanced at the door. It was shut, but she had the feeling it wasn't locked. Not that it would have mattered, she told herself firmly. Her implants would have woken her if someone had entered the room while she slept.

"Good morning, My Lady," a smarmy voice said. "Would you care for breakfast?"

"You're not human," Belinda said, automatically. "Are you?"

"Indeed not, My Lady," the voice said. "I am a Mark-XII Stupid Intelligence, capable of responding to over a billion different commands, verbal tones and other human interaction cues. My operation specifications are as follows..."

"Stop," Belinda said. She'd used expert programs – *stupid intelligences*, as they were called – before, but they had always been buggy. To use one in a house was a sign of either staggering wealth or sheer desperation. A stupid intelligence couldn't be argued into submission by a bratty teenage daughter. "I need to wash."

"The washroom is connected to your suite," the stupid intelligence informed her. A door clicked open as she climbed out of bed. "You may shower or bathe as you see fit. Can I take your order for breakfast?"

Belinda had to smile as she walked over to the washroom and peered inside. There was a shower, but also a large bath with a built-in Jacuzzi. It wasn't something she was used to from Marine Transport Ships, where there was a strict limit of two minutes to shower and dry one's body. She clicked a switch and water started to run into the bathtub, hot enough to scald her. It took several moments of experimentation to find out how to lower the temperature enough to bathe properly.

"I don't know," she said. "What can I order for breakfast?"

A hologram appeared in front of her as she undressed, displaying a menu which started with bacon and eggs and then went on to increasingly exotic and expensive dishes, some of which she'd never even heard of before leaving her homeworld. Clearly, Augustus had hired a catering staff from somewhere, perhaps from whoever owned the apartment block. They did the cooking, then shipped it up to the living room. It was both impressive and rather lazy.

"I'd like a full English Breakfast with coffee and orange juice," she said, "but only when I'm out of the bath."

"I will have it held in stasis for you," the stupid intelligence said. "Please inform me when you are ready to eat."

Belinda hesitated, on the verge of removing her panties. "Is there a visual monitor in this room?"

"No," the stupid intelligence said. "Privacy concerns do not allow the use of visual monitors without permission. However, I am capable of monitoring your location through heat sensors within the room itself."

And I can believe as much or little of that as I like, Belinda said, as she pulled off her panties and climbed into the bathtub. The water was hot enough to relax her muscles. *A stupid intelligence will say what it's ordered to say.*

"Miss Violet likes having music when she bathes," the stupid intelligence offered. "Do you wish music too?"

"No, thank you," Belinda said. Whoever had designed the system's Turing Interface had done a remarkable job, circumventing many of the prohibitions on developing genuine artificial intelligence. But it still bothered her at a very primal level. "But can I have a news round-up?"

There was a pause. When the stupid intelligence spoke again, the voice was very different, almost business-like.

"News round-up," it stated. "The Governor has declared a state of emergency over Terra Nova, invoking the Emergency Powers Act. Rioters are currently being held indefinitely under the terms of the Emergency Powers Act. Legal experts will discuss the constitutionality of the Emergency Powers later today. All former police and military personnel have been ordered to report to their nearest police station for conscription into the security forces. Princess Belldandy has been sighted leaving the Westside Arena after skipping out on a pledge to sing and dance for her fans."

"Stop," Belinda ordered. "What was that about conscription?"

There was another pause. "All former police and military personnel have been ordered to report for service," a third voice said. "Failure to report within one day of receiving a conscription notice, as stated in the terms of separation from the security forces and/or armed services, will result in automatic court martial for dereliction of duty."

Belinda rubbed her head as the voice twittered on. Everyone who had served in the military, regardless of their rank or responsibilities, was liable to be called back to the colours if necessary. It had never happened in her experience, save for a handful of individuals with specialist knowledge, but if it was happening now...she cursed under her breath as she realised *she* would be expected to report in as soon as possible. Her cover identity classed her as a military policewoman.

On one hand, it would let her get into the security forces, she told herself. But on the other hand, it would be a major headache. And yet, she couldn't think of a way to escape without making it impossible for her to do her duty.

She sighed, then pulled herself up and out of the bath. "Please have my breakfast ready now," she ordered, as she reached for a towel and dried her body. "I'll dress and come out of the room."

"Your new clothes have been ordered and are waiting for you," the stupid intelligence said. "If you place your old clothes in the hamper, they will be washed and returned within the hour."

Belinda's eyes narrowed as she walked out of the bathroom. When had anyone had a chance to take her measurements? But the clothes on the bed – and they hadn't been there before – were definitely in her size, close-fitting enough to require only a little alteration to be perfectly serviceable. Augustus, if Augustus had chosen them, had done well. The white dress suited her, setting off her hair nicely, without making her look too sexy or undignified.

You might have to cut off your hair if they do conscript you, McQueen pointed out. *You don't look like a Marine.*

I thought that was the point, Belinda thought back. *You didn't look like much of a Marine either.*

The dining room proved to be yet another example of elegant taste, mixed with the undeniable presence of a bratty teenage girl. Violet sat on a wooden stool – hand-carved, if Belinda was any judge – picking at a breakfast large enough to feed a grown Marine. Belinda eyed it in puzzlement, then realised that Violet was picking out the best pieces of meat and planning to discard the rest of her dinner. If she hadn't had some genetic modifications, like Prince Roland, her poor diet would have probably killed her by now. As it was, she really needed to eat more.

I'm not playing nursemaid again, she told herself, firmly. *Once was quite bad enough.*

I could play nursemaid, Pug offered. He wolf-whistled, loudly. *She's hot.*

Belinda ignored him as she found her breakfast waiting in a stasis chamber. The whole system, she realised, was a cleverly-built dumbwaiter, shipping food up from the kitchens and then holding it in stasis until the occupants were ready to eat. She carried the tray over to the table and sat down, then started to eat. It tasted far better than she'd expected.

"You can really put it away," Violet observed. "Why aren't you fat?"

"Exercise," Belinda said. She'd never met a fat Marine, at least outside the sections of Boot Camp that handled overweight recruits. Either they lost weight sharply or they quit in horror at discovering the physical requirements were inflexible. "I have to work hard for a living."

"Fucking my father?" Violet asked. "Is that hard work?"

Belinda looked up at her, feeling a mixture of rage and pity. She knew what would have happened to her, or any of her siblings, if they'd talked like that at home. But Violet was neglected by her family and probably largely home-schooled, or at least kept isolated from kids who weren't Old Money. And she probably didn't really have anyone to teach her how to behave.

"I'm a spacer," Belinda said, "and I used to be a military policewoman. *That* was hard work."

Violet smiled. "Do you arrest people?"

"I used to arrest soldiers," Belinda lied, smoothly. "They were always the worst when on leave. And they always used to like stealing my redcap and running away with it. Tradition stated that they got to keep the cap if they managed to get back to the barracks without being caught."

"Oh," Violet said. "Is that true?"

"Yes," Belinda said, although she didn't bother to mention that she'd been one of the ones who had stolen a cap, rather than one of the military policewomen who'd lost her cap. It had been a game at the time, back on a world everyone called Shithole. They'd been more interested in having fun than following the rules to the letter. "It was very embarrassing to lose a cap."

Violet smiled. "What happened to you?"

"The rules said that whoever lost a cap had to buy the drinks next time the unit went out on the pre-leave booze-up," Belinda said. "And if you couldn't afford the drinks, you had to take a buffet from everyone in the squad and ended up sore for days."

"A buffet," Violet repeated. "What's that?"

"A punch," Belinda said. She smirked. "And there were units that used paddles instead."

Violet looked doubtful. Privately, Belinda tended to agree. Military units had always insulted and mocked their fellow units, building up a rivalry that sometimes proved a hindrance on the battlefield. The military police got the worst of it, as the war-fighters saw them as nothing more than prissy spoilsports while the paper-pushers saw them as incompetents who couldn't hold down a proper job. But she was sure that most of the rumours were nothing more than absolute nonsense.

"I see," Violet said, finally. "Did you arrest people? With handcuffs and everything?"

"Sometimes," Belinda said.

"I saw them leading prisoners away on the viewscreen," Violet said, after a moment. "It wasn't fair."

"Life isn't," Belinda grunted. She knew that most of the rioters had just gotten caught up in the excitement, but she also knew the after-effects of their fun and games would last for years, if the economic damage didn't send Terra Nova the same way as Earth. It was quite likely that several of the Core Worlds definitely *would* fall into anarchy. "And they were breaking things."

"They wanted some fun," Violet said. "And some of the guys were hot."

Belinda looked up at her. She'd always been good at reading people and, in a moment of insight, she saw Violet's future. She would rebel against her father, even though he never tried to control her or steer her into less harmful occupations, until it led to her death or destruction. Maybe it would kill her, if she found the wrong boyfriend or the wrong cocktail of drugs, or maybe it would just ruin her life.

And Belinda felt she owed Augustus enough to try to save his daughter. "Bad boys are always attractive, aren't they? They seem daring and defiant and brave enough to do anything. We tell ourselves that we can smooth off their rough edges, if we're perceptive enough to see them. And yet we're almost always wrong."

Violet stared back at her. "I don't understand," she said. "What do you *mean*?"

"You should beware of people who act bad," Belinda warned. There were times when she felt there would be fewer problems with rapists if pretty girls didn't keep rewarding bad behaviour. "Because they often *are* bad – or trying to act like it. And they will turn out badly in the end."

She finished her breakfast, then placed the dishes in the dumbwaiter. There was a faint hum from the device, then it clicked open again, revealing an empty space. Belinda smiled, charmed despite herself, then turned to walk back to her room. There was a terminal there, waiting for her.

"Wait," Violet called after her. "What should I *do*?"

Belinda hesitated, then turned to face her. "How do you mean?"

"My father hates me," Violet said. "My mother never talks to me. And I don't understand my life."

"I don't think your father hates you," Belinda said. When had Violet decided *Belinda* was a proper confidante? "Like most men, he probably doesn't know how to handle a daughter very well without a wife or mother. And as for my honest advice, I would suggest you went to a proper school or bought land somewhere well away from the Core Worlds."

She turned back and walked into the bedroom. The terminal was a civilian model, but when she turned it on she noted that it had access to some of the secure databases. She shrugged, dismissing the thought of probing the datanet for sensitive data, then accessed her message account. The first message on the display, apart from a dozen pieces of junk mail, ordered her to report to the nearest police station within two days. There would be no grounds for claiming she'd missed the message.

"Blast," she muttered. Once she was in the system, she could be assigned anywhere. Her former experience – or at least the experience her cover identity had – would probably see her assigned to prisoner services, which would be annoying and frustrating. And it would make it harder to get access to the information the Commandant needed. "And damn..."

She looked up as Augustus tapped on the open door. "Belinda?"

"I received a draft message," Belinda said, shortly. "Someone must have noticed me at the riot."

"You did more than anyone else there," Augustus pointed out.

Belinda snorted. She'd done very little – and nothing that anyone else couldn't have done, if they'd thought of it. Things would have been a great deal worse if the rioters had reached the inhabited floors of the building, of that she was sure.

"I can have you assigned to me instead," Augustus said. "I...I will need security officers."

"I think I'd better report for duty," Belinda said. If nothing else, given a few minutes with a database access node she could ensure she was assigned to wherever she needed to go. And she would be inside the fire-walls protecting the most secure data on the planet. "But thank you for the offer."

"Violet was saying she approved of you," Augustus said. "What did you say to her?"

"Not much," Belinda said, surprised.

Augustus leaned forward. "I will pay you far more than you can hope to make as a security officer or a spacer," he said, "if you stay and serve as Violet's bodyguard."

Belinda shook her head. Close-protection duty was never fun, even when the person being protected was smart enough to understand why it was important that she did as she was told, rather than running off on her own whenever she had the chance. Violet would be a horrific person to guard, Belinda was sure. It wouldn't have been long, Belinda suspected, before she gave into the temptation to start treating Violet as a prisoner – or simply threw in the towel and resigned.

And besides, she thought, *I have a job to do for the Commandant.*

"I know my duty," she said, out loud. She sensed his surprise and sighed, inwardly. On the face of it, his offer would never be bettered. "My honest advice for Violet would be to send her to a private school well away from the Core Worlds."

Chesty Academy, Doug's voice said. *I went there and look what it made of me.*

"Chesty Academy, perhaps," Belinda offered. She'd been told that the school often took in pupils from wealthy families and made men out of them. Doug had said it also made mincemeat out of the brattier ones, but she hoped he'd been joking. "Or somewhere else, as long as it's somewhere safe, well away from the Core Worlds."

Augustus's eyes sharpened. "You think Terra Nova is going to go the same way as Earth?"

"I wouldn't bet against it," Belinda admitted. There were differences, she had to admit, but too much of the setting was identical. The only question was how well the Governor could adapt to the changing circumstances. But given what she knew of his family, she wouldn't be surprised if he'd manipulated the situation to claim supreme power. "And you might want to get yourself and your family well away from Terra Nova."

"I will see what I can do for Violet," Augustus said. "But I won't abandon what I've built here."

He stepped forward and gave her an oddly light kiss on the forehead, then a tight hug.

"Bill will run you over to the station," he said, softly. "And don't hesitate to contact me if you need anything – and I mean *anything*. I owe you quite a bit."

"Thank you," Belinda said. "And tell Violet she can contact me, if she likes. But she might not like what I have to say."

TWENTY

For example, there were a multitude of religions that believed that one sex was superior to the other. Therefore, despite Imperial Law enshrining equality before the law, the locals kept their own social system intact. This posed considerable problems for any attempt to enforce Imperial Law.

- Professor Leo Caesius, *The Decline of Law and Order and the Rise of Anarchy*

"I'll need you to handle the processing," Glen said, as they parked the van outside the Arena and clambered out of the giant vehicle. "It wouldn't be right for me to assist you."

"Lazy bastard," Isabel shot back. "I bet you organised everything so all you had to do was sit and do nothing."

Glen smirked. "Aren't I clever?"

He sobered as they walked towards the main doors. Handling large numbers of prisoners was always dangerous, even when the prisoners looked to have been weakened by their arrest and unexpected detention. No matter what every chicks in prison flick suggested – and most of them were even less realistic than Hero Cop – scared or desperate girls could be as dangerous as scared or desperate men. He checked the guards, noted that they'd been relieved only an hour ago, thankfully, then led the way through the gates and up into the observation booth, where two marshals were watching the prisoners through a network of security monitors. It didn't look as though any of them were causing trouble.

"We have five hundred prisoners now," Marshal Levier explained. "They brought in some more from other riot zones nearby, sir."

Glen shook his head tiredly. Overall, there were hundreds of thousands of prisoners on the entire world. The Empire's penal system had *definitely* never been intended to handle so many people at once. Normally, judgement would be passed – if bribes weren't forthcoming – as soon as possible, with deportation or execution the standard punishment. Now... he looked at the prisoners and shook his head. God alone knew how long it would be before the courts caught up with the backlog of cases.

Isabel leaned forward. "Did they give you any trouble while I was gone?"

"Not really," Levier said. "There were a handful of fights among the prisoners, but we turned water hoses on the girls and broke them up. I didn't have the manpower to do anything else."

"Understandable," Glen grunted. Fights in prisons or holding pens could be used to cover an escape attempt. The prisoners didn't look organised enough to do anything, apart from sit and wait for their fate, but appearances could be deceiving. He cast an eye over the screens, then shook his head. Levier had done the right thing. "We'll set up the processing centre in the medical bay, then."

"Make sure you take them all one by one," Levier warned. "I'd prefer not to have to deal with an outright riot, sir. I tried to get a medic out here, but none were available."

"Oh," Isabel said. "Why am I not surprised?"

Glen shrugged. There were countless injured among the innocents and security forces, too many for the planet's medical centres to handle quickly. It was unlikely that anyone would permit doctors and nurses to be diverted to the makeshift holding pens, no matter how many prisoners were badly injured. Right now, the Governor was not feeling merciful. And how could anyone blame him?

But the parents will, Glen thought, as he checked the monitors. *And it could easily get out of hand.*

He shrugged again, then led the way down to the medical centre. It was surprisingly advanced, something that bemused him until he realised that the famous gladiators would demand – and receive – the very latest in medical care. Life might be cheap in the Arena, with hundreds of people being killed each week, but those who made it through the first few hurdles were worth preserving. Or so their backers thought.

"Help me lock away the junk," he ordered, once they had assessed the room. "And then we can go to work."

"I'll take Falcone," Isabel said. "You and Davis concentrate on bringing the prisoners here, one by one."

Glen sighed, inwardly. Five hundred prisoners. Even assuming that most of them required nothing more than the standard search, then transport to the holding camps, it would still take hours to process them all. And when they asked questions...some of the prisoners were likely to know who had helped start the riot and fan the flames. Some of them would have to be isolated and held in the vans, until they could be interrogated at a later date. It was going to be a complete nightmare.

"Have the three vans brought to the entrance," he said. *Hours* was probably an optimistic estimate. *Days* was far more likely. "Designate Van One for general population, Van Two for sources and Van Three for *agent provocateurs*, assuming we catch any."

"Aye, sir," Marshal Harris said.

Glen waited until the vans were in place, the corridors were checked and every unnecessary door was firmly locked, then led the way down to the Arena itself. It was astonishing just how much like a prison it actually was, he decided, as they reached the innermost waiting rooms. The doors could be all locked from the main security office, while almost every inch of the Arena was heavily monitored. It seemed that the price for becoming a gladiator was giving up one's privacy. He shook his head in disbelief, privately relieved he didn't have a son to be seduced by the call of the Arena, then opened the main doors. Inside, the prisoners turned to stare at him.

They looked a pitiful sight, he saw. The girls looked scared to death, only a handful looking defiant or aware, watching for the chance to escape. Glen looked from face to face and saw fear looking back at him. They would all have heard stories about what happened to nubile young girls who were arrested by the Civil Guard. Now, they were prisoners and all-too-aware of their own helplessness. Glen just hoped it would keep them docile. If the Marshals lost control of the makeshift prison, the Civil Guard would definitely be sent in to replace them.

"You," he ordered, stabbing a finger at one of the defiant girls. "Come with me."

Her eyes flickered with fear for a long moment, before she forced herself to stand upright. Glen half-expected defiance, but instead she just walked towards him and halted in front of his face. Up close, it was evident that she was far too young to be involved in anything, something he found almost as pitiful as the rest of the prisoners. But the Empire condoned far too much from the young, he knew. They were never given a chance to learn how to handle growing up before they were overwhelmed with the pleasures of adulthood, offered far too soon.

"Walk this way," he ordered, and urged the girl through the gate. It closed behind them, leaving the prisoners in the Arena alone. "Place your hands on your head and keep them there unless we tell you otherwise. Do you understand?"

The girl nodded, but said nothing as they walked into the medical centre. Isabel was seated at a desk, looking forbidding. Glen gently pushed the girl into standing in front of the desk, then stood behind her, looking as intimidating as possible. It was wasted effort. The girl didn't look back at him as she swayed on her feet, clearly far too close to fainting. Glen silently judged that, for all her defiance, the girl had never come face-to-face with any agent of law and order beforehand. Much of her attempted confidence was nothing more than failed bravado.

Be grateful, he told himself. *It could be worse.*

Isabel looked up, sharply. "Name?"

"Ah...Cynthia," the girl stammered. "I want to see a lawyer."

"Surname too," Isabel snapped.

"Cynthia Gardner," the girl said. "I want..."

"Never mind what you want," Isabel barked. "You are currently being held under the Emergency Powers Act, which was invoked last night after your disgraceful riot in the centre of Landing City. You can be held for as long as we feel like it – and no, you can't see a lawyer. If you cooperate, you will be placed in line for early release; fail to cooperate and you will be held for the duration of the emergency."

She paused. "What were you doing before the riot began?"

The girl swallowed, noticeably. "What's going to happen to me?"

"It depends on how much cooperation you give us," Isabel said, shortly. "Don't make me repeat my questions."

"I...we...were told that there would be some excitement in the city centre," the girl said, slowly. "We used to go there to admire the shops; this time, we were told there would be some excitement and..."

"What sort of excitement?" Isabel demanded. "And who told you there would be some...*excitement*?"

"Harry did," Cynthia said. "He's...he's Gamma's boyfriend, one of the most daring people in the apartment. Everyone does what he says. They all thought it would be funny."

"I dare say it was to the idiots who managed to get away on time," Isabel mused. "And why didn't you run when it got *exciting*?"

"I was caught up in the crowds," Cynthia confessed. "I *couldn't* get away."

Glen nodded, sourly. It sounded true – and besides, there was no way to confirm or deny her words through security footage. Most of the security monitors had been smashed as soon as the riot began, indicating a high level of organisation. He listened as Isabel asked a few more questions, identifying Cynthia's family and home apartment, then checked her words against the records. Cynthia had never been in trouble before, but her mother had a citation for unregistered prostitution and her brother had been cautioned for intimidating behaviour in public. Reading between the lines, Glen suspected he'd merely been swinging his arms when a particularly pompous security officer had reported him.

Isabel rose to her feet. "Very well," she said, tartly. "You will now be strip-searched and then processed into custody. Follow my orders and the whole process can be conducted with the minimum amount of discomfort. If you attempt to resist, we will have to hold you down and complete the procedure. Do you understand me?"

Cynthia glanced at Glen. "In front of them?"

"They won't take advantage of you," Isabel assured her. "And as long as you behave, they won't even watch."

Glen turned his back and listened, carefully, as the girl slowly undressed. Isabel carefully catalogued every last item of clothing, then ordered the girl to squat and cough, in case she had anything hidden in her orifices. Glen didn't expect that any of the prisoners had managed to conceal anything during their confinement, but it was standard procedure to check. And besides, it helped convince the prisoners that their lives were no longer their own. It helped keep them docile.

And isn't that the same excuse, he asked himself, *that the Civil Guard uses?*

He turned back on Isabel's command. Cynthia was now wearing an ill-fitting orange jumpsuit, with her hands cuffed behind her back and shackles wrapped around her ankles, making it impossible for her to walk quickly. She looked torn between outrage and fear, somewhat to Glen's amusement, as Isabel signalled for two other Marshals to take Cynthia to the van. The prisoners would have to wait until the van was full before they were transported to the holding camps. Glen shook his head in tired pity – it wouldn't be an easy time for any of them – and then turned to collect the next prisoner.

"We need to check up on William Finsbury," Isabel said. "He was apparently one of the ringleaders."

"Understood," Glen said. "But we may not have time to follow it up."

The next seven prisoners went through the same routine. Three of them admitted to knowing in advance that there was going to be some 'excitement' – Glen was starting to hate that word – while the other four had just been swept up in the riot. Their lives would be ruined, Glen knew, because of their momentary weakness. But how could they be blamed when the riot was the most exciting event they'd ever seen? Life on Terra Nova was boring for the vast majority of citizens. They didn't have the gumption to leave the planet, despite all the incentives, or even try to make a life for themselves that wasn't centred around the viewscreen and foul-tasting government-supplied food.

"I would like to cut a deal," the ninth girl said. Unlike the others, she was either a very good actor or felt no fear. "I have information I can share."

Glen studied her for a long moment. She had claimed to be around seventeen, but he would have placed her at nineteen or twenty. If the apartment block records hadn't checked out, he would have assumed she was lying and threatened to use enhanced methods of interrogation to get at the truth. Even wearing the remains of a scanty set of clothes, she managed to look confident and determined.

"I see," Isabel said, finally. "And what is that information, so we can judge its value?"

"Oh, no," the girl said. "You have to agree to release me in exchange for my information."

Glen clenched his fists, calling on years of training and discipline to keep himself from simply jumping forward and pounding hell out of the silly girl. Didn't she know what the Civil Guard would do to her if they thought she was withholding information? She'd be beaten, then raped, if she refused to talk...and by then the Guardsmen would probably have forgotten that they were supposed to be extracting information in the first place. But she was his problem rather than anyone else's.

"We could make whatever deal we like and break it afterwards," Isabel pointed out, sardonically. "I suggest, young lady, that you tell us what you know and we will take it into consideration."

"Not good enough," the girl said.

Glen cleared his throat. "In the event of the information panning out, we will release you," he said. He did have the authority to make such an offer, but it was always risky. Criminals had been known to manipulate the system to escape punishment for far worse crimes than rioting in public. "However, if the information does not pan out, or if you commit further crimes afterwards, you will be re-arrested and charged with your previous crimes as well as your later crimes."

The girl looked at him for a long moment. She really was strikingly beautiful, he noted, an odd flower amongst the cold CityBlocks. The girls tended to look beaten down, particularly if they were alone, because they grew up without any real security at all. And the girls on Earth were worse. They jumped at their own shadows.

And now they're dead, he thought, morbidly. *Very dead.*

"I trust you," she said, with a sly smile. "My name is Verona. And I was in charge of organising our side of the riot."

Isabel snorted. "You're in deep shit," she said to Glen. "I hope this is worth it."

Verona smiled. "I am – I *was* – a communal organiser," she said. "I used to be in charge of organising the playrooms for teenage children in my CityBlock. It was a boring job, really, unless one wanted to be mean and petty. And then I was bribed to organise an anarchist club for young men and women."

Glen leaned forward. "Bribed? By whom?"

"They claimed to be anarchists," Verona said. "I never knew their real names. But they wanted to deliver a mob on command. I thought it was just the same as the other mobs. It wasn't until we got to the city centre and they started handing out masks and weapons that I realised things weren't what I'd thought. And then all hell broke loose."

Glen and Isabel exchanged glances as Verona kept talking. Her words would have to be checked – and checked carefully. But there was no way the riot had happened by accident, even if it had swept a number of young idiots into the madness. Someone had planned it from the start and then... and then what? Were they really anarchists or...Nihilists? Or what?

"You will be transferred to a holding camp until we can check your words," Isabel said, finally. "If they pan out, you will be released."

Glen watched as Verona submitted with icy dignity to the strip search, then donned the prison uniform and handcuffs without protest. Somehow, she still managed to look attractive. He shook his head as Verona was led out of the building, then hastily made notes for support staff to start following up on her words. The Civil Guard couldn't be trusted not to accidentally obliterate the evidence if they went blundering in, loaded for bear.

"She was involved," Isabel said. "Legally, she was obliged to report anything suspicious to her block's security."

"I doubt she trusted them," Glen said. In theory, each CityBlock was closely monitored; in practice, most of the security officers were either on the take or incompetent. The block he'd grown up in on Earth had had almost no security at all, which explained why the gangs had been able to take such complete control of the inhabitants. "And I wouldn't either, in her place."

"Silly girl," Isabel said. "At least she knew who else to consider potential suspects. One of them might lead us to the people behind the riot."

"Yeah," Glen agreed. He rubbed his tired eyes. Had it really been only a few short hours since he'd been in bed? "Or it might be just a giant waste of time."

"You'd better hope otherwise," Isabel said. "Making that deal with her will look pretty damn bad on your resume."

"Thank you," Glen said, crossly. "It's nice to know you're looking out for me."

"I try," Isabel said.

CHAPTER
TWENTY-ONE

This was not, of course, the only problem. Local laws could and did conflict regularly with Imperial Law in hundreds of different ways. One planet might not allow outsiders to testify in court, another might insist that people who followed the wrong religion were not considered equal to those who followed the acceptable religion.

- Professor Leo Caesius, *The Decline of Law and Order and the Rise of Anarchy*

The station was a towering monstrosity of concrete and glass, Belinda discovered, as she climbed out of the car and strode briskly towards the main entrance. There didn't seem to be many conscripts reporting for duty, not entirely to her surprise, and the guards at the door eyed her suspiciously as she climbed up the steps. Inside, the complex had been designed to take a bomb blast without serious damage, to the point of lining the interior of the reception with starship hullmetal. Belinda honestly wasn't sure if she should be impressed or start laughing hysterically.

"Belinda Lawson," she said, as she stopped in front of the desk. She dropped her fake ID chip on the wooden table and gave the officer a charming smile. "I'm reporting for duty."

The officer gaped at her. Belinda concealed her amusement with an effort. She knew, perfectly well, that she didn't *look* like a military policewoman, still less a Marine. The long blonde hair was most unmilitary. But Pathfinders weren't *meant* to look military, she'd been told often enough. It had been immensely difficult to lose habits like standing up straight, saluting senior officers and generally keeping herself neat and tidy at all times. And she still felt like a slob every so often.

"Ah, ok," he said, finally. He took her chip and plugged it into the system. "We're a little shorthanded at the moment, so this might take some time."

Belinda shrugged, then glanced around the reception. It was dull and barren, save for a number of metal chairs firmly bolted to the floor and a pair of doors that looked to be built to the same specifications as starship airlocks. Absently, she wondered if those specifications included a lock that could be opened hastily from the outside, if necessary. It was a precaution that had saved her life on more than one occasion. There was no one else in the room at all. Indeed, it was clear that the building was largely deserted.

They're all out on the streets, she thought, with grim amusement. The thought of paper-pushers trying to keep the peace wasn't funny, but she couldn't help a twisted smile. *Or trying to come up with some very good reasons why they shouldn't be on the streets. I wonder if any of them will put forward practicality as a reason.*

"You served on several different worlds, but not Terra Nova," the receptionist said. "I'll need to forward your file to the Colonel."

"No worries," Belinda assured him. She gave him another smile. "I can wait."

She paced over to the closest chair and sat down, crossing her legs as she took a deep breath. The room smelt of fear and too many humans in close proximity, a stench that reminded her of her first days in barracks. It was funny how quickly she'd grown used to sleeping next to sweaty men and women, but then she'd been too tired to do anything but go to bed. There certainly hadn't been time for hanky-panky. But for prisoners brought to the reception, she decided, the smell was merely one part of their nightmare.

The receptionist cleared his throat. "The Colonel is on his way," he said. "He wishes to see you personally."

Belinda nodded, wondering if her service record was really *that* impressive. Senior officers never came to see junior officers, at least in her experience, unless they'd won the Medal of Honour, which entitled the bearer to a salute from anyone who hadn't won it for themselves. But then, the security officers wouldn't want strangers running around inside the station without escort. The Colonel, whoever he was, might prefer to keep an eye on her himself rather than detail a subordinate to serve as her escort.

The airlock opened, revealing a dark-skinned man in a wheelchair. Belinda rose to her feet as she took in his uniform, then saluted. The man returned the salute, his dark eyes looking her up and down carefully, then beckoned for her to follow him. She couldn't help noticing that despite missing a leg, his upper body was strong and healthy.

A very impressive man, Doug said. *You should watch him.*

"I'm Colonel Christopher Fraser," the Colonel said, as they rode the elevator up to the seventh floor. "Your service record is very impressive."

"Thank you, sir," Belinda said. She wondered, absently, what he would have made of her *real* service record. "It was my pleasure to serve."

"Not enough, or you would never have left," Fraser told her, darkly. He patted the wheelchair, as if it were a dog or a cat. "And to think I stayed in the service after having one of my legs cut off by a terrorist shithead."

Belinda had wondered why he was still in the military. The Imperial Army was not allowed to discriminate, even when it was blindingly obvious that a man in a wheelchair was incapable of serving in the infantry. Some of them became clerks and did good work, she had to admit, but others were nothing more than oxygen thieves. And even they weren't as bad as the ones who claimed that being fat was a kind of disability. Maybe it was, she considered, but it was one that could be overcome. It wasn't like losing a leg.

She gave him a sidelong look. "Why didn't you have the leg regrown?"

"Doctors say my body will reject a force-grown leg," Fraser said. He didn't show any irritation at the question, surprisingly. "And I don't seem to work well with prosthetics."

"I'm sorry," Belinda said, as they entered his office. It was rare for someone to remain crippled, in a universe where bodily parts could be replaced with ease, but it did happen. "I didn't mean to pry."

"Everyone does," Fraser grunted. He waved her to a seat, then motored his way around the desk. "You have an impressive service record, for a redcap."

"Thank you, sir," Belinda said.

"You're welcome," Fraser said, dryly. "Thank me after you've completed your first assignments."

He paused. "Have you kept up with your skills?"

"Yes, sir," Belinda said. "I've been working out daily and shooting weekly, in a makeshift shooting range."

"Not since you landed, of course," Fraser muttered. "Bloody morons keep insisting that I should cut down on shooting practice, just to prevent accidents. It isn't enough to use low-power ammunition, not now. They want shooting practice cancelled altogether."

Belinda winced. Low-power ammunition was only 'safe' in the deluded minds of politicians who knew nothing about guns or ammunition. Bullets could still kill if fired from a low-power gun, while normal ammunition felt quite different when fired in combat. Using low-power ammunition on a shooting range was actually hampering soldiers when they went into action, she knew, recalling some of the other problems the Imperial Army had had. But the politicians were more concerned with pandering to their base than practicalities.

Fraser cleared his throat. "You've worked as a team leader," he added, "so I'm assigning you to a snatch squad. We're sorting out names and faces of suspects now, which you will be in charge of arresting once we have them all listed. You may have to impose yourself on the team."

Wonderful, McQueen said. *This guy is setting you up to take the fall.*

Belinda nodded, inwardly. It made no sense to assign *her* to command a team, not when there had to be hundreds of officers more familiar with Terra Nova and, for that matter, on active service. Her fake record clearly stated that she hadn't seen active service for over ten years. But if someone was concerned about losing his job, or about the effects on the efficiency of his department, it made sense to assign the task to a newcomer. Belinda had no powerful patrons who might intervene on her behalf.

"It's been quite some time since I commanded anyone in action," she said. It was true enough, unless one counted Roland. "Will your team accept me?"

"Probably," Fraser grunted. "Most of them are newcomers anyway. We don't have enough experienced officers to go around."

Belinda didn't try to argue any further. Being team leader would offer her more opportunity to look around without being noticed. She didn't want to argue so hard Fraser actually gave her what he thought she wanted. Instead, she rose to her feet, stood at parade rest and waited for orders.

"Your team is being assembled now," he told her. "I was looking for a commanding officer when you arrived."

He wheeled his chair around the desk and headed towards the door. "Come with me," he added, as the door hissed open. "You can meet your new subordinates."

Belinda coughed. "That quickly?"

"This is a state of emergency," Fraser reminded her. He powered his way down the corridor, narrowly missing a young officer in a skirt so short Belinda could see the underside of her ass when she walked. "There isn't time to go through the entire process of recruiting and vetting you again, Lieutenant Lawson. We'll catch up later."

And probably cheat you of some of your pay, Pug put in. *Wanker.*

Shut up, Belinda thought.

Another door hissed open, revealing a large room holding five men and one woman. Belinda looked from face to face, noting that two of the men looked like thugs and the woman looked alternatively scared or furious. The remaining men eyed Belinda with obvious interest, but said nothing out loud. It was clear, from their sloppy appearance, that it had been years since they'd been in the service. And none of them were Marines.

"This is Lieutenant Lawson," Fraser said, by way of introduction. "She's your new CO. You can spend the next hour or so getting acquainted, then you can go out on your first mission. I expect nothing, but the best from all of you."

He turned and wheeled his way out of the room, leaving Belinda facing the team alone. One of the thugs rose to his feet and stamped over to Belinda, trying to look intimidating. It would have worked, she freely admitted, if she hadn't had years of training as a Marine and then a Pathfinder. He was so strongly muscled that she rather thought he had muscles on his muscles, quite literally. But years of experience told her that all he really had going for him was brute force.

"I don't take orders from bitches," he hissed, as he forced himself into Belinda's personal space. "And I only have women under me..."

Belinda hit him in the chest, hard. He doubled over as she darted back, clutching his chest as he coughed, loudly. She wondered what he would have thought if he'd known she'd pulled her punch. One blow with augmented strength and she would have put her fist right through his chest, leaving him dying on the floor.

"Let's get one thing straight," Belinda said, as the thug recovered from her blow. "I am in charge and you will do what I say, or I will beat the living shit out of you."

She studied the thug closely, wondering just what sort of person he was. Would he be so offended at being beaten by a mere female that he'd undermine her constantly or would he accept that she was strong enough to serve as leader and do as he was told? She'd seen precedent for both in the Marine Corps, although it was muted. Anyone who reached a rank above Rifleman had definitely been tested and not found wanting. There was no need for anything more than a little tomfoolery when a new CO arrived.

But it was different in the Imperial Army. And worse in the Civil Guard.

"Bitch," the brute muttered.

"That's *Lieutenant* Bitch to you," Belinda said. "Name and rank, *please.*"

"Günter Hammerfest," he muttered. "Former Private in the Civil Guard."

Belinda nodded, resolving to read Hammerfest's file as soon as possible. Someone like him would have been ideal for the Civil Guard, which meant there had to be a very good reason why he hadn't been allowed to remain on active service. It was quite possible that he'd been given the boot for excessive violence – which would have taken some doing in the Civil Guard – or that he'd beaten up the wrong person at the wrong time. She'd just have to keep an eye on him and hope for the best.

She collected names from the rest of her team and filed them all away for later consideration, when she had a moment to herself. The men, at least, were fighters; the woman – Bella Jackson - had been a paper-pusher before she'd retired, two years ago. Belinda honestly had no idea what Fraser had thought when he'd assigned her to the snatch squad. She didn't have any combat record at all, not even minor policing. Indeed, it was quite possible she didn't know how to use a gun. Unlike the Marines, the Imperial Army didn't train its bureaucrats in using weapons. It was a weakness that had been exploited before and no doubt would be exploited again.

"Right," she said, firmly. "We all know each other now. Grab your kit and we will go down to the shooting range. I want to make damn sure you can all shoot."

Hammerfest grinned. "Really?"

"Yes, really," Belinda said. In a state of emergency, she wouldn't have to worry about the paperwork for firing off a crate or two of practice ammunition. Normally, there was so much paperwork that the army's sergeants rarely bothered, even before a known deployment to a trouble spot. The effect it had on readiness for action was depressingly predictable. "And then we will be practicing with everything from stunners to capture nets."

She led the way down to the shooting range, then ordered up weapons – they hadn't been issued, which made her roll her eyes in disgust – and put her team to work. None of them were even remotely up to Marine standards, she decided, after watching them clown around for five minutes. If she'd had to lead them into an actual fight, they would have been more dangerous to their allies than the enemy. But the raw material was there, if she had time to turn them into soldiers.

Don't forget that you have other work to do, Doug warned. *You can't become their leader in truth.*

Belinda sighed, then nodded.

"A word with you, Bella," she said. Bella was unquestionably the worst of the bunch, at least when it came to shooting. The gun she'd picked up the first time had nearly knocked her over with the recoil, even though they'd been using training ammunition. "Come over here."

She led Bella into a corner, directing the men to continue shooting practice while she talked to their comrade. Up close, it was clear that Bella was utterly terrified. Belinda honestly had no idea why she'd joined the military at all, let alone returned when the state of emergency was declared. It was alarmingly clear that Bella had no loyalty to the military, let alone anything else. And there was no time to nursemaid her.

"You don't know how to fire a gun," Belinda said, shortly. "And you're sloppy, very sloppy, in your uniform. What are you doing here?"

"I was called up with everyone else," Bella said. "I expected to go back into staff work and..."

"Yeah," Belinda said. "I'm sure you did."

She shook her head. "You really shouldn't be here," she said, tartly. Given a few hours without supervision, Hammerfest would probably have attempted to force himself on Bella. Belinda had met far too many people like him in her life. He wouldn't have considered it rape, not if Bella was too scared to say no. "I want you to stay behind and do the team's paperwork, when it arrives. In fact, I want you to start requisitioning training supplies for us, the more the better."

Bella didn't even *try* to argue. That, more than anything else, proved that Belinda was right and she really didn't belong with the team.

"I will," she said. "But what about the numbers? Snatch squads are meant to have at least seven members..."

"Let me worry about that," Belinda said. Five men behind her, at least one of whom had to be watched at all times...she didn't need more problems. "I can make do with five men if necessary. You concentrate on filling out all the paperwork when it finally arrives."

Bella nodded. "And do you want me for anything else?"

It took Belinda a moment to realise what Bella meant. When she did, she had to fight the urge to bang her head off the concrete wall. She'd known that senior officers in the Imperial Army chose their assistants for other reasons than competence – and staff officers weren't expected to have to fight, in any case – but it was still a shock. Was Bella seriously expecting Belinda to take her to bed?

Hell, yes, Pug's voice said.

"I want you for the paperwork," Belinda said. It was a shame there was no way to reach inside her head and strangle a little voice. "And that is *all* you are going to do."

"Yes, Lieutenant," Bella said. "I won't let you down."

Just think of everything you could do with her, Pug added. *Girl-on-Girl is HOT!*

Belinda shook her head. Hearing voices was never a good sign...and hearing such suggestions was worse. Were they her imagination, a reflection of aspects of her own mind, or the first sign of madness? God knew she'd taken enough of a beating to leave her permanently unstable. She should have been retired after the disastrous mission on Earth.

And if they're drawn from my impressions of my teammates, she asked herself, *what does that say about me?*

CHAPTER
TWENTY-TWO

Indeed, even interrogating suspects could be a headache for any interstellar law enforcement official. The planet Rand, for example, forbade any form of interrogation unless there was solid evidence that a crime had been committed, while the planet Boskone permitted any form of information-gathering, up to and including torture, to retrieve information from suspects.

- Professor Leo Caesius, *The Decline of Law and Order and the Rise of Anarchy*

"This is a bloody fucking awful place to live," Hammerfest said, as the van parked outside a medium-sized house. "I wouldn't live here if you paid me."

Belinda gave him an odd look. The house was situated within a garden, surrounded by a wall that ensured a certain amount of privacy for its inhabitants. This far from Landing City, it was relatively safe and isolated from the chaos simmering in the giant CityBlocks. It wasn't exactly as natural as the farmsteads on her homeworld, but it was far superior to a poky little apartment in a CityBlock.

And the people who live here are staggeringly wealthy, she thought. She'd had a bad feeling about this mission ever since she'd read the handful of briefing notes. *They can afford to live far from the maddening crowds.*

She sighed, then turned to face her team. They all carried pistols, stunners and zip-ties – and would have carried more, if she'd let them. Instead, she'd been careful to ensure they weren't overloaded if they had to drop everything and fight. She wasn't expecting resistance, but she'd been surprised before in her life. It was better to take precautions than wind up having to improvise on the spot.

"You are not to hurt anyone unless absolutely necessary," she said. Snatch missions in hostile territory were often dangerous, but this wasn't precisely hostile territory. "If you hurt anyone without a very good reason I will take it out of your hides afterwards. Do you understand me?"

There were nods. Like most brutal men, they followed orders from people who were clearly stronger and more capable than themselves, once the point had been proven. Belinda had won their respect by knocking Hammerfest down, then making it quite clear that she could do it again and again if necessary. But she still wouldn't sleep comfortably near them. Bella wouldn't sleep near them at all.

Belinda opened the van, then stepped outside to admire the house. It had almost no visible security, a testament to just how secure the gated estate was. The guards had hemmed and hawed for nearly ten minutes before letting the snatch team through the wire fence without alerting anyone inside. Belinda had no doubt that they were already passing the word to their superiors, who would call their political contacts as soon as they heard. It would only make their job more complicated.

And that's why they sent us here, she thought. *We're expendable.*

She took a long breath, enjoying the taste of the countryside in the air, then led the way up to the gate. It wasn't even locked! She rolled her eyes as she pushed it open, then strode up to the doorway and rang the bell. Her enhanced senses picked up the sound of someone moving inside before the door opened, revealing a middle-aged woman wearing an apron and a long skirt that reached down to her ankles.

"Mrs Armstrong?" Belinda asked. She had no doubt of the answer. "We're here to take you and your family into custody."

The woman stared at her, then started to scream. Belinda had no idea what was going through her mind, nor did she care. The screaming might convince anyone else in the house to run for their lives. She pushed the woman to one side, then ran into the house, glancing into each doorway as she passed. Their primary target, Gavin Armstrong, was rising to his feet in the living room as the team crashed in, stunners at the ready.

Armstrong gaped at her. "What is the meaning of this...?"

"Get down on the ground, hands behind your back," Belinda snapped. The target stared at her for a long moment, then obeyed. Belinda secured his hands, searched him roughly, then picked him up and deposited him on the sofa. His wife joined him there a moment later, still screaming. "Search the rest of the house."

Another shriek – from upstairs – caught her attention. She cursed and ran up the stairs, just in time to see Hammerfest securing a girl who couldn't be more than nineteen years old, wearing a dress that was barely there. Belinda eyed him suspiciously, but there was no evidence he'd done anything inappropriate and she knew it. Cursing under her breath, she motioned for Hammerfest to take the girl downstairs and checked the remainder of the rooms herself. According to the files, Armstrong had a teenage son as well as a daughter...

She paused as her enhanced sensors picked up the sound of breathing on the other side of a half-opened door. Someone was waiting there, lying in wait. He'd have done better, part of her mind noted, to try to breathe normally. There was nothing so conspicuous than someone trying to remain inconspicuous.

"You may as well come out of there," she said, softly. There was no point in dragging the young man out by force if there was any alternative. "I can shoot through the door, if necessary."

There was a long pause, then a face peeked out at her. Belinda fought down the urge to snicker – the boy couldn't have been older than fifteen – as he put the chair down on the ground and stared up at her, nervously. At least he'd tried to fight, Belinda told herself as she secured his hands and marched him downstairs. He had more nerve in him than most children from over-rich homes. Judging by the luxury surrounding her, the family had plenty of money.

"This is an outrage," Armstrong said. "Why are we being arrested?"

Belinda had wondered about that herself. The file hadn't been clear on who Armstrong actually was – it was hard to imagine someone like him planning the riots – but she'd looked him up afterwards and discovered that he was a political operator for one of the Governor's political opponents. The Governor having him arrested wasn't a good sign, she suspected. If his position was under threat, after Earth's collapse into chaos, he might start trying to secure it by taking out his potential enemies.

But he might be responsible for the riots, part of her mind offered. *He would certainly benefit if his patron took power, if the Governor fell.*

"On suspicion of helping to ignite the riots," Belinda said. She looked around for a blanket, then draped it over the man's daughter. Hammerfest had positioned her so adroitly that her bare breasts were clearly visible. "And various other charges, yet to be determined."

She sighed, then motioned for them to stand up. "As long as you do as you are told," she said, "you won't be hurt."

The team led the four prisoners to the van, doing their best to ignore the gathering crowd of people who were staring in horror, or filming the procession with their pocket communicators. Belinda thought about confiscating them, then decided it wasn't worth the effort. Instead, she kept an eye on the daughter to make sure she didn't lose her blanket as she was helped into the van. Moments later, all four were secured and the van lurched into life.

"Take us to the camp," Belinda ordered, shortly.

"I have money," Armstrong said. He was starting to sound desperate. Unlike most civilians, he would probably know just how far the Governor could go under the Emergency Powers Act. He would be quite within his legal rights to have the prisoners executed on the spot, if they were charged with undermining the safety and security of the Empire. "I could pay you to take us somewhere else..."

"Not interested," Belinda said, sharply. "And besides, where would you go?"

Armstrong looked puzzled, then alarmed. Belinda understood. He would understand how to move in high circles, but not how to keep his family hidden in the CityBlocks. And the orbital tower would be watched. He'd need contacts to get his family off-world without being caught and she rather doubted he had contacts in the right place. And even if he did, they wouldn't be so inclined to help him if he'd lost his position. There would be nothing he could do for them in return.

He may have some money stashed away in an unnumbered bank account, she thought, coldly. *He might be able to get away.*

She shook her head. Being in a camp would be unpleasant, but it would be relatively safe.

"We could take him up on it," Hammerfest said. "I could do with a bonus."

Belinda studied him, coldly. "And all of his accounts are frozen," she said, carefully not raising the possibility of an unnumbered – and thus unknown – account. "Where is he going to get the money? And even if he did, how would you take the money without making it blatantly obvious that you've accepted a bribe?"

Hammerfest snorted, more impressed by the first argument than the second. Belinda kept an eye on him, resisting the urge to roll her eyes in irritation. The second argument was much more impressive, at least in her view. Bribery might be an accepted part of life as a Civil Guardsman, but if the Governor was rounding up his political enemies, he would definitely notice if one of them happened to escape after being taken into custody. From that, it wouldn't be long before an investigator worked out that the team had taken bribes and jumped on them. But Hammerfest wasn't used to thinking through the consequences of his actions.

She kept her thoughts to herself as the van drove down the long road, heading further and further into the undeveloped regions of the planet. Terra Nova would have been covered in cities by now, she was sure, if the government hadn't tried to avoid at least one of the mistakes of Earth. It said something about their determination to maintain part of the planet's environment that no one had tried to turn the landscape into a factory or yet another megacity, although it might also have been prevented by a moribund economy. The plans to produce a second orbital tower had faltered, too. It was unlikely the planet would ever manage to put it into service before it was too late.

This world is doomed, she thought, grimly. Society was starting to unravel, the economic chaos had barely begun and the infrastructure was breaking down. *It might be time to urge people to leave.*

But that was impossible, she knew. Even if every last ship in the Imperial Navy had been massed in one place, it couldn't have even started to evacuate the entire planet. Countless billions were going to die when the infrastructure finally collapsed, just like it had on Earth...

"Here we are," Hammerfest called. "Can I say goodbye to the little girl?"

"No," Belinda snapped. "Stay there and keep the engine running."

She rose to her feet as the van lurched to a halt, then opened the door and looked outside. The camp looked remarkably small for the number of prisoners she knew to have been taken over the last couple of days, but perhaps it was intended for the Governor's political enemies. Judging from the way it was built, he wasn't expecting anyone to actually try to *rescue* the prisoners. She saw a handful of people inside the camp and saved their images for later analysis. It might be interesting to see who else the Governor deemed worthy of arresting and throwing into a camp.

"All right," she said, as she beckoned Armstrong and his family out of the van. "Walk through that gate there and the guards will take care of you."

She watched, feeling an odd twinge of guilt, as the four walked into the camp. People like Armstrong, political fixers were among her least-liked people, but his family didn't deserve to be rounded up with him. And his daughter looked weak and vulnerable, just like Bella. It was easy to imagine her going through hell in the camp, even if men and women were kept separate. And she'd been on the ground if – when – society finally collapsed.

But she will be isolated from the megacities, she thought. *This part of Terra Nova might survive.*

Shaking her head, Belinda climbed back into the van and glanced at the terminal. There were no new orders, so she told Hammerfest to head back to the station, which would give her a chance to check the local news channels. Unsurprisingly, there was nothing being reported about the purge; indeed, several of the more independent-minded newsreaders had vanished from the airwaves. Belinda had no great regard for newsreaders either – most of them merely read what they were told to read, without bothering to think about it – but she couldn't help thinking that it was an ominous sign. The Governor's grip was tightening.

"You can take a few hours to rest," she said, when they arrived at the station. "But keep your wristcoms with you at all times."

Hammerfest smiled. "Even in the whorehouse?"

Belinda gritted her teeth. It was impossible to tell if he had finally accepted her as one of the guys or if he was trying to disconcert her. But it didn't really matter right now.

"Particularly in the whorehouse," she said. The thought of Hammerfest grunting over a whore was thoroughly unpleasant, all the more so as he might be feeling emasculated after she'd knocked him down so easily. She felt a moment of sympathy for the whore, which she pushed aside with more difficulty than she'd expected. "I want you to come the moment I call you."

She ignored his pitiful rejoinder and walked up to Fraser's office, where she made a brief report. Fraser listened, then congratulated her and told her to get some sleep. Belinda shrugged, then walked down to the female barracks and lay down. But, instead of sleeping, she started to use her implants to access the datanet. As she'd expected, it was yet another mass-produced system, rather than anything new. Slipping into the system was depressingly easy. And the first thing she looked at was the list of people to be arrested.

It was a surprisingly long list. She'd seen arrest lists for planets in open revolt that were shorter. There were thousands of names, most of them belonging to the Governor's political or commercial opponents. Thomas Augustus wasn't included, thankfully, but there were quite a number of CEOs included, all of whom worked – had worked – for Earth-based corporations. Belinda puzzled over it for a long moment, then guessed that the Governor was clearing the decks for a nationalisation of all corporate-owned facilities. Or, at least, the facilities that were owned by corporations based outside the system.

Most of them are gone, Belinda thought. Just about every interstellar corporation had been based on Earth, even if the manufacturing complexes were elsewhere. They hadn't had a choice, not when they'd needed to keep the Grand Senate sweet. Jobs for the boys and girls on Earth went down well, particularly when it was accompanied by large bribes. *But their CEOs are still being pains about who actually owns the complexes.*

She sighed. She'd never studied economics – it was hardly one of her five Military Occupation Specialities – but she'd seen enough broken-down societies to understand what worked and what didn't. There was no time for a dispute, as Augustus had said, over who owned what when the economy was on the verge of collapse. But the CEOs might fear losing everything if, by some miracle, their superiors survived and demanded an accounting of their time in independent command.

Shaking her head, she filed the information away for later consideration and started to review everything else. Her suspicions about how badly undermanned the various security forces actually were stood confirmed. She'd wondered why Bella had been accepted and then sent to a snatch squad; now, she understood that the security forces were desperate. They simply didn't have the manpower to keep a lid on the whole planet if it exploded into chaos.

And someone is trying to make it do just that, Belinda thought. *But why?*

She worked her way through the evidence, piece by piece. But nothing seemed to make sense. The Nihilists had shipped a vast quantity of arms to the planet – and then lost them, in an astonishing display of incompetence, to the Civil Guard. And then they had launched attacks on the planet's infrastructure that had been unredeemed and unredeemable failures. And then there had been the riots...which the Governor had used as a justification to invoke the Emergency Powers Act, giving him the right to clamp down on the entire planet...

Did the Governor, she asked herself, *arrange for the attacks himself?*

It was a bitter thought, but one she found very believable. She'd seen too much of the Governor's family – and just what they'd been prepared to do to an innocent boy to maintain their power. Surely, if they were prepared to cripple the Crown Prince, they would be prepared to mount a few false flag operations and start a few riots. And dangling guns in front of the Civil Guard rather than risk them falling into the hands of *genuine* Nihilists?

It would be dangerous to risk using them too much, she thought. Arming terrorists and rebel groups had a tendency to backfire. *And yet, everyone knows they're a threat. Their mere existence justifies all kinds of precautions.*

She sighed, then started to look for files on the conference. There were, it turned out, quite a number, all hidden behind the firewall. It was almost a relief to discover, finally, some evidence it actually existed – and that it was going to take place.

Because, in truth, she'd been starting to have doubts.

CHAPTER
TWENTY-THREE

The Empire's law enforcement rested on three services; Planetary Police, the Civil Guard and the Imperial Marshals. In theory, the Planetary Police would handle law and order, the Imperial Marshals would handle interstellar criminal affairs and the Civil Guard would handle riots, rebellions and outright military invasions that were beyond the ability of the police to handle.

- Professor Leo Caesius, *The Decline of Law and Order and the Rise of Anarchy*

"So we have a few leads?"

"Yes, boss," Glen said. "But not many. Most of the prisoners were just swept up in the riots, while the ringleaders fucked off as soon as we arrived."

"Surprise, surprise," Patty muttered. "It wasn't as if we wanted to contain everyone within the central district."

Glen nodded in agreement. Trying to trap all of the rioters would have resulted in more deaths, injuries and property damage. Patty had made the right call, although he knew the Governor and the Civil Guard might feel differently. No, they *would* feel differently. Who cared about death or injuries when there had been a chance to capture some of the people behind the riot?

But they'd still give a damn about property damage, he thought, sourly. *We'd just have to make it clear that there would have been more damage.*

He sighed, recalling the preliminary reports from the central district. It was early days, they'd been warned, but the shop owners were looking at over ten million credits worth of repairs before they could open for business. A staggering sum of money at any time, Glen knew, yet many of the owners would have difficulty raising it, given the current state of the economy. It would be easier to sell the patches of land they'd turned into shops, assuming they owned them directly, and then go into business somewhere else. No wonder the owners were loudly demanding the harshest of punishment for the rioters.

"I am sick of this," Patty announced, shaking her head as she paced her office floor. "And it's been getting worse. Do you know who's been targeted?"

Glen shook his head, worried. He'd worked with Patty for over nine years and he'd never seen her so frustrated, or worried for the future of the Marshals themselves. But Earth was dead and all the old certainties had died with it. The Marshal service might find itself split up and scattered over a dozen independent states, or simply abolished altogether. It was not a pleasant thought.

"The Governor has been targeting his political enemies," Patty said. "I believe the snatch squads have rounded up over three hundred people, either political or economic enemies of the Governor. It's only adding to the chaos, Glen, rather than stamping on it."

Glen winced. "Why?"

"Fucked if I know," Patty said. She shook her head. "It might be a response to the prospect of a change in government, now that Earth is gone. But no one knows just how the government will function in the future anyway. So it could be something altogether different, Glen. We might face the prospect of our esteemed Governor becoming Emperor of Terra Nova. Where are our loyalties then?"

Glen considered it. He'd sworn an oath to the Empire, as had the remaining Marshals. But, without Earth and the Grand Senate, what *was* the Empire? Glen had no illusions about the popularity of the Empire's rule, at least outside the Core Worlds. Hundreds of worlds, ranging from stage-one colonies to ancestral homes, would take advantage of the chaos to break free, now their oppressors were dead. But losing so many colonies would devastate the Core World economies.

And if the Empire was gone, who gave the orders?

He sighed. There was no room for idealism in a Marshal. He knew far too well just how the Empire worked, how those born to power wielded it and how those born without power rarely managed to reach the rarefied levels of the Grand Senate. Hell, even in the Marshals, external power and influence could ensure a promotion or demotion for someone who pleased or offended the Empire's power structure. And he found himself curiously unconcerned about losing the Grand Senate. And yet...what would take its place?

"I don't know," he confessed.

Governor Theodore Onge had been selected by the Grand Senate, at least officially. In reality, he'd won the post of Governor because his family had *always* held the post of Governor, at least in the last seven hundred years or thereabouts. Certainly, the power structure of Terra Nova was designed to support their primacy. But without Earth's backing, he asked himself, was there a prospect for change? And, if there was, would the change be better or worse?

And what price the Marshals, he asked himself, if the Governor could arrest his political enemies and hold them without trial?

"Me neither," Patty said. Her voice tightened. "It would be so wonderful if we could just enforce law and order without having to worry about politics."

Glen couldn't disagree. There were crimes that were thoroughly illegal to all levels of society, but there was no point in prosecuting if the criminal happened to be from the aristocracy. No matter how disgusting the crime, he knew, as long as the victims happened to be lower class no one from High Society would give a damn. And then, politics made it impossible to actually bring justice to the economic criminals too. The corporations that slowly killed their own workers would never face justice, because they were too intermeshed with the Grand Senate. And he knew of far worse crimes in the Empire...

What is the point, he'd asked himself more than once, *of punishing the little fish when the bigger fish swim freely?*

"It would," he said. "But would we be allowed to operate independently?"

Patty shrugged. "Probably not," she said. She paused, looking him up and down. "Have you made any further progress on tracking down the Nihilists?"

"I've been dealing with the aftermath of the riot," Glen pointed out, crossly. "I haven't had time."

"That could come back to haunt us," Patty observed. "Unless the riot was actually staged by the Nihilists..."

"The body count was surprisingly low," Glen noted. But he couldn't disagree. The Nihilists presented the greater threat by far, if only because they had no goal beyond killing as many people as possible, yet he hadn't had time to go after them since the riots. They just didn't have the manpower to spare any longer. "And none of the suspects showed any trace of Nihilistic beliefs."

Patty shrugged. "You may be reassigned in the next few days," she said. "I've been asked to put forward an officer for special duties and your name came up."

Glen stared at her. "With all due respect..."

"I don't need respect," Patty said, darkly. "Right now, I'm trying to balance a dozen competing requirements. Do you realise that the Governor is building up yet another security force, composed of people who are effectively mercenaries?"

"I hadn't known," Glen said. "Why...?"

"He doesn't trust us," Patty said. "I'm not really sure he trusts the Civil Guard either."

She shook her head. "We have too much of a reputation for upholding the Empire's laws, I guess," she added. "And the Governor is starting to think about his own political future."

Glen frowned. "You think he means to declare independence?"

"He's already effectively independent," Patty said. She cleared her throat. "You should be aware that you may be reassigned at any moment. If that happens, transfer your files on the Nihilists to me and I'll make sure someone else is assigned to chase them."

"Yes, boss," Glen said. "Where am I going?"

"Right now? Home," Patty said. "And make sure that partner of yours gets a good night's sleep too. You both need it."

Glen felt a sudden rush of affection for his boss. She looked out for her people, unlike some of his previous superiors – and the Civil Guard's commanding officers. For every officer who genuinely gave a damn about his subordinates, there were ten who stole their pay, forced them to work overtime or simply treated his men like shit. No wonder some Civil Guard units were composed of brutes or in a constant state of simmering upheaval. It was hard to blame them for wanting to mutiny if they were treated so badly by their own leaders.

"I should stay here," he said. "I..."

"Go home," Patty said. "I'll expect to see you at your desk at 0900 tomorrow and you'd better be sober."

Glen snorted – Marshals were not encouraged to drink, smoke or take drugs – but obeyed, walking out of the office and heading to Isabel's cubicle. She'd fallen asleep at her desk and was snoring loudly, so Glen poked her gently and then half-carried her down to the garage, where their car was waiting. She was still half-asleep when he drove her back to her house and handed her over to her partners, then drove to his apartment. This time, there were more security officers on deployment, who insisted on checking his ID before they let him through the garage gates.

Bastards, he thought. The Governor's conscription program was not a great success. Far too many corporations were also interested in recruiting security staff, particularly from experienced military or police officers. The men and women defending the apartment block really should have been part of the new force, but their new employers would ensure they weren't conscripted. Unless, of course, the Governor decided to make himself some new political enemies by insisting the corporations give up their manpower.

He sighed heavily as the elevator rode up to his floor. Where *did* their loyalties lie if the Governor decided to make himself Emperor of Terra Nova? It would have been outright treason a year ago, but Earth and the Grand Senate was now gone. Who held ultimate authority in the Empire now? And how many people would really give a damn if the Governor seized power for himself? And how much difference would it really make?

The thought didn't comfort him. He knew of local authorities, even Colony Marshals, who'd gone into rebellion against the Empire. They'd seen too much abuse of power to stick to their neutrality – and they'd been loyal to their new homeworld over the Empire as a whole. It was hard to fault their decision when justice was a joke and the people they were meant to protect were abused by their far-distant masters. But the Governor of Terra Nova was part of the old power structure. Would it really make any difference if he declared himself Emperor?

He pushed the thought aside as he stepped into his apartment. Helen was sitting on the sofa, watching the news. The newsreader was babbling on about the Governor's plans for an economic revival, starting with a financial program to give a boost to industries that had faltered after the Fall of Earth, but Glen was not impressed. In his observation, any attempt to infuse government money into a corporation ended up with most of the money being stolen.

"Welcome home," Helen said. She stood and smiled at him, looking younger than ever. "I finished the last set of puzzles."

Glen smiled back at her. "I think we'll have to get you more," he said, although he wasn't sure where to go now. The riot had convinced a number of shops to close and, as far as he knew, they hadn't reopened. He had a nasty feeling that there might be food riots in a few days, if the shops stayed closed. Not everyone kept enough food to tide themselves over for more than a few days, not when buying so much food could result in being asked hard questions. "Or perhaps find you something new to watch."

"I didn't like *Family High*," Helen confessed, as she followed him into the kitchen. "They were all so *stupid!*"

"It's all the rage," Glen protested, without heat. *Family High* was an entertainment drama for young children, featuring handsome men, beautiful women, pimped out dresses and a complete absence of any real consistency. But then, given that the show had been running for over twenty years, it was hard to keep the storylines consistent. "Don't you like the stars?"

"They're stupid," Helen said. "Shelia won't marry Austin because Austin is a dick, but she's willing to make love to him, while Henry is too much of a coward to declare his love for her and Robert is too busy stealing the family jewels to give a damn about his girlfriend. And they all wear those silly dresses, when they're not walking around in the nude."

"I think the show is meant to showcase the dresses," Glen said. He didn't know why the producers bothered. Most of the dresses were only available on Earth, which meant they had been largely unavailable even before Earth had died. "Or perhaps cause civil unrest."

He smiled at the thought as he sorted out the food. "What would you like to do this evening?"

"Play chess," Helen said. She gave him a suddenly nervous look. "Do you play?"

"I've been known to," Glen said. "We'll have to use the viewscreen to represent the board, though. I don't have a physical one."

"Uncle Rolf used to play me," Helen said. "He used to bet sweets that I couldn't beat him."

Glen concealed his amusement. "My uncles played cards with me," he said. "It wasn't until I was nine that I realised they were actually *letting* me win, so they could give me some pocket money."

Helen snickered. "And what did you do then?"

"I kept the money," Glen said. "They *were* trying to give it to me, after all."

He smiled at the memory as he placed the food on the table. His uncles had wanted to teach him something about the value of earning money, rather than simply being given cash for nothing. It was against the law – there were laws stating that children had to be given pocket money by their parents, no matter what they did or didn't do – but Glen hadn't cared. Earning it for himself, at least in theory, felt better than simply taking it. And yet, it had been a struggle to rise out of the dependency culture when he'd become an adult. So many people never managed to escape.

They'll have to escape soon, he thought, darkly. *What happens when the economic crash finally destroys the welfare state?*

"Glen?" Helen asked. "Are you alright?"

"I was just thinking," Glen said. How long could Terra Nova afford to feed its unemployed and unemployable population? "Maybe we should go live somewhere else."

Helen looked down at her food. "But what about my parents?"

Glen winced, feeling an odd chill gripping his heart. When had Helen managed to make her way into his heart? What would he do if she was taken away? Or what would *she* do if her parents were arrested and exiled for their role in shipping weapons to Terra Nova?

She isn't a pet, he told himself, savagely. *And you should know better than to let yourself care.*

He cursed himself under his breath as he finished his meal and placed the dishes in the sink for later attention. They'd been warned never to develop emotional attachments to suspects, no matter how sweet and harmless they seemed. Helen was not, technically, a suspect, but it made no difference. What would happen when the issue of her status was finally resolved?

It might not matter, he told himself, *if Terra Nova falls.*

"Set up the chessboard," he ordered. "And then we can play."

Helen smiled. "Of course," she said. "Prepare to be thrashed."

She was right, Glen discovered, twenty minutes later. Helen was a brilliant player, certainly better than he'd been at her age. Her uncle certainly hadn't been *letting* her win, he decided, as she pushed his pieces back across the board. There might be a great deal of nonsense published on making sure children had a win or two, to help build their self-esteem, but Helen didn't seem to need it. On the board, she was confident, definitely brilliant. It made up for her shyness...

She grew up on a starship, he thought. *There wouldn't have been so much else to do.*

"Checkmate," Helen announced. Her face was lit up with a brilliant smile. "You want to play again?"

Glen reset the board. "Why not?"

The second game was more even than the first – he didn't underestimate her – but Helen still won, slowly but surely. Glen congratulated her on her victory, then helped her to her feet when she started to yawn. She clutched his hand tightly for a long moment, before walking into her bedroom. Glen watched as she closed the door, then sat back on the sofa feeling tired and drained. And concerned about the future. What would happen to Helen after the investigation was wrapped up? And what would happen to *him*?

"It might be time to apply for a Colony Marshal post," he muttered. He could do it, if he applied. God knew he had the experience and then some. But it would mean abandoning Terra Nova. And he'd be practically kidnapping Helen. "But what would I do with her?"

He closed his eyes and went to sleep. It felt like mere seconds before his terminal started to bleep.

"Glen," the dispatcher said, when he keyed it, "we've had a breakthrough. The boss wants you to report to the station ASAP."

Glen glanced at the time. It was 0632.

"Understood," he said. "Do I have time for a shower and a change of clothes?"

"Boss wants you in at 0700," the dispatcher said. "You might want to hurry."

"Right," Glen said. He swore, mentally. Getting to the station on time would be tricky even if he left immediately. There would be no time for anything, but a can of cold coffee. "I'm on my way."

CHAPTER
TWENTY-FOUR

The Planetary Police were raised and trained on their homeworlds. They were not always perfect, but they did have ties to the locals and the ability to know what should and what shouldn't be in their local areas. Furthermore, they were well-trained and equipped for forensic work. And they were often quite popular.

- Professor Leo Caesius, *The Decline of Law
and Order and the Rise of Anarchy*

"Glad you're both here," Patty said, as Glen and Isabel entered her office. "There's work for you to do."

Glen exchanged a glance with Isabel. "Work, boss?"

"Yes, work," Patty said. She sounded as if she'd managed to catch some sleep between sending Glen home and recalling him to the office. "The tasks you do for a living."

She cleared her throat, loudly. "The backroom staff kept grinding through the data recovered from the warehouse and the shipping firm," she said. "They came up with a lead that needs to be investigated, as soon as possible. As you are already working the case, you will take the lead on this."

"I'm starting to get whiplash," Isabel commented, wryly. "How are we supposed to get anything done if we keep hopping from case to case?"

"I can start cutting your spare hours, if you like," Patty offered. She tapped a switch and a holographic image appeared in front of them. "This gentleman is called Wayland Nards."

Glen leaned forward, studying the image. Nards looked young, no older than Isabel, but he had an air of indolence that suggested he wasn't used to working with his hands for a living. And his paunch, and his balding head, suggested he didn't really care what he looked like, as he could probably have afforded cosmetic surgery.

"A bureaucrat," Glen guessed.

"A Senior Shipping Officer," Patty corrected. She smirked. "Which is pretty much the same thing, really. Point is – this is the gentleman who cleared the crates of weapons to pass through the security network without inspection and who signed the covering papers for the transhipment warehouse. There should have been at least two inspections of the crates as they were moved down to the surface. This...*person* cleared them without inspection."

Glen's eyes narrowed. "Is he a Nihilist?"

"We assume he was bribed," Patty said. "His account shows a number of payments from various single-use accounts that were, we assume, created specifically to fund Nards. Each of them were just under the reporting limits, but collectively they add up to quite a considerable sum of money. His lifestyle is also too luxurious for his legal income."

"He probably collects a lot of bribes," Isabel said. "Shipping delays alone can be more costly than paying off the bureaucrats supervising the process."

"No doubt," Patty agreed. She looked up, meeting Glen's eyes. "This guy might be able to lead us to the Nihilists, Glen. We need to take him alive."

Glen nodded, slowly. One bureaucrat without any combat training. It shouldn't be a problem, but they'd take every precaution, regardless. A glance at the file showed him that Nards lived in a built-up area, rather than one of the gated estates normally occupied by government workers. It was an odd choice, even assuming Nards was trying to make a show of living within his means. But there were no prying eyes in the place he'd made his home.

"There isn't any manpower available to assist you," Patty warned. "And that place is notoriously restive. I'm assigning a snatch squad to accompany you."

"Those clowns," Isabel said. "I thought they would be busy beating up the wrong people."

"There's no one else to send," Patty said. "And you may be grateful to have them."

Glen sighed, then nodded. "We'll go now," he said. He thought, briefly, of trying to call Nards into the office and grabbing him there, but it was quite likely that the bureaucrat would smell a rat. The bureaucrats had great working hours and no overtime. "Or do we have time to wait for him to return to the office?"

"No," Patty said. "We're looking at his backlog now, but we don't know how many crates he might have let through the net. I think we need to snatch him up as soon as possible."

"Understood," Glen said. "Will there be additional backup?"

"Only if desperately necessary," Patty said. "There's a handful of SWAT teams on standby to serve as emergency reinforcements, but just about everyone else is out on the streets, trying to keep the lid on. And it isn't enough."

Glen nodded, sourly.

———

Belinda lifted an eyebrow as the door to the communal shower opened so slowly that she just *knew* the person behind the door was trying to sneak into the room. Adjusting her position as water ran down her naked body, she watched with some amusement as Hammerfest peeked around the corner and looked for her. His eyes went wide as he saw her naked body, then he fell backwards as she punched him in the nose. She stepped over him and dried herself as he struggled to pull himself back together.

"You know, the next person you try to spy on might just put a bullet between your eyes," Belinda said, pleasantly. She'd expected trouble, although nothing *quite* so blatant. "And where would you be then?"

"Worth it," Hammerfest said. He managed to sit upright, one hand rubbing his bleeding nose. "You're gorgeous."

"And deadly," Belinda said. Being naked in front of him didn't bother her, not after years in various barracks. "Next time, I'll break something less vital than your nose."

It took Hammerfest a moment to realise what she meant. And then he howled with laughter, honest genuine laughter, as if she'd made a hilariously funny joke. Belinda rolled her eyes, then reached for her uniform and dressed quickly. Hammerfest made no move closer to her, even after he stumbled to his feet. His nose was a crooked bloodstained mess.

"Go have that fixed," Belinda ordered. Broken noses were common injuries in the Marines and, she assumed, it was true of the Civil Guard too. "And then report to the briefing room."

She finished dressing as he stumbled out of the room, then followed him down towards the briefing room, where Fraser was waiting for her. The remainder of the squad had already joined him, somewhat to Belinda's annoyance. She wasn't actually *late* – the meeting wasn't due to begin for another ten minutes – but it made her look inefficient. She controlled her irritation as Hammerfest entered the room, a surgical mask placed carefully over his nose, and took a seat next to her. His raspy breathing was more irritating than his half-assed attempt to spy on her in the shower.

"There have been developments," Fraser said. If he was curious about Hammerfest's broken nose, he showed no sign of it. "You and your squad will be accompanying the Marshals as they make an arrest."

Belinda leaned forward, interested. "The Marshals?"

"Indeed," Fraser said. "They have a lead and they need some armed backup. You'll get the rest of the briefing from the agent in charge, so draw your weapons from the locker and remember the rules of engagement."

"Of course, sir," Hammerfest said, too loudly.

Belinda winced, inwardly. Rules of engagement were problematic even when highly-trained Marines were involved – and their practically-minded superiors were responsible for drawing up the ROE. The ROE she'd been given as part of a snatch squad looked to have been written by several different sets of lawyers, each one with different priorities. She was authorised to use whatever level of violence she deemed necessary, but she was also to avoid doing anything that might alarm civilians or result in a bloodbath. There were so many contradictions within the ROE that she would have made an official complaint, if she'd thought it would get her anywhere. It was impossible to do almost anything without infringing one of the contradictory requirements.

They could justify or punish anything, just by pointing at the right part of the ROE, she thought, crossly. *And idiots like Hammerfest will always err on the side of violence.*

"Thank you, sir," she said. She rose to her feet and motioned for the squad to follow her down to the weapons locker. As always, there was a bureaucrat sitting outside, ready to demand paperwork in triplicate. Belinda ignored him and turned to face her subordinates, her expression as grim as she could make it. "Take weapons and stunners, but leave the weapons unloaded until I give the command."

Hammerfest snorted, rudely. "And what happens if we need to open fire?"

"I will order you to load your weapons and open fire," Belinda said. She'd seen the team shoot – and she had a private suspicion that they would be more dangerous to each other than the enemy. Hammerfest wasn't a bad shot, she had to admit, but the others were appallingly bad. If there had been time, she would have forced them to go back to the shooting range and practice time and time again. "Until then, you will keep your weapons unloaded on pain of a beating."

She glared at him until he lowered his eyes. Dumb muscle. That was all he was, with a little lechery and misogyny rolled in. Someone too stupid to realise how his career was at risk, someone so thick-headed that the only way to get him to obey was to beat hell out of him every time he questioned his orders. She longed, so intensely it was almost painful, for a trained company of Marines. Hell, she would settle for Auxiliaries with some proper weapons training. So far, she hadn't seen Hammerfest point his gun at his own head, but she was sure it was just a matter of time.

"The van's outside," she said, once they were tooled up. She had no idea why Hammerfest wanted so many weapons, but she wasn't disposed to argue. "Let's go."

"Why the fuck does he live here?" Isabel asked. "It's a fucking dump."

Glen nodded in agreement. Kinabalu District might have been nice, once upon a time, but it was definitely suffering now. The houses were dirty and grimy, huge piles of uncollected rubbish lay everywhere and the handful of people on the street kept looking down, refusing to make eye contact. He caught sight of a number of children playing in a side alley, wearing nothing more than rags, and winced inwardly. There were no social services here, no one who might take the children away from unfit parents. But then, the people who lived in the district might actually fight back.

"We really should move them to a CityBlock," Isabel added. "They could be cared for properly there."

"That would also cost the government money," Glen said, as they passed another pile of rubbish. "And how many of them would want to move?"

He considered it as they drove past a burned-out shop. The CityBlocks were meant to be able to supply everything their customers wanted or needed, from food and drink to clothes, entertainment and employment. But Glen knew better. The food was bland, the drinks were often poor and there was little chance of actual employment. And the Block would be dominated by a gang of social workers or outright thugs, depending on how strong the administration actually was. There were probably good reasons for the residents of Kinabalu to stay where they were.

Isabel turned to look at him as they reached the unnamed street. "And why is Nards living here?"

"The atmosphere," Glen guessed. He parked the van, then opened the door. The stench – he didn't want to think about what was producing it - struck him like a physical blow. "Or maybe he just wants to be out of public view."

"I'd say he succeeded," Isabel said. "There aren't any cameras here, are there?"

Glen shook his head as the snatch squad parked behind them. The squad itself looked terrifyingly incompetent, save for the blonde-haired leader, who carried her stunner as if she'd been born to handle a weapon. She had to be impressive if she managed to dominate her subordinates,

Glen decided, then he pushed the thought to one side and turned to walk towards the targeted house. God alone knew what they'd find inside.

"Come on," he ordered. "Let's move."

The house was as dark and grimy as the remaining houses – and seemingly deserted. Glen knocked on the door and listened, carefully, but heard nothing. He hesitated for a long moment, then pulled a multitool off his belt and went to work on the lock. There was a click as the door opened, allowing him to step into the house. The scent of rotting meat greeted his nostrils as he slipped inside, shining his flashlight from place to place.

"That's dead flesh," someone muttered. It took Glen a moment to realise it was the blonde woman. "And it's been dead for quite some time."

"Stay here," Glen ordered.

He stepped forward and peered into the living room – and froze. A dead body sat on a chair, peering accusingly at him. It wasn't hard to identify the body as belonging to Nards. He swore, then took his camera from his belt and started taking pictures of the crime scene, recording as much as possible for the backroom experts. It was unlikely the crime scene would remain undisturbed once the locals realised the house had been effectively abandoned.

"Cause of death; slashed throat," Isabel said. She leaned close to the body without actually touching it. "No other obvious signs of damage."

Glen nodded, then let her inspect the body while he checked the rest of the house. It was surprisingly bare, given how much money Nards had been collecting; Glen puzzled over it for a long moment, before putting the issue on the backburner. Maybe Nards had been courting a wealthy high-class woman, or had a gambling addiction. It was certainly not unknown among the ones who longed to be rich and powerful. He peered into the bedroom and swore out loud. Four bodies lay on the bed; one woman, three children. They all looked surprisingly peaceful.

"No obvious cause of death," he said, for the benefit of the record-ers. He took a handful of photographs, then took a closer look. One of the children had lips that had turned blue. "Poison seems the most likely cause, based on observation. There are no signs of sexual or other forms of assault or restraint. Time of death unknown, but judging from the lack of visible decay probably not more than two or three days ago."

"The forensic staff will have to come out here," Isabel said, as she entered the room. "If the killers left clues behind..."

Glen shook his head. "They're not likely to come," he said. "Everyone is busy with the rioters right now. And...well, here."

Isabel made a face. "Shit," she said. "So...what do we do? Take the bodies with us?"

"There's no alternative," Glen said. "Send one of the team to pick up some body bags, Isabel. We'll have to carry them back to the station."

They searched the rest of the house, taking photographs as they moved. There was very little to indicate that Nards was a rich man, which bothered Glen more than he cared to admit. The file hadn't shown any problem with drinking or gambling, or anything else that might explain why Nards wasn't living in the lap of luxury. He'd had three children, Glen knew, and bringing them up in Kinabalu was asking for trouble. Glen wouldn't have been too surprised if the boy, just entering his teens, was already a member of a gang. What sort of parent would bring his children up in such a place if he had a choice?

"It makes no sense," Isabel agreed, when he outlined his thoughts. "He must have had debts of some kind. We can do a spending analysis when we get back to the station, if the eggheads haven't done it already. See if he was spewing out money as fast as it was coming in."

She frowned, searching for alternate suggestions. "Maybe he was a committed Nihilist and just couldn't take the strain of living any longer."

Glen shrugged. The Nihilists rarely committed suicide without taking as many people as possible down with them. Nards might have poisoned his family – there was no sign of a struggle upstairs – but it was still a remarkably low body-count. Normally, even a single Nihilist aimed to kill dozens of innocent victims. He slapped his head, angrily. Nothing about the case made *sense*!

"It's odd," he said, softly. He turned to walk back to the living room. "But if he killed himself, what happened to the knife?"

"Point," Isabel said. They returned to the body and inspected the surroundings, but found no sign of the knife. "He couldn't have hidden it before he died, not with that slash in his throat. Someone else definitely killed him, probably to cover their tracks."

"It looks that way," Glen agreed. If Nards *hadn't* been anything more than an easily-bribed official, the Nihilists would have killed him to ensure he couldn't betray them afterwards. It was so common that he honestly wondered why *anyone* would accept a bribe from the Nihilists...unless, of course, Nards had had no idea who'd bribed him. "Or maybe there's something else going on."

He sighed. "Get the bodies bagged up," he ordered. He reached for one of the bags, then opened it up and eyed the body, wondering how best to tackle the job. The bodies would be contaminated, damaging the chain of evidence, no matter what they did. It might be harder to secure a conviction. "We'll take them home."

"Of course," Isabel said. She took a smaller bag and started to walk towards the stairs. "And..."

She broke off as a deafening explosion shook the entire house. "The hell...?"

CHAPTER
TWENTY-FIVE

Imperial Marshals, by contrast, worked cases that extended beyond a single planet in the Empire. A Marshal commanded vast authority; in theory, they were superior to both policemen and guardsmen wherever they went. However, their authority was not always recognised by their so-called allies.

- Professor Leo Caesius, *The Decline of Law and Order and the Rise of Anarchy*

Belinda spun around and swore out loud as she saw the vans explode into a fireball. She gripped her weapon as the mob appeared, swarming out of the nearby houses and heading towards them with deadly intent. Mobs were always dangerous, particularly in close confines where there was nowhere to run. She cursed under her breath, then snapped a command to load weapons as the mob came closer.

"We have to get out the back," she snapped, thinking hard. There was no point in trying to stand and fight, not with only a handful of men. "Hurry!"

Two of her men looked to be on the verge of panic. She slapped them both, hard enough to sting, then shoved them towards the door. The lack of real training was harming them now, she knew, although training for mobs was never easy. There was something brutally *primal* about the sheer force of a mob that scared people to death, even though they had training and weapons and even powered combat armour. But if they'd had armour, she knew, they would have been safe. The only problem would have been keeping her men from tearing through the mob like paper.

The Marshals looked up in surprise as she urged her men into the house and through the kitchen. One of them, a middle-aged man with a reassuring air of competence, tossed her a questioning look. Belinda motioned for him and his partner to start moving, then gabbled out an explanation.

"There's a mob approaching the house and the vans are gone," she snapped. What had destroyed the vans? They weren't tanks, but they *were* heavily armoured. Did the locals have antitank weapons or homemade RPGs at their disposal? "We have to get out of here."

She hit the emergency beacon, summoning help, then followed them out the rear door. The back garden was a desolate wasteland, the grass dying through lack of care. Belinda had no time to take in the sight; ahead of her, there was a wall that was high enough to pose a real barrier to some of her team. She pulled out an explosive charge, cursing their lack of training as she keyed the trigger, then darted backwards. The sound of the explosion would reveal their position to anyone who wasn't already sure of where they were. Moments later, the wall collapsed as the charge detonated, sending pieces of shattered brick flying everywhere. Behind her, she could hear the mob rampaging through the house.

"Run, she snapped, urging the Marshals through the gap. She unhooked a stun grenade from her belt and threw it backwards, as the mob came crashing into the garden. Blue-white light flared, sending tingles down her spine. The mob howled in outrage as a dozen bodies were sent tumbling to the ground, but there were just too many people in the crowd for them all to be knocked out. "Hurry!"

She watched grimly as the team ran for their lives, bringing up the rear. She'd seen enough mobs to know the dangers of being caught, but there was no way to know if the mob was carrying out an organised plan or if it was purely spontaneous. If the former, they might well run into another mob as they tried to beat a retreat, which would force them to take up residence in one of the houses and hope they could hold out long enough for backup to arrive before they died. But if it was the latter, they might well manage to escape by running.

A piece of stone crashed down beside her, thrown from an uppermost window. Something seemed to have broken in the district, she decided, as she fought back the temptation to open fire. The locals, never very inclined to obey authority, had decided to just lash out at the Marshals and their support staff. But were they primed to explode or was it just a coincidence? She contemplated the possibilities, then pushed the thought aside. Her one priority was getting the Marshals and her team out alive.

"Assholes," Hammerfest shouted, as more pieces of rubbish cascaded down from upper-floor windows. "Fuck off and die, you pricks!"

"Ignore them and keep running," Belinda snapped. *She* could have outrun or evaded the mob with ease, but she couldn't simply abandon the team. "Get your weapons loaded, but don't shoot..."

She swore as they spun around a corner and saw another mob at the far end. Belinda hesitated, then unslung her rifle and fired a handful of rounds over their heads. The mob seemed to quiver for a long moment, then rushed forward, the ones in front pushed by the ones behind. Belinda swore, then pointed the Marshals towards an alleyway, feeling sweat trickling down her back as they ran for their lives. But the alley was a dead end, save for a metal staircase leading up to the rooftops.

"Get up there," Belinda ordered. "Hurry!"

She reached for her second stun grenade, then moved her hand to an HE grenade instead. It made a satisfying *clang* as she slammed it against the lower levels of the staircase. She ran after the others up the stairs, feeling the metal shifting under her feet as she climbed, then triggered the grenade as soon as she reached the rooftop. There was an explosion – she felt a twinge of guilt as she heard screams from below – and the staircase toppled away from the building.

"Keep moving," she bellowed. The mob wouldn't take long to break into the apartment block and climb up to the roof. "Get over to the edge."

The lead Marshal stopped on the edge. "You want us to climb down here?"

"I want you to jump," Belinda said. There was only a metre between the two apartment blocks. Down below, the mob was gathering, some of them carrying bottles of liquid. It didn't take a military genius to realise they were Molotov Cocktails. "Move!"

"You have got to be fucking kidding," Hammerfest said. "I can't jump that far."

213

"Then stay here for the mob," Belinda said. The noise from below was growing louder. She had no doubt that anyone who fell into their hands was in deep shit. "You – *Marshal*. Jump!"

The female Marshal hesitated, then ran towards the edge and jumped. Fear propelled her forward, Belinda noted, for she landed safely. The others followed her one by one, just as bullets started to crack through the air around them. Belinda made her own jump, then activated her implants, hunting for the source of the bullets. A sniper was perched on top of a nearby tower, shooting at them. She lifted her rifle, took careful aim, and fired a single shot back, using her implants to assist her. The sniper jerked, then tumbled off the tower and fell to his death.

Hammerfest gaped at her. "Nice shot," he said.

Belinda concealed her amusement. There were Marine snipers, specialists, who routinely fired at targets over three kilometres away and hit them, often without them ever knowing they were being scoped out for death. Indeed, the snipers were so lethal that they were often too good for urban combat, or simply couldn't take the long-distance shots they so loved. Sniping wasn't one of her MOS, but she'd had enhanced training and implants to assist. It would have been more astonishing if she'd missed.

"Keep moving," she ordered. She glanced down at her terminal, but there was no ETA for backup. "And run for your lives."

They jumped three more buildings in quick succession, then reached the end of the row of apartment blocks. Belinda cursed as more bullets started flying around them, then led the way down the metal steps, grenades in hand. As soon as the mob appeared, she primed the grenades, then threw them down towards the mob. There was a thunderous explosion and the mob recoiled, with dozens injured, perhaps killed. They reached the bottom and started to run.

"You killed them," the Marshal said. "You..."

"There isn't a choice," Belinda snapped. "Kill or be killed."

She swore as shooters started to open fire, raining bullets down towards the team. It was a struggle to find cover; she barked orders to her men, using them to lay down covering fire in hopes of suppressing the shooters. Where had the weapons even come from? She shook her head, then looked back towards the mob. It had collected itself and was starting to advance again. Belinda looked around, trying to see a way out, but saw nothing. If they ran, they would be exposed to the shooters; if they stayed where they were, the mob would get them...

"Cover me," Hammerfest said. He sprang out of cover and opened fire, keeping his finger on the trigger and spewing out bullets towards the shooters. His fire was hopelessly inaccurate, but it forced the shooters to duck for cover. "Hurry..."

A shot struck him as Belinda rose to her feet and began shooting herself, with calm dispassionate precision. His body struck the ground, bleeding from a head wound she knew would be fatal, unless he was rushed to hospital at once. There were no Marine Corpsmen around, no medics who would save his life...she silently noted his death, then shouted for the rest of her team to follow her. The shooters stayed down long enough for the team to put some distance between itself and the mob. And then another shot rang out...

...And the female Marshal tumbled to the ground.

Belinda swore, first silently then out loud as her partner turned back for her. She could admire loyalty, but it was clear that his partner was already dead. Gritting her teeth, she scooped the body up with enhanced strength and inspected it rapidly, while the remainder of her team covered her. There was no point in trying to revive her, Belinda saw at once. The bullet had torn through her brain, killing her instantly.

The snipers seem to like headshots, she thought, savagely. First Hammerfest and...it struck her, suddenly, that she didn't know the woman's name. *And they have us in their sights.*

"Stay low," she snapped. She would have preferred to abandon the body – there was no way it could be carried safely – but she had a feeling the dead woman's partner wouldn't allow it. "And run..."

Her terminal buzzed. Help was on the way...she glanced at the screen, then urged her team to run faster. High overhead, she heard the sound of rotor blades as a pair of helicopters swooped overhead, decked out in the silver and gold livery of the Civil Guard. Belinda hoped – prayed – that the locals didn't have any HVMs in their illicit armoury or the helicopters were dead. It was alarmingly obvious that their pilots had no experience flying over a combat zone.

But instead the mob just melted away and the guns fell silent.

One of the helicopters flew top cover, twisting and turning to show off the weapons underneath its stubby wings, while the second dropped down to the ground. Belinda hesitated as the rest of the team scrambled onboard, wondering if she should run back for Hammerfest's body, but when she looked the body was missing. The mob must have scooped it up, she realised, as she climbed into the helicopter. She gritted her teeth as the noise of the engines grew louder, then the craft shuddered as it rose into the air and made its way out of the area.

"We could have died there," Abdul said. He was one of the other team-mates, someone who had seemed in awe of Hammerfest – and uncertain what to make of Belinda. "We could have died."

"We could have died," Belinda agreed. Very few of the planet's Civil Guardsmen had been anywhere near a genuine war zone. They'd been on the verge of panic when the mob had appeared, despite having weapons and discipline. "But we made it out alive."

She felt another pang when she thought of Hammerfest. He'd been a thug, a brute, probably a rapist...and he was dead. She held no affection for him – he wasn't a good-natured brute, like some of the Marines she'd known, but a violent thug – and yet he'd died bravely. If he'd been a Marine, she knew, she would have taken whatever risks were necessary to recover his body. Instead, she felt nothing...and it bothered her that she felt nothing.

You fought beside him, Doug said. *Doesn't that give you a bond even though he would have forced himself on you if he'd had the chance?*

I would like to have seen him try, Pug injected. *I happen to know what you used to stick up your...*

"Shut up," Belinda said, out loud.

Abdul stared at her. "I didn't say a word!"

Belinda shook her head, then peered through the hatch as the helicopter made its way over the city. It was clear that another riot or set of riots was underway, with smoke pouring up from a dozen locations and more helicopters flying over the city, weapons at the ready. She couldn't hear much over the noise of the helicopter, but her audio-discrimination programs insisted that there was quite a bit of gunfire over the city, as well as the noise of angry crowds. Terra Nova might be on the brink of complete anarchy.

She turned her attention away from the hatch and peered towards the Marshal. He looked broken, his head resting in his hands Belinda felt another pang of sympathy, then shook her head. Death was part of life for anyone who fought to defend civilisation, from Marines to the lowest Police Officer. She understood grief, but she also understood that grief could not be allowed to dominate a person's life.

And who are you to say that? Doug asked her. *You've kept us around as part of your mind.*

Belinda sighed, then ignored the voice.

The helicopter flew over the centre of the city and dropped down towards a military camp established in the middle of the Central Park. Belinda felt a moment of sadness for how much natural beauty had been destroyed, then braced herself as the helicopter hit the ground hard enough to shake the entire craft. A team of armed Guardsmen surrounded the helicopter, as if they expected to be attacked at any second. Belinda smiled as she rose to her feet, noting just how tired the remainder of her team looked. They didn't have anything like her endurance.

And you might want to pretend to be wasted, McQueen offered. *You can't afford to look too good.*

Belinda nodded as she stepped outside. Central Park had been utterly devastated. The trees had been cut down to provide landing zones for helicopters, while tents had been erected to serve as barracks for the conscripted security forces. Belinda wondered why they hadn't simply taken over a few nearby buildings, but she had a feeling the answer probably involved large bribes. Why go for the smart and practical option when it would put a few wealthy noses out of joint?

"Have the body moved to the tent," Fraser said. He was sitting in his wheelchair, seemingly unbothered by their tired faces. "What happened, Lawson?"

Belinda looked at her remaining men, then looked back at Fraser. "The shit hit the fan," she said, simply. "And we had to run."

She met Abdul's eyes. "Get him somewhere to lie down," she ordered, indicating the Marshal with one hand. "I'll finish up here."

"You seem to have lost a man," Fraser said, a clear note of warning in his voice. "And one of the Marshals…"

"Snipers, sir," Belinda said. "They caught us in the open."

She thought, briefly, of the warehouse the Civil Guard had found, crammed with weapons destined for the Nihilists. Had there been another delivery that had been completely missed? It was quite possible. Terra Nova's security struck her as disturbingly lax.

You can't secure a whole planet as easily as a military base, McQueen said. *Planets are big.*

And we found a lot of crap in that base we secured on Tannins, Pug added. *How many porn magazines and drugs crap did we recover and burn?*

Fraser eyed her for a long moment. Belinda wondered, absently, what he was thinking. If he had an inkling that something wasn't entirely right with her, he might well have insisted that she return to civilian life – if, of course, it was an option. But if the Governor was insistent on cripples returning to duty, it was unlikely he'd be able to discharge her without some very searching questions being asked.

"Go get some rest," he said, "and make sure your men do too. There may be more questions later."

"Yes, sir," Belinda said. She needed to think – and assess what she'd learned, before she was sent out on another mission. And she needed to decide if the Governor was up to something or if he was merely taking harsh, but necessary steps. "Is there a tent for us?"

"Go back to the station," Fraser ordered. "Your barracks are still there."

Belinda nodded, then turned and walked towards the edge of the park. It wasn't far to the station, she knew, and most of the streets would be deserted. She'd have a chance to think about her next move.

"And Lawson," Fraser called after her, "good work."

"Thank you, sir," Belinda said.

But we fucked up, she thought, as she rounded up her men. *A little less luck and we'd all be dead.*

CHAPTER
TWENTY-SIX

However, the Empire had good reason to believe their system was workable. Had they had the funds to keep it balanced, they might have been able to maintain law and order throughout the Core Worlds, even after the Fall of Earth.

- Professor Leo Caesius, *The Decline of Law and Order and the Rise of Anarchy*

Isabel was dead.

Glen stared down at his hands, half-convinced they were covered in blood. Isabel was dead. His partner of five years was dead. And...and he no longer felt as if he could go on.

It had been a long time since they'd first been introduced. She'd been a rookie, newly-trained; he'd been nervous about working with her, knowing that rookies made stupid mistakes every day. But she'd done well and they'd become friends as well as partners, working together...and now she was gone.

I always thought I'd die first, he thought, bitterly. Isabel had had so much to live for; her partners, her children, her career...Glen had only ever had his career. She'd been able to go home and relax, while Glen had only ever been able to brood. *It should have been me who was killed.*

He shook his head, angrily. The mob would never be brought to justice, he knew, not when it was composed of thousands of people in one of the poorer districts of the city. And the bodies they'd found had probably been destroyed, or eaten, if there was any truth to the rumours about cannibalisation. The only evidence they had were the photographs they'd taken, which would be insufficient to lead them to the killers. Isabel had died for nothing.

It should have been me, Glen thought. *Not her.*

"Glen," Patty's voice said. "Come into my office."

Glen sighed, then picked himself up and walked into the office. It felt like too much effort to move, as if he just wanted to sit down and never move again. But somehow he managed to walk into her office and sit down. She pressed a cold glass into his hand a moment later, inviting him to take a sip. The cheap wine tasted like paint stripper against his tongue.

"I'm sorry about Isabel," Patty said. She sat down next to him, rather than behind her desk, and patted his shoulder awkwardly. "She was a good cop."

"I know," Glen whispered. They always said the dead were good cops, even if they'd been corrupt or incompetent. There was no point in slandering the dead. But Isabel had been more than just good, she'd been brilliant. He mentally replayed some of their shared cases and cursed, feeling the bitter pang of loss. She'd been a *very* good cop. "She deserved much better."

"Yes, she did," Patty agreed. "We will hold a ceremony for her as soon as the city calms down."

Glen shook his head. There were more riots underway, he'd heard as he'd stumbled back to the station. People rising up and attacking the very infrastructure that kept them alive, no longer caring about the law or the prospect of being punished. By the time the day was over, he was sure, hundreds – perhaps thousands – would be dead and thousands more would be in the makeshift prison camps, where feeding them would be one hell of a burden on an already overstretched system. Or maybe the Governor would just start sending them off-world as quickly as possible.

"And when," he asked, "will that be?"

"I do not know," Patty said. She patted his back, trying to offer comfort. "I wish I could give you a few days off, Glen, a few days to yourself."

"I know," Glen said. He wasn't sure what to feel. Part of him suspected he would have taken the opportunity to put a gun in his mouth and blow his head off. "You need to keep us working."

He sighed and stared down at the floor, trying to understand. He'd seen so much evil in his time, ever since he'd graduated; he'd seen everything from murder and rape to theft and mass slaughter. Humans were very good at inventing new crimes and carrying them out, all the while practicing very old ones. He'd lost his innocence long ago, if anyone truly kept theirs in the Empire. And yet, Isabel had kept going.

And now she was gone.

"I should be assigned to the riot squad," he said. "The investigation into the Nihilists has hit a dead end."

"So it would seem," Patty agreed. "We can try to sweep the house for evidence, but they would have covered their traces."

Glen looked up at her. "What about your source?"

"Gone silent, for the moment," Patty said. "He could easily have been silenced, or he could have gone into deep cover. We will have to wait to see if he resurfaces."

She took a deep breath. "I can't leave you on the case, Glen," she added. "You're far too involved, now."

"I know," Glen said. He hated the thought of leaving the case unfinished, even if the rioting had torn him away from his duty, but there was no choice. Isabel's death had destroyed his objectivity. Hero Cop would have made a big fuss about being removed from the case, he knew, yet Patty was right. He *was* too emotionally involved. "Who will take over?"

"Davis, I think," Patty said. "He broke a leg yesterday and he's confined to the station, so he can handle the number-crunching and deploy snatch squads if necessary."

"He won't be able to do the legwork himself," Glen objected. "What about Gwen? Or Patrick?"

"They're both assigned to street patrols," Patty said. "I can't spare any able-bodied officer."

She sighed. "Your next assignment will be quite different," she added. "You're going to go into space."

Glen blinked. "Space?"

Patty straightened up. "This is all highly classified, at least for the moment, so you have to keep your mouth shut," she warned. She waited for his acknowledgement, then went on thoughtfully. "Our Governor is going to hold a summit of the various planetary leaders and military officers, men and women who control the remains of the Empire. This summit will, hopefully, devise a new system of power-sharing that will allow us to salvage as much as possible from the wreckage."

Glen frowned. "You think the Empire's already gone?"

"Earth is gone," Patty said, bluntly. "I think nothing will ever be the same again."

She paused, then met his eyes. "They want an Imperial Marshal to handle security," she told him. "I'm assigning you to the role."

"I see," Glen said. He wanted a chance to sit down and think, but he knew she'd want an immediate answer. Besides, he wasn't really being given a choice. "Where is the conference being held?"

"Island One," Patty said. "The Governor himself will be in attendance, as well as leaders from across the Core Worlds. I don't need to tell you, I hope, that you will need tact and diplomacy as well as a badge and a gun."

Glen smiled, despite the grief threatening to overpower him. "How many officers will I have under my command?"

"The Island One security staff," Patty said. "You may have others, but I'm still trying to see who can be reassigned without crippling us still further. It will be a challenge."

"Yes," Glen agreed. "It will be."

Under other circumstances, he suspected, he would have enjoyed the challenge. The most secure location he'd ever visited had been heavily guarded, with guests subjected to full body and cavity searches before they were allowed to pass through the gates. But he rather doubted that senior government and military officials would allow him to conduct such searches as they arrived for the conference. There would be too great a risk of a diplomatic incident. He would have to rely on other methods to secure the conference location.

At least it isn't on the planet's surface, he thought. *That would have created a nightmare.*

And Isabel would have enjoyed it too...

The pang of bitter guilt tore at his heart. How could he go to Isabel's family and report her death? But he would *have* to go...he owed them an explanation. And they would hate him for getting her killed...

"I'll have the files transferred to your terminal," Patty said. "Barring unexpected delays, I will expect you to be on Island One in four days. I would suggest that you take the next day off to rest, but I know you won't."

Glen nodded. "How long will the conference take?"

"Fucked if I know," Patty said. She shook her head, slowly. "How do you think the Governor can convince a hundred suspicious individuals to work together? It didn't work out that well in the days of Mountbatten the Great."

"No," Glen agreed. "It didn't."

He sighed. Mountbatten the Great had been a warlord in the days before the Unification Wars, one of the few historical figures to be remembered in the dying days of the Empire. He'd been a conqueror, absorbing nearly a thousand star systems under his banner, but he'd been assassinated by one of his subordinates, who had then proven unable to keep the warlord's empire under his control. The disparate generals and admirals had ripped it apart, then started to fight each other. And then their territory had been swallowed up by the expanding Empire.

At least the First Emperor managed to provide for his own death, Glen thought, without heat or anger. *His Empire wasn't dependent on him.*

But it wasn't a pleasant thought. The Empire had been centred on Earth, on the Grand Senate and the Admiralty. Now, Earth was gone and all its subordinates – including Terra Nova's Governor – were effectively independent. Would they choose a new Emperor, he asked himself, or would they start fighting to remain independent? A thought struck him and he leaned forward. Would they even come in person?

"I think some of them will send representatives," Patty said, when he asked. "The guest list has yet to be finalised."

"I see," Glen said. It would definitely be a challenge. "How long should I prepare to stay on Island One?"

"As long as necessary," Patty said. She smirked. "There are staff who will tend to your every need, of course. You'll be cosseted and treated like a king when you're off-duty. I will expect a full report when you return, of course."

Glen groaned. "You do realise I can't afford it?"

"You do realise that the Governor is paying for everything?" Patty asked. "You'll have a place to stay and access to the services, when you're off-duty."

Glen nodded. Island One was a luxury resort, a giant space habitat resting in the Lagrange point between Terra Nova and its sole moon. Only the very wealthy could afford to visit, much less to live there. Even the staff were treated well, he'd been told. Competition for places on the space habitat was fierce.

Patty cleared her throat. "You can take Helen along," she added. "There's a school – a well-run one – on the station, so she can attend if she feels up to it. Or she would have the same access to the datanet as she'd have on the planet. Or she could even go exploring, if she wished."

Glen nodded. Island One was *safe*. There was no need for a heavy security presence because no one ever got on to the station without being heavily vetted. Children could run freely through the streets – and the gardens – without needing to fear predators, bullies or murderers. It was a grim reminder, to Glen, that security was only possible if one had the money to spend. The common folk on Terra Nova would never know true security.

"It will remind her of her home," he said. He cleared his throat, embarrassed. "Has there been any news of her parents or their ship?"

"None," Patty said. She lifted an eyebrow. "I thought you would be watching for any contact."

"I didn't look," Glen said, embarrassed. How could he explain that he'd been dreading the day her parents returned to Terra Nova? And yet, wasn't it thoroughly selfish of him to treat her almost as a pet? He should be hoping for some settlement of Helen's affairs. "I was busy."

"Careless," Patty reprimanded him. She shrugged. "Take care of her, but remember that protecting the conference comes first."

"I know," Glen said. He hadn't forgotten his duty. "Is there any other business?"

"Try to relax, then start planning," Patty ordered. She pointed a finger at the glass in his hand. "And finish that before I take it back."

Glen considered it, then passed the glass back to her. He'd never cared for heavy drinking, even when he'd been a young man. It was too easy to allow alcohol to take control, then move on to hard drugs and completely waste his life. He'd walked into far too many opium or cocaine dens where the victims would just lie there and inject themselves, only to be kicked out when they ran out of credit. They often died shortly afterwards.

"A wise choice," Patty said. She placed the glass on her table, then helped Glen to his feet. "I wish I had more comforting words to offer you, Glen. All I can really say is that the pain will fade eventually."

"I know," Glen said. But he didn't really believe her. His wife's death had left him in mourning for years. Even now, thinking of her brought nothing, but pain. And Helen was the same age as his daughter would have been, had she lived. "It's no comfort right now."

He shook his head. Death was a constant risk in his profession. The man he tried to arrest might have a concealed weapon, the woman he caught robbing the till might be desperate enough to fight rather than surrender quietly, even children could be vicious when rounded up by the security forces. He'd lost count of the number of mourning ceremonies he'd attended in his time, for Marshals and Civil Guardsmen who'd died in the line of duty...he shuddered, bitterly. Isabel had deserved better than a cold patch of land somewhere near the city. The only consolation was that her body wouldn't be violated by the thugs who'd killed her.

"I know," Patty said. "Go get some rest."

Glen nodded, then walked out of the door. Outside, the station seemed as busy as ever, although he could tell it was being run on a skeleton staff. The vast majority of Patty's subordinates were out on the streets, trying to bring them back under control. He paused outside the operations room and peered inside, catching sight of dozens of red icons flashing on the giant street map. There were hundreds of crimes, from simple theft to outright riots, being reported. And most of them, he knew, wouldn't be handled. The Marshals simply didn't have the manpower.

"Glen," a voice said. He turned to see one of the auxiliaries, civilians who volunteered to serve with the Marshals. "I had her body moved down to the morgue and placed in a stasis chamber. Do you happen to know if she had any particular requests?"

"I haven't had a chance to open her will," Glen snarled. Patty would take care of it, once the chaos died down. It was one of her responsibilities. "I imagine she would have wanted to be buried with the rest of us. Leave her body in stasis for the moment."

"Yes, sir," the auxiliary said.

He scurried off before Glen could give in to the temptation to strike him. Auxiliaries were often strange and rarely trained, unless they'd had some prior military or policing experience before volunteering to assist the Marshals. Most of them, in his opinion, were oxygen thieves. But it helped free up manpower to patrol the streets.

But the snatch squad's leader did very well, Glen thought. He hadn't expected anything beyond thuggish behaviour from the snatch squad – they'd barely been active a week and they'd already earned a bad reputation – but the blonde-haired woman had been brilliant. *She saved most of our lives.*

"Riot on Langford Street," someone called, from inside the operations room. "Dispatch a squad to investigate."

"New prisoners, forty-two male, twenty-five female," another voice said. "They're being sent to Clearing House Alpha."

Glen shook his head tiredly, then walked down towards the garage. His car was waiting for him, gleaming in the brilliant light. He sat down in the driver's seat and breathed in the faint scent of Isabel, then cursed himself under his breath. No matter how much he missed her, he would never see her again, never have her watching his back as they carried out a raid or arrested people on the streets. And one day, it would be his body in the morgue, with his new partner mourning his death.

Maybe it's time to leave, he thought, as he started the car. *Finish the Island One job first, then hand in my retirement and go to a colony world. Or maybe even stay on Island One.*

He shook his head. Even if they accepted him, and they might well, it would be still far too close to Terra Nova. He'd be happier leaving the Core

Worlds completely, maybe heading out to a planet along the Rim. There was never any shortage of demand for trained and experienced officers, he knew. He'd been headhunted more than once after his wife had died.

Outside, the streets seemed largely deserted. The only people within eyesight were armed Guardsmen, escorting a handful of prisoners to the station. Glen couldn't help noticing that the prisoners looked as though they'd been roughed up; one of them, a girl, had had her shirt torn away, revealing her bare breasts. He felt a moment of pity, but he knew there was nothing he could do for her. An official complaint to the Guardsman's superiors would simply be ignored.

Poor bitch, he thought. What were the Marshals if they couldn't prevent the citizens from being abused. *It's definitely time to leave.*

CHAPTER
TWENTY-SEVEN

Needless to say, it didn't work out as planned. The Empire's colossal budget-crunch in the years prior to its collapse effectively crippled the Planetary Police forces. Local governments placed more and more responsibilities on the Civil Guard, trusting the Guardsmen to handle everything from street patrolling to criminal investigation.

- Professor Leo Caesius, *The Decline of Law and Order and the Rise of Anarchy*

Belinda lay on her bunk, staring up at the ceiling.

The secure datanet held no secrets from her, not now. She could poke into any datacore connected to the network, without triggering any alarms. But she knew, better than most, just how easy it was to believe that she knew everything. All she really knew was what was entered into the database and it could easily be lies, or simple mistakes. The Marines had faced too many situations on the ground that simply didn't match the data in the Empire's files.

But what she'd found had left her with a dilemma. The conference was to be held on Island One. It wasn't a bad decision, she had to admit; Island One would be far easier to secure than any facility on the planet's surface, even one on a island thousands of miles from the closest city. And yet, getting there would be difficult. The Governor had no reason to allow her to visit Island One, let alone stay there. She wondered, briefly, if Augustus would be attending – the files suggested the Governor wouldn't be alone – but how could she ask him? It was impossible to ask him without revealing her cover.

She sat upright as a low chime ran through the complex, followed by an announcement.

"Attention, all personnel," it said. "The Governor will be addressing the population through all channels in ten minutes. You are required to watch."

Belinda silently cursed the announcer under her breath as she swung her legs over the side of the bunk and dropped down to the ground. Typical bloody bureaucrat, working a nine-till-five job and forgetting that others had to work different hours. Her team, trying to catch a nap in the male barracks, would be shocked awake, then would have to somehow look presentable while they listened to the Governor's speech. She gritted her teeth, pulled her boots on and inspected herself in the mirror. Thankfully, she looked reasonably presentable, once she bound her hair into a ponytail.

She walked down to the lounge and frowned, inwardly, as she saw just how few officers and men were present. Clearly, the riots were proving an even bigger drain on manpower than she'd been led to expect. She wondered, as she found herself a mug of coffee, just what the men on the streets would be expected to do when the speech began. Stop fighting to contain the rioters just to listen? Would the speech be pumped over the channels dedicated to the security forces? She wouldn't have been surprised.

"Ah, Lawson," Fraser said, as he wheeled his way into the room. "Coffee would be very nice, thank you."

Belinda bit down the response that came to mind and made Fraser a mug of coffee, taking a petty revenge by preparing it to Marine standards. It was rare to come across a Marine who didn't insist on taking it black, no sugar, although she had a suspicion it was nothing more than a display of pointless macho behaviour. *She'd* always preferred to drink with milk, no sugar. Fraser showed no reaction when she put the mug on the table next to him, somewhat to her disappointment. Instead, he just started to drink.

"Your team will be reassigned later today," he warned her. "I don't have a position for you, yet."

"That's quite all right, sir," Belinda said, truthfully. She needed time to think, not another mission into a hellish part of town. Terra Nova would soon need more soldiers than the Empire had deployed at the height of its power to maintain order. "I will await your orders."

She wondered, absently, what he had in mind as the viewscreen ticked down the seconds to the Governor's speech. There were no shortage of officers who would look for a young and pretty personal assistant, but in truth she didn't think Fraser was that type. Besides, he was stuck in a wheelchair. *And* he was smart enough to know not to waste someone's talents.

The viewscreen darkened suddenly, before clearing to show the face of Governor Onge. He didn't look much like the Grand Senator, Belinda discovered, but he did look as though his face had been carefully designed to project an impression of strength and resolve. The politicians believed that looks were important, that people would vote for politicians who looked good, and unfortunately they tended to be right. But then, voting hadn't changed anything for years. The Empire was a dictatorship of the aristocracy in all, but name.

But that might change, Belinda thought. *Who knows what will happen now the Grand Senate is gone?*

"My fellow citizens," the Governor said. "We have seen many changes in the last three months and some of us have speculated that they mean the end. There have been riots on the streets and mass civil discontent as it has sunk in, slowly, that Earth is gone. The Empire has changed...

"Yes, the Empire has changed. It has not fallen, but it has changed.

"I understand that many of you are worrying about the future," he continued. "I cannot blame you. So much is at stake, so much is at risk, now that Earth is gone. Old certainties are crumbling everywhere. From the highest to the lowest, everyone has been asking the same question. Where do we go from here?"

Good question, Belinda thought. The Governor sounded convincing, but he would. She'd seen enough to know that the speech would have been practiced time and time again, then recorded. This was no live broadcast from Government House. *Where do we go from here?*

"I have been in contact with many other planetary governors who are facing the same questions and issues as myself," the Governor said. "Without Earth, are we doomed to fragment into thousands of competing planets, a nightmare that will eventually lead to interstellar war on a colossal scale? Or will we seek a way through the chaos and emerge stronger than ever before? I intend to work for the latter.

"We are one empire. Earth may be gone, but the Empire lives on."

Unlikely, Belinda thought, coldly. The Core Worlds might buy into imperial unity, but the outer worlds would think differently. *And what do you want to do about it?*

"We will hold a conference in two weeks that will determine the future of the Empire," the Governor said. "That conference will sort out the niggling questions of just who own what, allowing us to restart the economy and defeat the economic crash. There will be jobs for everyone as we move to replace Earth. Everyone who wants a job will be able to work towards getting one."

Belinda frowned. Earth's industry had once been the largest in the known universe, but it had only ever employed a small percentage of Earth's eighty billion strong population. And even Earth had had trouble finding enough educated men and women to work in the massive industrial complexes out in the belt. The educational system would need to be completely reformed, quickly, to produce more educated workers on Terra Nova, yet she doubted that was even possible. There were just too many rotten teachers and a complete lack of discipline within the system.

And even if they do succeed, she thought, *they still won't be able to provide jobs for everyone.*

The Governor was still speaking. "I ask all of you to have patience and bear with us as we move through the storm," he said. "There is a light at the end of the tunnel. But we must not break down the engine before we finally reach that light and progress forward into a whole new world. I thank you for your time."

He bowed, then his image vanished. In his place, there was a Talking Head who promptly started to expound on the meaning of it all. Belinda tuned the woman out as soon as she realised that the woman knew nothing, at least nothing new. Judging from the way she spoke, she didn't entirely agree with the words put in front of her. But defying her bosses was a good way to get sacked, without even the prospect of another job. Belinda shook her head, then turned to leave. She needed to think.

"Report to my office tomorrow morning," Fraser said. "I may have a job for you."

"Yes, sir," Belinda said. "I'll be there."

She left the room, thinking hard. The Commandant had said that the conference had to go ahead, which meant she had to be there. She knew, without false modesty, that a Pathfinder would make an excellent security officer. But she also knew that she wouldn't be able to board Island One, not without assistance from someone on the planet's surface. As a newcomer to Terra Nova, it was unlikely she would be allowed within a hundred miles of the conference. She needed a way to get onto the security team.

Augustus might be able to get me up there, she thought. *But I'd have to tell him everything.*

She frowned as she accessed the files again and skimmed through the list of assigned agents. One name – a familiar name – jumped out at her. Glen Cheal.

He won't want to see you, Pug warned. *His partner died on your watch.*

But he could get me to Island One, Belinda thought back. *And he has an excellent motive to keep the delegates safe.*

If you convince him of your identity, McQueen offered. *And what happens if he refuses to listen to you? Or reports you to planetary security?*

Belinda frowned. Technically, there was nothing wrong with her being on Terra Nova, but she was definitely using false papers, rather than openly declaring herself to be a Marine. It was possible they'd shrug – it wouldn't be the first time Pathfinders had posed as other ranks – but it was equally possible they'd be outraged. Belinda had seen both reactions in her time, when the local authorities had been less stressed, or independent. The prospect of having to fight her way out or submit to captivity was thoroughly unpleasant.

"I'll take that chance," she said out loud, as she downloaded the file. Glen Cheal was older than her, she noted, and a widower. Oddly, there was no hint he'd shown any interest in women since his wife had died. "And what other choice do we have?"

She checked the security situation, then collected her paperwork and walked out of the station. The streets were nearly deserted, save for roving patrols of Civil Guardsmen, but she could hear the sound of rioting in the distance, carried over from the poorer parts of the city. It was worse in the megacities, she knew, where everyone was confined in towering blocks of concrete and steel. When riots began, she knew from her experience on Earth, they spread like wildfire. But how could she blame them, when they were confined to a tiny apartment and trapped within a CityBlock that might as well be a prison?

They could leave, if they wished, Doug pointed out. *There are no shortages of flights to colony worlds. And there are bonuses to anyone who leaves voluntarily.*

After being so ill-prepared for life, McQueen countered. *What can they learn about life on a colony in a CityBlock school?*

Belinda shrugged as she reached her destination. It was tiny, compared to the CityBlocks of Earth, but it was still large enough to house over five thousand people in reasonable comfort, as well as providing them with free food and drink. And it was more orderly, according to the files, unlike the CityBlocks of Earth. It was a testament to the sheer durability of the design that only a handful of CityBlocks had failed completely before the Fall of Earth, despite constant attacks on their infrastructure. Honestly! What sort of idiot would attack the systems keeping him and his family alive?

An idiot from Earth, she told herself. *Someone too ignorant to know where air, food and water comes from.*

She snorted, then walked into the main entrance, showing her security ID as she passed the guard. The guard didn't look very alert, she noted, as she walked past him; he might have looked intimidating to a local, but she knew she could have forced her way past him if necessary. He didn't even seem to carry a weapon, apart from a stunner. It wouldn't be effective if someone wore protection, or injected themselves with a stimulant beforehand.

They prefer the illusion of protection to the reality, McQueen said, as she entered the elevator. It demanded a security code, but a quick twist of her multitool ensured the device came to believe she'd provided one. *And besides, someone could get hurt. And sue.*

Belinda rolled her eyes. Lawsuits were almost unknown on her home-world, where taking the blame for something that was one's own fault was considered the honourable way to behave. There was no need to hire lawyers, not really. But, on Earth and the rest of the Core Worlds, *any-thing* could serve as grounds for a lawsuit. Even coming to someone else's assistance could result in a lawsuit, if something went wrong. It explained a great deal about Earth, Belinda felt, and why it had collapsed into chaos. No one dared assist anyone else for fear of becoming the next victim.

And so they became utterly dependent on the Government, she thought. The unemployment rate on Earth had been over seventy percent. Most of the workers had gone into dead-end jobs that had barely paid a liv-ing wage, then lost half of their income to taxes. *And, no matter how the Government tried, it couldn't look after everyone.*

She pushed the thought aside as the elevator stopped at the correct floor, then opened the doors. Belinda stepped outside, glancing around with interest. The walls seemed closer than the walls of Earth, painted in an eerie dark style that left shadows everywhere. Belinda felt a chill running down her spine as she contemplated the effect, wondering why it was tolerated on a world like Terra Nova. Anything could hide within the shadows, anything at all. But then, maybe that was the point. The residents didn't want to see anything that might hurt them.

Shaking her head, she walked down the corridor until she found the correct door. There was nothing on it, apart from a number; no name, no ID card...there wasn't even a buzzer. She hesitated, then tapped firmly on the door. There was no response. A second tap brought nothing, not even a whisper of sound from inside the apartment. Cheal might be asleep or he might be elsewhere. Or he might be feeling paranoid. She rather doubted anyone would open the door to a visitor, now that night was fall-ing over the city. The vast majority of the population would have locked their doors by now. There was no way to know without entering the apart-ment for herself.

Belinda hesitated, then reached for her multitool and pressed it against the lock. Breaking and entering wasn't the best way to introduce herself, she suspected, but she couldn't think of an alternative. There was a click as the lock opened, allowing her to enter the apartment. It was dark inside, but her implants allowed her to see through the shadows. Someone was talking in the distance, the faintly-tinny sound suggesting that it was a viewscreen or – perhaps – a datanet program. Belinda hesitated, listening carefully. No one seemed to have heard the sound of her entering the apartment. And that was worrying.

He lost his partner, she thought, remembering how badly she'd reacted to losing her teammates. She might well have considered suicide if she hadn't known it was a form of giving up. *He might have killed himself – or drunk himself into a stupor. Or...*

"Freeze," a voice snapped. The lights came on at the same instant. They would have blinded her if her implants hadn't adjusted instantly. "Put your hands in the air!"

Impressive, Belinda noted, as she obeyed. She didn't normally keep her implants stepped up – they tended to pick up more sound than could be easily processed – but Cheal had managed to come up behind her, without being heard. There were few Marines who could have done it better, all Pathfinders. *Very impressive.*

"Put your hands behind your head, then get down on your knees," Cheal ordered. "Interlock your fingers as you move!"

Clever, Belinda thought. She obeyed, after considering her options. Cheal was too close to her for his own safety, although he would have been safe enough if she hadn't been an enhanced human. But knocking him out would have made it even harder to convince him to listen to her. *He must have been woken by my knocks and hidden himself behind me.*

"Lie down," Cheal ordered, after a moment. "Hands behind your back."

She grunted as she obeyed, feeling his gun pressing into her back. Moments later, he had snapped on the cuffs and searched her roughly, but professionally. He didn't take advantage of her apparent helplessness to cop a feel. Belinda smiled as he rolled her over, then stared down in disbelief. Whatever he'd been expecting to see as he nabbed someone he'd thought was a burglar, it hadn't been her.

"You?"

"Me," Belinda confirmed. He *was* professional. Surprised or not, he kept his gun firmly pointed at her head. Clearly, he didn't have any great confidence in his cuffs. "And we do need to talk."

Cheal looked at her for a long moment. "Very well," he said, finally. "Talk."

CHAPTER
TWENTY-EIGHT

This was disastrous. The Civil Guardsmen were often deeply corrupt. They were certainly not trained to handle anything that required delicacy. Their conduct as policemen was poor, to say the least. Rumours rapidly spread that they took bribes (they did), they shook people down for money (they did) and that they sold prisoners to various colony trusts (they did). Faith in the Empire's law and order plunged rapidly in the core worlds.

- Professor Leo Caesius, *The Decline of Law and Order and the Rise of Anarchy*

Glen had had to deal with burglars before, in his previous apartment. He'd certainly given them a nasty shock when he'd emerged from his bedroom, carrying his oversized pistol in one hand and a set of cuffs in the other. And he had very little faith in the security guards on the lower floors to keep unwanted guests out of his apartment. Indeed, he had no friends in the building and no one could visit without signing in at the desk first, which would alert him to their presence. He'd come out and positioned himself as soon as he heard the knocking...

...And then arrested the leader of the snatch squad.

He stared at her in frank disbelief. There were so many contradictions surrounding her appearance that he *knew* she had to be playing a role. She looked young – he would have placed her age at twenty-five, perhaps younger – and yet she held herself with the ease of a seasoned officer. Indeed, despite being cuffed and searched, she didn't *look* helpless. Glen's instincts were screaming at him, warning him that this was no one to underestimate. And he thought he would have known better than to underestimate her even if she hadn't saved his life.

And lost Isabel's, he thought, with sudden bitterness. *But at least she saved the body.*

Talk," he repeated. "You broke into my house."

"You didn't answer the door," Belinda Lawson said. "I knocked. Twice."

"No one answers the door here," Glen muttered. He'd expected someone trying to rob him, with an excuse prepared if the apartment had actually been occupied. And he'd given Helen strict orders to ignore anyone knocking at the door. The thought of what might have happened if someone had broken into the apartment when she was alone was horrifying. "I normally have people buzzed through the security gates."

"Oh," Belinda said. She sounded torn between amusement and irritation. "Do you know who I am?"

Glen shrugged. "A snatch squad leader of surprising competence?"

Belinda's nose wrinkled at his words, as if she'd smelled something bad. "I assumed you would have read my file," she said. "Didn't you have a chance?"

"Not really," Glen said. There had been too many other files to read and, truthfully, he hadn't expected much from their escorts. They'd been incredibly lucky he was wrong. "I assumed you'd been conscripted, as they wouldn't have wasted experienced officers on us."

"True enough," Belinda said. "My file – officially – states that I was a military policewoman before I retired."

"I'm sure that made you popular," Glen grunted. Military policemen were rather less popular than regular policemen, at least among the ranks of those they patrolled. "Or is that a lie?"

"Yes," Belinda said. "I'm a Marine. A *Pathfinder* Marine."

Glen looked at her, then started to laugh. "You are a Marine," he repeated. He allowed his voice to become sarcastic. "Correct me if I'm wrong, young lady, but aren't Marines supposed to have bald heads? Your hair is long enough to touch your shoulders. And why are you wearing that awful uniform anyway?"

"A Pathfinder isn't supposed to look like a regular Marine," Belinda said, without heat. "And I'm undercover, which is why I'm wearing this uniform."

"I think I've seen far too many posers in my time," Glen said. "Do you know how many criminal thugs claim to have military experience? They get paid more if they manage to convince their masters that they can actually *fight*."

And yet, despite the sheer unlikelihood of the situation, he couldn't help wondering if she was telling the truth. She'd displayed genuine combat skills during the riot, rather than running around screaming or firing madly into the maddened crowd.

He took a breath. "Prove it."

Belinda looked up at him and smirked, then flexed her arms. The handcuffs shattered. Glen stared as pieces of chain fell to the floor – he'd checked the handcuffs personally before he'd signed for them and they were in excellent condition – and then watched as she tore the bracelets off her wrists. And she'd done it so quickly that he hadn't had a chance to raise his gun. If she'd attacked him...

"Enhanced strength and reinforcement," Belinda said. She ran her fingertips along her arm, trailing the bone. "A normal human, no matter how strong, could not have done that without damaging herself."

"True," Glen said. He glanced at her wrists, but the skin seemed utterly unmarked. If she was *that* heavily enhanced, she *had* to come out of a government facility. "How did you manage to pass through the security sensors?"

"I know how to spoof them," Belinda said. She rose to her feet, her blonde hair spilling around her heart-shaped face. "Can we talk now?"

Glen looked at her for a long moment, then returned his gun to his belt. If she meant him harm, she could have killed him by now, the moment he'd relaxed after snapping on the cuffs. It had been brave of her to let him cuff her – he might have shot her at once or found something capable of holding her – and he felt a flicker of respect. And he found himself wondering if she was telling the truth.

"We can," he said. "Would you care for a cup of coffee?"

"Milk, no sugar," Belinda said, as she followed him into the kitchen. "I...hi!"

Glen turned to see Helen, staring at the older woman. "This is Belinda," he said, quickly. "She's come to visit."

Helen looked doubtful – how much of their conversation had she overheard? – but nodded and went back into the lounge. Glen hadn't really spoken to her since he'd returned from the station, choosing instead to sit in his room and brood. He felt a stab of guilt as he sorted out two mugs of coffee, then motioned for Belinda to take one of the chairs. She sat, with all the daintiness of a cat. Up close, now he knew what to look for, there were more signs of intensive training in her movements.

"I'm looking after her," he said, by way of explanation. He hadn't missed the puzzled look Belinda had thrown at Helen. Glen's file would not have mentioned a child living with him, either natural-born or adopted. "It's a long story."

Belinda crossed her legs as she sipped her coffee. "Mine is also a long story," she said. "The short version is that I was sent here to make sure the conference, the conference the Governor just made public, goes ahead without a hitch."

Glen's eyes narrowed. "Do you have any reason to believe it would be threatened?"

"Quite a number," Belinda said. She shrugged, expressively. "Do you have any idea just how many factions there are that would like to see the Empire shatter?"

"I could guess," Glen said. "Do you have any information on *specific* threats?"

"No," Belinda said. "I would venture a guess that most people haven't heard of the conference, not until now. But your Governor had to invite others and word might be spreading."

"Very well," Glen said. He sighed. "And do you have a prime suspect?"

Her eyes darkened, long enough to worry him. "I suspect that some-one is planning trouble," she said. "There are too many worrying signs. The warehouse full of weapons might just be the tip of the iceberg. But I don't think it's the Nihilists, unless they've learned how to be patient."

"Explain," Glen ordered.

"The Nihilists believe that life is ultimately futile and ending it, for themselves as well as others, to be the only sane response," Belinda said. "Their attacks on the planetary infrastructure fit in with the pattern we saw on Earth, but they were too weak to succeed and only managed to place the security forces on their guard. The attacks were worse than useless, from their point of view."

"I concede the point," Glen said. He'd wondered the same himself. "But who else would be mad enough to launch attacks that could have devastated the planet's population?"

Belinda's blue eyes met his. "They started with a plan that was doomed to fail from the start," she said. "It makes no sense, so I started wondering if they *meant* to fail. And then I started wondering who benefited from the failed attacks."

Glen frowned. "But no one benefited from the attacks."

"Someone did," Belinda said. "The attacks – and the riots – gave the Governor a chance to declare a state of emergency and take supreme power for himself. And he's been using snatch squads like mine to round up political and corporate enemies, people who might stand in his way. He's now in control of the entire system, without anyone to oppose or countermand him."

Glen felt his blood run cold. He'd never considered the possibility, except...it did make a certain kind of sense. Without Earth, Terra Nova was the most important planet in the Empire. Whoever controlled Terra Nova would be in a good position to become Emperor in his own right, or at least shape and control the successor state as it took on shape and form.

"The warehouse," he said, slowly. He'd wondered why the Nihilists hadn't hastened to scatter the weapons across a number of safe houses as soon as possible. "Were we *meant* to stumble across the weapons?"

"It's quite possible," Belinda agreed. She rubbed her chin, thoughtfully. "The Governor might be trying to ensure that he is in the best possible position to take power."

Glen cursed under his breath. If it was the Governor...there was no real hope of bringing him to trial. He could take what they had to Patty, but she'd point out that they had nothing more than suspicions, without any real proof. And even if they did have proof, who would try the Governor of Terra Nova? Three-quarters of the men and women in high places owed their positions to the Governor. They'd resist any attempt to remove him from power.

"We don't have any proof," he said, out loud. Just about everything the Governor had done, even snatching his political opponents, could be justified. He needed to keep the peace long enough to hold the conference and sort out the Empire's future. "And it could easily be someone else."

Belinda's eyes flickered. "Like who?"

"Someone who benefits from seeing Terra Nova go up in flames," Glen said, frankly. "Hell, do we have any proof that the existence of the warehouses, and someone manipulating the rioters, is connected to the conference?"

"...No," Belinda said. "But the Governor is still the most likely suspect."

Her face twisted. There was something personal there, Glen was sure, or he couldn't read people at all. And that meant that Belinda would hardly be impartial on the subject of the Governor. She'd be predisposed to believe the worst of him. And, even if she was right, it would blind her to the facts.

"Then someone could easily be trying to cause a disaster without being aware of the conference," Glen offered. "The Nihilists could have lost their senior leaders in the warehouse and their subordinates are lashing out desperately, without a clear plan."

Belinda snorted. "Wishful thinking," she said. "And how do you account for the arrival of outside commandos?"

"Point," Glen said. The Nihilists had proven themselves immensely difficult to eradicate, just like any other organisation composed of fanatics. Earth had never managed to crush the movement right up until its final days. "But were the commandos working for the Governor or someone else?"

"They wouldn't want the weapons to fall into the hands of *real* Nihilists," Belinda offered, dryly. "Fanatics are dangerously unpredictable."

She sighed. "We have to make sure the conference goes ahead," she said, "all the while watching our backs."

"And we have to consider all possibilities," Glen said. "How do I know *you're* not here to stop the conference?"

Belinda looked oddly hurt. "Because I wouldn't have come to talk to you if I intended to sabotage Island One," she said. "I would have sneaked onto Island One as part of the security detachment and done my dirty work there. If I managed to get myself into the security forces on the ground, it wouldn't be much harder to get onto Island One."

"It will be once I'm in charge," Glen said. "I'll make sure that everyone boarding the station is scanned thoroughly."

"Good luck," Belinda said, dryly. "I think we should work together."

Glen studied her for a long moment. She wasn't Isabel, he knew, and she was a dangerous rogue element. What if she was involved in the plot, even though her actions made no sense if she *was* involved? She was right. All she really had to do was keep her head down until the time came to sabotage the conference. But there were too many imponderables for him to be happy about anything.

Logically, he should inform Patty of her presence and ask for orders. And yet, if the Governor was behind the entire plot – for whatever twisted reason made sense to him – asking for orders would be a form of suicide. He knew what to do when confronted with a thief, a rapist or a murderer, but political crimes were beyond him. What was the right course of action?

"Very well," he said, finally. It would be better to have Belinda under his wing than running loose on her own. "I'll request your presence as part of my security team."

"That would work," Belinda assured him. "And you'd have a good reason to ask for me."

"I suppose," Glen said, shortly.

He stood up and started to pace the tiny room. "I think we should take advantage of the next two days," he added. "I'm going to find out what happened to the source, the one that betrayed the warehouse."

"I may be able to tease it out of the computers," Belinda said. "My implants have built-in hacking software."

"Brilliant," Glen muttered. "That's how you got through the security network, isn't it?"

"More or less," Belinda confirmed. "But my level of augmentation is quite rare. Few people can endure so much enhancement, much less operate effectively afterwards."

"Even a hidden nerve-burst implant can be dangerous," Glen muttered. He'd heard plenty of horror stories about people with hidden augmentation breaking out of custody or murdering policemen when they were caught. "Is there a way to counter it?"

"Only from the inside," Belinda said. "I can help you with that, if necessary."

"It will be," Glen said. He took a breath. It was night outside and the curfew would be in full effect. "When are you expected back at your barracks?"

"I have an appointment with my superior tomorrow," Belinda said, "but I'm not actually expected back before then. They seem to find me surplus to requirements."

"Too competent to be wasted on a snatch squad, too new to be given a more trusted position," Glen guessed. He knew he would give his eye-teeth for a handful of competent subordinates, particularly if *he* was in charge of the conscripts. But Belinda was beautiful as well as competent. "Or does he have something else in mind?"

"I hope not," Belinda said. She gave him a sharp look. "What do you want to do?"

"You stay here," Glen said. "There's a couch in the living room – Isabel slept there once or twice, when she had a fight with her partners – and you can spend the night there. I'll call the boss, get you transferred over to my command and look for the source. We can investigate just where the tip-off actually came from tomorrow."

Belinda hesitated, then nodded. Glen wondered just what was going through her head; if she was half as capable as she claimed to be, she wouldn't be scared of falling asleep near him, even if he *was* a near-stranger. But then, he wasn't helpless either.

"But I do need more proof of your credentials," he added. "Is there any way to prove your identity?"

"There's a code you can send to the Imperial Army database," Belinda said. She reached for a piece of paper and scribbled down a set of numbers. "You have to send it to the automated system you use for checking ID numbers, not the desk officer. You'll get a response from them confirming that it belongs to a Marine."

"That doesn't prove anything," Glen pointed out. "The code could belong to *any* Marine."

"Check the message path," Belinda said. "You'll find it comes right out of the Marine subsection of the datanet. They'll certainly confirm the code could only be used by an active-service Marine."

She shrugged. "Details of active-service Marines are restricted, for obvious reasons," she added. "It would be very irritating if someone ran my DNA against the files and discovered who I really was."

"Irritating," Glen repeated. There were so many holes in the files that an entire battlefleet could fly through one without scraping the edges. "I suppose I'll have to trust you."

Belinda stood. She was taller than him, Glen noted, suddenly. He scowled, cursing his oversight. It hadn't been obvious from the way she moved and it damn well should have been. But it was another hint that she'd been very carefully trained to move, utterly unnoticed, through any environment. Any description he'd given of her would be badly skewed.

"Yes, you will," she said. "Because I think your entire planet depends on the conference going ahead, without delay."

CHAPTER
TWENTY-NINE

Worse, the Civil Guard was entirely unsuited to any form of detective work. They could respond rapidly against open attacks, but they were unable to track down terrorists, such as the Nihilists. Indeed, their actions helped make the Nihilists far more dangerous. Local civilians, hating and fearing the Civil Guardsmen who were supposed to be keeping them safe, were often quite willing to supply help to the Nihilists.

- Professor Leo Caesius, *The Decline of Law and Order and the Rise of Anarchy*

Belinda wasn't too surprised that Glen – she supposed she could call him Glen now – was still a little suspicious of her. She'd come out of nowhere, after all, when he was emotionally vulnerable and weakened. And she really had no definite way to prove her identity. Carrying anything other than the Marine code would have risked exposure, while the code itself could be used by any Marine. He had to consider the possibility that, augmentation or no, she was a poser.

But she really had no choice, except to convince him to trust her.

"I'm going to make a few calls," Glen said. "Can you wait in the living room?"

Belinda nodded. It was obvious that Glen wanted to check her out, then perhaps ask his superiors about their source in the Nihilists. She rose to her feet and walked into the next room, where the little girl was watching the viewscreen in a manner that suggested she was tenser than she'd like to admit. Belinda had no difficulty in recognising a lost soul, or someone afraid that the universe was going to change on them again. But why was the girl even here in the first place? Glen's file hadn't mentioned a daughter or a niece.

"My name is Helen," the girl said, eying Belinda doubtfully. "What's your name?"

"Belinda," Belinda said. The girl seemed thinner than she should be, but otherwise healthy and well. She might not look so pretty now, Belinda decided, yet those cheekbones would give her a definite presence when she was a little bit older. "I'm working with your..."

"Caretaker," Helen supplied. "It's just until my mommy and father come back."

Belinda frowned, inwardly. The girl seemed to believe her words, yet there was something in her tone that suggested otherwise, that she knew her parents would never return. She wondered, absently, just what the story was, then made a mental note to ask Glen once he returned. It might not be important, but her instincts were telling her she should be paying attention. But, thankfully, the girl didn't look as though she was being abused.

You really think she would have been abused? Pug asked. *Glen's a nice guy.*

You know how many bastards there are in uniform, Belinda thought back, feeling yet another flicker of guilt. *Remember Han?*

She shuddered at the memory. The Imperial Administrators had made matters far worse on an already-staggering planet by abusing the population. One of them had collected under-aged children, making the others seem almost reasonable and pleasant by comparison. She had no idea if the administrator had always been a monster or if the complete lack of oversight had gotten to him, but it hardly mattered. He'd helped fuel a revolt that had cost millions of lives.

Helen turned to look at Belinda, her gaze suddenly serious. "Are you going to marry him?"

Belinda had to choke back a laugh. "I don't think so," she said, dryly. Glen was attractive, but she didn't want to risk damaging their fragile relationship by sleeping with him, let alone marrying him. "Why do you think I would?"

"There's a girl in *Romantic Relationships*," Helen said. "She met a guy, slept with him and then married him, all on the same day."

"That only works out when you have a scriptwriter on your side," Belinda said. She hated to admit it, but she had watched a few episodes of *Romantic Relationships*. It was really nothing more than hundreds of sex scenes, joined together by a very flimsy plot. None of the actors were very good at their jobs, but they hadn't been hired for their acting talent. "How would you know, after one date, that you wanted to spend the rest of your life with him?"

"I don't know," Helen said. "Do you have a boyfriend?"

"No," Belinda said, flatly. Romantic relationships were never easy for female Marines – and harder still for Pathfinders. She had to either keep her boyfriends in the dark or watch them shy away from her when she revealed the truth. The only person who had made a pass at her after she'd revealed herself was Prince Roland. "I don't have a boyfriend."

"That's sad," Helen said. "*Romantic Relationships* says that no one is happy without a partner."

Belinda rolled her eyes, blatantly enough to make Helen giggle. "Soap operas say a lot of things," she said, sarcastically. Once, they'd tried to shock; now, there was little they could do that *would* shock their jaded viewers. "You have to bear in mind they don't have any interest in showing happy, but single people."

She allowed her smile to grow wider. "Do *you* have a boyfriend?"

Helen shook her head. "I was on a ship, without anyone apart from my parents," she said, softly. "The only time I met boys was at a Meet – and there wasn't time to do more than chat."

"Probably for the best," Belinda said. Helen couldn't be older than fourteen, physically old enough to have a relationship but probably not mature enough to handle it. "Wait until you're older."

"That's what my mother said," Helen commented. "I don't think she ever understood me."

"My mother understood me all too well," Belinda said. Her mother had been kind and caring, but she'd never put up with any nonsense from her children. "And when I had to leave, she waved me goodbye and wished me luck."

"I'll have to leave one day," Helen said, morbidly. "If I marry someone from another ship, I'll have to go live with him and his family. My parents wouldn't want someone else joining us, not even if he was young and handsome."

Belinda nodded, feeling pity. Helen's words concealed a harsher reality. To prevent inbreeding, the Traders often traded daughters from ship to ship, sometimes without the daughter's consent. It was a habit that had persisted despite the existence of genetic modification technology – but then, the Traders did prefer to use the simple option, if possible. One day, Helen might be sent to live elsewhere...

Or she might find someone and be happy, Belinda thought. *There's no reason it has to end in tragedy.*

Helen clicked on the viewscreen again, then started a flick. Belinda smiled to herself as she realised it was one of the dreadfully unfunny attempts at comedy produced on Earth, then settled back to watch it anyway. They were always unfunny, she knew, because the producers were desperate to avoid offending anyone. And just about *anything* could be offensive, to the right person. The only acceptable targets were Traders, colonists and anyone else who wanted to live outside the Empire.

Glen stepped into the living room, looking calmer than he'd been while they'd been talking. "Your code checks out," he said, as he sat down facing her. "Thank you."

"That's good," Belinda said. She glanced at the sofa, then back at him. "Where do I sleep?"

"Helen, bed," Glen said, firmly. He gave Belinda a sidelong look. "Perhaps you could read her a bedtime story?"

Belinda shrugged, then rose to her feet and waited for Helen to prepare for bed. She hadn't tried to argue, somewhat to Belinda's surprise, although she wouldn't have expected an argument from someone raised on a starship. Traders kept strict hours and rarely stayed up late. Or perhaps Helen was merely tired. The memory of how her siblings had kept crawling out of bed after their mother had put them into bed and tucked them in brought another stab of guilt. She hadn't been the easiest daughter to raise.

And that was lucky for us, Doug pointed out. *You would never have made it if you'd been a submissive little girl.*

But you would have been more obedient, Pug added snidely. *You wouldn't have disobeyed orders under fire.*

I didn't have a choice, Belinda thought, rubbing her temple. *And you know it.*

Helen readied herself for bed quickly and efficiently, to Belinda's amusement. The girl undressed, washed and then donned a pair of flowery pyjamas before climbing under the covers and giving Belinda an expectant look. Belinda smiled back at her, feeling as if she finally understood why her mother hadn't booted her out of the house after the first few instances of childish disobedience. There was something about a smile from a child that made it all worthwhile.

"A story," she said, out loud. "Let me see."

She took a breath, remembering one that had been popular on her homeworld.

"Once upon a time, there was a family of pigs who lived together in a very large house," she said. It had been one of her favourite stories, to the point her mother had flatly refused to recite it for her after several months of repeating it time and time again. "One day, Papa Pig went out and found a wolf cub lost in the forest. He picked up the cub and took him back to the house."

She paused. "Over the years, Little Wolf became their servant," she continued. "He did whatever he was told, even as he grew bigger and bigger. The pigs didn't hesitate to keep putting him down, though. They insulted and mocked and belittled him to his face."

Helen sat upright. "Why?"

"People are stupid," Belinda said. "And idiotic too.

"Little Wolf kept growing bigger and bigger," she said. "And yet he stayed obedient until the day they finally pushed him too far. They wanted him to fight other wolves for them! And so Little Wolf turned on the pigs. He ate Papa Pig and Mama Pig and Big Pig and Middle Pig and Little Pig. He even crunched up Little Pig's doll. And that was the end of the piggy family. Little Wolf brought his mother to the house and they lived there, happily ever after.

"Apart from the pigs, of course."

Helen twisted her face in contemplation. "But they treated him really badly," she said, finally. "Why shouldn't he eat them?"

"Good question," Belinda said. "The moral of the story is that treating someone badly can come back to haunt you."

Her father had once argued, in the weeks before Belinda left for Boot Camp, that the whole story was a metaphor for the Empire itself. On one hand, the Empire needed warriors to defend it; on the other hand, the Empire hated and feared its defenders. What was to stop the sheepdogs from deciding it was better to act like wolves? Belinda had never seriously considered turning against the Empire – the Marine Corps trained its people better than that – but she could understand why others would be tempted. Why would an Admiral *not* consider becoming a warlord when the Grand Senate could break him at will?

And she'd always liked Little Wolf. The story of the oppressed over-throwing the oppressor struck a chord with her, but she knew from bitter experience that the oppressed often became the oppressors when the tables were turned. Little Wolf, on the other hand, had simply managed to take over Papa Pig's house, after killing his family. But then, it was a children's story. The unfortunate implications that would have been present in an adult story were missing.

And we should be grateful for that, she thought, crossly. *What would happen to our children if we read them stories about murder, rape and oppression?*

She tucked Helen in, then rose to her feet and slipped out of the room. Outside, Glen was sitting on the sofa, waiting for her. Belinda hesitated, then sat down facing him.

"There's a blanket under the sofa," he said, shortly. "We'll wake up at 0800, if that's alright with you."

"I guess so," Belinda said, feeling oddly hollow. Telling the story had cost her more than she wanted to admit. There were VR simulations where people, men and women, went back to childhood, but she'd always held them in contempt. And yet, she thought she understood now. There was not only innocence in childhood, but escape as well. "Do you have to go back to the office?"

"Not for a day or two," Glen said. His face shadowed as he remembered his partner. "I was told to take a break."

"Your boss must dislike you," Belinda said. Someone like Glen would be better off working until the pain had a chance to dull. Being alone wouldn't help, really. "Or is she trying to be kind?"

"Kind, I think," Glen said. He shook his head. "I need to do more than just sit around on my ass."

Belinda nodded, looking him up and down. He wasn't unattractive, not by any means, even if he was older than her. And he was definitely fit. His face showed more lines than Doug or even the Commandant had ever shown. She considered, very briefly, making love to him. It had been a long time for her and, she thought, longer for him. But she knew it would destroy their working relationship, as flimsy as it was.

"Try to sleep," she urged, instead. "We'll talk in the morning."

Glen nodded slowly – perhaps he'd been having amorous thoughts too – then rose to his feet and walked out of the room. Belinda took off her shoes, then found the blanket and lay down on the sofa. Oddly, she realised in the moments before she slipped her implants into sleep mode, she felt more comfortable in Glen's home than she had in Augustus's apartment. It was nowhere near as pretentious.

The next thing she knew, it was morning and she could hear the sounds of someone making breakfast. She stumbled to her feet, feeling oddly grimy in her uniform, then walked into the bathroom and splashed water on her face. It honestly hadn't occurred to her to bring a spare uniform, let alone toiletries. Going without washing wasn't something she enjoyed, although she was used to it. She'd been unable to wash during the Crucible and, by the time her team had finished, they had all stunk so badly the Drill Instructors had practically shoved them into the showers and threatened to lock the door.

"You can use the shower, if you like," Glen called from the kitchen. "There's no water rationing yet."

"It's only a matter of time," Belinda called back, as she undressed and climbed into the shower. The water pressure was pathetic, compared to the showers she'd used on the *Chesty Puller*. "They'll start drawing water from working apartment blocks to blocks without water purification equipment soon enough."

She washed herself quickly, dried herself with a towel and dressed in her uniform, then walked out into the kitchen. Glen was frying something that smelt heavenly in a pan, while there was bread and orange juice on the table. Belinda took a glass, sighed inwardly at the smell of heavily-processed juice, then drank it anyway. She still missed pure juice from her homeworld, where there were no petty regulations to ensure that all the fun was drained from life.

Glen put a plate of bacon and eggs in front of her, then sat down with his own. It must have cost a great deal of money, Belinda thought as she ate, but it was possible that Glen considered it comfort food. He ate quickly, using pieces of bread to wipe up egg yolk in a manner that reminded Belinda of her brother. She had to smile, wondering if Glen had irritated his father as much as Kevin had irritated hers, but it wasn't something she could ever ask. Glen's parents, according to his file, were dead.

"You did well with Helen," Glen said. "Thank you."

He explained, quickly, why she was staying with him. Belinda silently approved. It would have been easy to have Helen handed over to the Civil Guard, where she would probably have been sold – if she was lucky – to a colonial development corporation. Easy, but not right. Taking her in, if only for a short space of time, meant that Glen was a better person than most of the Empire's population. But then, helping each other was strongly discouraged by the government.

"You're a better man than I am," she said, when he'd finished. "And she's a sweet kid."

"I suppose," Glen said. He paused. "I spoke to my boss."

Belinda frowned. "And?"

"And she says that we are to keep our noses away from the source," Glen said. "I'm to take the next day off, then concentrate on building up the security force for Island One. I put in a request for you" – Belinda tensed – "and you should have orders to report to me officially tomorrow."

He paused. "I didn't mention your real identity," he added. "Just...just that I admired your competence."

"Very good," Belinda said. She finished her breakfast, then leaned forward. "I think I should have a word with the source anyway, Glen. Your boss didn't forbid *me* from checking him out."

Glen nodded, slowly. "But how will you know how to find him?"

Belinda tapped the side of her head, then winked. "Leave that to me," she said. "You spend the day trying to relax, understand? Go do something mindless."

"I'll be going through the files," Glen said. "I'm damned if I'm sitting about doing nothing."

I definitely like him, Doug's voice said. *He would have made a good Marine, if things had been different.*

Better get after him, Pug added. *The boss likes the cut of his jib.*

Belinda told both voices, firmly, to shut up.

CHAPTER

THIRTY

This might have seemed suicidal. The Nihilists were the enemies of all. They killed without conscience, without mercy. But they looked better than the government and that was all that mattered.

- Professor Leo Caesius, The Decline of Law
and Order and the Rise of Anarchy

"You're being reassigned," Fraser said, as soon as Belinda walked into his office. "Marshal Cheal has requested your services."

"Yes, sir," Belinda said, trying to look surprised. "What does he want me for?"

"It doesn't say," Fraser said. "I shall be sorry to lose you, but orders are orders."

He paused. "You are to wait until called, then report to him," he added. "Your team has already been reassigned to other duties, so you can wait without worrying about them."

"Thank you, sir," Belinda said. "Has there been any progress on tracking down the rioters – or the snipers?"

"No," Fraser said. "We don't have the manpower to track them down. Some people just want to bombard the area at random, in hopes of making an impression, but the Governor overruled them."

"Oh," Belinda said. It was the first humane act she'd seen from a member of the Governor's family. Was it a genuine concern for the innocents who would die, she asked herself, or an attempt to prevent another upheaval? There was no way to know. "Should I wait in the barracks?"

"Wait wherever you please," Fraser said, dryly. "Just make sure you're ready when he calls, Belinda. It was priority-one."

Belinda nodded, then saluted and left the office. Outside, it seemed busier than before, with newer conscripts reporting for duty. She smiled to herself as she walked into the barracks – there were several more occupied beds – and checked her message inbox. A note from Violet popped up in front of her, asking when Belinda was next going to visit her father. It concluded with a warning that Augustus would be off-world next week and thus unavailable.

Unless he's going to Island One, Belinda thought. It made sense; Augustus was the largest economic operator in the system, so he'd definitely want input. And the Governor would value his advice. *I might see them there.*

And it might turn into a stupid romantic comedy, Pug added. *You might...*

Shut up, Belinda thought.

She lay back on her bunk, then accessed the secure network through her neural link. It didn't take long to find the sealed files on the warehouse – there really had been enough weapons to outfit a small army resting there when they'd been recovered by the Civil Guard – and through it identify the source. He was, apparently, a deep cover agent sent in by the Marshals, someone capable of posing as Nihilist for quite some time. Belinda was moderately impressed. *She* knew how to play roles, but deep cover agents never had an easy time of it. If nothing else, there was the very real risk of being accidentally killed by their own side.

Downloading the file into her implants, she stood up and headed for the garage. A wave of her ID was enough to get a driver to take her back to her hotel, which seemed almost empty as guests and tourists fled the city. The bellhop paid almost no attention to her, which surprised her until she remembered she was still wearing her uniform. Once she was in her room – someone had searched it twice, she noted – she showered again, then changed into a civilian outfit. She had to pass unnoticed as she walked into the middle-class district of the city.

Just make sure you don't get seen by the Civil Guard, McQueen warned. *You don't have time to fight off rapists.*

Belinda nodded, checked that her weapons and IDs were safely concealed, then headed out of the door and down to the lobby. The doorkeeper hurried to open the door for her, something that always left her feeling slightly awkward, then muttered something about it not being safe on the streets. Belinda gave him a charming smile, then started to walk towards the universities. It hadn't been a surprise to discover that the deep cover agent lived close to the primary source of recruits for the Nihilists.

They should shut the place down, she thought, recalling the role Imperial University had played in the Fall of Earth. Teaching children – teenagers – how to work was one thing, filling their heads with radical ideas and political correctness was quite another. No wonder the Nihilists were so popular on campus. Their doctrine was the epitome of the pointlessness of existence, the complete lack of morality, that students were taught by their tutors. And any tutor who actually tried to teach the kids how to think would swiftly get the boot.

She gritted her teeth as a handful of male students wolf-whistled at her as she passed. They were on the streets to show their defiance, which would have been brave of them if the university district had actually been patrolled heavily by the Civil Guard. She fought down the urge to lure them into an alleyway and administer a quick beating, settling instead for ignoring them as contemptuously as possible. The simple absence of any female students on the streets spoke volumes about the dangers of being out alone.

Bastards, she thought, nastily.

The student accommodation was nothing more than a series of apartment blocks, very similar to Glen's home. There were no official guards, somewhat to her surprise, but several students stood outside the building, carrying makeshift clubs and other weapons. They'd be in deep shit if the Civil Guard saw them, Belinda knew, wondering if they were actually prepared to *use* the weapons. It was quite likely that, sooner or later, the growing anarchy would find its way into the university district.

She walked past them, nose in the air, and pressed her fingertips against the scanner. It bleeped as her implants interfaced with the system, convincing it that she had a right to enter the building. The student guards ignored her, confident that the system wouldn't have let her in without permission. Belinda, who knew just how easy it was to spoof just about any automatic system with the right preparation, knew better. But the students wouldn't have been taught to doubt the computers. Or the security cameras, even though a quick check revealed that they'd been disabled long ago.

And yet someone, with the right training, could make sure he graduates with the highest of marks, she thought. There had been a scandal on Earth, she recalled, where a pair of computer geniuses had fiddled their own marks. She hadn't seen the point of it, she recalled, because degrees from Imperial University were largely worthless anyway. The students wouldn't have gone straight to the top even if they graduated with perfect marks. *Or rob them blind before they even notice they've become victims.*

Inside, the corridors were warm and brightly lit – and decorated with countless posters from movie flicks. Belinda sighed as she saw a poster for Psychopathic Marine VI – a very popular, if utterly unrealistic flick featuring a crazy Marine – and firmly resisted the urge to tear it down and rip it to shreds. Instead, she walked up the stairs, glancing into each floor as she passed. Half of them were deserted, but one of the corridors had been turned into makeshift sleeping space and another seemed to be hosting a party. But, when she reached the source's floor, it was deserted. She wrinkled her nose at the smell, then walked up to the door and checked it. It was locked.

She tapped the door and waited, then used her multitool to open the lock. It clicked open, allowing her to step inside. This time, she resolved not to be surprised, but as her eyes adjusted rapidly to the gloom she realised it wouldn't be necessary. The source – a young man called Richard Keystone – was lying on the sofa, his body stiff and cold. Belinda closed the door behind her, then crept forward, every sense alert for the presence of someone else in the apartment. But there was no one.

"Shit," she muttered, as she pulled on her gloves. There was no mistaking Keystone for anyone else. He looked roughly nineteen – his file stated he was twenty-five – and looked alarmingly sloppy, just like a regular student. Belinda felt a moment of professional kinship, then leaned down to examine the body. There was no apparent cause of death. "Why..."

She saw the headband on the ground and picked it up, then swore. A neural simulator, one designed to feed a program directly into the wearer's head. The technology was dangerously addictive – among other things, it activated the pleasure centres in the human brain – but largely unrestricted. It was considered an affront to human dignity to ban it.

And it helps keep the masses under control, she thought, as her implants scanned the headband's processors. It swiftly became apparent that there had been a glitch in the system, which had caused immediate and fatal brain trauma. Keystone would have died instantly, maybe as little as two to three days ago, without ever knowing what had hit him. *And why did no one come to visit?*

She put the headband back down on the ground where it had fallen, then searched his body thoroughly. There was nothing, apart from a handful of datachips, including five marked as belonging to various university modules. Belinda considered taking them for later inspection, then decided it was probably futile. Keystone wouldn't have survived for years as a deep cover agent if he had hidden anything incriminating in his apartment.

Straightening up, she started to search the rest of the room. There were several piles of paper books, including a number that were considered restricted, and literally hundreds of datachips scattered on the floor. She glanced at a few of the titles – most of them seemed to be pornographic – and then left them where they'd fallen. But something was missing, something so obvious...it took her several minutes to realise what was gone. Keystone should have had a computer, something to use to read datachips and type out his essays for his professors – assuming he'd bothered to write any, of course. Attendance was hardly mandatory. Students could get a passing grade just by signing up for the class.

So where was the computer? It was inconceivable he didn't have one. The universities handed them out for free to their students, just to make sure they were all on the same level when they started. But, no matter how hard she looked, she couldn't see one or any sign it had ever existed. Whoever had rigged the headband to kill the wearer, and make it look like a dreadful accident, had come back afterwards and stolen the computer. There was no other possible conclusion.

He could have given it to someone else, McQueen offered.

Pug snickered. *What sort of student would surrender his computer?*

Belinda ignored the voices as she considered the order of events. The headband had been rigged, then Keystone had put it on naturally. There was no hint that he'd been forced to wear it and activate a program – and he had had some genuine training. If he'd believed he was being forced to commit suicide, he would have fought and there was no sign of a struggle. No, he hadn't known he was about to die. But his killer had crept back afterwards, searched the apartment himself and stolen the computer. It would need a dedicated forensic team to find any clues he might have left behind. Sighing, she stepped into the next room.

The bedroom stank so badly she wondered if he had wet the bed, but when she turned on the light it became clear that he hadn't bothered to clean away the food he'd eaten before his untimely death. There were a handful of female garments hanging from a line in the washroom, she discovered, all labels with a different name. But then, Keystone would have had to sleep around to keep up his cover.

I'm sure he hated every last moment of it, Pug said, archly.

The kitchen was almost completely bare, she discovered. There was no food in the fridge, apart from a handful of pre-prepared meals and a couple of bottles of cheap rotgut. Someone had been making it themselves, she guessed after taking a sniff, and selling it to students too dumb to consider the potential risks. Belinda had drunk plenty of homemade beer and wine on her homeworld, but the brewers had generally known what they'd been doing. The illicit still-owners in the university might well not know anything, beyond the basics. And where did they get the ingredients anyway?

She snorted at the thought, then checked the rest of the kitchen. There were only a handful of pieces of cutlery, all plastic. Clearly, the university was so obsessed with safety that they'd banned metal knives and forks, as well as weapons and common sense. She snickered at the thought of anyone trying to cut through meat with a plastic knife, then sobered as she remembered the pre-packaged meals. They were *designed* to be eaten with plastic spoons, she decided. The administrators were trying to install learned helplessness in their students.

Idiots, she thought, as she went through the cupboards. They were empty, without any trace of food or drink. *What the hell were they supposed to eat?*

Belinda sighed, then walked back into the living room and sat down next to the body, thinking hard. Keystone had known about the warehouse, somehow. He had to have known if he'd tipped Glen off. But he'd died, within a day or two of the warehouse being captured and the weapons impounded. Had the Nihilists realised he'd betrayed them, she asked herself, or had someone else murdered him to cover their tracks? There were too many things about the whole affair that didn't make sense.

"What did you know?" She asked the corpse. "And why were you killed?"

There was no reply. Belinda looked at him for a long moment, then rose to her feet. There was no point in taking anything from the apartment. Keystone hadn't left anything behind that could lead to the Nihilists – and if he'd set up a dead man's drop, it hadn't activated yet. She took one last look around the apartment, then slipped out of the door, closing and locking it behind her. Glen could make a call to the campus police and have them 'discover' the body. His superiors would have to dispatch a forensic team after their source was found dead.

She headed down the stairs, then froze as she heard the sound of a struggle. The cold and rational part of her mind told her to ignore it, but she headed towards the sound anyway. A woman was struggling and arguing...Belinda turned the corner and saw a young girl, probably in her first year of studying, trying to get away from a much larger male. He looked too old to be a student, Belinda considered, although that proved nothing. His hand was reaching down into the girl's blouse as his body pinned her firmly against the wall. No matter how she struggled, she was trapped like a butterfly in a case. She cried out as her bare breasts bobbled free...

Belinda threw herself forward and slapped the back of the man's head with augmented strength. His skull cracked under the blow and he collapsed, his body hitting the ground like a sack of potatoes. Belinda felt a flicker of regret, then dismissed it. The bastard was unlikely to face any form of justice, even for nearly raping a younger student. She looked up at his would-be victim, who seemed to be going into shock, and sighed. There was no way she could allow the girl to tell anyone she'd been there.

She had authority to kill unwanted witnesses, if necessary. But she'd never liked the thought of killing innocents, even if it ran the risk of them reporting her presence.

"Where is your apartment?" She asked. The girl was shaking too hard to answer. "Where is your apartment?"

"There," the girl said, pointing towards an unmarked door. She stuttered so badly that she seemed to be on the verge of fainting. "I...I..."

Belinda picked her up, then carried her though the door and into a messy apartment. Thankfully, there was no one else in the room. She placed the shaking girl on the floor and injected her with one of the needles implanted in her fingertips, then watched as the girl fell into a restful sleep. Her short term memories would be scrambled, leaving her unsure what was real and what was a dream. She certainly wouldn't be able to make a viable witness report. Belinda sighed, cursing the schools for not teaching children how to defend themselves, then walked out of the apartment. The corridor was still deserted, so she picked up the dead body and stuffed it in a storage compartment before walking out of the building and onto the streets. By the time they found the body, she planned, she would be a very long way from the university.

Poor bitch, she thought. The girl would have been raped, right there and then, if Belinda hadn't intervened. Nothing would have been done to the rapist, leaving the girl to pick up her life as best as she could. Suicide was far from uncommon after such violation. *And damn those who tried to keep her safe.*

At least you intervened, Doug offered. *How many others would have watched or simply joined in?*

Belinda shuddered. The campus police had low crime stats. But they'd done it by ensuring that there was no actual 'crimes' on the books. The students had responded by doing whatever they liked, because if nothing was criminal nothing was actually wrong. It was hard to escape the sense that Terra Nova was definitely doomed. She thought of Violet, and then Helen, and shuddered. Would they be going to university soon too?

Doomed, she thought. *Definitely doomed.*

CHAPTER
THIRTY-ONE

Worst of all, it was not long before the Civil Guard was thoroughly penetrated by organised crime. This was nothing as simple as a handful of Guardsmen on the criminal payroll. No, it was far more dangerous; senior officers, some with powerful connections, were bribed into compliance.

- Professor Leo Caesius, *The Decline of Law and Order and the Rise of Anarchy*

"I'm glad you took care of the rapist," Glen said. "Not everyone would have intervened."

He sat back at his desk and looked up at Belinda. Her report had been complete, comprehensive and extremely detailed, even though nothing had actually been written down on the datanet. Richard Keystone was dead, any leads he might have had to the Nihilists had died with him and they'd hit another dead end.

"I know," Belinda said. "But I found nothing apart from a dead body." She paused. "If Keystone was killed," she added, "why?"

Glen shrugged. His imagination could provide too many possible answers. The Nihilists had killed him for betraying them. The Governor – or an outside force – had killed Keystone after using him. Or...it was quite possible that the glitch in Keystone's headband had been genuine, with his death nothing more than an unfortunate coincidence. Glen rather doubted it – the odds against it were quite high – but it was possible. The prospect had to be taken into account.

"I wish I knew," he said. He looked down at his terminal. "The Campus Police *did* find the body, so there will be a forensic team dispatched once his death starts alerting people. And if one isn't dispatched, it will raise more problems for us."

Belinda nodded, then started to pace the small office. "Have you sorted out a security team yet?"

"I'm asking for three more Marshals as well as you and the security staff already on Island One," Glen said. "I may not get the Marshals, Belinda. Everyone is considerably overstretched at the moment."

"I wish I was surprised," Belinda said. "Have you thought about asking for a Marine security detail?"

"There aren't any Marines on the planet, apart from you," Glen reminded her. "And you said the Slaughterhouse was gone. Where should we send the request?"

"Point," Belinda said. She didn't seem inclined to answer the question. "Have you seen the list of attendees?"

Glen nodded. Half of the military and civil leaders in the Core Worlds were attending in person, while the remainder were sending representatives. They'd be escorted, too, by battle squadrons of their own, threatening bloody mayhem if anything happened to them while they were on Island One. It would rapidly turn into a nightmare if anything *did*.

"We need to hold the conference somewhere in interstellar space," he muttered. "But where could they go that would suit them?"

He sighed. The list of instructions for Island One's staff had been clear. They were to provide the delegates with maximum luxury, up to and including courtesans from a high-class escort agency if requested. The courtesans alone would be a security headache; they'd need a great deal of very expensive soothing before they agreed that whatever happened on Island One would remain a secret, come what may. Their owners had a habit of supplementing their income by using pillow talk as a source of political intelligence. It said a great deal about human nature that it still worked, even through everyone knew about it.

And then there was the food, the drink and the luxury accommodation, all of which would pose its own brand of headache...

"It would be efficient, but it would not suit their dignity," Belinda said. "What do you have in mind?"

She looked at the datapad Glen passed her. They and the remainder of the staff would move to Island One as soon as possible, taking security equipment from Terra Nova and transferring it to their new posting. The staff, including the courtesans, would arrive the following day, after being inspected before they left the planet and inspected again when they arrived on the space habitat. Food and drink supplies would be drawn from Island One's stockpiles, if possible, and supplemented from Terra Nova after another security check if not.

And, after that, there would be no further contact between Terra Nova and Island One until the conference was over.

Glen sighed. Island One should have been easy to secure, but he had a nasty feeling there would be problems. The delegates would need to be inspected, yet they'd probably take that as a personal affront, disrupting the conference. And their aides, security guards and others would also need to be inspected, which would cause further problems. It was going to be a horrible nightmare, even if nothing went badly wrong.

"We'll have to search Island One from top to bottom," Belinda said, when she'd finished scanning the datapad. "And what about the residents?"

"They have a guaranteed right to stay on the habitat," Glen said. "But they were all heavily vetted by the owners and there's nothing wrong or alarming with them."

"I hope so," Belinda said. "But you might want to ask them to consider moving for the duration of the conference."

"I will," Glen said. "But they didn't go to Island One because they wanted a pleasant view, Belinda. They wanted security. And moving away would compromise it."

"True," Belinda agreed.

Glen's terminal buzzed. "One moment."

He picked it off his belt and glanced at it. "We're getting two more Marshals," he said, "and a handful of security officers trained in space operations. But not much else."

"Drat," Belinda said. "You'd better hope the staff is up to scratch."

Glen sighed. "I'll give orders for them to meet us at the spaceport," he added. "We'll get the equipment sorted out and then get onboard the shuttle."

"And pick up Helen, of course," Belinda offered. "She'll enjoy her time on Island One."

Glen had no doubt of it. Island One had plenty of wilderness that was safe for children; indeed, the brochures he'd accessed had shown tree houses and lakes suitable for swimming without the threat of hostile wild-life. There were so many pleasures available to the filthy rich that were simply not available to the children of the poor, trapped in box-like apart-ments on Terra Nova. He envied them more than he cared to admit.

"Lucky kids," he said, out loud. He flickered through the terminal until it showed a picture of a treehouse. "I would have loved to have a treehouse as a child."

"I had one," Belinda said. "We built it for ourselves – actually, we had to rebuild it several times because it kept falling down until we mastered how to secure it properly."

She took the terminal and shrugged. "That one was built by qualified engineers," she added, "not children. It's far too good to be made by a group of children."

Glen sighed. "Where were you born?"

"Greenway," Belinda said. "It's out on the Rim. My family had to learn to look after itself."

"I've often thought about going out to the Rim," Glen admitted. "Is it a good place to live?"

Belinda opened her mouth, then paused. "It depends what you want from life," she said, after a moment's thought. "There are no social security networks along the Rim, no one willing and obliged to take care of you if you run into trouble. You have to learn to work with your neighbours – help them and they'll help you. And there are dangers out there that you don't see on places like Earth.

"But, on the other hand, you can build a life of your own," she added. "There won't be anyone to force you to conform, or to do as the govern-ment tells you. You'll live and die by your own merits."

Glen had to smile. "It sounds like paradise," he said.

"You have genuine experience," Belinda said. "Go to Greenway if you like, after the conference, or sign up for a stint as a Colonial Marshal. You might find you fit in very well."

"I'll find a way out," Glen promised. He rose to his feet. "Do you want to go fetch Helen while we load up the shuttle?"

Belinda smiled. "Why not?"

———

Belinda had more experience than Glen, she suspected, in securing space stations against intrusions, but she hadn't been able to find anything wrong with his plans. He didn't really have the manpower she thought he needed, yet he'd been right; there really was very little manpower to draw on, now that chaos was gripping the streets. A company of Terran Marines would have been ideal, but they wouldn't be forthcoming. They were on their own.

The real question, she mulled over as she drove back to Glen's apartment, was just what the Governor had in mind. Did he plan to declare himself Emperor? No matter how she looked at it, she couldn't imagine it sticking. Or did he intend to capture the delegates and force them to surrender their power to him? With so many warships primed to enter the system, it struck her as insane to try. Terra Nova would be destroyed in the crossfire if fighting broke out. Or was he genuinely trying to get them to work together?

It wasn't a thought she wanted to contemplate, but it had to be considered. There was more to be gained from pooling resources and power than there was from a civil war, particularly as the Empire would not survive a major conflict without Earth. The Governor might be willing to share the pie if he managed to control it, or get an agreement sorted out for sharing power – or even recognising his independence. But, if it wasn't the Governor who was behind the bizarre plot, who was? How many other suspects were there?

The only people she thought would actually *benefit* from a civil war were the Nihilists themselves. Outright war would destroy the infrastructure of the Core Worlds. Billions would die in the fighting, trillions more would starve as interstellar trade broke down and entire planetary populations ran out of food. The Core Worlds couldn't feed their vast populations without technology. If they lost it, they were doomed.

And, she asked herself, *would that be a bad thing?*

It was a terrifying thought. Even *she* couldn't grasp the sheer enormity of losing the eighty billion lives on Earth, let alone the twenty billion on Terra Nova and several other Core Worlds. One death was graspable, which made it a tragedy, but over a trillion deaths were completely beyond her imagination. But she could see advantages to watching as the Core Worlds died. The colonies, the smaller worlds that weren't degraded or crushed by the Empire's all-encompassing bureaucracy, would have a chance to breathe free.

Horrific, Doug snapped. *Would you condone the deaths of trillions on the off-chance the colonies might manage to rebuild civilisation?*

Belinda parked the car, then put her head in her hands. Doug – or his ghost – was right. The thought of casually sentencing so many people to death was horrific. And yet, part of her regarded the idea with curious detachment. It was tempting. It could be rationalised into becoming acceptable, if she tried. She had no love for the couch potatoes who made up much of the population of the Core Worlds. The Empire might never have started to fall if they'd stood up and forced the politicians to be reasonable.

And yet, was it *right* to sentence them all to death?

She shuddered, remembering something she'd been told right back at the start of her training. It wasn't easy to find men and women who could be trusted with control over planet-killing weapons, then be trusted to fire them upon command. They had a tendency to become reluctant to press the button or, on the other hand, became obsessed with pushing the button. And, her instructors had added, several of them *had* fooled around with weapons that could destroy planets. If the security precautions had failed at any point...

They wanted us to be the perfect operatives, she thought, as she wiped tears from her eyes. *But even we break under the right level of stress.*

The voices were silent as she walked up the stairs and pressed her fingers against Glen's sensor. It acknowledged her, allowing her to step into his apartment. Helen was sitting in front of the terminal, playing a game of chess with someone online. Belinda sighed inwardly, then cleared her throat. Helen looked up at her, then smiled.

"Is it time to go?" She asked. "Really?"

Belinda nodded, heavily. "Yes," she said. "Abandon the game, grab your bag and let's go."

"This guy didn't believe me when I told him my age," Helen said. "He thought I was an adult."

"People born in the Core Worlds are less intelligent than people born in space," Belinda said, although she knew it wasn't just a matter of birth. "Chances are he wouldn't have been allowed to develop his intelligence at a rate that suited him, Helen. He would have been held back by his tutors until he considered it to be natural."

Helen stood up, after forfeiting the game. Belinda glanced at the stats and lifted her eyebrows, impressed. For someone who was only thirteen, Helen had won a surprising number of games against human opponents. No wonder they didn't believe her, Belinda realised, as she closed down the console. Child geniuses were very rare on the Core Worlds.

Because they go into the same educational stream as everyone else, Belinda thought. *And whatever intelligence they have naturally is soon ground out of them.*

"They could use teaching machines," Helen said. "I had one of them teaching *me.*"

"There are unions blocking it," Belinda explained, shortly. The teachers union had managed to prevent the large-scale use of computerised teaching, claiming that students needed human contact, both with their tutors and other students. There were so many unfortunate implications in their words that Belinda was mildly surprised the judge hadn't died laughing, but somehow the union had won the case. "You have to understand that most people care more for their own interests than for the interests of everyone else."

Helen gave her a puzzled look. "Why?"

"Because one person can become disconnected from hundreds of people," Belinda said. "And because we're hardwired to care more about ourselves and our families than anyone else."

"That's stupid," Helen protested.

Belinda nodded. Teaching machines were better than the Empire's current crop of teachers; they both taught by rote, but teaching machines moved their students along as fast as they could, while they didn't try to grope or otherwise abuse their charges. Indeed, separating students from one another might have made it easier for them to learn. Belinda had never been unfortunate enough to study in a classroom on Earth, but she'd heard enough horror stories to know she never wanted her children to go there. Unfortunately, most parents and children on Earth were never given a choice.

"Yes, it is," Belinda said. "Pass me your bag and we'll go down to the car."

Helen seemed oddly reluctant to leave the apartment, something that didn't really surprise Belinda at all, considering her origins. She was quite likely to have problems with wide open spaces, like most people who were born and bred in space. But, somehow, Helen managed to walk down to the garage, clutching Belinda's hand in a surprisingly strong grip. Belinda felt an odd trace of affection and realised, for the first time, why Glen wanted to keep Helen around. There was something about her that invited love and affection.

She isn't as cynical as the kids here, she thought. Children were taught to fear and suspect everyone, either through government-sponsored teaching or simple observation. It didn't take long for kids to realise that the government and their teachers didn't really give a damn about them either. *And she isn't as tainted.*

The streets seemed more crowded as she drove towards the spaceport. She clicked on the radio at Helen's request and logged into a news station, which was babbling on and on about the conference and what it might mean for Terra Nova. The Governor hadn't said anything else, publically, but his Talking Heads were talking up a storm. If the conference failed, if all their hopes fell through, there would almost certainly be outrage on the planet's surface. It was easy to imagine the riots growing out of hand and tearing through whatever remained of the planet's infrastructure. And then Terra Nova would die.

She glanced at Helen, sitting in her seat. "Are you glad to be going back to space?"

"Yes," Helen said. "But will my parents be there?"

"I don't know," Belinda said. "I wish I did."

The thought made her wince. She'd read the file. Helen's parents hadn't been seen since their ship left orbit and headed out beyond the Phase Limit. It was possible they'd return, if they thought their daughter was a hostage, but it was also possible that they would assume the worst and never return. Or that they were already dead. If the unknown plotters had killed several people on Terra Nova to cover their tracks, why not a pair of Traders?

But if they killed her parents, she thought, *why did they leave Helen alive?*

She had nothing good to say about the death-worshippers. But even she had to admit they weren't given to assaulting women or children. Sex, after all, was just another pointless act in their doctrine. Why try to seek pleasure when there was none to be had? Helen could have been killed, perhaps poisoned, and had her body dumped somewhere it would never be found. Instead, they'd kept her. Maybe she had been a hostage after all...

And there's no point in keeping a hostage if there's no one who would be affected by her death, Doug said, at the back of her mind. *Her parents must still be alive.*

I know, Belinda thought back. *But where?*

CHAPTER
THIRTY-TWO

Accordingly, as respect for the law collapsed, chaos threatened to overwhelm large parts of the Core Worlds. The law-keepers were no longer familiar, the law-keepers were, in their own way, threats to the general population. Indeed, there was no justice left in the Empire.

- Professor Leo Caesius, *The Decline of Law and Order and the Rise of Anarchy*

Island One, Glen considered, was beautiful.

The design actually predated space travel, according to the files. It was a giant wheel, spinning slowly against the inky darkness of space, with an entire ecosystem inside the wheel itself. The complex at the centre of the wheel – the hub – was a small industrial base in its own right, geared to keeping the rest of the habitat functional. As they flew closer, they could see greenery inside the wheel, as well as blue lakes of water. Glen couldn't help feeling a stab of envy for the men, women and children who lived in the wheel.

Belinda put her head next to his. "We already know their security is lax," she said. "We're already within missile range. They should have challenged us by now."

Glen winced. She was right. Space combat wasn't his forte, but he knew a laser head warhead could be detonated and inflict colossal damage on the space habitat from considerably further away. Island One was heavily armoured, true, yet it didn't have the defences of a battlestation or the mobility of a starship. It was very much a sitting duck if the shit hit the fan.

He gritted his teeth, then waited as the shuttlecraft flew over the wheel and into the hub. The artificial gravity field took hold of the shuttle, making it rock slightly, as it touched down in the shuttlebay. Moments later, a docking tube appeared from the side of the bay and advanced on the shuttle, linking to the hatch. The shuttlebay itself, Glen noted, was never actually pressurised. He wasn't sure if it was a security precaution or merely a quirk of the unusual design. Island One had been built in the days before artificial gravity had been commonplace and it showed.

The hatch opened with a click, allowing them to leave the shuttle and walk through into the arrival lounge. Glen would have been impressed if he'd been a visiting tourist, he decided, for there was luxury everywhere. But there was very little actual security. Their bags weren't searched, their bodies weren't scanned...there wasn't even a physical search. And, given Belinda's nature, the failure to check the newcomers could prove fatal.

He looked up as a man emerged from a wooden door – a *wooden* door – on the far side of the lounge. Glen had to resist the temptation to roll his eyes like a rude schoolgirl; the man wore a uniform that made him look alarmingly like a raspberry, while even the best tailoring couldn't hide the fact he was developing a paunch. His face had been engineered to show confidence and reliability, which would have been more impressive if it hadn't been so clear that it *was* engineering. The nasty part of Glen's mind wondered what he'd looked like beforehand, the remainder wondered just how easy it would be to slip an entire shuttlecraft of illicit goods past Island One's security. He didn't like the answer.

"Marshal Cheal," the newcomer said. "I'm Luke Doyenne, the Head of Security..."

Glen eyed him, sharply. "And why are you not doing your job?"

Doyenne blinked at him. "I am doing my job..."

Glen lunged forward, catching Doyenne's neck in his hand. The Head of Security gasped, but did nothing. If he was augmented in some way, he wasn't able or willing to use it to break free of Glen's grip. Indeed, he didn't *feel* as if he was used to physical fighting. Glen had seen similar problems among private security officers on the planet's surface. They were never truly tested and so lost condition quickly, leaving them in deep trouble when all hell broke loose. Several had died during the first set of riots on Terra Nova.

"You are not doing your job," Glen snarled, feeling the frustrations of the past week bubbling up within him. "You let us, a group of strangers, land a shuttlecraft in your station without vetting us before we landed. You let us bring weapons onto the station before checking our identities. You didn't check the equipment we brought on the shuttle – a single nuke could have taken out the entire habitat, killing the people you are pledged to defend. You even came to greet us in person rather than sending a minion. We could have taken the hub by now because of your carelessness."

"But...but you're Marshals," Doyenne protested. "You're..."

"You didn't *know* we were Marshals," Glen snapped. He let go of Doyenne and watched, with bitter contempt, as the man rubbed his throat. "You are going to be hosting a conference featuring the most powerful men and women in the galaxy or their designated representatives – and if one of them so much as breaks a nail, it could mean war. Your security is *shit!*"

"We're not supposed to be intrusive," Doyenne said. "And we did have your IDs..."

"Shuttles can be hijacked," Glen pointed out. "IDs can be copied or faked. You didn't *know* who we were and it could easily have gotten everyone killed."

And you missed Belinda too, he added, in the privacy of his own mind. It wasn't something he wanted to point out. Having an ace up his sleeve might come in handy, if the shit really did hit the fan. Besides, she needed to remain undercover until the end of the conference.

"Now," he said, after a moment to let Doyenne recover, "you can show us to our quarters. I will expect a full briefing on Island One's security and current situation in one hour, after which I will take command of the station. You will serve as my second-in-command, but your main duties will consist of working with the various bodyguards to come to a mutually-acceptable agreement on what is considered acceptable. I believe you have done such operations before?"

"I have," Doyenne said. "But these aren't normal security officers."

"I know," Glen said. "I hope your diplomatic skills are up to it."

He smiled at Doyenne. "You'll need some time to recover," he added, darkly. "You'd better find someone else to give us the tour."

"Of course," Doyenne said. His voice sounded harsh, although Glen knew he hadn't inflicted any real damage. "Stacy will show you to your apartments, then assist you in unloading your shuttle."

Glen rolled his eyes as Stacy stepped into the room. She was young, barely older than nineteen, with long blonde hair and a shapely body her maid's uniform was designed to show off to watching eyes. Glen privately supposed that if he had enough money to hire servants, he might well dress them as maids too, just to enjoy the view. But then, Stacy probably made more money than he did, as well as living on Island One. He didn't know many people who *wouldn't* put up with a humiliating uniform in exchange for being isolated from the chaos on the planet below.

Stacy bowed low, exposing her breasts, then straightened up with a smile. "If you'll come with me," she said, "I'll take you to the transit tubes."

Glen followed her, carefully keeping his eyes away from her dangerously short skirt. It was designed to distract as well as entice, he suspected, based on rumours about the lives of people so wealthy they didn't have to give a damn about the Empire's laws. None of Island One's permanent residents would ever see the inside of a courtroom, no matter what they'd done. It galled him to know that there were people even the Marshals could never touch, but he was used to it by now. There was no point in wasting time grumbling about the untouchables.

Besides, they're all up on Island One, he thought. *They won't be causing trouble down on the planet.*

He pushed the thought aside as they reached the transit tubes. Island One was large enough to require public transport, although the transit pods seemed surprisingly luxurious for vehicles that would only be used for a few minutes at most. Stacy started to play tour guide, outlining the vehicle's functions, but Glen tuned her out. It didn't matter to him how the pods functioned, merely how they could be secured. The pod hummed as soon as the doors hissed closed and started to move. There was almost no sense of acceleration at all.

"Pretty good compensators," Belinda commented, from beside him. "And fast too."

Glen nodded as they broke through into the transparent tube. For a moment, his head swum as he tried to grasp the fact that they seemed to be racing *upwards* towards the ground. It was so confusing that he had to look away, but neither Belinda nor Helen seemed to be bothered by the view. The pod must be rotating within the tube, he decided, as they entered the giant wheel and the view vanished again. There was a faint quiver, then the pod's doors hissed open again. He hadn't even felt the pod slow to a halt.

"There are twelve spokes in all," Stacy said, as they walked out of the pod. "Each one houses a transit station you can use to get back to the hub, if necessary. There are additional stations scattered around the wheel and under each of the mansions, but they're not linked to the hub, so you have to change at one of the spokes. It was deemed safer for the children if the systems were separate."

"Clever," Glen said, dryly.

Stacy's expression didn't change as she led them out of a door and into the midst of a forest. Glen stared, utterly charmed. There were trees everywhere, surrounded by flowers and grass; in the distance, he could hear the sound of birds and insects buzzing through the trees. A motion caught his eye and he reached for his pistol, before realising that it was a giant red butterfly. He hadn't seen one outside the zoo in his entire life. They were long since extinct on Earth.

"This is fantastic," Marshal Sitka Singh said. "I..."

"It does have that effect on people," Stacy said, as she led them towards a grassy path. She pointed to a large tree with red and green fruit hanging from the branches. "I should tell you that you can eat just about all of the fruit – and anything else, if you have an enhanced digestive system. If you don't, pick the fruit and check it against the datanet. That should tell you what is safe to eat."

"You actually eat food grown in the wild?" Marshal Gerry Alongshore asked. He'd grown up on Earth. "Really?"

"The habitat is designed to be completely safe," Stacy assured him. "Anything dangerous was simply not permitted to enter the biosphere.

There aren't even any plants or animals here from other worlds, apart from Earth."

Belinda leaned forward. "No dangerous animals?"

"None at all," Stacy said. "Most of the animals we introduced to the habitat are small and harmless. The only dangerous critters allowed here are guard dogs, which aren't really part of the biosphere. It's perfectly safe."

"Good," Glen said.

He couldn't help being torn between feeling impressed and a strange kind of contempt as they walked over a stone bridge – there were so many fish in the stream that it seemed to be teeming with life – and up to the shores of a silver lake. There were a dozen small huts, resting on stilts, with wooden staircases leading down into the water. He saw a large fish – a dolphin, if he identified it correctly – break the water, then vanish back under the waves. It seemed alarmingly safe and tranquil.

"These are your quarters," Stacy said. She seemed unaware of their astonishment as she led them over the bridge to the huts. "Each of them has access to the datanet, food distribution network and everything else you might need. If you want to swim, you can just undress and walk down the stairs into the water. There's small boats and toys in the furthest hut..."

Glen cleared his throat. "We're not here for a holiday," he said, although he knew that part of him would be very tempted to simply relax. Maybe Doyenne had an excuse for his lax attitude after all. If the landscape hadn't curved slightly, it would be alarmingly easy to forget that they were on a space habitat. "We have work to do."

"Of course," Stacy said. "But we were told to offer you our best guest accommodations."

Glen stepped into the nearest hut and shook his head. It managed to combine primitivism with modern luxury, pleasing both. There was a large double-sized bed, a smaller bed in a separate room he suspected was intended for Helen, a viewscreen, a cabinet full of expensive alcohol and a computer terminal. In one corner, there was a glass sheet allowing him to peer down into the water below. Hundreds of fish were swimming around the stilts, glimmering with light and life.

"It's unnatural," Belinda said, quietly. "And it may not be sustainable."

Helen looked up at her. "Why?"

"They only added the life they wanted," Belinda said. "If they didn't copy Earth's biosphere, even on a limited basis, there will be all sorts of holes. I'd expect the biosphere to fall apart without constant maintenance."

She turned to look at Stacy, who had been showing the other Marshals their huts. "Where do you stay when you're not working?"

"There's a section on the other side of the wheel for us," Stacy explained. "It's not quite as nice as here" – she waved a hand to indicate the hut – "but it's pretty good and accommodation is free. We spend seven hours on duty each day, then the rest of the time is ours. The only real downside is that we can't go to the planet."

"That's something of a blessing," Glen assured her. "Right now, you should be glad to be here."

"I am," Stacy said. "I could spend the rest of my life here."

Belinda leaned forward. "What's it like working here?"

"It isn't bad," Stacy said. She shrugged. "I can't give you specifics, though."

"Of course not," Belinda said. "But do you have fun?"

"Mostly," Stacy said. "There are always some issues, of course, that need to be handled. But otherwise we have fun."

"Thank you," Glen said.

"We're always available," Stacy assured him. "Just call if you need us."

Too much luxury, Glen thought.

He rubbed his forehead as Stacy turned away. The sheer luxury surrounding them would dull their senses and leave them calm, too calm. It would be easy to lose their edge, which could prove fatal if the conference was attacked. He scowled, then reached for the datapad and glanced at the list of services Stacy had mentioned. They ranged from childcare, which was unsurprising, to massages and outright sexual services. There were no prices mentioned, he noted, which wasn't really a surprise. Anyone who could afford to visit Island One, even for a few days, would be rich enough to pay.

"This place is strange," Helen announced. "Like it's in space but not in space."

"True," Belinda agreed. She looked around the room, then smiled at Glen. "Where were you planning to sleep?"

Glen felt his cheeks heat like a schoolboy's. He hadn't told the staff to arrange a double bed; hell, he wasn't even sure how that had happened. There were several other huts, he knew; it was quite possible that one of them was intended for Belinda. And then he realised he was being teased.

"You can have one of the other huts," he said, stiffly. It didn't help when Belinda started to giggle at him. "And what about...about S-C-H-O-O-L?"

"I can spell," Helen said, sounding offended. "And it wouldn't be so bad up here."

Glen sighed. Helen had watched a series of programs set in planetary schools and she'd been thoroughly horrified. The hell of it was that the programs hadn't been particularly exaggerated. If someone happened to be tough, good at sports and capable of looking after himself, schooling wasn't too bad. But if someone happened to be weak, unpopular and incapable of self-defence...being in school on a planet would be a foretaste of hell.

"No, it probably won't," he said. The documents he'd seen had made school on Island One sound like heaven. "But we'll see to it tomorrow."

Belinda elbowed him. "Growing lax already?"

"Unfortunately," Glen said. "Maybe we should sleep on the floor, just to keep ourselves in the proper vile mood for security work. And then we should not bother to wash either."

"I think there would be complaints," Belinda said. She smirked. "Unless you happen to enjoy walking around smelling like recruits staggering off the training field for the first time."

"Yuk," Helen said.

"You have no idea," Belinda said.

Glen glanced at his watch. "We'll eat, then go back to the security centre and start going through procedures, one by one," he said. "And then we can hold drills until the attendees finally arrive. How does that sound?"

"Lazy," Belinda said. She smiled, then turned to step out onto the balcony. "But it's probably the best idea."

"Good," Glen said. He followed her out and stared at the silver lake. Belinda was right. The more he looked at it, the more unnatural it seemed. "Where are you planning to sleep?"

"I think I'll stay here," Belinda said. "It's a comfortable floor."

Glen looked down at the wooden floor, then laughed nervously. "You have got to be kidding."

"Try sleeping in a swamp sometime," Belinda muttered. She cleared her throat. "Besides, I really think we should stay close together."

CHAPTER

THIRTY-THREE

A rich man could buy his way out of trouble. Everyone knew it. Furthermore, there was no way a poor man could get out of trouble. This had always been true, but it was now utterly unmistakable. As rumours got out about how the Civil Guard treated prisoners, the general population hovered on the brink of revolt.

- Professor Leo Caesius, *The Decline of Law and Order and the Rise of Anarchy*

Belinda didn't blame Glen and his team for being impressed with Island One. It was a remarkable creation, after all, even if the technology behind the space habitat was deceptively simple. But the more she looked at it, the more convinced she became that the entire system was simply not designed to serve as a secure conference facility. The residents might be rich and powerful, but even they hadn't designed their home to stand off a battlefleet.

Not that they could have done so, she thought, as Doyenne talked them though the security system. *The station that can stop a battlefleet hasn't been built.*

She allowed her mind to wander, probing the habitat's datanet, only to discover that it was actually more secure than anything she'd seen on Terra Nova. There was a public datanet, accessible everywhere, that didn't seem to be connected to the private datanet; indeed, there seemed to be *two* private datanets. It appeared to be impossible to alter one of them without direct access to the computer core, while the second didn't actually seem to do anything. She made a mental note to ask why there were two, then she started to skim through the public datanet. Half of it seemed to be nothing more than entertainment, ranging from flicks and blue porno movies to VR simulations, while the remainder appeared to be centred around household management. The staff had regular access to the system.

Maybe the second private network is for corporate staff, she thought. It was as good a theory as any. *Or maybe there are more datanets out of my sensor range, one for each corporation.*

"You're experienced," Glen said, breaking into her thoughts. "How would you attack Island One?"

Belinda considered it, carefully. How would *she* do it? And what would she actually *want*?

"It would depend," she said, finally. "If I wanted to take hostages, I'd try to surround the station with battleships and force it to surrender. But that isn't likely to work here."

Glen nodded. Each of the delegates would be bringing a small fleet of escorts with them, while Terra Nova's defence forces were far from insignificant, even though Belinda had her doubts about how many of them were fit for action. The Nihilists – or whoever – would consider launching a direct military attack futile, assuming they had the firepower to try.

"They'd have to get people onboard," Glen mused. "And that would be difficult."

"Yeah," Belinda said. Glen had revamped the security procedures as soon as they'd started work. No one else would be permitted to land on Island One without a full security sweep, even though it would put a lot of pressure on the staff. "And then they'd have to get away from the station afterwards."

She winced. Hostage-rescue missions were always tricky, even at the best of times, and dealing with hostage-takers was even worse. They would want to hang on to the hostages long enough to escape, while the security forces would want the hostages back as soon as possible. It was never easy to balance the two competing requirements, even without the prospect of outright treachery. She'd been on the ground when a planetary governor *had* been treacherous and all five of the hostages had been killed in the crossfire.

"But if they're Nihilists, they'll want to die," Glen mused. "And if they can take the station with them..."

"They got a shitload of weapons from somewhere," Belinda said, although that was no surprise. The Core Worlds might be thoroughly hoplophobic, but ask in the right place and almost anything could be purchased. "Maybe they could get a nuke. Or simply rig one up with the right equipment."

"Bastards," Glen muttered. "Why are they never controlled?"

Belinda shrugged. "Because making nukes is easy, because finding the raw materials is easy too and because there are plenty of people with both the skills to make them and the desire to use them for perfectly legitimate purposes."

Glen nodded. "But why aren't they secured?"

"Because it can take years to get a permit to use a nuke for any purpose," Belinda said. "It's often quicker to build a nuke for yourself than apply for permission."

She shook her head, slowly. The blunt fact was that if the Nihilists managed to detonate a nuke onboard Island One, they were all going to die. Even a near-miss would be dangerous, despite the hullmetal sheathing the giant space habitat. They'd have to run through a whole series of emergency drills, just to make sure the population knew what to do if the shit hit the fan. It was quite likely that emergency drills had been reduced or cancelled altogether, just to keep the wealthy residents happy. No one ever paid any attention to the endless flight safety announcements made before shuttlecraft departed, in any case.

"Wankers," Glen said.

Belinda paid close attention as they ran through an endless series of checks and rechecks, then finally headed back to the wheel for dinner. Marshal Singh didn't seem to like her very much, Belinda noted, although she was definitely competent. Belinda had a suspicion that Singh regarded either the Civil Guard or the Military Police as buffoons, a description that wouldn't have been too inaccurate. Her dislike certainly didn't seem to be *personal*. Her partner, Marshal Alongside, seemed quiet, but very competent. Belinda couldn't help feeling relieved, even though she would have preferred Marines. They wouldn't have bitched so much about adding extra levels of security to Island One.

And we could have tested it properly too, Belinda thought. She knew the Governor had only had a month to set up the conference, but surely he could have assigned additional firepower to guard the conference chambers? Or was he worried about having so many armed guards around proud and touchy men? He wasn't the Emperor, after all, or even a Grand Senator.

"It's a good thing they're not going to charge us for this," Marshal Alongside said, when they were back at the huts. There was no dining hall, it seemed; the food was served in a massive clearing, in the open air. "The food here is staggeringly expensive."

Belinda glanced at the menu. Growing up on Greenway and then serving in the Marine Corps had left her with very little food snobbery. The more she ate, the better; taste was always a secondary concern. Food was food – and childish likes and dislikes were embarrassing liabilities in the field. But if she'd had expensive tastes and the money to afford them, Island One would have had something for her. There were hundreds of dishes on the menu, sourced from all over the galaxy. She couldn't help wondering how long they would still be available as interstellar trade ground to a halt.

"Indulge yourself," Glen said, "but no alcohol. Or anything else that would render you unfit for duty."

"Like drugs," Belinda offered, brightly. She pretended not to see the sharp look Marshal Singh aimed at her. "There's a whole list of available substances here."

Glen looked annoyed, although not at her. It took Belinda a moment to realise that most of the substances were illegal, even on Earth and the Core Worlds. Seeing them offered so blatantly had to offend his lawman's soul. But then, he'd never seen the luxuries offered to Prince Roland to keep him from actually trying to think for himself. There had always been one set of laws for the rich and another for the poor.

"Eat what you can," she advised. She tapped the menu, choosing a large steak and fries for herself. It would provide enough substance for several days, if necessary. "And then we can get some sleep."

Night slowly fell over Island One as they ate, the giant light-tube dimming until the stars started to come out overhead. They seemed to be moving slowly, something that puzzled her until she recalled that the wheel was spinning. Flickering dots of light, high overhead, had to be the network of security satellites and automated weapons platforms surrounding the Island One. It looked impressive, on paper, but Belinda had no illusions. They wouldn't be able to stand up to a determined assault.

"Look," Helen called. "What are *those*?"

Belinda followed her gaze. Dancing flickers of light hung in the air, spinning through the trees at the edge of the clearing. There was a faint buzzing as they grew closer, barely audible even to her enhanced hearing, then faded away as they withdrew into the forest and vanished. It was an utterly charming sight.

"Fireflies, I think," she said. They might well have been enhanced by the biologists, but there was no way to be sure. She'd never seen them glowing so brightly before. "They only come out at night."

She had to smile at Helen's expression. The girl would have grown up on her starship, spending only a small amount of her life on space stations or settled asteroids. None of them, she suspected, would be like Island One. RockRats had a tendency to grow wild gardens in their asteroids, but Traders tended to shy away from plants and gardens. They preferred to grow their foodstuffs in vats.

But they miss out on natural beauty, she thought, as her enhanced vision caught sight of other animals moving through the trees. A snowy white owl flew overhead, calling out to its prey as it faded into the distance. None of the animals seemed very scared of humanity, something that amused her; it was unlikely that Island One's residents tried to hunt. Or maybe they did, on the far side of the wheel. There was no shortage of land space that could be turned into a hunting ground.

But it wouldn't be quite the same, she mused. *Nothing like hunting for real.*

She looked down at her steak and fries as they arrived, then started to eat. Helen had ordered a burger and fries on Glen's advice, although Belinda doubted Helen could eat the whole meal. The burger alone was larger than her head! The other two Marshals had ordered meals from other worlds, featuring very rare animals. They probably cost more, Belinda noted, than their entire salary for the year. She wondered, vaguely, what Stacy and the others ate, then decided she didn't want to know. Island One's residents would never notice if their staff ate steak and fries every day.

Her steak was perfect, absolutely tender. She shook her head in amused irritation, wondering what Augustus would have made of Island One. He probably owned a home on the habitat, judging by the list of other wealthy men and women who had places to stay well away from Terra Nova. Keeping Violet on Island One might not have been a favour to her though, Belinda knew. It was quite possible that the kids were spoilt brats.

Or would they play with the servant families?

The thought made her shudder. Greenway hadn't had any real social classes, but there had been some colonist families who were more equal than others. On Earth, it would be literally impossible – *would* have been literally impossible, she corrected herself – for someone from a lower class background to meet and befriend someone from the Grand Families. Even if they did, there would always be envy between the two. What would happen if Island One ever had to exist on its own, isolated from the rest of the universe?

"You're being quiet," Glen said. "Penny for your thoughts?"

"My thoughts are a credit apiece," Belinda said. "I'll be glad when this is over?"

And what will I do then? She asked herself. *I can't go back to the Pathfinders – or even be a Rifleman.*

The ghosts offered no answer. But then, she hadn't really expected one.

Helen yawned, then pushed the rest of her burger aside. Belinda scowled, remembering precisely what her mother would have said about wasting food, then decided it wasn't really Helen's fault. Besides, she'd eaten three-fourths of the burger and all of her fries. It was impressive, given how thin she was. The genetic engineers must have given her one hell of a metabolism.

"Come on," Glen said. "We'll go back to the hut."

Belinda followed them, allowing her enhanced senses to peer through the darkness. The lake was glowing faintly, allowing her to see fish still swimming in the water. She started as a much larger fish swam through the water, then vanished back into the darkness. It didn't look harmful, but she would have been astonished if she'd been swimming and run right into the creature. She wondered, absently, if it only ever came out at night.

The interior of the hut was brightly lit, somewhat to her amusement. Glen lowered the lights, then escorted Helen into her bedroom and pointed her towards the bed. Helen didn't argue, a sure sign of tiredness; she merely picked up her bag and started searching through it for nightclothes. Belinda watched, then turned and walked onto the balcony. Silence descended at once, even to her enhanced ears. The only sound she could hear was water lapping against the stilts, far below.

"She's in bed," Glen said, as he walked out beside her. "And I think she was completely exhausted."

"She probably did some exploring while we were in the security complex," Belinda said, practically. "You make a good dad."

Glen looked away, his face twisting into bitter grief. Belinda cursed her own mistake under her breath. Standards of medical care in the Core Worlds had been slipping for years, at least partly because of an obsession with quotas rather than actual healthcare, but it was still rare to lose a wife and child in childbirth. She couldn't blame him for latching on to Helen, even if it was potentially quite dangerous. He still *wanted* to be a dad.

But what will you do, Belinda asked silently, *when her parents come back?*

She sighed, then reached out and tapped his shoulder. "Fancy a midnight swim?"

"I don't have any swimming gear," Glen said. At least he could *swim*. Roland hadn't been able to swim until Belinda had taught him. "I could find some..."

"Or you could swim naked," Belinda said. She had to fight to keep from giggling at his expression. For a man who'd grown up on Earth, he had a surprising amount of body-modesty. "It's not very cold down there."

She shucked off her shirt, then her trousers, before she could think better of it, dropping them down on the wooden balcony. Glen stared at her in disbelief as her underwear landed on top of the pile of clothing, then she turned and made her way down the steps into the water. It was warmer than she'd expected, warm enough to be comfortable instantly. Compared to the water tests of the Crucible, it was paradise itself.

"Come on in," she called. "The water's lovely."

Glen hesitated, then undressed too. Belinda turned away, granting him some privacy as he stepped down to join her, concealing her amusement at how he tried to look everywhere, but directly at her. His reaction was definitely odd, for a man from Earth. People were so closely jammed together in the megacities that modesty was rare. Women had a harder time of it, but then they always did. Rape was so common on Earth that it was barely noticed by anyone other than the victim.

Bastards, she thought.

She winked at him, then swam away with easy strokes. Glen followed her. He wasn't as good as her in the water, even without augmentations, but he was better than she'd expected. There were no deep swimming pools on Earth, at least in the megacities. Someone might get hurt or drowned and then there would be lawsuits. The last time she'd looked, the liability waivers on Earth were hundreds of pages long and covered contingencies she rather doubted happened in real life.

"We shouldn't get distracted," Glen said. "I..."

Belinda ducked beneath the water, then caught his feet and yanked, hard. Glen went down under the water as Belinda popped up again, then surfaced, coughing and sputtering.

"You need to relax," Belinda said. She kicked herself upwards, allowing her breasts to bobble in front of her. His eyes followed them, then he looked away. "Really."

Glen splashed her with water, then gave chase as she started to swim away from him. Belinda giggled, then let him chase her back to the hut and up the steps, then into the shower room. It was easily large enough for two people...she saw him hesitate, then sighed. He was far from unattractive, and it had been far too long.

Try harder, Pug offered. *Most men are too dumb to notice that you're trying to seduce them.*

Shut up, Belinda thought. *Please.*

She looked at Glen and threw caution to the winds. "Come here," she ordered, and pulled him into the shower. She felt his body respond to her as soon as she touched him. It would have been grossly unprofessional at any other time, but it felt right now. "We both need to relax."

He opened his mouth, then stopped as she kissed him. His arms encircled her and held her, tightly. Belinda smiled to herself, then kissed him again as she felt him hardening. It had been too long for both of them. She felt him tense as she pushed him down and straddled him, then relax as she kissed him again. And then she mounted him and pushed down, hard.

Afterwards, they washed themselves clean, walked over to the bed and fell asleep, hand in hand. And the ghosts in her head remained silent.

CHAPTER
THIRTY-FOUR

And laws were now being passed for the benefit of the powerful, rather than the population as a whole. Who could respect a law that destroyed all businessmen without powerful connections? That criminalised activity that was utterly harmless? That took law enforcement officials away from serious crimes to enforce laws that made no sense or destroyed lives?

- Professor Leo Caesius, *The Decline of Law and Order and the Rise of Anarchy*

Glen jerked awake as he heard someone screaming, then looked around as one hand scrabbled for the pistol he normally kept within arm's reach. Beside him, Belinda sat upright, one hand extended in a pointing gesture that would have looked absurd, if he hadn't known how many weapons implants had been inserted into her body. She looked at him, then jumped out of bed and headed towards Helen's room. Glen followed, after yanking on a dressing gown. The last thing Helen needed to see was both of them naked.

"Stay here," he ordered, as he opened the door. Helen was rolling backwards and forwards on her bed, tangling in her bedding, screaming even though she was still asleep. "Helen!"

Helen's entire body shook violently, then fell limp on the bed. Her eyes opened a moment later, wide and frightened. Sweat dripped from her forehead as she stared at him, numbly, as if she wasn't quite sure where she was. Glen remembered the nightmares she'd had earlier and cursed himself for assuming they'd gone away for good. He should have organised some help for her before they reasserted their grip on her mind.

He stepped forward, sat down next to her and wrapped her in a hug. Her entire body was shaking, her nightclothes so drenched in sweat that he thought for a horrified moment that she'd wet herself. He hadn't seen anyone have so violent a nightmare since raiding a den of drug addicts who'd cut their star dust with something that definitely wasn't even remotely safe to smoke, even in small doses. Five of the seven young men he'd seen hadn't survived the experience. But Helen wasn't taking anything to make her have such awful nightmares.

"It's ok," he said. She clung to him as if he were a life preserver. "It's going to be ok."

Belinda stepped into the room, wearing a dressing gown that concealed almost all of her body. Glen couldn't tell if she was trying to be reassuring or if she was regretting their one-night stand. He cursed his own weakness, but without heat. It had been far too long since he'd last slept with anyone and, despite Isabel's best efforts, he'd never dated anyone since his wife had died. Part of him would always wonder if he'd killed his wife and unborn daughter by getting her pregnant.

"Dreams can be really bad," Belinda said. She knelt beside Glen and stroked Helen's head. "What did you see in your dream, Helen?"

"They were cutting me open," Helen said. "I could *feel* them cutting into my body and..."

She shuddered, again. "It hurt so much and it just wouldn't *stop!*"

"It sounds like a bad nightmare," Belinda said. She looked over at Glen. "Has she had these nightmares before?"

"Sometimes," Glen said, grimly. "Do you think there's a real problem?"

"Maybe," Belinda said. "but I've always had odd dreams when I moved from posting to posting."

Glen scowled. He'd had nightmares too, shortly after his wife had died, and *they'd* never truly faded. Patty had advised him to visit the headshrinkers, but he'd never cared to risk his career to their whims. Headshrinkers were rarely helpful, while a word from them could destroy a career, if said to the right person. He hadn't wanted to be told that he had a rare psychological disorder and be summarily sacked. It had happened far too often.

He considered checking to see if there was a psychologist on Island One, before dismissing the idea. Even if there was, he didn't want to see Helen sectioned by the mental health authorities or thrown into care...or, for that matter, face the barrage of accusations he *knew* would be hurled at him. Every little dispute could be blamed on abuse, even if the so-called victim denied it. And the stigma from such accusations would never fade away.

Years ago, he'd arrested a young man whose social worker had ruined his life. It had been hard, very hard, to blame him for murdering the silly bitch. But the law was inflexible when the suspect was poor. He'd been transported to a colony world, where he'd been sentenced to twenty years of indentured servitude. Somehow, Glen suspected that he'd be happier as an indent than a citizen on Terra Nova.

"You'll be fine," Belinda said. "We just have to learn to move with the changes in our lives."

She helped Helen to her feet, then led her towards the shower. Glen watched them go, then stood and walked back into the main room, where he checked the terminal. Thankfully, the soundproofing on the hut was good enough to prevent the others from hearing the screaming and charging in with guns drawn. The chances of an accident would be far too high.

He sat down at the desk and checked his messages, then sighed. What had they been doing last night? Had it been a one-night stand or the start of something better? Or was he just being a silly old man worrying about it. Neither of them had time to consider the prospects for a relationship when they were meant to be securing Island One, with a dangerously understaffed force. The security staff weren't *that* bad, he'd decided after he'd reminded them of the dangers involved in taking anything for granted, but they were still undermanned and inexperienced. Glen had been seriously considering begging for extra manpower when it had become clear there would be none to be had.

The important messages were short and to the point. Island One would receive its first guests later in the day, including the Governor, Patty and Thomas Augustus. Glen had heard of him – who hadn't? – and suspected he would make a reasonable delegate to represent Terra Nova's industry. The remainder of the delegates would arrive over the next two days – there was some leeway built into the schedule – and the conference would begin as soon as they were all assembled. It was, Glen suspected, a testament to the sheer urgency of the conference that most of the formalities were being skipped.

And that no one has any actual experience of holding a summit conference, he added, in the privacy of his own mind. He'd checked, just out of curiosity, and the last time the Empire had ever negotiated with *anyone* as an equal had been towards the end of the Unification Wars. *Normally, they'd just send a battlefleet to hand out the demands and administer a thumping if anyone decided to reject the demands.*

He shook his head, tiredly, the list of attendees was long, with representatives coming from all over the Core Worlds and even a few of the closer colonies. It would be a pain to organise, even with the best will in the world, while there were plenty of worlds that wouldn't even *know* about the conference until it was too late. Even the fastest starships took six months to travel from Earth to the edge of the Empire. Hell, he knew, there would be worlds that hadn't heard about the Fall of Earth yet.

It had normally been a major problem for the Empire that it took so long to send out the orders, then get a report back from the people on the ground. But, for once, the time delay might be working in the Empire's favour. By the time the rest of the Empire knew that Earth was gone, the Governor might have hammered out a compromise that would leave the rest of the Core Worlds intact, ready to deal with any disobedient colony worlds. There would still be a great deal of chaos, not least because of how badly the Empire's military had been pruned back before the Fall of Earth, but it would be survivable. Or so the Governor clearly hoped.

"Glen," Belinda said. She stepped back into the room and sat down on the bed. "I think Helen needs some stability in her life."

Glen nodded. It made sense, he supposed. Starship life was very stable. Helen had probably reacted badly to being taken off her ship and held as a hostage, then living with Glen, because it was inherently unpredictable. And then she'd had to change homes again...

"I was planning to go out to the colonies," he said. "If Helen's parents don't show up by the end of the conference, I'll take her with me."

"You might go into trading instead," Belinda offered. "Helen would prefer that, I think. If, of course, you're serious about adopting her."

Glen considered, then nodded. It wasn't the sort of life he'd care for, but it would have its upsides. Part of him was tempted to ask if Belinda would like to come with him, yet he couldn't get the words through his lips. It would have been tempting fate.

He stood and checked his watch. "We'll go for breakfast once we've showered and dressed," he said. "And then take Helen to school."

Breakfast was as staggeringly luxurious as dinner – and, if anything, even more elaborate. Glen ordered a small plate of bacon and eggs – careful to specify a small plate – and shook his head in disbelief when a giant plate of food was placed in front of him. Belinda ordered a large plate and ended up with an even bigger pile of food. Somehow, she managed to eat it all, while Helen ate a plate of bacon sandwiches and scrambled eggs. Glen honestly had no idea how she managed to remain so thin when she ate so much. But she hadn't shown so large an appetite on Terra Nova.

"I checked the updates," he said, and outlined what he'd been told. "If I go to greet my superiors, will you keep an eye on the security lounge?"

"I should say hello to Mr. Augustus," Belinda said. "But that can wait."

Glen gave her a sidelong look. "You know him?"

"We've met," Belinda said. She shrugged. "He offered me a job."

"Well," Glen said, after a long moment. "If I hadn't believed you beforehand, Belinda, I certainly believe you now."

Belinda giggled.

"It would have been tempting if I hadn't had another task," she said. "Has there been any progress on identifying Keystone's killer?"

"None," Glen said. "I specifically requested that I be informed if anything were found, but..."

He shrugged. He'd been ordered to concentrate on the conference and leave the whole issue of the Nihilists and their warehouse to other Marshals. Given how few Marshals there were, it was quite possible that the whole issue had been left in limbo. It was insane, in his view, to leave a group of known terrorists free to act as they saw fit, but there was little choice, not if they wanted to maintain such a strong presence on the streets.

And he who would be strong everywhere is strong nowhere, he thought, remembering Isabel's death. If there had been more reaction forces poised, ready to spring...she might have survived. *We don't even have the manpower to patrol the streets.*

Belinda sighed. "Do you know if they even sent a team to investigate?"

"They should have done," Glen said. "The Campus Police were informed. And there was a second body in the apartment."

He shrugged, again. "They might not give a damn now," he added. "What use is a dead student?"

Belinda snorted. "What use is a *living* student?"

Glen watched the servants take the plates away, including quite a bit of leftover food, and then stood. "Come on," he said. "Let's go find the schoolhouse."

The tube station was nearby, buried underground. Glen was moderately impressed; the tube system was fast and efficient, not something that could be said of public transport on the planet below. When they emerged from the station, they found themselves in the midst of a small village. A sign identified it as Hundred-Acre Woodsville.

Helen frowned. "What's an Acre?"

"It's an old style of measurement," Belinda said. She paused, obviously consulting her implants. "Roughly four thousand square metres, I believe."

"So the village is really called Four Hundred Thousand Square Metres?" Helen asked. "Why the odd name?"

"It's just a name," Belinda said. "Give us a few thousand years and people might forget what kilometres are too."

"It isn't the first name to hang around without anyone knowing what it actually means," Glen offered. The village looked natural, too natural. One long look was enough to tell him that it was designed to an ideal, rather than reality. "There's a planet called Washington, but who or what was Washington?"

"A great military leader and rebel," Belinda supplied. "The Empire removed him and most of his allies from the history books. The last thing they want is to encourage rebellions against their authority."

Glen smiled, then walked down towards the schoolhouse. It was already open, with a friendly-looking teacher standing in front of the door, waving a handful of children into the classroom. She looked so friendly that Glen wondered, for a long moment, if she actually *was* the teacher. Most of the teachers he'd met looked stressed out, their eyes flickering to and fro as if they could prevent mischief if only they saw it. They tended to take early retirement after working long enough to earn their pension.

But here, there won't be any bad kids, he thought. *And even if there were, the teacher is being paid enough to deal with them.*

"Marshal Cheal, Lieutenant Lawson," the teacher said. "I'm Mrs Teacher."

Belinda gaped. "Seriously?"

"Working name," the teacher said, with a shrug. She motioned for them to enter the classroom. "We have teaching machines here for the morning, then the children engage in unstructured play or enhanced learning. I understand your charge has never been in a planetary classroom?"

"Correct," Glen said.

"Lucky you," the teacher said. She looked down at Helen. "Do you have any educational certificates?"

"Not with me," Helen said, very quietly.

"And we're not sure how long we're going to have you," the teacher mused. "We'll start you on a handful of basic exams, then start proper learning tomorrow once we know where you stand. Or we can take more exams for certificates, if you like."

"Don't worry about it," Glen said. He had enough contacts to obtain the certificates, if necessary. No doubt it would be, if Helen ever decided she wanted to work on one of the Core Worlds. "Just work on her education."

The teacher smiled. "Of course," she said. "Do you want a quick tour?"

"Yes, please," Glen said.

His school on Earth had been horrific. Indeed, one of the reasons he'd gone into law enforcement was through having too close a view of the very worst of human nature. There had been no order, no discipline... and the stronger students had bullied the younger ones mercilessly. Even now, he wouldn't have willingly walked into one of those schools without a platoon of armed guards in powered combat armour.

But Island One's school was lovely. There were no bad children, clearly, as nothing was nailed down or cheap enough not to be missed, if it were stolen. A handful of kids sat in front of teaching machines, while several others were working together. Oddly, they seemed to range from seven to fifteen. And none of them looked unpleasant. They even threw shy smiles at Helen.

"Acceptable," he said, feeling a stab of bitterness. If he'd had a chance for proper schooling, he asked himself, would it have made his life better? "We'll come back for her tonight?"

"That's fine," the teacher assured him. "The parents often come back late for their children, so the school is actually open 24/7. If she needs a nap, there's a bedroom through there and we have food and drink shipped in. Does she have any special requirements? I notice she's not on the system."

Neural link, Glen thought. "No, she doesn't," he said. "Just...take care of her."

He waved goodbye to Helen as she sat down in front of one of the teaching machines, activating it with easy competence. Belinda nodded, then followed Glen as he walked out of the schoolhouse and back towards the tube station. The village was slowly coming to life, he noted, with men and women emerging from their homes and heading to work. They must be rich enough to afford a home on Island One, but not among the richest people in the system, he decided. But merely living on Island One would give their kids an enviable start at life.

"She'll be fine," Belinda reassured him. "And she will have to resume her education wherever she goes."

"I know," Glen admitted. "But I will still worry about her."

"Dad-shock," Belinda diagnosed. "It gets them every time."

Glen looked down at the stone pathway, then grinned. "Let's hold a security drill," he said. "That always cheers people up."

"I suppose it would," Belinda said. "But you'll also have them mad at you. And plotting revenge."

"I'll survive," Glen said. The great advantage of drills was that it allowed mistakes to be made – and learned from – without a real emergency. But the disadvantage was that too many drills could convince people not to take them seriously. "And they need the practice."

"Yeah," Belinda said. She lowered her voice as they passed a pair of teenage girls, both looking remarkably unafraid at sighting strangers. "Just remember – this isn't a military base. You can't hold them to the same standards."

Glen snorted. "No," he said. "I'll hold them to higher standards."

THIRTY-FIVE

Indeed, laws were being passed that made being in debt a criminal offense. A debtor could be seized and arrested, then sold to a settlement corporation – slavery, in other words – merely for being in debt. And yet, there was hardly anyone in the Empire who was free from debt.

- Professor Leo Caesius, *The Decline of Law and Order and the Rise of Anarchy*

The staff were looking rather harried, Belinda noted, as she stepped into Island One's command centre. Two days of relentless drills had that effect, as Glen forced them to run through their procedures for each and every conceivable emergency. By now, they considered themselves ready for anything, although Belinda had her doubts. It was her experience that preparing for the expected – or the probable – tended to weaken one's resistance to the unexpected.

She sucked in her breath as she caught sight of the holographic display. Hundreds of starships were slowly circling Island One, each one watching the others warily. Belinda felt a pang of loss as she realised that, to all intents and purposes, the battle squadrons might as well belong to different fleets. The Imperial Navy had been fragmenting for years, as squadron commanders started to consider their interests ahead of the service, but the Fall of Earth had shattered the remaining ties. They were no longer part of the same navy.

"We have thirty-seven different squadrons within range," the operator said. He was young enough to be Belinda's son, assuming she'd started early. "So far, they're not doing anything hostile, but their sensors are at full capacity and they've rejected the idea of leave on Terra Nova."

"Hard to blame them," Belinda muttered. The latest outbreak of violence had threatened to consume an entire megacity. It was impossible to tell if the riots were being planned by an outside force or if they were random, but it hardly mattered. Terra Nova was on the brink of falling into complete chaos. "What about our own defences?"

"Ready to spring to life," the operator assured her. He was too young to grasp the truth. If the fleets started firing at each other, Island One would be destroyed in the crossfire. There were thirty-two heavily armoured battleships out there and Island One was flimsy by comparison. "But we have them stepped down for the moment."

"Then keep them stepped down unless the shit hits the fan," Belinda ordered. There was far too much tension out there. The Governors, Admirals and outright Warlords who had been invited to the conference distrusted each other, not without reason. Only the prospect of a share in the pie without fighting had brought them to the negotiation table. "And then be prepared to cover Island One alone."

. She walked over to another console and watched as the shuttles flew towards Island One. It had taken nearly an hour of argument before the visitors had agreed to allow Island One's shuttles to pick them up, rather than use their own. They had to agree it was more secure – and everyone would be under the same restriction – but it didn't befit their dignity. Belinda wasn't surprised, but she was more than a little disappointed. The Fall of Earth should have told them just how serious the situation had become.

One by one, the shuttles landed, their occupants greeted by the Governor and his team of advisors. Island One's staff had done a good job, Belinda conceded reluctantly, at assigning the visitors to houses of their own. The Governor spoke a few brief words of greeting – he used the same words every time – and then allowed the staff to take the visitors to the assigned quarters. Perhaps the sheer luxury of the space habitat would help them to relax, Belinda considered, or perhaps they'd see it as an attempt to soften them up before negotiations began. There was no way to know.

"Keep an eye on them," she warned, as she wandered back to the near-orbit display. "And let me know if anything changes."

She scowled up at the display. The starships were still watching each other, but so far nothing had gone seriously wrong. But the presence of so much firepower, under so many different commands, worried her. There hadn't been anything like it since the Unification Wars. Would they really fire on their former comrades? Or bombard a planet that was almost as important, historically speaking, as Earth?

Probably, she thought. Apart from the Marines, who shared the same basic training regardless of their eventual destination, there was no truly unified military force within the Empire. The Imperial Navy had long been assigned to homeports, the Imperial Army's regiments were raised from separate planets, as was the Civil Guard. *They're no longer capable of being loyal to an abstract concept like the Empire.*

The thought bothered her more than she cared to admit. It was impossible to ignore the fact that someone had destroyed the Slaughterhouse, that the Marine Corps was homeless and largely friendless. What would happen to *them* if the conference failed? She looked back at the image of the Governor, greeting yet another party of newcomers, and gritted her teeth. That damned family would not hesitate to find a use for the Corps – or destroy them. In either case, nothing would survive of the Marines.

They never trusted us, she thought, thinking of the Grand Senate. The Marine Corps was designed to resist outside influence, swearing loyalty to the Emperor and the Imperial Constitution. They'd never been infiltrated by patronage networks and corrupted into servitude to their political superiors. *And now they have a chance to destroy us once and for all.*

Pushing the bitterness aside, she found a chair and forced herself to relax.

––––––

"This is an outrage," a woman snapped. "We cannot be searched."

Glen somehow managed to keep his face expressionless as the woman snapped and snarled at his subordinates. He'd expected trouble with the delegates, but so far most of it seemed to have come from their subordinates rather than the governors themselves. The men and women who had risen high by clinging to the coattails of powerful men seemed more inclined to stand on their dignity and resist any form of search procedure, even when it was definitely necessary.

"You cannot enter the station until you have been scanned, along with your luggage," he said, tiredly. Hadn't he been fresh this morning, only an hour ago? "Your superior, Governor Niles, accepted the restrictions when he agreed to attend the conference."

"But surely those restrictions don't apply to *me*," the woman protested.

Glen looked at her. Her file had been largely blank, apart from a name, which was worrying. He would have thought lover, or courtesan, but Governor Niles wasn't known for moderation in his desires, or for trying to hide them. Someone brought along for sexual purposes would have been listed as such. But the woman was ugly, and alarmingly fat, so huge it was clear she cared nothing for her appearance. An hour in the surgery – or any half-way decently designed autodoc – would strip the fat from her body, then adjust her appearance to match the latest fashions for beauty.

"They apply to everyone," he said. "Please step into the scanner or I will have no choice, but to hold you here until Governor Niles can be informed. I'm sure he would be pleased with you for delaying procedures."

The woman gave him a long look, then smiled suddenly. "Can't you pat me down instead?"

"No," Glen said. A pat-down wouldn't reveal any implants, let alone anything else that might be missed. Besides, it was much less personal. "Please step into the scanner."

He watched as the woman stepped into the device, then pressed a key, activating the scan. It ran quickly, revealing almost nothing apart from a neural link and a replacement eye. Glen was unwillingly impressed. He'd looked the woman in the eye more than once and hadn't realised that one of them had been replaced by an artificial eye. A camera, he guessed, recording everything it saw for later analysis. And that probably meant he was looking at the Governor's personal PR manager.

The woman leaned forward. "Have you finished undressing me yet?"

Glen ignored her, concentrating on the scan. Her body was stronger than he'd expected, with some genetic enhancement boosting her muscles, but there was no biological danger. There was nothing else to worry him, nothing that posed a threat. He checked her neural link anyway, out of habit, then stepped back to allow the woman to step out of the scanner. She was clean.

"You can proceed through the gate," he said, pointing to the gate in the distance. "Once you're through, you will be escorted to the rest of your party."

He sighed as the woman waddled off, then turned to meet the next one. His instincts started screaming at once, telling him that he was looking at a soldier. The young man didn't smile or show any other trace of emotion. He merely stepped into the scanner and waited. Glen tapped a switch and watched as the scan results built up in front of him. There was no tech augmentation, but the soldier didn't seem to need it. He'd had enough biological enhancement to make him a dangerous opponent. Everything seemed to be practically perfect in every way.

And he even looks like he stepped off a recruiting poster, Glen thought. There were no implants, nothing remotely comparable to Belinda's augmentations, but that proved nothing. He wasn't foolish enough to believe an unarmed man was incapable of being dangerous. *But we have no grounds to bar him from the station.*

He sighed, then waved the soldier through the gate.

"Sir," one of his subordinates called. "I think you should see this."

Glen shrugged, then walked through the door into one of the side rooms. Each piece of luggage was scanned, then physically searched. Glen had enough experience to know that the scanners weren't always reliable, particularly when weapons and other pieces of equipment could be dismantled, leaving them looking harmless to automated systems. It took a human eye and mind to spot a disassembled weapon.

The officer was peering down at a large suitcase, which was open in front of him. Glen couldn't help noticing that most of its contents consisted of frilly underwear, all very definitely feminine despite the tag identifying the owner as a man. The officer was holding up a device that looked like a metallic octopus, complete with shiny tentacles. Glen shook his head in amused disbelief as he recognised it. It wasn't something he would have expected to find in a diplomatic delegation's luggage.

"Sir," the officer said. "What is it?"

"It's a sex toy," Glen said. He looked down at the device, silently grateful that his people were wearing gloves. It wasn't pleasant to consider where the device had been. "What else does he have?"

"Thirty pairs of underwear, two pants and shirts, nine pairs of socks and a number of VR simulation chips," the officer said. "They're all unmarked, but they have a blue border."

"Which means they're pornographic," Glen mused. The Empire's moral guardians hadn't even been able to put a tiny dent in sales of pornography, but they had managed to extract the concession that all pornographic datachips would be blue. Given that most porn was downloaded from the datanet, it was pretty much a pointless victory, but they seemed happy with it. "But it isn't something we can bitch about, really."

He shrugged. "Pack up the bag, then pass it on," he ordered. "We're not here to be the moral guardians of anyone. Their...perversions are of no concern to us as long as they're not actively harmful to Island One or anyone living here."

"Yes, sir," the officer said.

Glen nodded. "What else have you found?"

"There's a complete list on the datanet," the officer said, as he started to repack the bag, piece by piece. "Mostly clothes and a handful of pieces of personal equipment. The only really interesting discovery was several bottles of expensive alcohol, from Governor Standish's batman."

"Probably planning to drink in private," Glen speculated. It didn't really matter. "Just keep checking everything."

He sighed as he walked back through the door. Security checks were a nightmare, even on a place as restricted as Island One. They annoyed visitors – he had no doubt that some of the guests were already planning to file complaints – while it was far too easy to miss something dangerous, or something that could become dangerous in the wrong hands. And the longer they worked, the sloppier his staff became. If he'd had more manpower he would have rotated them through on half-hourly shifts, just to ensure they stayed fresh.

His wristcom buzzed. "Glen, the boss wishes to see you," Marshal Sitka Singh said. "I'm to take over here."

"Understood," Glen said. Marshal Sitka Singh was young, but she had enough experience and tact to handle the gates. "Tell her I'm on my way."

He passed her as he walked through the hatch and into the security complex. He'd taken it over completely, pushing out half of Island One's staff to another office, and equipped it with everything he'd been able to requisition from Terra Nova. It felt astonishingly good to have a full budget for once, but it was frustrating too. The one thing he needed – additional manpower – was the one thing he couldn't have.

Patty turned to face him as he entered the security lounge. Monitors were embedded in the walls, showing the live feed from hundreds of sensors scattered around the habitat. Some of them were in very intrusive places, leading him to wonder if they'd picked up his tryst with Belinda. Patty would have good reason to be annoyed with him if they had, even though relationships between superiors and subordinates were far from unknown in the Empire.

"It seems to be going well," Patty said. "I assume everyone will be on the station by local nightfall?"

"I believe so," Glen said. "So far, we haven't discovered anything *dangerous*."

"They hardly need it," Patty said, jerking a thumb towards the near-orbit display. "There's enough firepower out there to turn Terra Nova into a floating cloud of ash."

She shrugged. "The Governor will be hosting a dinner at nightfall for the guests, then they will get down to the nitty-gritty of actually trying to hammer out an agreement the following morning. You'll be glad to hear you're not invited to attend."

"Thank God," Glen said.

Patty gave him a thin-lipped smile. "I will be invited, of course," she said, darkly. "Can you call me out after...say, ten minutes?"

"I think that would upset the Governor," Glen said. He was fairly sure she was joking. As the senior Marshal on Terra Nova, her presence would be mandatory. "You'll just have to grin and bear it."

"Rats," Patty said. She shook her head. "You've done a good job, Glen. Just don't let anything go wrong until the conference is over and we have a working agreement."

"I'll do my best," Glen said. He glanced at his terminal as it bleeped. "We have five new complaints about the security procedures."

"Copy them to me," Patty said. "I'll have a word with the Governor. Everyone agreed to intensive security procedures for entry and...and these aren't particularly intrusive."

Glen nodded. The security procedures for entering prison – or a secure military base – were incredibly intrusive. A criminal could expect to be stripped, prodded and then scanned down to subatomic levels before being allowed to enter the complex. The paranoid side of Glen's mind insisted that it wasn't a bad idea, but the practical side knew it would be a diplomatic nightmare. There had to be a compromise between security and a diplomatic incident that would derail the conference.

"Keep an eye on things," Patty ordered, finally. "And don't hesitate to alert me if you need assistance, even if it's just superior verbal firepower."

"I won't," Glen promised. He smiled as she rose to her feet. "This place is astonishing."

"And well beyond your expense allowance," Patty said, "Enjoy it while you can."

———

"We will be attending the dinner, of course," Augustus said. He'd been astonished, but delighted to hear from Belinda again. "Well, I will be. Violet will be with the children of Island One."

Belinda smiled. "There will be at least one other new child there," she said. Helen had been invited too, somewhat to her surprise. Spacer or not, Helen was nowhere near as well-connected as the children who'd grown up on Island One. "Why didn't you keep Violet there?"

"I wanted to keep her with me," Augustus said. "Do you think I did the right thing?"

"Parenting is a mix between too little oversight and too much," Belinda said. It was possible to let one's child grow up into a wild thing, but it was equally possible to smother them with too much attention and oversight. "I think you gave her too much of the wrong oversight."

"Oh," Augustus said. He cleared his throat, loudly. "Do you have any insights into the guests?"

"None, apart from the fact they all want some kind of agreement," Belinda said. She'd observed the visitors, but most of them were smart enough to know they were probably under observation and kept their comments bland and inoffensive. "But you can work with that, I think."

"I sure as hell hope so," Augustus grumbled. "The Governor is leaning towards nationalising everything belonging to corporations on Earth. We don't have a choice if we can't save what remains of the interstellar economy. And yet that will open a whole new can of worms."

He shrugged, then changed the subject. "Will you do me the honour of serving as my escort tonight?"

"I have my duty," Belinda said. And besides, there was Glen. How could she expect him to understand what she was doing when she wasn't sure she understood it herself? "Ask me after the conference is over."

CHAPTER
THIRTY-SIX

Worse, perhaps, the debts were impossible to repay. Everyone knew it. The economy was contracting, hence few could get a job and start repaying their loans. It was only a matter of time before the bubble burst and the economy collapsed.

- Professor Leo Caesius, *The Decline of Law and Order and the Rise of Anarchy*

Stacy didn't mind her job on Island One.

Sure, there was almost no privacy, and many of the wealthy residents would make passes at her whenever they thought they could, but she knew it was far better than a job on Terra Nova – if, of course, there had been a job for her. On Island One, she shared an apartment with another girl and could enjoy the facilities when she wasn't on duty – and she was *safe*. It wasn't like growing up on Terra Nova, where she'd had to sneak around for fear of running into a monster in human form. If she ever had children, she knew she would want them to grow up on Island One.

But that wasn't likely to happen, unless she married one of the permanent residents. And that wasn't easy. She had no illusions about the difference between her, or any of the other staff, and the residents, all of whom could buy and sell the staff on a whim. They'd understand the reasons a young and beautiful girl would throw herself at them, all right, and while she didn't mind putting out, she would have liked some security in return. It was why she had traded two nights of duty in Home Sweet Home for a place supervising the children as the guests started their banquet.

The children were sweet – sometimes *spoiled* sweet, but sweet – but that wasn't why she had taken the job. Several of the children had no mothers, either because the mothers were gold-diggers who had moved on to the next mark or simply because the fathers had simply bought some donated DNA and grown their children in an exowomb. If she could worm her way into their hearts, she was sure, their fathers would take notice. *Someone* had to look after the children, after all. And the fathers doted on their children.

She cast her eye over the kids and smiled to herself. They ran the gauntlet from six to fourteen, boys wearing black suits and ties while the girls wore a whole series of fancy dresses that probably cost more than her salary for a decade. The girls looked sweet and the boys looked just adorable, although they would probably hate her for pointing it out. It was easy to like them, and easier still to consider playing mother.

Calmly, she clapped her hands together.

"The food is in the next room," she said. The kids had been playing several different games, the older ones hanging back until – eventually - they'd let go of their dignity and started to have fun. "Let us go through and eat."

The younger kids cheered and ran through the door, the older ones following with less enthusiasm. Stacy concealed her amusement at their attempts to act like their fathers, then followed them. The sound of cheers could be heard as the younger kids saw the food laid out for them, the entire table covered in treats and sweet things. They probably ate the same food all the time at home, Stacy knew, but this was different. This was a party...and food always tasted better at a party.

She motioned for the older kids to take their seats – the younger ones were already grabbing for food – and did a quick headcount. Her blood ran cold as she realised there were nineteen kids in all, instead of twenty-one. It was unlikely that any of the kids had run into any real danger – Island One was *safe* – but it was still worrying. She'd be in deep shit if any of the kids decided to wander off back home. Shaking her head, she walked back into the playroom and looked around. She saw nothing.

They're probably in the bathroom, she thought. Both of the missing girls were old enough to be toilet-trained, thankfully. The boys and girls she recalled from her childhood had used to fling their own waste around for fun, but the children of Island One were far more civilised. She walked up to the door and checked inside, then glanced into the next room. The two girls were standing there, one stock still, the other tugging at her arm.

Stacy walked into the room, relief flowing through her veins. "It's time to eat," she said, softly. "I..."

She broke off as the older girl – Violet Augustus – turned to look at her. "She's not moving," she said, urgently. There was a faint hint of panic in her tone. "She isn't moving!"

Stacy leaned forward. Violet was older than she would have preferred, if she had to play mother, but her father was stupendously rich. It might have been worth the effort of trying to lure him into her arms. But she pushed the thought aside as she checked the other girl. She was standing completely rigid, her body as stiff as a board. Alarm bells rang in Stacy's mind as she reached for her wristcom. If something was wrong, she would need to summon a medical team as quickly as possible and...

The girl spun around with blinding speed, one hand lifted up...

...And Stacy knew no more.

———

"They're making the boring speeches," Glen commented. They were seated together in the security booth, watching the show through emplaced sensors. "Is that normal?"

Belinda nodded. "It's why people talk about the weather," she said. "They're breaking the ice without discussing something so controversial that they would have a falling out."

Glen sighed. Dealing with the entry procedures had been bad enough, but he'd hoped to have a break between the last of the arrivals and the dinner party. Instead, he'd had to deal with a dispute between two sets of bodyguards and another over which guest had the biggest guest house. It wouldn't have mattered to *him* if he'd been given the mansion with ten bedrooms or the mansion with fifteen, but it did seem to matter to the guests. Why they felt the urge to squabble over such petty things mystified him. The Empire was dying!

"Let us hope so," he said. On the display, Governor Hamilton was rising to his feet, readying himself to make a speech of his own. Another display showed a flight of Island One's drone transports as they moved luggage from one mansion to another. "Have you ever met such badly-behaved guests?"

Belinda smiled. "You should have seen the reporters we had to take to a hellhole called Blake's Town," she said. "The General in command thought he was going to win a staggering victory over the forces of darkness – he always called his enemies the Forces of Darkness – so he invited a few hundred reporters to witness it. I'd...ah, pissed off my superior and I found myself being offered a choice between being flogged or helping to guard the reporters. If I'd known how bad it was going to be, I'd have taken the flogging."

Glen blinked. "Marine officers are allowed to flog their subordinates?"

"I think he was joking," Belinda said. "Marine regulations take a dim view of an officer who actually lays hands on his subordinates. That's the sergeant's job."

She smirked, then sobered. "I wasn't joking. I would sooner have charged the enemy stark naked than put up with those assholes for another microsecond."

Glen had to smile at the mental image, then leaned forward. "Just how bad were they?"

"Awful," Belinda said. "They asked the most stupid questions, chatted up younger officers, three of them were seriously injured because they didn't follow instructions and one of them even tried to follow me into the bathroom. We had a couple of good ones, but they were few and far between."

She sighed. "And then the glorious victory failed to materialise, so the reporters were sent home and I went back to my unit," she added. "The reports of the campaign bore no resemblance to reality."

Glen shook his head. "If that's true," he said, "why has the Empire survived for so long?"

"One of my Drill Instructors had a theory," Belinda said. "He was a tough-minded old bastard, but he softened every time we passed a test and told us his thoughts while we were recuperating. His theory was that successive generations grew less and less able to handle challenges because they were never seriously challenged."

"I see," Glen said. It sounded reasonable enough. "But there are all sorts of challenges."

Belinda looked down at her hands. "On the Slaughterhouse," she said, "there's a final test for recruits – the Crucible. Pass the Crucible and you're a Marine, no questions asked. But no one, not even I, could have passed the Crucible without years of Boot Camp and then the Slaughterhouse. The Empire, collectively, doesn't have challenges that force it to adapt, react and overcome. And now there *is* such a challenge, it is incapable of meeting it."

Glen sighed. "I hope you're wrong," he said.

"So do I," Belinda admitted.

————

Normally, there wasn't a guard at the spokes that led back to the hub. The residents rarely left the wheel unless they were leaving the station, while the staff knew better than to enter the hub without permission. But with so many visitors, the new Head of Security had felt it advisable to place a guard on each of the spokes. Corporal Lewis, who had drawn the short straw, bitterly resented it. The security officers didn't need an outsider to point out their problems, or to force them to drill and drill again. They were already prepared for anything.

He sighed. Normally, guarding the residents directly was a good way to earn tips and make contacts. He had no intention of staying on Island One indefinitely and, with his savings and references from some of the richest men in the system, he could practically write his own ticket. He'd even seen the conference as a chance to meet contacts from right across the Core Worlds. But how the hell was he supposed to meet the visitors, something that would be hard enough at any time, without actually being near them? They'd be in the best possible mood after the dinner.

There was a click. He looked up, in time to see someone step into the station. The lights flickered and failed a moment later, casting the entire complex into darkness. Lewis groped for the flashlight hanging from his belt with one hand, cursing his decision to secure it to the leather for greater security, then flicked it on. He saw nothing...

...And then something crashed into his head with staggering force. He was dead before his body hit the ground.

———

Belinda had always disliked waiting. Patience had been hammered into her at the Slaughterhouse, but she'd been taught that she would probably never make a sniper or even an observer, let alone a deep cover agent. Indeed, being a Pathfinder had been hard enough. But now, all she could really do was watch and wait as the delegates made speech after speech, each one so bland that it made her grind her teeth in irritation. Even Glen had fallen silent after the speeches had started to blur together into a single mass.

Fuck him again, Pug offered. *You liked it last time.*

Don't be fucking stupid, Doug snapped back. *You're on duty.*

Fuck the pair of you, Belinda thought. Somehow, she wasn't surprised that the ghosts had returned. *This is serious.*

That would be against regulations, Pug pointed out. *You don't have anything stopping you from making love to him.*

Belinda rubbed her forehead, resisting the urge to groan. She'd wondered, once, why someone she'd known had put a gun in his mouth and killed himself, after having mental problems. She understood now. The ghosts were always there, even if they were just figments of her imagination. And she refused to accept the possibility they might be real. Outside bad flicks and worse stories, there were no such thing as ghosts. Or the Slaughterhouse would be haunted by the remains of thousands of dead recruits.

You like him, Pug urged. *And what is going to go wrong?*

Shut up, Belinda thought. Pug had been famous for chasing woman – and, as a Marine, he was up against some pretty stiff competition. But he'd known better than to violate the regulations banning Marines from developing sexual feelings for one another. He'd certainly never made a pass at her. *You're just a figment of my imagination.*

And how, Pug asked, *would you know?*

You'd be encouraging me to chase women instead, Belinda thought. Pug had been aggressively heterosexual. *But you're encouraging me to chase men.*

She's got you there, McQueen put in. *You always hated the thought of dipping your wick in a man.*

Belinda smirked, then stood up and started to pace. The dinner was still going on...and would be going on for hours to come, unless the guests started fighting. She rather hoped they wouldn't, knowing it could mean war. The hundreds of starships outside could do a great deal of damage to the system – and smash Island One to rubble – before they left. If, of course, they were forced to leave. A handful of them might already have made alliances to work together if the shit hit the fan.

Glen looked up at her. "Are you all right?"

"I think so," Belinda lied. She didn't want to confess to any form of mental instability. Once, she'd mocked films featuring crazy or homicidal Marines. They didn't seem so funny now, as the voices in her head grew louder. Imagination or not, having them as part of her was more than a little worrying. "Just bored."

"It's always boring on stake-out too," Glen commented. "You feel the urge to do something – anything – to relieve the boredom. But almost anything you do would only alert your target. All you can really do is watch and wait."

"How very reassuring," Belinda said.

An alarm started to bleep on the console. Glen looked over at it – and froze. "There's an emergency alert," he said, straightening. "It's coming from the nursery!"

Belinda froze. "Helen and Violet are there," she said. She checked her pistol as she headed for the hatch. "Coming?"

"Marshal Singh can take over the observation booth," Glen said. "I'm right behind you."

———

Luke Doyenne knew, without false modesty, that he wouldn't have earned his job if he hadn't been related to one of the owners of Island One. It wasn't a post that could be trusted to anyone who wasn't a relative, not when staggering amounts of wealth and intellectual capital were based on the giant spinning wheel. There was too much risk of corruption, even of subversion, no matter how much the security officers were paid each month. And, to be honest, he knew he hadn't been bad at his job.

But you never really expected to host a diplomatic gathering, he reminded himself. His security precautions had been geared around preventing undesirables from entering the wheel. Much of the vetting was done before the prospective recruit ever saw Island One, let alone passed through security. *And you got lax.*

He sighed. Marshal Cheal had been arrogant, obnoxious and unpleasant, but he'd also been right. It wasn't easy to admit it, yet there was no alternative. The worst Luke and his staff had ever faced was a handful of drunkards who'd had too much to drink and ended up acting like idiots. Compared to the multiple challenges facing the police on a planet's surface, it was almost nothing. And he...

The hatch hissed open. Luke spun around in surprise. The compartment was meant to be completely sealed, no one permitted in or out without the proper codes. Indeed, even most of his staff didn't have the right codes. Marshal Cheal had insisted on changing them every day, just to be certain they weren't copied and stored by the guests. They could cause trouble, he'd warned, even without weapons. But the person standing in the hatchway was no diplomat...

There was a brilliant flash of light, then Luke knew no more.

———

Glen ran down the pathway towards the nursery, forcing himself to run as fast as he could, despite the growing stitch in his side. Belinda paced him, holding her pistol in one hand, somehow giving the impression she could easily have outrun him if necessary. He wanted to urge her to do just that, but the words wouldn't come by the time they arrived at the nursery. A young boy, barely old enough to be considered a teenager, was standing at the entrance, his face pale.

"Stacy is asleep," he said. "And Violet is freaking out."

Asleep, Glen thought. He had a very bad feeling about the whole affair. Stacy hadn't struck him as someone likely to sleep on duty. *Asleep – or dead?*

He pushed his way into the room and froze. Stacy was very definitely dead. The side of her head was caved in, allowing brain tissue to leak onto the floor. Violet trembled in a corner, unable to take her eyes from the body. Belinda knelt down next to her, wrapping the younger girl in a hug. Glen blessed her silently as he looked down at Stacy. The damage to her head looked to have been done by something small, like a closed fist...

The lights flickered, then failed. Glen straightened up, then peered out of the window. Apart from the dull glow of bioluminescent plants, the lights had failed everywhere. The houses and mansions of the rich and powerful were as dark and silent as the grave.

"It was Helen," Violet said, suddenly. Her voice was terrifyingly shrill in the darkness. "She...she hit Stacy and ran."

Somehow, it didn't occur to Glen to doubt her words.

CHAPTER
THIRTY-SEVEN

And so there was no longer any respect for the law. Why should there be? The law-makers had long since abandoned any pretence of being on anyone's side, but their own.

- Professor Leo Caesius, The Decline of Law
and Order and the Rise of Anarchy

Belinda helped Violet to her feet, then stepped over to inspect Stacy's body. Up close, it was clear the murder weapon was nothing more than a human fist, driven with augmented strength. She'd seen similar wounds in people she'd killed herself. Her implants clicked to life, examining the damage and comparing it to her observations of Helen. There was a strong chance, they concluded, that Helen was indeed the killer.

"Helen," she mused. "Helen of Troy. A Trojan Horse. The threat was hidden in plain sight all along."

Glen was staring down at the body, almost in shock. Belinda didn't blame him – he'd felt a fatherly love for Helen ever since she'd entered his life – but there was no time for him to snap out of it naturally. She braced herself, then slapped him lightly across the face. Glen started, swung around to face her with his fists clenched, then forced himself to calm down.

"We found her at the warehouse," Glen said. He sounded furious, yet there was an undertone of despair that worried Belinda. "And with so many weapons and supplies waiting there, we never gave a second thought to Helen."

"The diversion can be bigger than the actual threat," Belinda said. She'd been on enough operations where a company had launched a frontal attack, hammering the enemy's front lines, while a platoon had crept around the enemy positions and launched a flanking attack from the side. "But she's clearly augmented..."

She broke off as she remembered Helen's nightmare. Someone had taken a young girl and cut her open, turning her into a weapon. But who? Pathfinder-level tech wasn't available outside the Marine Corps or Special Operations Command. Even Prince Roland hadn't been granted any form of physical augmentation. And yet, the evidence was undeniable.

"Patty," Glen said, slowly. "She *knew*."

Belinda looked at him. "What...?"

"She was the one who told me to look after Helen, she was the one who told me about this job and she was the one who told me to take Helen with me," Glen said. His voice steadied, after a chilling moment. Betrayal was never easy to take. "We took the weapon through the defences ourselves, then closed the barn door after the horse had fled."

"So it would seem," Belinda said. She tried to ping the nearest processor node, then swore under her breath as it rejected her intrusion. Someone – Helen, no doubt – had uploaded subversion software into the system and taken it over. And there was only one place it could be done. "She's in the Hub."

She thought rapidly, running through all the plans she'd downloaded into her implants. The only way to reach the Hub was through the spokes – and the spokes would be closed. And then...she gritted her teeth. There was another way to get through to the Hub, but it would be risky, even for her.

"I'll go after Helen," she said, fighting down the fear she felt for the girl. Helen was no Pathfinder, no volunteer for her work. She hadn't known about her augmentations or she would never have told them about the dreams. And...Belinda shuddered, recalling how *young* Helen was. It was quite likely that her next growth spurt would kill her, if the augmentation wasn't designed to keep her permanently young. "You need to go back to the delegates and warn them."

She thought, fast. Helen was one person, augment or no. Were there others on Island One, ready to join her? Or was she truly alone, with rein- forcements on the way? Or was she already looking for a way to kill every- one on Island One? Her augments would drive her forward remorselessly until she was dead. And then Belinda realised the next step of the plan.

"I think she'll try to take control of the drones," she said, softly. "They could be turned into weapons, Glen, and most of our weapons aren't designed to handle them."

"I'll go for the weapons stash," Glen said. He looked down at the body, then towards the room where the children were waiting. "What about them?"

"There's nothing we can do right now," Belinda said. "Tell them to get into the shelters, then see to your weapons."

She turned and walked out of the nursery, her sensors scanning the surrounding landscape for anything she could use. There should have been hundreds of network nodes, just waiting for access, free to all. But none of them were active, save for one that was beaming out vast, impossibly-complex signals. Belinda frowned, then gave it a wide berth. It was just possible that Helen was trying to infiltrate neural links and subvert their owners. Most military-grade models were impossible to take over, but she knew that some civilian designs were vulnerable to direct attack. It was one of the reasons why they weren't in common use outside the very wealthy.

The Governor can't be behind this, she thought, as she broke into a run. *He'd have to be completely out of his mind, because his life is at risk too.*

She almost tripped over the next body on the pathway, then halted long enough to take a look at the corpse. It was beheaded, the head itself missing, probably lying somewhere within the forest surrounding the path. Belinda absently noted the position of the body, then resumed her run. Judging from its location, Helen had been running too and simply slammed her augmented fist into the man's neck, slicing right through his neck. Or maybe she had a weapon of some kind.

But that might have been detected, Belinda knew. It wasn't impos- sible to fool a security scanner – she'd done it herself – but secondary systems might realise that the primary system had been subverted. *No, whoever was behind this was very clever...and wanted to snare everyone in the habitat.*

She kept running through possible scenarios as she made her way up to the spoke and slipped inside. It was as dark and cold as the grave, but her implants rapidly saw through the darkness, revealing a sealed hatch blocking access to the transit tubes and another dead body on the ground. Glen had left someone there to watch for intruders, she recalled, something that had struck her as properly paranoid. There was no shortage of stupid things people could do, if they didn't know the rules for where they were. Opening an airlock without wearing a spacesuit was the least of them.

She checked the body, removing the flashlight and anything else that struck her as useful, then turned her attention to the hatch. But no matter what she did to it, the hatch refused to budge. Helen had scrambled the entire system, then depowered it completely, making it impossible to gain access to the tubes. And the whole system was made of hullmetal, which could only be damaged by starship-level weapons. She had nothing that could burn through the hatch. Cursing, she found an emergency door and pecked at the handle, then kicked it with superhuman force. It shattered, allowing her to slip into the maintenance shaft and climb upwards, into the parts of the station that were rarely seen by outsiders.

Darkness pressed around her like a physical thing. It was so dark that even her implants had to struggle to pick up on anything. Cursing, she unhooked the flashlight from her belt and turned it on, then shone it up as she climbed up the shaft. The gravity field seemed to get lighter as she rose higher, but never faded completely. Belinda wasn't surprised; Island One's gravity was natural, generated by spinning the wheel. It wasn't a proper antigravity generator.

It felt like hours – her implants informed her that it was ten minutes – before she reached the top of the shaft and pushed open the hatch. The tube opened up into a set of passageways intended to carry goods from one part of the wheel to another, well out of sight of the rich residents below. Belinda glanced out the window and looked down towards the landscape below – dark and shadowy, barely illuminated at all – then looked up at the stars overhead. Some of them were moving rapidly, suggesting that the starships outside were changing position. Someone had clearly realised that something was very wrong.

If she has command of the network, Doug pointed out, *she could open fire on the starships outside, starting a war.*

Belinda shivered, then paced over to the maintenance hatch and tried to get into the tube. It wouldn't open. She bit down a curse, then walked over to the airlock and hunted for a spacesuit. Legally, there should be at least one general-purpose suit on hand at all times, but there was none. She cursed out loud at the thought of having to walk in space without a spacesuit – it hadn't been fun the last time she'd tried – and then opened the airlock. Inside, a man was lying against the far hatch, a spear rooted in his body. Beside him, a drone spun to life. Belinda threw herself back as it came right at her, waving its manipulators around as it tried to end her life. She drew her pistol and looked for a target, then realised the robot was too tough for her pistol to hurt.

She jumped backwards again, then threw herself up in the air with augmented strength and clung on to the ceiling. The drone buzzed underneath her, seemingly unable to think of a way to reach her, which suggested there wasn't a human mind in control. Someone had probably wiped the Asimov Protocols that all robots were required to have, by law, and uploaded something a little more aggressive. She considered the possibilities, then clambered over to the hatch leading down to the station. The drone snapped below her all the way like an angry crab.

Bracing herself, Belinda drew her multitool from her belt, then dropped down and landed on top of the drone. It's manipulators snapped at her, but not quickly enough to prevent her using the modified multitool to take out its optical sensors. The drone buzzed angrily as she hopped off, then started to search for her by touch. Belinda dropped back down again, opened the hatch and waited as the machine rushed forward. It fell through the hatch and plummeted to its death.

Those things are nasty, Pug observed, in her mind. For once, he was being serious. *I'd hate to face one without a plasma cannon.*

Belinda ignored him as she made her way back to the airlock. The man inside must have had the same idea as her, she reasoned. She pulled his body out of the airlock, stripped the suit off him and slapped an emergency repair plaster over the damaged material. There was no helping the blood, not now. Pulling it on, she used her augments to link to the suit's processors and run a status check. Oxygen levels were low and there was no provision for human waste, while the radio was completely wrecked, but everything else was in order. And besides, she had no alternative.

Gritting her teeth, she stepped through the airlock and out into space. Island One rose above her, its vast immensity staggering to behold – and, beyond her, the moving lights of starships glittered against the inky darkness of space. The suit had no way to contact them and ask for help, something that worried her. Someone on the outside, without any way of knowing what was actually going on, might well do something stupid, given half a chance. She briefly considered pulling a Dutchman and diving into space in hopes of being seen and rescued, but common sense told her it would be stupid. Something the size of a spacesuit might well be missed if the warships were already fighting...

Another flicker of light caught her attention. The warships *were* fighting. Helen had to have turned on the defences and pointed them at every ship within range, Belinda guessed, or the people behind the plot had sent warships of their own to pick a fight. Or...she shook her head as she reached the spoke, then concentrated on climbing up towards the hub. At least the gravity field was still fading, making it easier and easier to move.

Move faster, Doug advised. *Whoever wins the fighting outside is going to want answers.*

Belinda ignored the voice as she drove forward. The suit made it hard to move with her normal speed; if she hadn't been all too aware of the dangers of relying on her implants in vacuum she would have seriously considered stripping it off. But her last exposure to hard vacuum had almost killed her. It didn't seem like it was worth taking the risk.

Uh-oh, Pug said. *Trouble inbound.*

Belinda looked up to see a line of drones making their way down the spoke towards the wheel. The drones didn't seem to be paying attention to her, but looking at the way their manipulators snapped at empty vacuum she found herself hoping that Glen had found some heavy weapons.

Or...what if they forced open the airlocks? The standard safety precautions could be subverted, with enough effort. What would happen if they cracked open the airlock she'd used to reach the outside of the habitat?

Gravity would keep the atmosphere in, I think, McQueen offered. *This isn't a starship where the atmosphere would whistle out of a hull breech.*

Belinda didn't know, so she forced herself forward. There was nothing she could do about the drones now, no matter what happened. Instead, she just kept moving until she finally approached the hub. The airlock dead ahead of her was a very welcome sight, particularly when she realised that the designers had obeyed Imperial Law and ensured it could be opened from the outside. Helen would know she was there, of course, but she couldn't keep Belinda from gaining entry. The automatic systems wouldn't allow it.

She forced the airlock open, then tumbled forward as the hatch closed behind her. Moments later, the second opened, revealing an empty corridor. Belinda stepped forward as she heard a rattling noise, then swore as two more drones came into view. They didn't look as tough as the one she'd tricked, but her pistol was in the suit and she had no time to draw it. Instead, she waited until they both lunged at her, then threw herself to one side. The two machines crashed together, ensnared in one another's manipulators. Belinda allowed herself a smirk, then ran past them, slamming the hatch shut as she passed. Clearly, whatever software was controlling Helen and the army of drones wasn't very smart.

Don't get overconfident, Doug's voice warned her. *This might well be an adaptive program rather than a simple subvert and destroy system. And you don't* know *that Helen isn't anything more than a meat puppet.*

Belinda shuddered, recalling her own fears. Direct mental access, through the neural link, could be abused easily, given an unscrupulous doctor or programmer. Indeed, she'd worried about being controlled herself, back when she'd been invited to join the Pathfinders. It was quite possible, she knew, that someone could have wired *her* mind for outside control and she would never know it. And even if she believed the Marine Corps would never do anything of the sort, someone else certainly would. There had once been a fashion for servants who were implanted to keep them obedient, sickening though it was.

And we are deadly weapons, McQueen offered. *Would they not want to ensure they could control us?*

She pushed the paranoia aside as she approached the security complex. The absence of drones worried her – had Helen sent them all to the wheel or had she kept one or two back for personal defence. Belinda considered the options, then took a detour to the weapons locker and glanced down the corridor. Three drones stood guard outside it, with a handful of bodies scattered around them. Belinda shuddered, calculating the odds, then decided it wasn't worth the risk. She'd have to do with her implanted weapons when she faced Helen.

If worst comes to worst, use the charge, Doug warned. *There may be no other choice.*

Belinda nodded as she approached a access hatch. It was locked, but a little fiddling with the multitool disconnected it from the main command network and allowed her to open it up. She braced herself, expecting to face another drone on the far side, but the corridor was empty. Instead, as she moved forward, her implants warned of nerve gas. It was a security precaution, she remembered from the briefing, that no one had expected to have to use. And it would have killed her, if she hadn't been augmented. Even standard Marine immunisations wouldn't have been enough.

Good thing they don't have this in the wheel, Doug said. He was right. *Everyone would be dead.*

And their little dogs too, Pug injected. *Good thing they don't have a self-destruct either. I guess they paid a huge bribe to gain exemption from the rules.*

Doug snorted. *For once, corruption works in our favour,* he agreed. *And thank the gods for that, I think.*

Belinda ignored them both as she keyed open the door to the security centre. Helen couldn't be anywhere else, she knew. There was no other place that could be used to control the security systems, turning them against their rightful owners. And, as she stepped into the room, she felt her eyes going wide with horror.

"Helen," she said, as the girl turned to face her. "What have they *done* to you?"

CHAPTER

THIRTY-EIGHT

And this, perhaps, explains why there was so much support for the Nihilists. Why would anyone care about maintaining society when society so clearly didn't give a damn about them?

- Professor Leo Caesius, *The Decline of Law and Order and the Rise of Anarchy*

Glen tapped his wristcom as he ran, but it refused to function. It shouldn't have surprised him. Island One's datanet acted as an exchange hub for all communications and it honestly hadn't occurred to him to bring a communicator that didn't rely on the local system. That oversight could easily get them all killed.

High overhead, he heard the sounds of drones moving through the twilight. They wouldn't be armed, he knew, but from what he recalled of their designs they would be formidable foes, if aimed at bodyguards armed only with pistols. Patty had known about the conference from the start, he knew, and she'd had time to devise a plot that took advantage of the location's weaknesses. It was fortunate that she hadn't managed to convince the Governor to hold the talks on a military base. She could simply have triggered the self-destruct and blown them all to hell.

The taste of betrayal was foul in his mouth. Marshals worked together, he'd been taught, fighting to defend the Empire's population from crime and anarchy. But Patty had betrayed him, betrayed all of them. She'd sold out...to whom? The plot hadn't been her own work, of that Glen was sure. But she'd betrayed her oaths and her fellow Marshals to make it work.

And she tricked us all, Glen thought, bitterly. He'd taken Helen at face value; hell, he'd trusted Patty when she'd told him to take the girl. The argument she'd used had been perfect, if she'd wanted to manipulate him. She'd known he would never have let an innocent young girl fall into the hands of the Civil Guard if it could be avoided. Taking Helen in had seemed so simple...and his growing affection for her had helped blind him to the risks. He'd been manipulated right down the line.

He pushed the thought aside as he ducked down and entered the complex he'd taken over and turned into a storage dump. Marshal Alongshore should have been on guard, but there was no sign of him. Glen drew his pistol and glanced from side to side, peering into the darkness until he spotted the body lying in the corner. Someone had shot him in the head, Glen realised, killing him instantly. There was no time to mourn. Glen nodded briefly to the corpse, then started to walk down towards the weapons locker. Someone was already there, ahead of him, and he had a fair idea who it was.

The sound of someone tapping the keyboard echoed down the corridor as he approached, walking as quietly as possible. Patty was standing in front of the secure hatch, trying to open it with her access codes. Glen smirked inwardly as he remembered he hadn't shared the codes with Patty, in ironic obedience to her commands to keep security codes and suchlike as close to him as possible. She probably hadn't realised that he hadn't used a Marshal-issue safe for the weapons. Her override codes were useless.

He lifted his pistol, then clicked on his flashlight. "Freeze!"

Patty froze, then slowly turned to face him. "Glen," she said. "I need to get to the weapons. Open the hatch."

"Helen *was* a weapon," Glen said. Had she been meant to kill him before she started her murderous rampage? There was no way to know – but, without him, no one would have made the connection between a young girl and the sudden loss of power. "You had me take the weapon right into the heart of the conference."

Patty's eyes narrowed. "Glen, we don't have time for games," she said. "What are you playing at?"

Glen kept his weapon aimed firmly at her forehead. "I think you were planning it all along," he said. "You used Keystone to set up a Nihilist cell, which took delivery of the weapons – and Helen. Then you used Keystone to tip me off, knowing I'd lead a raid – and I suppose, if I'd asked you for orders, you would just have told me to launch the raid anyway. And then you put Helen into my care and moved me off the case – I think you thought I wouldn't be involved enough to notice the discrepancies. The riots must have been a stroke of luck – or did you have a hand in triggering them?"

"Conspiracy theories," Patty said. She sounded regretful, rather than angry. "I'd expected better of you, Glen."

"Nards was corrupt, but his living accommodation made no sense," Glen continued. "If he was a rich man, he wouldn't be living in such a shitty hovel. There was no sign of wealth in that house. I think you were using him too. What did you tell him? That he was part of a sting operation and he was to take the money, then hold it for later use? His records show a dedicated bureaucrat, so I think he would have been happy to work for you."

He paused. "And then you killed them both to cover your tracks," he added. "It must have been a nightmare for you when we found the bodies – and had to run from the mob. You practically ordered me to take the rest of the week off, before assuming my post here. I think you didn't dare risk any more disruption to your plans."

"If that was true," Patty pointed out, "I could have taken Helen to Island One myself."

"Not unless you were looking after her," Glen said. "I had an apartment to myself; your quarters were at the heart of the station. You couldn't have taken her under your wing without questions being asked. Hell, a random security sweep might have identified her as a weapon. So you gave her to me, then gave me the task of securing Island One, knowing that I'd carry your weapon with me. I never considered her a potential threat."

"Imagination has always been your weakness," Patty said. It was a very double-edged comment. "Do you really think that anyone will believe such a flimsy tissue of lies?"

Glen met her eyes. "I think it stands up to scrutiny," he said. "Who are you working for?"

"I'm not working for anyone," Patty snapped.

"You didn't come up with anything like this on your own," Glen snapped back. He heard a whining sound in the distance and winced. It sounded like an antigravity lifter going badly wrong. "Who are you working for?"

"Glen, this is nonsense," Patty said. "You have to listen to me..."

"Get down on the ground, ankles and hands crossed," Glen ordered. "You know the drill. I..."

Patty sprang, leaping forward with astonishing speed. Glen fired, instinctively, the bullet lodging in her upper chest. She wasn't augmented, he realised, as she stumbled and hit the ground. An augmented soldier like Belinda would have shrugged off the bullet and kept coming. Instead, Patty was injured, perhaps dying. He looked down at her, keeping his gun aimed at her head, and cursed. If she died, there was no way to trace her backers.

"Why?" He asked quietly. "What was all this for?"

"There's no justice," Patty coughed. "No matter what we did, it didn't bring justice to the people. We did as we were told, enforced stupid laws and bullied those who sought freedom, while our leaders committed unimaginable crimes. One day, I just gave up."

She closed her eyes. Moments later, her entire body shuddered, then lay still.

A suicide implant, Glen thought, as he rose to his feet. Patty's backers wouldn't have risked her falling into enemy hands, not when she could have pointed investigators towards clues that might have revealed her identity. *And there still isn't time to mourn.*

Shaking his head, he tapped the code into the hatch and watched it hiss open. Thankfully, the whole system had its own power supply. Inside, there were a handful of boxes of heavy weapons, ready for use. He'd only brought them along at Belinda's insistence, he recalled, as he opened one of the crates and picked up a handheld plasma cannon. There hadn't seemed any need for them when he'd been designing the security plans.

He placed the remaining weapons on an antigravity trolley, then started to run, tugging the weapons after him. There almost certainly wasn't very much time left before the shit hit the fan. The night seemed even darker as he pulled the trolley through the village and down towards the dining hall. He could hear the sounds of people shouting in panic, but saw no one. The rich and powerful, hidden away on Island One, suddenly felt vulnerable. A nasty part of his mind pointed out that it was how everyone felt, on Earth. The remainder felt a stab of pity for the children.

Marshal Singh met him as he entered the dining hall. Behind her, the Governor was trying desperately to calm the delegates, none of whom were able to contact their ships. Helen must have done something to the network nodes, Glen realised, as he gabbled out an explanation and started handing out weapons. Even a handheld wristcom that wasn't linked to the local network could be jammed, with the right precautions.

"Take the weapons," he said, passing one to the Governor. The Governor looked bemused, but took it anyway. "We have to hold this compound..."

They were only just in time. Moments later, the first swarm of drones appeared and swooped down on the hall.

———

Belinda had seen many horrors since joining the Marine Corps. She knew, all too well, just how evil humans could be to their fellow humans. She'd seen the mass graves of people killed for daring to be the wrong religion, ethnic group or merely for being in the way. She'd seen men, women and children raped just to send a message to their fellows. But she'd honestly never seen anything as horrific as a young girl turned into a living weapon.

Helen stood in the centre of the room, a curious slackness around her posture that indicated she was being directly controlled by the implants. There was none of the smooth motions Belinda had tried to develop, nothing to suggest she was in command of herself. Helen was no Pathfinder, Belinda concluded, no volunteer out to destroy the entire habitat. She was just another innocent victim, in a universe where there were already too many of them.

There was no point in trying to talk, Belinda knew. Helen wasn't in control and the program directing her body – and probably considering the best way to kill Belinda, right now – wouldn't be interested in listening to arguments. The only grounds for optimism was that the program wouldn't have the imagination of a living person, let alone a tactical expert. It was far more likely to run down a checklist rather than devise plans on its own.

She took a step forward, then started to circle the girl. Helen turned to face Belinda, her body jerking as if she was a puppet, dangling on strings. Belinda pushed her horror aside into a tight little box in her mind, forcing herself to remain calm. Helen was expendable, if worst came to worst. The entire habitat was at serious risk. One girl's life was nothing compared to everyone on Island One.

But she still wanted to save Helen, if she could.

The girl's hand snapped upright, then fired a tiny dart towards her. Belinda jumped to one side reflexively, then fired back one of her own from her implanted weapons. Helen didn't move. The dart struck her in the shoulder, but nothing happened. Belinda realised, grimly, that Helen had to have augmentations capable of pushing her body beyond its natural limits...hell, having a controlling program probably made it easier to ignore stun darts. She jumped forward, then twisted in the air as Helen's arm blocked her. Helen had the speed of a Pathfinder, if not the strength. But with augmentation, her smaller build didn't matter.

Belinda threw herself into the fight. Helen was faster, but there was a curious pattern to how she moved. It took Belinda a moment to realise that her earlier thought had been correct and Helen was definitely being controlled by an adaptive program. She'd fought simulated opponents during her Pathfinder training who'd had similar fighting patterns, patterns that were always predictable – eventually. Belinda's implants started to analyse the patterns as she dodged and weaved, then tried to strike out at Helen. The girl showed no reaction when Belinda hit her arm, even though the force of the blow would have broken bones, if Helen hadn't been enhanced.

Her implants reported an endless stream of data flowing from Helen into the main computers. The power level was surprisingly low – Helen might have had no choice, but to go to the security office even if it hadn't been locked down – but Belinda had no difficulty in reasoning it out. The adaptive program had been uploaded into the main computers and taken them over, crippling Island One. It was going to try to kill them no matter what happened to Helen. Cold rage flared through Belinda's mind as she forced herself forward, shrugging off a blow that would have killed a normal person. The entire galaxy was at risk of falling into civil war because of...whom?

Concentrate on your fighting, Doug advised. *You can't take your mind off her.*

Belinda nodded, then threw another punch as Helen ducked backwards. She was sure she could stop the girl, if only she could hit her hard enough to actually damage her. But Helen was too quick to be hit easily...and she was still an innocent victim. Belinda's mind raced, searching for options, trying to think of something – anything – that would knock Helen out long enough to get her into a stasis tube. Or wipe out her controlling implants. Or...

A thought occurred to her and she hesitated, then faked a move. As she had expected, Helen's program took advantage of her mistake – and then she switched into a different plan, lunging forward. Helen's fist caught her in the stomach – augmented or not, she felt two of her ribs crack under the blow – but it was too late. Belinda slammed into the smaller girl, knocking her to the floor, then gripped her head with both hands. She could have snapped Helen's neck like a twig. Instead, she used her implants to force her way into Helen's implants, through the connection the girl had used to access the main computers.

Helen's tactical program showed a flicker of indecision. It didn't last – the program was quick to react to the unexpected, even if it had no imagination – but it was too late. Belinda's hacking programs forced their way into the implants, then ordered the systems to shut down completely. Helen shuddered under her, proving – if Belinda had any doubt – that she was under outside control – then went limp. The stream of data from her implants to the main computers stopped dead. Belinda relaxed, slightly, then rolled off Helen and swatted at her wristcom. It bleeped once, then stopped.

You need to move, Pug said. The urgency in his voice shocked her. *This place isn't safe.*

He's right, Doug added. *The computer will do whatever it takes to get you out of there.*

And you can't destroy the system, even if you could get access, McQueen warned. *The whole system is distributed through the habitat. You'd have to vaporise Island One to destroy the network.*

Belinda nodded, then inspected Helen quickly. The girl had gone into a catatonic state, lying on the ground helplessly. She looked small and frail, so weak that Belinda felt a stab of guilt despite knowing she'd had no choice. The impulse to just sit down and cry was almost overwhelming. She found herself wiping tears from her eyes as she inspected Helen, then started to check the security computers. They were locked out. Somehow, she wasn't surprised.

Carefully, she activated her implants...and swore as red alarms flared up in front of her eyes. Whatever was in the main computers was *very* aggressive, copying itself into every network processor that attached itself to the datanet. And it wouldn't be just the drones, she knew. A simple terminal would become a spy for the computer if it linked to the network. If her implants hadn't been secure, she would have been subverted and used as a weapon herself, just like Helen. There was a reason why the Empire had shied away from any form of true artificial intelligence. They were just not human.

And they could not be trusted, she thought. There were horror stories about alien races wiped out completely, all traces of their existence obliterated, for daring to exist in a universe with humanity. They were myths, she was sure, but she suspected they would have been true if aliens had actually existed. But humanity was alone in the universe.

Bracing herself, she tried again. The security network was thoroughly infected, as was the command and control network, but the civilian network was barely damaged. Belinda puzzled over it for a moment, then realised the system was designed to prevent tampering, particularly from outsiders. She felt a moment of hope, which dimmed as she realised just how many limitations were *also* designed into the system. It was impossible to use it to take control of the habitat.

Use it to send a message, McQueen urged. *That* was certainly possible. *Or...*

Shit, Belinda thought. She hadn't realised that the monitoring network could be accessed through the civilian datanet, but it made a certain kind of sense. A number of drones had started to attack the conference hall, while others were still out in space. And they were hacking away at the spokes holding the wheel to the hub. Given enough time, the habitat's spin would rip it apart. *I have to warn Glen...*

Throwing caution to the winds, she plunged her mind back into the network.

THIRTY-NINE

This made life impossible for lawmen genuinely concerned with keeping the peace and enforcing the law. Civilians were uncooperative, criminals could buy their way out of trouble or even have energetic lawmen fired, if necessary.
- Professor Leo Caesius, *The Decline of Law and Order and the Rise of Anarchy*

"You're a good shot, sir," Glen said.

"Thank you," the Governor said. He'd taken one of the plasma cannons and, so far, had shot down seven drones. "It's hunting and shooting in the woods that helps."

Glen smiled, then turned his attention back to the battlefield. The drones didn't seem to have any real tactical awareness, thanks be to God. Their only tactic seemed to be rushing forward, manipulators extended, intending to crush the humans under their treads. It made them easy targets, too easy. He couldn't escape the sense that he was missing something obvious. But there was no time to think. Stupid tactics or not, if the drones got into crushing range they were dead. Normal weapons just bounced off their metal bodies.

He took aim at another drone and blew it into flaming debris. The plasma cannon grew warm in his hands and he eyed it carefully, then relaxed – slightly – as the weapon started to cool again. Plasma cannons had a nasty tendency to explode if allowed to overheat and an explosion, in the confined space, would be devastating. He watched two more drones shot down in quick succession, then winced as a third lanced down from high overhead and landed on top of one of the delegates. The drone was killed a second later, but it was already too late for its target. He'd had his body crushed by the impact.

"We need to find somewhere more defensible," General Coombs shouted. "This place isn't safe."

"There isn't anywhere safe," Glen snapped back. The General wasn't wrong, but the drones would crunch through the houses and mansions of Island One like a hot knife through butter, no matter where they tried to hide. It was just lucky that whatever program was controlling the drones wasn't smart enough to think of using the debris as missiles. "We have to make our stand here."

A crack, so loud it sounded like thunder, echoed through the entire habitat ring. Glen looked upwards, unsure of what he'd just heard. Antigravity generators didn't produce sonic booms and yet he could think of no other explanation. But when he peered at the spoke, barely visible against the stars, he thought he saw pieces of debris drifting away from the structure...

His wristcom bleeped. "Glen! Can you hear me?"

Glen hesitated, then clicked the switch. "I can," he said. He silently thanked all the powers that were that he hadn't thrown the wristcom away when he'd decided it was useless – or, worse, that it could be used to track him. "What's happening?"

"The main computer is trying to kill us," Belinda said. "I've stunned Helen, for the moment, but Island One is on the verge of breaking up. The drones are trying to cut the wheel away from the hub."

Glen swore out loud. He wasn't sure what would happen to the atmosphere if the wheel opened into space. Would gravity keep it clinging to the wheel or would it explode out into space, as would happen on a normal starship? No one had seriously considered such questions since artificial gravity had been invented. But it didn't matter, he realised. If the habitat started to come apart, the gravity generated by the spin would do the rest. They were all about to die.

"I see," he said. "Can you call for help?"

"No," Belinda said. There was a grim note to her voice that told her what she was about to say before she said it. "The fleets are exchanging fire."

"Fuck," Glen said. He thought, rapidly. There were shelters, in case of a hull breach, but would there be enough of them to use? And if the drones had been subverted, were the shelters still intact? "I don't know if we can trust the shelters."

He swung around and sought out Marshal Singh. "Go check the shelters," he ordered. There should be one under every house, buried within the bedrock that made up the wheel's innermost layers. In theory, they were safe from everything, apart from the complete destruction of the station. But could the drones bore through and tear the shelters open, exposing them to the open air? "And then get back to me."

"I think I can get Helen and myself out of the hub," Belinda said. "But I can't guarantee we'd be able to get in touch with the fleets. I doubt the shuttles are still working."

Glen nodded. The shuttle control processors were linked to Island One. Whatever had taken over the main computer would be sure to infect the shuttles as well. They *could* be flown manually, if there was no other choice, but it would take longer than they had to prepare the shuttles for flight. And there was no way to get up to the shuttlebays in any case.

Marshal Singh appeared from the basement. "The shelters are jammed," she called. Another loud crack from high overhead underlined her words. "And something has fucked the control processors."

"Someone's head is going to roll," the Governor muttered.

Glen rather suspected that none of them were going to have time to exact revenge, but he pushed the thought aside. There were no spacesuits in his supplies and he rather doubted they could trust any from Island One, if there were any in reach. The houses wouldn't be airtight and, in any case, the drones could smash through them. A dull quiver ran through the entire habitat ring, suggesting that one of the spokes had already been severed. It wouldn't be long before the entire structure started to tear itself apart.

"Think outside the box," Belinda said. "Anything *inside* the box will already have been countered."

"I know," Glen said. Patty's superiors, whoever they were, would have had plenty of time to work their way through the standard responses and devise a counter to each and every one of them. They needed something unexpected. But what? "I..."

A thought stuck him and he smiled. "Get yourself off the hub," he ordered. "I know where we're going."

Belinda sounded doubtful. "Where?"

Glen told her.

————

Belinda shook her head at the plan, but she couldn't think of a better one. The worrying possibility was that whoever was behind the plot had already thought of it and taken countermeasures. Their plan would have succeeded already if she hadn't been there, she knew, and it might still succeed. But there was nothing more she could do in the hub.

She picked up Helen and checked her, again. The implants remained completely shut down, but Helen was barely breathing. It was quite possible she was already brain dead. Belinda looked down at the girl's pale face for a long moment, then slung Helen over her shoulder and walked through the hatch. Outside, the nerve gas stung her face, but did no harm. She could only pray that Helen was similarly immune.

They used Pathfinder-level tech to create her, she thought, grimly. *Whoever did this to her is very well connected. But who?*

The thought tormented her as she finally reached the shuttlebay. A handful of maintenance technicians lay on the deck, their bodies torn and broken. Belinda looked around, expecting to see a drone emerging from the shadows to attack her, but saw nothing. The drones must have been redirected to the forces attacking the spokes, she decided, as she hunted through the room for spacesuits and survival balls. There would always be a handful hidden away, no matter what regulations said. People who worked in space tended to get properly paranoid about their environment – or they ended up dead.

"I'm sorry, Helen," she said, as she found a ball and pumped it up. "But you'll have to go in here."

There was no response, but she hadn't expected one. She finished pumping up the ball, then inspected the emergency pack. The control nodes weren't scrambled, suggesting that whoever had hidden the balls in the emergency locker hadn't wanted them found by security officers. Belinda wondered, absently, if they'd been running a smuggling ring, then decided it didn't matter. All that mattered, right now, was getting off Island One before the structure started to come apart.

The spacesuit in the next locker was in good condition, but the radio was useless. Belinda poked it twice, then gave up in annoyance and picked up the ball holding Helen. If she made it out alive, she resolved, she would have sharp words with the designer of Island One, even if she had to dig him up and reanimate him first. Linking everything together had no doubt seemed a good idea, but it had made sabotaging the entire station remarkably easy.

She carried Helen's ball over to the airlock, then opened the hatch and stepped inside. There was a dull hiss, then the outer hatch opened, exposing them both to the vacuum. Keeping a firm hand on the ball, she triggered the gas jets and boosted them both upwards, away from Island One. Helen's distress beacon sprang to life, screaming for help.

Belinda could only pray there was someone listening.

———

The drones seemed to grow less frantic as the small party made their way towards the underground station. Glen looked from face to face, noting just how many had been killed in the chaos, then hurried them down into the station. The children, bringing up the rear, looked utterly terrified. The sounds from high overhead were getting louder, suggesting that the transparent canopy was on the verge of shattering. And when it did...

Inside, the transit tubes were waiting for them. Glen motioned for the armed men to guard the entrance, then walked over to the nearest tube and went to work. It was sealed, but not tightly enough to prevent him from inserting a multitool and powering the entrance from a single power cell. The hatch hissed open, revealing a train large enough for fifty people.

"Get the children in here," he called, as he clicked on the life support. Thankfully, *that* was a separate system. "Fill up the rest with delegates. And at least two armed men with them."

The children hastened past him, into the tube. Glen took a moment to ensure that the main control processor was completely deactivated – the main computer might reason that it could take control of the trains, override the safety precautions and then slam one train into another – then stepped back out. The transit trains were airtight, a safety precaution that had been largely forgotten in the days since Island One had been built. Glen only hoped they would remain airtight long enough for them to escape.

He wondered, briefly, what had happened to Belinda, then opened up the next train. This one was smaller, but it still held enough room for thirty passengers. Glen hurried the remaining delegates into the tube, then turned to the third one, just as the drones started to force their way into the station. There was only one way in, he knew; the walls of the compartment were sheathed in hullmetal. If the drones had carried anything capable of burning through, they'd all be dead by now.

"We can't hold them indefinitely," Marshal Singh called. "Not if we want to get into the tubes."

"Hold them long enough," Glen called back. He opened up the third tube, then motioned for the remaining servants and staff to get inside. "We don't have much longer..."

The habitat shuddered, a dull sensation that – this time – refused to fade. Glen turned, just in time to see the drones falling back, taking to the air and flying away from the station. They must have decided the station was impregnable, he guessed, as he motioned for Singh to take her place in the tubes. He followed the drones back to the surface and looked up as the shuddering grew worse. Giant cracks were forming high overhead as the transparent canopy finally started to shatter. Beyond it, he could see one of the spokes coming apart. It wouldn't be long now.

A deafening crash echoed through the structure as a piece of the canopy broke loose and fell inwards, striking the inner wheel with all the force of a large asteroid. The ground seemed to heave beneath his feet as shockwaves ran out in all directions, knocking over trees and buildings. He hoped – he prayed – that the hullmetal that made up the wheel's outer layer would remain intact. If it didn't, they were dead.

The temperature started to drop rapidly as earthquakes ran through the giant structure. Glen watched, almost hypnotised by the sight, as the air started to flow out of the wheel. It moved slowly, hesitatingly, but there was no escaping the fact that Island One was dying. He wondered just how many others were still alive on the wheel, how many were going to die because they hadn't been able to gain shelter in time. Losing Island One, and many of the wealthy residents, would do considerable damage to the economy.

They won, he thought, as another piece of debris struck the ground. *The conference has been torpedoed and some of the delegates are dead. And the remains of the Empire will die with them.*

He flinched as the shockwave slapped his face, knocking him to the ground. The shock jarred him out of his trance. He pulled himself to his feet, then turned to run back to the trains, cold terror snapping at his heels. He'd done some training for emergency decompressions, but they'd always assumed that survival gear would be within reach. If it wasn't, the instructor had pointed out, there was no point in doing anything other than kissing one's ass goodbye. Only a heavily-enhanced human could survive in outer space without protection.

The train was waiting for him, door gaping open invitingly. Glen jumped inside, then pushed the door shut with all his might. And then the shaking really started.

———

Belinda turned her spacesuit so she could watch as Island One slowly tore itself apart. It was slow, slower than she'd expected, but there was a cold inevitability about it that sent chills down her spine. The spokes shattered, one by one, throwing pieces of debris into trajectories that would impact the wheel. Belinda doubted they carried enough weight to smash the hull-metal, but they would definitely mess up the interior. If there was anyone left on the surface, they were dead.

A movement caught her eye and she shivered. The hub was stronger than the spokes, but it was starting to come apart anyway. More pieces of debris spiralled out into interplanetary space, some drifting towards Terra Nova as they were knocked away from the Lagrange Point. The planetary defences would stop them long before they posed a threat, she hoped, if the defences remained intact. No matter how she tried, she couldn't get an idea of how the fighting had gone. The flashes of light in deep space told her nothing.

And, oddly, it was surprisingly beautiful.

I'm sorry, Glen, she thought. She wondered, briefly, if there was a prospect of sharing a life together. Her emotions were such a tangled mass that she had no idea where she stood. But if he was dead, there was no point in tormenting herself. *I'm sorry.*

She had failed, she knew. The conference had failed. Even if it were to be reconvened somewhere else, on Terra Nova perhaps, there would be so much suspicion it would be impossible to come to an agreement. She peered into interstellar space and wondered just how many people were going to die, if civil war broke out. There was little hope of salvaging anything from the wreckage now.

And then light flared around her as a shuttlecraft approached.

Belinda closed her eyes, taking a moment to centre herself. If they were about to be picked up by enemies, she wanted to fight. But she was tired, so tired. It was hard to think straight any longer. Perhaps this truly was the end.

No giving up now, Doug's voice said. *You're not dead yet.*

I know, Belinda thought. *But what do I do now?*

You survive, Doug said. His voice held nothing, but confidence. He'd always believed in her, once she'd proved herself. *It isn't in you to give up while there's breath in your body.*

The shuttlecraft opened its hatch, then slipped forward, sucking both Helen's ball and Belinda's spacesuit into its gaping maw. Belinda grunted in pain as gravity reasserted itself and she plummeted to the deck, then staggered to her feet as the inner hatch opened, revealing two men in white uniforms. The uniforms were unfamiliar, something that bothered her more than she cared to admit. It was yet another sign of the collapse of the unity that had made the Empire strong.

"Greetings," one of them said, as she pulled off her helmet. Her voice was concerned; she leaned forward, holding a medical scanner towards Belinda. "What happened to you?"

"You need to get a stasis tube," Belinda said, ignoring the question. She'd try to save Helen, because it was the right thing to do. Glen would thank her for it, if he'd survived. She wasn't used to caring this much about someone who wasn't a Marine.

Oh, you've got it bad, Pug mocked. *Not that I can blame you. He could give you something you couldn't get from your past boyfriends.*

Belinda ignored him. "And then you need to start looking for survivors", she ordered. Glen's crazy plan might have worked. But even if it had, there wouldn't be long before the life support failed. "They're in the transit cars."

"Understood," the woman said. "We'll get right on it."

"Good," Belinda said. She wondered about the fighting, then cursed herself. She'd have to tell them something, just to stop the crossfire. "And get me to a radio. I have something to tell the fleets."

"If you think they'll listen," the woman said doubtfully, "you can certainly try."

CHAPTER

FORTY

And so the Empire continued its steady descent into catastrophe.
- Professor Leo Caesius, *The Decline of Law
and Order and the Rise of Anarchy*

Glen hadn't been sure what would happen to him after he'd been rescued from the transit car, once the various fleets had backed off. There had been a long debriefing, a brief – and very polite – chat with the Governor and finally an invitation to leave the system on a starship belonging to the Marine Corps. His superiors had raised no objections, which rather suggested to him that Belinda must have arranged it. It didn't bother him, not really. He missed her more than he cared to admit.

He missed Helen too. The girl had brought something into his life he'd known was missing, but she'd been a disguised weapon. He mourned for the young life, ruined by the shadowy masterminds behind the attack on Island One, and swore privately that he would do whatever it took to bring them to justice. And yet, if his private theory was correct, it would be almost impossible to find them. Perhaps, just perhaps, the Marines could help. The thought had encouraged him to board their starship when he'd known he could easily refuse.

But, when his starship had docked with another ship, he found himself escorted through a maze of gunmetal-grey corridors and into an advanced sickbay. The room was impressive, the very latest in Imperial medical technology. There was only one bed in the room, surrounded by a faint blue glow that warned of an active stasis field. And, lying on the bed, was Helen.

"A pleasure to meet you, Marshal Cheal," an unfamiliar voice said. Glen turned to see a short man wearing an urban combat uniform, with a single golden star pinned where his rank stripes should be. "You did well, I am told."

"Thank you," Glen said. He wasn't in the mood for games. "And you are...?"

"Major General Jeremy Damiani, Commandant of the Terran Marine Corps," the man said. "Perhaps the *last* Commandant of the Terran Marine Corps, but we will see."

Glen shrugged, unimpressed. He'd heard that the Marines practically worshipped their Commandant, but he'd worshipped Patty – he'd liked, trusted and respected Patty – and she'd turned out to be a traitor. The Governor had made noises about offering Glen her post, something else that had prompted him to go with the Marines. He didn't want to be tied down to a desk. It was quite easy to wonder if *that* had driven Patty mad.

He looked down at Helen, instead. "What have you done to her?"

The Commandant looked up. "Doctor?"

A thin brown-skinned woman emerged from the rear of the compartment, carrying a datapad in one hand. "The patient is currently stable," she said, "but she's going to have a very nasty few months. We need to remove most of her augmentation before she starts her next growth spurt."

Glen winced. Children grew up rapidly as they entered their teenage years. But Helen's bones, replaced or enhanced by solid metal, wouldn't grow with her body. She would be doomed by her own growth, if something wasn't done first. Whoever had turned her into a cybernetic killing machine had known she would die, if she somehow managed to wander away from the Nihilists – or Glen. Her implants would probably destroy themselves – and her – before she grew up.

He looked up at the doctor. "*Can* you remove the implants?"

"We can break most of them down," the doctor assured him. "A combination of tailored nanomachines and various....*classified*...treatments will take care of them. The remainder will either have to be removed surgically or simply left in place, for fear of doing worse damage as we try to take them out. But none of them should be *dangerous*. Belinda crippled the processors that took control of her."

Glen looked back at Helen. "Are you sure?"

"Yes," the doctor said. "We scanned every inch of her body as soon as we brought her into the sickbay. There isn't any room for a single piece of hardware to hide."

"Glad to hear it," Glen said. "Will she survive?"

"We think so, but it's never easy to judge with mental trauma," the doctor said. "She may blot it all out of her mind or she may be completely traumatised, assuming she wakes at all."

The Commandant frowned. "We will give her the best care we can muster," he said, quietly. "You have my word."

"Thank you," Glen said.

A hatch opened behind him, but he didn't look round.

"You're out of uniform, Specialist," the Commandant said. "Is there a reason for that?"

"Yes," Belinda said, as Glen turned to face her. She was wearing a shirt and long trousers, rather than the BDUs worn by the other Marines. "I'm off duty."

The Commandant gave her a sharp look, then motioned for them both to follow him into the next room. Belinda winked at Glen as soon as the Commandant's back was turned, then followed the Commandant. Glen brought up the rear, taking one last look at Helen before the hatch hissed closed behind him. They walked through a handful of unmarked corridors until they reached a small office. It had to belong to the Commandant.

"The conference failed," the Commandant said, without preamble. He waved them towards the coffee machine in the corner, then sat down behind his desk. "Ships from New Washington were reported in the Trinity System, presumably...*convincing* Governor Heston to join New Washington. There are several other reports of military manoeuvres, but we have yet to receive confirmation. I am not hopeful they will prove false."

Glen shuddered. Transit times between the Core Worlds were measured in days, not months. The failure of the conference would be common knowledge everywhere by now. And the surviving delegates had presumably left with nothing, but bitterness towards Terra Nova and the idea of saving what remained of the Empire. All hell was about to break loose.

"Yes, sir," Belinda said. "We underestimated our enemy."

"We don't know who our enemy is," the Commandant said. "Or do we?"

Glen leaned forward. "I have a theory," he said. "But I don't have any real proof."

"Go ahead," the Commandant said.

"The question facing any criminal investigator is means, motive and opportunity," Glen said. "How the crime was committed, why the crime was committed and when the crime was committed. Means and opportunity we have. I started to wonder about motive.

"The Governor has no motive for destroying his own conference," he continued, remembering how Belinda had thought it *was* the Governor. "He doesn't benefit from shattering any trust the rest of the Core Worlds might have placed in him."

"If any," Belinda said.

"If any," Glen agreed. "Nor do the other delegates have much to gain from sabotaging the conference. At best, they'd start a war, a war that could easily see their own power bases destroyed in the fighting. My belief is that whoever attacked the conference wanted to start a war – and believes himself immune to discovery or reprisals.

"And then there was the weapon herself," he added. "Helen had to have been modified some time prior to the conference being held. I think they knew, perhaps through Patty, about the conference as soon as it was planned, maybe even ahead of the rest of the delegates. And Helen was a trader, from a trader family, a family that hasn't reappeared since leaving Terra Nova. That much about her origins checks out.

"I think our enemy is numbered among the traders – or perhaps the RockRats," he concluded, slowly. "They could have taken Helen and turned her into a weapon, then used her own parents to deliver her. A war that tore the Core Worlds apart would leave them alone, without having to suffer under repressive regulations that cripple their activities. *And,* perhaps most telling of all, Patty was involved in an attempt by a large interstellar corporation to drive independent traders out of a particular system. She was trying to defend the traders when she was reassigned to Terra Nova."

"You think she was sympathetic to them?" The Commandant asked. "It seems too thin."

"There's no one else who has a plausible motive, as well as means and opportunity," Glen said. "The Nihilists would never have lured Patty into their clutches – and if they had, they could have depopulated Terra Nova by now. They weren't involved, I suspect, apart from being used to force the Governor to ramp up security. Patty could get away with a lot under martial law. No one would think to question her."

He paused. "She once talked to me about our role in the Empire," he added. "I think she might have been trying to recruit me."

"Good thing she failed," the Commandant said.

Belinda coughed. "Wouldn't the traders suffer if the Core Worlds were destroyed?"

"They'd have a chance to survive, if they tended to the worlds outside the Core," Glen said, slowly. "The Empire was strangling the life out of them. This way, they get some breathing space."

"While hundreds of billions of people die," the Commandant said. He looked down at the empty table. "They have to be mad."

Glen shook his head. "Their community is quite democratic, to the point where they even have a tradition of collective punishment," he said. It was impossible to apply their system to anything larger than a small town, but it hardly mattered. People from one society rarely understood that other societies could be different. "From their point of view, holding the entire population of the Core Worlds accountable makes a great deal of sense."

"I see," the Commandant said. "What do you suggest we do about it?"

"I was planning to leave Terra Nova," Glen said, frankly. He had no real intention of returning. Everything he'd left behind could be replaced, if necessary. Isabel was dead and he'd built up no real ties to anyone else. "I intended to go with Helen and become a trader, but I could go alone. Given time, I could hunt down the people responsible for the disaster..."

"If you had a ship and a cover story," the Commandant mused. "It might be workable. We could see to getting you a ship. And Helen would be able to join you, if she recovered."

"Yes, sir," Glen said.

The Commandant looked up, meeting his eyes. "You do realise you might be completely wrong?"

"I know, sir," Glen said. "And I might never work my way into their counsels. But I cannot think of anyone else who has the means, motive and opportunity."

"The Traders have always tried to push the limits of technology," Belinda added. "Helen's implants weren't exactly Pathfinder-grade, but they were alarmingly close. What might they have become if they'd been merged with a willing brain?"

"Something like you, perhaps," the Commandant said. He keyed a switch. "Molly, please show Marshal Cheal to his quarters. He can dine with us tonight."

"Marine-issue rations," Belinda said. "Men have cut off their own toes rather than eat them."

Glen smiled, then stood as Molly entered the room.

"You'll have my decision soon enough," the Commandant said. "Until then, I suggest you get some rest. I'll see you tonight."

Glen nodded, then left the compartment.

———

"I would like to resign, sir" Belinda said, as soon as the hatch was closed. "My conduct has not been in line with the traditions of the service."

The Commandant held up a hand before she could start enunciating her failures. "You saved many of the delegates," he pointed out. "Given how badly we were blindsided, it could easily have been a great deal worse."

"I know, sir," Belinda said. She felt the sudden urge to throw a tantrum and stamped on it, hard. Her emotional control was also slipping. "But I am starting to lose myself."

"If there was a way to help, I would take it," the Commandant said. "I told you, when this started, that I would prefer to keep you on the sidelines."

"Yes, sir," Belinda said. She took a breath. "I am becoming dangerous, to myself as well as my fellow Marines. That is not a good situation."

"No, it isn't," the Commandant agreed. "Do you believe the Marshal?"

"I think he has a point," Belinda said, slowly. "But I was prepared to blame the Governor for everything. I never really considered the possibility of someone *else* plotting to blow up Island One and kill everyone onboard."

She sighed. Augustus and Violet had survived, at least. God alone knew how long that would last. Terra Nova had a considerable amount of industry orbiting its star and the various warlords would definitely want to get their hands on it, even if the Governor didn't become a warlord in his own right. She'd considered sending them both a message, telling them to get out while they could, but she'd known it would be far too revealing.

"I am minded to let him take a starship and go," the Commandant said. "We have no other leads to follow."

Belinda looked at him. "Does it actually matter?"

The Commandant lifted his eyebrows. "Explain."

"The conference failed," Belinda said. "The war is about to begin, if it hasn't already started. Is there any point in hunting the people responsible down? And if we caught them, where would we try them?"

She'd seen enough High-Value Target snatch missions to know they were rarely effective. Often, the person captured would be replaced by another, who would promptly declare the previous person a martyr and use his name for propaganda. The war was about to begin. It seemed pointless to hunt the people responsible down, no matter how much revenge she wanted for Helen. There was no way they could be tried in front of a court.

"They have to be stopped before they do something worse," the Commandant said. "I believe they attacked the Slaughterhouse too. What will they do *next*?"

Belinda gritted her teeth. It made sense. The only people who would willingly destroy an entire biosphere were people who weren't dependent on biospheres of their own. RockRats or traders, they'd consider themselves independent from planets – and if the Core Worlds decided to use planet-killing weapons on each other, so much the better. Attacking the

Core Worlds to encourage the others to retaliate against the suspected culprits might help make the war worse.

The Commandant sighed. "I would like you to accompany him," he explained. "You will be effectively on detached duty. I imagine it will take months or even years to pick up a trail, if there is one to find. And if you find something, you will have the pleasure of dealing with it – or calling for help, if necessary."

"If there is help," Belinda said. How long could the Marine Corps survive in hiding? It wasn't in their nature to hide. "It would be workable."

She considered it. It wouldn't be the same as being on active duty, so she could relax and slowly fit into her new role. There would be less at stake, at least at first, with no real deadline. And she would be able to spend time with Glen. He wasn't a Pathfinder; hell, he wasn't even a Marine. But that didn't matter.

"Very well, sir," she said. "I will accept."

"Then you will depart in a week or so," the Commandant said. "You may as well give him the good news."

"Yes, sir," Belinda said.

Good for you, Doug said. *You get to have your cake and eat it too.*

Belinda sighed as she walked out of the hatch, then ignored the voice as best as she could.

————

Glen looked up as the hatch bleeped, then opened. His quarters on the ship were best described as tiny, with hardly enough room to swing a cat, although he was alone. The presence of other bunks suggested the room was intended to hold at least four occupants, when the ship was at full capacity.

"Glen," Belinda said. "I see they've put you in the guest quarters."

"I'm glad I'm not claustrophobic," Glen said, as he turned to face her. "What are the *real* quarters like?"

"Put it this way," Belinda said, as she sat down on the bunk. "We cram eight Marines into a room this size."

Glen looked from side to side, then shook his head in disbelief. Most of the Marines he'd seen on the ship had looked muscular, with a couple large enough to pass for gorillas. Fitting eight of them into the tiny compartment seemed impossible. He doubted he would be able to even wake up without banging his head on the bed overhead.

"It's true," Belinda assured him.

She smiled, then looked at him. "The Commandant has agreed to give you your ship, *provided*" – she held a hand up before he could say a word – "you take me along with you."

Glen looked into her blue eyes and smiled back. "I'd be delighted," he said. And he would be, he realised. Belinda wasn't Isabel, but she didn't have to be. "You did well on Terra Nova."

"I wish I felt that way," Belinda said. Her face twisted into sudden realisation. "And you know we have two hours before dinner?"

"Oh," Glen said, as she locked the hatch. "And what do you propose we do with that time?"

"We'll think of something," Belinda said. She smiled, mischievously. "Our papers will probably say we're husband and wife. We'd better start practicing."

And she leaned forward and kissed him on the lips.

The End

AFTERWORD

The Law is the true embodiment
Of everything that's excellent.
It has no kind of fault or flaw,
And I, my Lords, embody the Law.

-The Lord Chancellor, Iolanthe

It is a curious fact that the Roman Republic never had a police force. There was no disinterested force keeping the peace on Rome's streets, even though political disputes led to outright violence, murder and, to some extent, outright war between Rome and the other allied cities of Italy. Indeed, the lead up to both Sulla and Caesar's attacks on Rome were marred with intensive political violence and a marked disregard for the rule of law.

I believe, to some extent, that the failure to have a dedicated police service that upheld the peace, without fear or favour, played a large role in the collapse of the Roman Republic and the eventual rise of Emperor Augustus. Political disputes led to outright violence – the killing of Clodius by Milo, for example – while lawsuits brought against Roman politicians made failure something to be avoided at all costs. It was truly said that any Roman Governor needed three years in office; one to pay off the expenditure in rising to high office, one to make a fortune and one to amass the funds for legal defence after his term in office expired.

But, some would argue, the West does have dedicated police forces. Surely we can avoid the pitfalls facing the Roman Republic?

Perhaps we can. But, like so many of the other pillars of our society, the police forces are under threat. And, like the other threats, it contributes to the overall decline of our civilisation.

————

Equality before the law is a relatively new invention. The Romans had a court case that pitted a Roman Citizen against an Italian. The Roman won by reminding the (Roman) court that he was a citizen of Rome – would they rather listen to him or a foreigner? There was no other defence, but one wasn't necessary. He was acquitted.

The Western concept of equality is quite simple. Everything that can be used to separate one human from another (the diversity lauded by left-wing thinkers) is not taken into account. It does not matter if someone is male or female, black or white, religious or atheist, young or old – such matters are left out of the equation. The jury is expected to debate solely on the merits of the case – and, with a presumption of innocence, unless proven guilty. A suspect must *not* prove his innocence, the prosecution must prove his guilt. (If he can prove his innocence, all the better, but it isn't his responsibility.)

I mention this because there are two different kinds of civil police force extant in the world today. The first is the politically-neutral police force, typified by the idealised British Bobby; the second is the deeply corrupt and brutal police forces which can be found throughout almost any Third World state (and bear a great deal of the blame for *why* those states are counted among the Third World.)

This is actually quite important. Where justice is blind, there is justice; where justice sees, there is *no* justice. It is, in fact, an important precept of Western Law that *all* are equal before the law, that little things such as sex, race, wealth and so on are not taken into account when someone is put on trial and sentenced. This is, of course, the ideal. However, it is quite difficult for someone to use wealth or power in the West to create an ideal end result.

But this isn't true where police forces are deeply corrupt. Policemen in the Third World tend to be underpaid (hence willing to take bribes, then start soliciting them), brutal or simply biased in favour of one political faction or another. Part of the reason Iraq slipped into Civil War after Operation Iraqi Freedom was that the Shia made up most of the police force and the Shia wanted payback for years of Sunni oppression. Even without the chaos of civil war, police forces in the Third World can be utterly merciless to the poor, or those without political power.

The West's ideal of justice is blind.

And it is the task of the police force to police the population, while trying to be even-handed.

It isn't an easy job.

———

There will be people who say that society doesn't need policing, that decent people don't need to be watched constantly and that the police are parasites, drains on society. Such an attitude is badly flawed. As long as there is a concept of criminal behaviour, behaviour that is outside the pale, there will be criminals. And there will be a need for a police force to try to keep crime under control.

Some people will argue, as some did when I talked about this for the first time, that an armed citizenry can handle policing, without a force of uniformed officers. This harks back, I think, to the days when police officers were closer to the population (like the ideal western sheriff) rather than to any genuine concept. The problem with relying on civilians to handle law enforcement is that people can and do make mistakes, particularly when faced with a need to make a decision in a split-second. Let us assume, for example, that an armed man stumbles across a couple having sex in an alleyway. Is he witnessing a rape, and thus is perfectly justified in shooting the rapist, or merely a pair of horny idiots being unable to wait until they got a room? A mistake could result in tragedy.

[This also leads to the problem that one group of civilians may have more or less firepower than another group, thus leading to 'might makes right' instead of any form of 'justice.']

There are also the questions raised by prejudice. If you rely on what is, to all intents and purposes, mob justice, you will be encouraging discrimination against anyone who steps out of line. If someone dislikes homosexuality, what is to stop him from issuing 'justice' against homosexuals? Or, if a father dislikes his daughter's boyfriend, what is to stop him shooting the poor bastard and claiming he shot a rapist? Or what is to prevent someone imposing religious standards on a community? (This has already become a problem in religious communities across the West – the Muslims are the worst offenders, but they're not the only ones.)

Mob justice is a dangerous thing. It is a genie that should never be let out of the bottle.

But why do we have trials and lawyers and judges and juries? We have them to ensure that tempers cool, that both sides have a chance to present their arguments, that a honest and impartial jury stands in judgement and comes to a decision without fear or favour.

And to bring people to face a court, instead of mob justice, we need a police force.

———

But what is a crime, anyway?

It will not surprise anyone that the definition of crime has changed radically since the early days of mankind, when it could reasonably be summed up as 'anything the headman didn't like.' For example, the ancient civilisations were quite brutal by our standards and engaged in behaviour that we would consider criminal. The Spartans practiced homosexual relationships between older men and young boys that we would label paedophilia. Romans, on the other hand, married off their daughters young, often *very* young. Indeed, a girl was considered old enough to formalise (by having sex) the marriage as soon as she started her periods.

Other crimes are fairly new. Drugs were considered a social evil in Britain for years before anyone managed to ban opium dens (and, so far, no one has actually managed to ban tobacco and alcohol, which are arguably worse) and the concept of going to take drugs wasn't considered more than a bad habit. (Sherlock Holmes takes both cocaine and opium in canon stories, despite Watson's lectures.) Arranging a marriage for one's child wasn't considered unusual until around 1900 – and is still practiced in many parts of the world. The Age of Consent being 16 (in the UK) is relatively new too, while it is obviously different in other parts of the world.

Indeed, crimes like ebook piracy were impossible as little as twenty years ago because there were no such things as ebooks – and governments had enough problems without writing laws to cover imaginary crimes. There's no law against flying like Superman, for example, for the very real reason no one *can*. (But if that changes, expect there to be laws in short order.)

But the precise issue of just *what* is a crime is subject to so many arguments that it is tempting to believe that liberalism is intended to be nothing more than an assault on society itself. Given the chance, a person can rationalise their way into believing that almost anything should be legally permissible (an odd twist on the concept that anything is permitted if not forbidden) and thus wind up with arguments that they cling to, even though they disgust them.

Let me pose a moral argument for my readers. Teenagers are starting to have sex earlier and earlier (never mind that marriageable age in the past was often around 12, at least for girls). Let us assume that Bob (15) and Jill (14) have started a sexual relationship. They're bright kids, so they're using condoms to prevent an unexpected pregnancy. But they're both, legally, deemed incapable of giving consent.

And then Bob turns 16. Immediately, Bob is guilty of statutory rape. (A statutory crime is one that is *always* a crime, like sleeping with someone under the age of consent.) By the law, Bob should be arrested, charged with paedophilic rape (forced sex with a child) and thrown into jail as a sex offender. And he is *guilty*, because Jill is legally *unable* to give consent. It doesn't matter to the law that they talked their way through it, that they took precautions and that no force was involved. Bob is a paedophile.

I suspect that quite a few readers will disagree with that assertion. They will be horrified at the thought of Bob having his life ruined (and yes, it will be ruined.) In that case, they will demand the law be changed to allow for consenting teenagers below the age of 16 to have sex. Perhaps they would be right...except that would open the floodgate for adults to have sex with teenagers. If Bob and Jill are doing nothing wrong, people will ask, precisely why is it wrong for a 40-year-old to have sex with a 13-year-old?

This is not a question many liberals would find easy to answer. If we state that the age of consent is flexible, we are opening a legal pathway to argue that a paedophilic relationship is in fact legal. But if we consider the age of consent an insurmountable barrier, we cause hundreds of little tragedies and call the very judgement of the law into question.

But why do we have a fixed age of consent in the first place?

Judging the maturity of a teenager is never an easy task. It becomes impossible if one doesn't know the teenager in question. The law finds it easier to ban sexual relations involving anyone under the age of 16 than to try to handle each case individually. And, in many ways, it works. A 40-year-old man should know better than to try to start a relationship with a girl so very much younger than him. But the laws intended to prevent such predators also run the risk of catching innocent teenagers.

These problems are bad enough. But there are worse problems.

Humans are not one vast homogenous mass. I was raised in a culture where it was generally agreed that I would meet and marry someone for myself, that I wouldn't need the approval of my parents and that my wife wouldn't need the approval of *her* parents. But my culture is not the only one. There are cultures where children are expected to marry partners selected by their parents, with only a short meeting to decide, and are often forced into it if they refuse to wed willingly. To me, those marriages are rapes (with the possible twist of both partners being forced into a sexual relationship.) The parents in question should spend the rest of their lives in prison. But others will disagree.

Can culture be used as an excuse for criminal behaviour? Can religion be used as an excuse for criminal behaviour?

I would say no.

But others (again) will disagree. Do I have a right to force my culture, which insists that children should grow up to choose their own marital partners, on someone who grew up believing that his parents will choose his wife for him? Liberals will muddy the issue by claiming that this is a form of cultural imperialism (and they might, in a sense, be right.) But, on the other hand, such a relationship will involve coercion and innocents forced into an unwanted marriage. And *that* is what such hair-splitting forgets. There are innocent people at risk.

The police are needed to intervene if someone is forced into a marriage. Because few people directly involved will try.

———

And yet, throughout the West, police forces are held in increasingly greater fear and contempt and even outright hatred. Not from criminals, who might be expected to dislike the people charged with catching them, but from ordinary citizens, the people who need the police to protect them. Why is this true? If a patient wouldn't hate a doctor, why would a civilian hate a policeman? There's no logic in it, is there?

Well yes, there is. And it's the source of the problems affecting the law enforcement forces of the West today.

I recently considered a list of everyone I considered either a friend or an acquaintance. I have, it seems, precisely one friend who serves in the British Police Force. I have a feeling – I can't actually prove this – that there aren't that many people in Britain who *do* know a policeman out of uniform. This is a potential problem. Just as the shift from patrolling on foot to patrolling in cars made it harder for coppers to keep their fingers to the pulse of what was going on, it also put a barrier between policemen and civilians.

This alone is bad enough, but it gets worse. There has been no shortage, over the past few years of incidents in both Britain and America that call the judgement, competence and basic decency of the police forces into question. People have been arrested on flimsy pretexts, money has been confiscated (apparently, it's legal in the USA to confiscate money if the officer on the spot believes it is related to drugs, forcing the owner to prove their innocence rather than the law his guilt) and people have been killed in shootings or brutalised by excessive force. It's never easy to tell how much of the noise is just noise, but the overall picture seems to be alarming.

There are worse problems. For example, there was a nasty episode of rapes (including underage girls) in Oldham, England. There are some grounds to believe that local police chose to ignore the early signs and complaints because the perpetrators were Muslims, a problem caused by political correctness (i.e. a member of an ethnic/religious minority should be treated with kid gloves, because even looking at them funny is grounds for an investigation. In the US, an investigation against the New Black Panthers for voter intimidation was dismissed shortly after Obama won the election. (A coincidence? Even if it was, it stinks like Limburger.) And, also in America, the Department of Homeland Security seems to be more worried about survivalists and constructionists than either protecting the border or keeping an eye on Islamic terrorist groups.

This is a major problem. But it gets worse.

There is a fundamental difference between *personal* guilt and *institutional* guilt. *Personal* guilt exists when someone commits a crime, however defined. *Institutional* guilt, however, exists when the organisation chooses to cover up the crime or soft-pedal it, rather than carry out the hard task of punishment. Contrast, for example, the Catholic Church's tepid response to sexual abusers among the clergy in comparison to the US Army's response to Steven Green and his comrades. The Church has spent more time trying to deny the existence of paedophilic priests than actually removing them, while the Army reacted, investigated, tried the suspects, found them guilty and put them in jail. Guess which one is not *institutionally* guilty?

It isn't the Church.

For police officers, the growing separation between them and civilians leads to a belief that policemen, their comrades, are always in the right and/or picked on by ignorant civilians. There is some truth in that viewpoint. The arrest of Henry Louis Gates was a case of a police officer trying to follow procedure being lambasted for it by the chattering classes – including, in a dangerous foretaste of things to come, the President of the United States. It was not a case of racism, but – as always – the charge of racism requires the person accused to clear himself, rather than be proven guilty. Law enforcement officers were justly furious at both the accusations and the President's intervention.

This tends to lead to an 'us against them' attitude that is dangerous at the best of times. It is hard for humans to realise that 'us' may be in the wrong, or that 'one of us' isn't the fine fellow we like to think he is. Police officers thus tend to rally round other police officers, unless there is very clear evidence that the police officer in question is a criminal, corrupt or just a colossal asshole. There's one in every large organisation. 'Betraying' ones fellows is, in the eyes of many police officers, dangerously corrosive. Police officers have to trust each other to do their job. But this very trend – and the contempt it leads to for 'them' (i.e. the public) – destroys trust in the police force.

(Something similar may have played a role in SF fandom's unwillingness to contemplate the possibility that the charges against Marion Eleanor Zimmer and Walter H. Breen were rooted in reality. They were 'us' as far as fandom was concerned.)

And this is far from the only problem. Police officers don't actually sentence criminals to jail. That's the task of the courts. But the courts have become increasingly politicised over the last few years, with high-visibility cases further damaging confidence in law and order. The OJ Simpson case and the Traven Martin/George Zimmerman cases were both highly politicised, creating a situation that – no matter the result – a large percentage of America would be unhappy with the verdict. (The Zimmerman case saw the worst abuse of power in an attempt to find something – anything – to pin on Zimmerman.)

And then we have laws intended to stop terrorists being used for other purposes. Britain's anti-terrorist laws have been used to spy on civilians for reasons that have nothing to do with terrorists. Indeed, hate-spewing preachers have been allowed to go free and practice their vile art while ordinary citizens have been arrested for very minor crimes, if indeed they *are* minor crimes. (It is notable that the original builders of the Finsbury Park Mosque protested to the police about the takeover of the mosque by radicals, only to be ignored.)

If the population of a country – any country – doubts the prospect of a fair trial, they will have no motivation to submit to it. And if they have no respect for the law, a perception that it upholds the rights of the criminal over the rights of the victims, they will see no reason to support it. And that will prove fatal to society.

Right now, in Britain, there is a perception that certain classes of society can literally get away with murder. (This may or may not be true. The point is that a great many people *believe* it to be true.) Immigrants, for example, have often stalled deportation procedures for months or years, often taking the case to the European Court of Human Rights (and thus drawing the ECHR into disrepute). Ethnic minorities have been allowed to practice illegal cultural practices (arranged marriages) without much impediment. Religious extremists have been allowed to spread hatred, or go abroad to fight in enemy forces (the Islamic State of Iraq, for example.)

True or not, it threatens the underpinnings of society and breeds hatred.

————

With that in mind, how might we proceed to mend the damage to our law enforcement system?

First, we might as well redefine criminal acts. I would suggest borrowing a modified form of Heinlein's definition – 'a criminal act is an act that harms non-consenting people (or has a strong possibility of harming people),' with an assumption that children are *never* able to give consent. Homosexuality between consenting adults, for example, should not be considered a crime.

Second, we should insist on a right to trial by jury for all criminal acts. If necessary, jurors should sign the Official Secrets Act (in the UK) if cases include secret evidence that should not be made public. The jury should have the final say on the verdict, including the (declared) ability to dismiss the case at any point. They will therefore be able to make a more balanced decision than anyone else.

Third, sentences should be handed down as specified, with no time off for good behaviour (or immediate deportation if the suspect is a foreigner/immigrant). Certain crimes should result in permanent incarceration or the death penalty – serial killers, child molesters and terrorists. The idea is to prevent them causing further harm, not tend to their rights.

Fourth, police officers (or other law enforcement agents) accused of misbehaviour against the public are to be called to face a jury composed of members of the public. They will have a chance to present their defence and explain why they acted in the manner they did. If found guilty, they will be instantly dismissed from the police force and tried under the same conditions as civilians.

Fifth, politicians, reporters and celebrities are to be barred from commenting, speculating or otherwise attempting to influence the outcome of the trial. The bare facts are one thing, slanting the narrative is quite another. The Zimmerman trial was threatened by conflicting narratives established by both sides of the case, which would have almost certainly led to a retrial if the defence had lost.

Sixth, laws should be used for their intended purposes only. Laws for dealing with terrorists should not be used for other purposes, as they weaken faith in the laws themselves.

I do not know if these ideas are enough to start repairing the damage we have done, in the interests of liberalism and political correctness, but the problem is growing acute. Law and order are the foundations of our society – and they're starting to crumble. I don't think we will like it when they collapse for good.

Christopher G. Nuttall
2014

The *Empire's Corps* will return in…

NEVER SURRENDER

A NOTE FROM THE AUTHOR

Never Surrender is the direct sequel to *Retreat Hell*, but features several characters from *Reality Check*. Their backgrounds are detailed there.

As always, I would be grateful for any spelling corrections, grammar suggestions, nitpicking and suchlike. Please send reports directly to my email address or through Amazon.

Thanks for reading! If you liked the book, please write a review.

CGN

PROLOGUE

From: *The Day After: The Post-Empire Universe and its Wars*. Professor Leo Caesius. Avalon University Press. 46PE.

When the Empire fell, it fell into war. Planets that had been held under the crushing grip of the Empire fought to free themselves, military officers and planetary governors sought to claim power for themselves and old grudges, held in check by the Empire's overpowering military might, returned to haunt the human race. It is impossible to even guess at the sheer number of human lives snuffed out by war, or condemned to a horrific existence in the middle of a war zone, located in what was once a peaceful sector. Indeed, there was so much devastation in the former Core Worlds that putting together a viable picture of what actually happened when seems impossible.

However, of all these wars, the most important was, perhaps, the Commonwealth-Wolfbane War. It is also the one where we are able to access records held by both sides in the conflict.

They made an odd pair. The Commonwealth, based on Avalon, was an attempt to escape the mistakes that eventually, inevitably, doomed the Empire. It was a capitalist society, based around maximum personal liberty; indeed, unlike so many other successor states, the Commonwealth never had to force a member world to join. And it flourished. Five years after Avalon was abandoned by the Empire, and the Fall of Earth, it was perhaps one of the most advanced successor states in existence. Personal freedom and technological innovation went hand in hand. By sheer number of ships, the Commonwealth was puny; by technology, the Commonwealth was far stronger than it seemed.

Wolfbane, by contrast, was a corporate plutocracy. Governor Brown of Wolfbane successfully secured control of the sector's military, once he heard the news from Earth, and worked hard to put the sector on a self-sustaining footing. His skill at convincing corporate systems to work together, and his eye for talented manpower, allowed him to save Wolfbane from the chaos sweeping out of the Core Worlds. Indeed, two years after the Fall of Earth, Wolfbane was already expanding and snapping up worlds that would otherwise have remained independent, after cutting ties with the Empire.

It was natural that Wolfbane and the Commonwealth would come into conflict. In the marketplace of ideas, the Commonwealth held a natural advantage that Governor Brown could never hope to match, not without dismantling his own power base. Like other autocratic states, Wolfbane chose to launch an invasion rather than wait for their system to decay, or face violent rebellion when its population started to ask questions. The operation was carefully planned.

The Commonwealth had an Achilles Heel - a world called Thule. Thule was unusual in that it had a sizable minority of people who resisted the idea of joining the Commonwealth, mainly for local reasons. However, it was also an economic powerhouse that could not be disregarded. And so, when the local government, faced with an insurgency that was clearly receiving support from off-world, requested Commonwealth help and support, the Commonwealth reluctantly dispatched the first Commonwealth Expeditionary Force (CEF), under the command of Brigadier Jasmine Yamane, to uphold the planet's legitimate authority.

Those who held misgivings were proved right, however, when the long-dreaded war finally began. Wolfbane's forces surged across the border at several places, targeting - in particular - Thule and its industrial base. The Commonwealth Navy struggled to evacuate as much of the CEF as possible before it was too late, but a number of soldiers - including the CO - remained on the planet when the enemy ships entered orbit. They were forced to surrender.

But while Wolfbane seemed to be winning the war, cracks were already appearing in the enemy's defences...

CHAPTER
ONE

It will come as no surprise that the Empire was disinclined to coddle prisoners of war. As far as the Empire was concerned, it was the sole human power and all other states were in rebellion against it.

- Professor Leo Caesius, *The Empire and its Prisoners of War*

Meridian, Year 5 (PE)

Jasmine was not used to being alone.

In truth, she had never really been alone, save for her short stint as Admiral Singh's prisoner on Corinthian. Her family had been large, large enough for her to always be with her siblings or cousins, while no one was ever alone in the Terran Marine Corps. She had lived in barracks ever since joining the Marines, like her friends and comrades. But now, even though she was surrounded by hundreds of people, she felt truly alone.

The prison camp wasn't bad, not compared to Admiral Singh's dungeons or the cells used for the dreaded Conduct After Capture course. She had been primed to expect interrogation, perhaps drugs or torture; the Empire had shown no mercy to its prisoners and there was no reason to assume its enemies would do any better. But instead, the remains of the CEF had been transported to Meridian and dumped in a POW camp, some distance from whatever passed for civilisation on a stage-one colony world. It was a mercy part of her would have happily foregone.

She blamed herself. Each and every one of her decisions had been the best one at the time, she was sure, taking into account her limited options and incomplete knowledge. And yet, it had ended with her and her subordinates in a POW camp, while the Commonwealth was under attack. She had failed. She had failed the Commonwealth, the CEF and her fellow Marines. Guilt warred within her soul, demanding retribution for her failures. She was a prisoner, isolated from the war by countless light years, yet she wanted - needed - to get back to the Commonwealth. But how?

The POW camp wasn't quite standard, she'd noted when they'd been unceremoniously dumped off the shuttles and prodded through the gates. Instead of the standard prefabricated buildings, they'd been given barracks made of wood, suggesting the locals had built the POW camp for Wolfbane. They probably hadn't been given much of a choice, Jasmine was sure; a stage-one colony world couldn't hope to defend itself against a single orbiting destroyer, let alone the battle fleet that had hammered Thule into submission. But, non-standard or not, it was secure. There was no way for the prisoners to escape.

They don't care about us, she thought. On one hand, it was something of a relief; she'd expected interrogation precisely because she'd been in command of the CEF. But on the other, it suggested the enemy were very sure they would remain prisoners. *And they think we're irrelevant to the war.*

She closed her eyes, then opened them and looked around the barracks. The guards hadn't bothered to try to separate senior officers from their subordinates, let alone segregate the sexes. Jasmine wasn't bothered - she'd slept in the same barracks with men from the day she'd enlisted - but some of the other prisoners had taken it hard. Wolfbane had set up the POW camp long before the war had begun, she suspected, judging by some of the prisoners held behind barbed wire. *She'd* been in the camp for four days; *they'd* been in the camp for five *years*.

Cursing under her breath, she rose to her feet and walked towards the open door. Outside, rain was pouring from the sky, splashing down around the various buildings and collecting in great puddles under her feet. It would have been fun, the child in her acknowledged, if she hadn't been far too certain that it was wearing away at the wooden buildings. How long would it be, she asked herself, before the roofs started to collapse, or simply leaked water onto the bunk beds? And what would the guards do then?

She sighed, then walked into the rain and made her way slowly towards the edge of the camp, where the barbed wire held the prisoners firmly secure. It wasn't a bad design, the officer in her noted, even if she *was* on the wrong side of the wire. The POWs were all confined in one place, allowing the guards to keep them all under control - or simply hose them down with machine guns, if necessary. A prison riot might be left to burn itself out, or the guards would intervene with overwhelming force. Jasmine would have preferred somewhere more secure, she knew, but even if the prisoners overcame the guards they would still be stuck on Meridian. The only hope was to find a way to get off the planet.

The rain ran down her face and soaked her clothing as she walked away from the wire and around the side of one of the barracks, where two of her former subordinates were waiting for her. Riflemen Carl Watson and Thomas Stewart nodded politely to her - they'd agreed that salutes would only draw more attention to Jasmine - then glanced around, making sure they were alone. Jasmine looked behind her, then leaned against the wall, trying to look nonchalant. There was no one in view, but it was far too easy to imagine microscopic bugs being used to track their movements and monitor their conversation. The guards might have good reason to assume the camp was inescapable.

But if we assume we're doomed, we are doomed, she thought, morbidly. It was their duty to try to escape, no matter the risk. *And if the guards catch and kill us trying to escape, at least we will have tried.*

She knew better than to remain in the camp, if it could be avoided. The war would be won or lost - and if it were lost, Wolfbane would have a free hand to do whatever it liked to prisoners of war. The Empire had normally dumped POWs it considered to be beyond redemption on penal worlds, where they would either fight to subdue a world that could be later settled by the Empire or die, countless light years from home. Wolfbane might treat them better, but nothing Jasmine had heard from any of the other POWs suggested that Governor Brown was interested in anything other than efficiency. He might leave them on Meridian indefinitely - a stage-one colony world would welcome an influx of trained manpower - or he might just transfer them to a penal world. There were several candidates within the Wolfbane Sector alone.

"Brigadier," Watson said.

Jasmine sighed, inwardly. There had been a time when she'd been a Rifleman too...and she looked back to that time with a certain degree of nostalgia. She had been a Marine, one of many, and she hadn't had to worry about making more than tactical judgements in the heat of battle. Captain Stalker had been in command of the company and she'd just been one of his Marines. But the company had been scattered around the Commonwealth after they'd been abandoned by the Empire, leaving only a handful to continue serving as Marines. She envied Watson and Stewart more than she cared to admit.

"Let us hope they are not watching us," Jasmine said, curtly. "Have you met anyone interesting?"

"A handful," Stewart said. "It looks as though Meridian was used as a dumping point for quite a few people from Wolfbane."

Jasmine frowned. It wasn't common to put civilian and military prisoners together, but Governor Brown's people seemed to have ignored that stipulation. Maybe they only had one major POW camp...she shook her head, dismissing the absurd thought. It would have taken less effort, *much* less effort, to set up a POW camp on an isolated island on Wolfbane, well away from any hope of rescue. Anyone sent to Meridian had to be someone the Governor might want to keep alive, but didn't anticipate freeing for years, if at all.

"And a couple from Meridian itself," Watson added. "I think you might be able to talk to one of them, Brigadier. She won't talk to any of us."

"Understood," Jasmine said. She rubbed her scalp, where her short hair was itching under the downpour. "Anyone particularly important?"

"We seem to be sharing a POW camp with a former Imperial Army officer," Stewart said, with the air of a man making a dramatic announcement. "He claims to have been the former CO at Wolfbane, before the Governor took power for himself."

Jasmine felt her eyes narrow. "And he's still alive?"

"He was ranting and raving about how his clients wouldn't let him be killed," Stewart said, dryly. "I don't know how much of it to take seriously..."

"None of it," Watson said. "If he had enough clients to make himself a serious concern, he'd be dead, not mouldering away in a shithole on the edge of settled space."

Jasmine was inclined to agree. Patrons and clients had been the curse of the Empire's military, before the Fall of Earth; senior officers had promoted their own clients into important positions, rather than using competence as a yardstick for promotion. Each senior officer had enjoyed a network of clients, which had allowed them to bolster their positions... and probably set themselves up as warlords, once the Empire had collapsed into chaos. If this former CO had been outsmarted by Governor Brown, it was a wonder he was still alive. He wouldn't be dangerous once he was buried in a shallow grave.

And if he had enough of a power base to make himself a threat, he wouldn't have been removed so easily, she thought, darkly.

"Talk to him anyway, see what you can learn," she said. "What's his name?"

"Stubbins," Watson said. "General James Stubbins."

Jasmine shrugged. The name wasn't familiar, unsurprisingly. There had been literally hundreds of thousands of generals in the Imperial Army, ranging from competent officers who had been promoted through merit to idiots who had been given the title as a reward from their patrons. The latter had been incredibly common in the dying days of the Empire, if only because everyone knew a competent officer was also a *dangerous* officer. She told herself, firmly, not to let prejudice blind her to the possibility that Stubbins had merely been unlucky...

But if he had a power base, she thought again, *he shouldn't have been so easy to remove.*

"He has his aide with him," Watson added. "Paula Bartholomew. Very pretty woman - and smart too, I fancy."

"Then talk to her, see what she says too," Jasmine ordered. There was something about the whole affair that puzzled her, but there was no point in worrying about it. If Stubbins was a plant, someone charged with watching for trouble from the prisoners, they would just have to deal with him when he showed his true colours. "And see if you can separate her from him long enough to have a proper conversation."

Watson grinned. "Are you ordering me to seduce her?"

"Of course not," Jasmine said, dryly. "I would never *dream* of issuing an impossible order."

Stewart laughed as Watson glowered at both of them. "I don't think she was hired because she has a pretty face, my dear Watson," he said, mischievously. "And she certainly wouldn't have been sent out here if she hadn't been regarded as dangerous by *someone*."

"Unless they were making a clean sweep," Watson objected. "There have to be millions of pretty girls on Wolfbane."

"And if they were making a clean sweep," Jasmine pointed out, "they would have wiped out his whole patronage network."

She shook her head. "There's no way to know," she added. "Talk to him, see what he says...and then we can decide how to proceed."

"Getting out of the camp will be easy," Stewart said. "We just tunnel under the fence."

"Assuming they're not watching with sensors for us to start digging," Watson countered, darkly. "They might wait for us to pop up on the other side, then open fire."

"Then we will need a distraction," Jasmine said. She had thought about trying to dig a tunnel out of the camp, but the soaking ground would make it incredibly dangerous. And besides, the guards hadn't been fool enough to leave them any digging tools. "Something loud enough to keep their attention away from any sensors they might have."

"A riot would do nicely," Stewart said.

He broke off as the rain started to come to a halt. "The girl I mentioned - Kailee - is in Building 1," he said, quickly. "I think you should definitely talk to her."

Jasmine nodded, then glanced from Stewart to Watson. "We're going to get out of here," she said, firmly. "Whatever it takes, we're going to get out of here."

"Of course," Stewart said. "I never doubt it for a moment."

The rain came to a stop, leaving water dripping from the rooftops and splashing down to the muddy ground. Jasmine shook her head, cursing the prison uniform under her breath. It was bright orange, easy to see in semi-darkness...and it clung to her skin in a manner that revealed each and every one of her curves. Being exposed didn't bother her - she'd been through worse in basic training - but it was yet another problem. They would be alarmingly visible if they happened to be caught tunnelling under the fence.

She nodded to them both, then headed towards Building 1. It was simple in design, nothing more than a long rectangular building. Judging by the jungle just outside the fence, Meridian was not short of wood; hell, clearing woodland was probably one of the first tasks the settlers had had to do, when they'd landed. And they'd thrown away a small fortune, if they'd been able to get the wood to Earth before the Fall...

Inside, it was no more elaborate than Building 8, where she'd been placed, but it had an air of despondency that suggested the inhabitants had been prisoners for much longer. They'd reached a stage, she realised, where they'd come close to giving up. A handful of bunk beds were occupied, mainly by women, either sleeping or just staring listlessly up at the wooden ceiling. There was nothing to do in the camp, save eat rations and sleep; there were no footballs, no board games, nothing the prisoners could use to distract themselves from the numb tedium of their existence. Given enough time, Jasmine had a feeling that the ennui would wear her down too.

You expected torture, she thought.

It was a galling thought. Conduct After Capture had warned her to expect torture, mistreatment, even rape. Admiral Singh's goons *had* tortured her, intent on trying to break her will to resist. But the POW camp was nothing except mindless tedium. There was no gloating enemy to resist, no leering torturer to fight...merely her own mind. Perhaps, just perhaps, the true intent of the camp was to erode her will to resist by depriving her of an enemy to fight. And it might just work.

"You're new, I see," a voice said. An older woman smiled at her, revealing broken teeth, although there was a hint of wariness in her expression. "What are you in for?"

"I'm looking for Kailee," Jasmine said, shortly. The woman sounded cracked, like so many of the older prisoners. "Where is she?"

"There," the older woman said, pointing towards a dark-haired girl lying on the bunk. "Be gentle, my dear. She's had a rough time of it."

Jasmine nodded, then walked towards Kailee. She was young, around twenty, although it was hard to be sure. Like so many other colonists, she would have aged rapidly during the battle to settle a whole new world. She turned to look at Jasmine as she approached, her dark eyes fearful. Jasmine realised, grimly, that the girl had been through hell. No wonder she had refused to talk to either of the men.

"I'm Jasmine," she said, sitting down by the side of the bed. It reduced the height advantage, hopefully making it easier for Kailee to talk to her. "I understand you were born on Meridian."

"Earth," Kailee said. Her accent was definitely from Earth, although several years of being away from humanity's homeworld had weakened it. "I was born on Earth."

Jasmine frowned. "How did you wind up here?"

Kailee laughed, harshly. "I won a competition," she said. "I didn't enter the competition, but I won anyway. And they sent me out here, where I was happy after a while. And then they took me away and shoved me in the camp."

Jasmine frowned. She could understand imprisoning the planetary leadership, or anyone who might have military experience, but she rather doubted Kailee was either connected to the leadership or an experienced military officer. Indeed, Kailee held herself like someone from the lower classes of Earth, a sheep-girl who knew herself to be vulnerable. She wouldn't have survived an hour of Boot Camp, let alone six months.

"If you're from Earth," she said finally, "why are you here?"

"Because of Gary," Kailee said. "They want to keep him under control."

Jasmine felt her frown deepen. "Gary?"

"My...my boyfriend," Kailee said. "We came from Earth together and... and...I..."

She caught herself, then scowled at Jasmine. "There aren't many people here who like modern technology," she said. The bitterness in her tone was striking. "Gary's one of the few who do. And they wanted him to work for them, so they took me as a hostage."

"I see," Jasmine said. An idea was starting to flower at the back of her mind. "Tell me about him, please."

Kailee gave her a sharp look. "Why do you want to know?"

"Because it might be the key to getting out of here," Jasmine said. "And I need you to tell me everything you can."

CHAPTER
TWO

There was no distinction drawn between a previously-undiscovered human colony, that might object to being absorbed into the Empire, and members of an insurgency mounted against the Empire's overseers. They were all seen, legally, as being illegitimate combatants.

- Professor Leo Caesius, The Empire and its Prisoners of War

Avalon, Year 5 (PE)

"It isn't going well, is it?"

Colonel Edward Stalker shrugged. "It's always darkest before the dawn," he said, seriously. "And the first impressions are always the worst."

President Gabriella Cracker eyed him sardonically. "And now we've gone through a whole list of clichés," she said, "it isn't going well, is it?"

Ed shrugged, again. "No one has fought a war like this for hundreds of years," he said. He looked around his office, morbidly. "We're still learning and so are they."

He sighed. "There are five worlds currently under occupation, but only one of them - Thule - is a significant issue," he added. "The remainder don't add much to our combat power..."

"But they look bad on the display," Gaby said. She pointed a sharp finger towards five holographic icons, all glowing a baleful red. "The Wolves seem to be advancing forward in an unstoppable wave."

"But they're not," Ed said. "There's a long way between the front lines and Avalon."

"You know that and I know that," Gaby said, tiredly. "But I have to convince the population that we're not losing the war."

Ed nodded, reluctantly. Avalon had always had a more stalwart population than Earth or any of the other Core Worlds, but even colonists, used to setbacks, could falter if they thought defeat was inevitable. Wolfbane had captured five worlds, after all, and Gaby was right; it did look bad. And yet, he knew the worlds were largely immaterial. The war wouldn't be won or lost until one side managed to destroy the other's fleet, planetary defences and industrial base.

"They're actually being quite cautious," he said, softly. "I was expecting a stab at Avalon itself as a way to open the war, but instead they're proceeding carefully, taking system after system as they advance towards our heartland. That gives us time to rally and mount counterattacks into enemy-held territory."

"And take out their supply lines," Gaby agreed. "Are you sure we can keep them from continuing the offensive?"

"Nothing is certain in war, apart from the simple fact that professionals still study logistics instead of tactics," Ed said. "They will need regular resupplies to keep their fleets advancing forward, everything from missiles to spare parts and replacement crewmen. And if we can impede that, they will be unable to advance further."

"I hope you're right," Gaby said, again. "The council isn't taking the latest loss too well."

Ed sighed, inwardly. It took nearly three weeks to get a message from the front lines back to Avalon, three weeks during which anything could happen. The Empire had had all sorts of problems because the Grand Senate had tried to issue orders from Earth, orders that were already long out of date before they reached the Rim. Avalon was closer to the war front, but three weeks was still far too long to do anything but allow the local commanders freedom of action. It was the only way to hold the line.

At least we can trust our commanders, he thought. *The Empire never felt it could trust anyone.*

"Tell them that we are rallying and readying our counter-offensive," he said. It was true, although he had a feeling that it would be several months before the Commonwealth could mount more than heavy raids behind enemy lines. Trading space for time was the only practical course of action, but it wasn't very heroic. "Is Travis still being a pain in the ass?"

"Travis isn't calling the war itself into question," Gaby said, "but he's insisting we need new leadership at the top."

Ed sighed, again. It was typical of politicians - opposition politicians - that they carped and criticised, while they had no power or responsibilities. Gordon Travis might have a point, but it was lost behind the simple fact that he could - and did - say whatever he liked. It wasn't *him* who had to make the plans work, or write letters to the families of men and women killed in action. And Travis blamed Ed for the death of his son.

"Tell him to wait for the next election," he said. "Unless he can put together enough of a coalition to rout you."

"I don't think he can, yet," Gaby said. "But if we lose more worlds, Ed, the councillors from those worlds will be out for blood."

Ed nodded, cursing under his breath. He'd trained as a Marine, not as a combination of Admiral, General and Politician. He'd had to learn to balance all three roles on Avalon, after they'd been abandoned by the Empire, but none of them really fitted. He wanted to get back into action, to get stuck into the enemy...not to remain behind while men and women under his command went into danger. Part of him had almost been glad when the peace talks had blown up in their face, when he'd had to command a force under siege on a primitive world...

He shook his head, angrily. It might have been better, in the long run, if they'd been able to make a firm agreement with Wolfbane. But, knowing what he did now, he was sure that Wolfbane wouldn't have honoured the agreement for long. They had simply far too much at stake to risk a firm peace.

"Then we hold the line, in the council as well as the war," he said. "I think..."

He broke off as his intercom buzzed. "Yes?"

"Colonel Kitty Stevenson is here to see you, sir," his current aide said. "She says its urgent."

Ed and Gaby exchanged glances. Colonel Kitty Stevenson had been stationed on Avalon long before Stalker's Stalkers had arrived, simply because she'd managed to get on the bad side of one of her superior officers. Ed wasn't sure of the details, but he'd never doubted Kitty's competence; she'd had almost nothing to work with, on Avalon, yet she'd built up the bare bones of an intelligence network from scratch. Now, she was in charge of both espionage and counter-espionage.

"Show her in, please," he ordered.

"I'll leave you to it," Gaby said. "I need to go soothe a few troubled minds."

Ed smiled. "Good luck," he said. "And I'll see you tonight?"

"Unless there's another late sitting in the council chamber," Gaby said. "I don't get to steer matters *all* my own way."

Ed watched her go, smiling inwardly at how the former rebel leader had matured. His instincts had told him that he could compromise with Gaby, work with her to establish a lasting peace...and he'd been right. But, at the same time, Gaby was as limited as himself when it came to building an interstellar government. The Commonwealth was a ramshackle structure in many ways, built from various planetary governments rather than something designed for genuine interstellar governance. It wouldn't be long before cracks started to show in the edifice.

But changing that will require careful forethought, he considered, as the door closed behind his friend and lover. *The Empire wasn't a very effective interstellar government either.*

The door opened again, allowing Kitty Stevenson to step into the room. She was a tall redheaded woman, wearing a naval uniform without any rank insignia. Her jacket was open, revealing a surprising amount of cleavage, something that would have gotten her in trouble if she'd been a genuine naval officer. Ed - and his fellows - had worked hard to ensure that the old patronage networks that had plagued the Imperial Navy found no root in the Commonwealth Navy. And trading sex for advancement had been a favoured practice for the Empire's senior officers.

"Colonel," she said, as she produced a bug-sweeper from her uniform pocket and started to sweep the room. "I'm afraid I have bad news."

Ed's eyes narrowed. "How bad? Should we go to a secure room?"

"This room appears clean," Kitty said. "I'm just feeling a little paranoid."

She returned the sweeper to her pocket and sat down facing him. "I think we have a rat."

Ed blinked. "A spy?"

"Yes, sir," Kitty said. "And someone quite high up."

Ed met her eyes, tiredly. "Explain."

Kitty looked back at him, evenly. "Since the start of the war, sir, Commonwealth Intelligence has been installing monitors on the various deep-space communications transmitters," she said. "It wasn't quite legal, but it had to be done."

Ed scowled. The Empire had been in the habit of insisting that all commercial encryption programs included backdoors, allowing Imperial Intelligence to read encoded messages at will. Unsurprisingly, bribes had changed hands and powerful corporations had developed ways to read messages sent by their rivals. And then pirates and news agencies had started cracking messages at will, too. It hadn't encouraged new businesses, already staggering under the weight of oppressive regulations, to enter the marketplace.

The Commonwealth had banned the practice. Businesses, even civilians, could use whatever encryption programs they liked, without ever having to leave backdoors for Commonwealth Intelligence. If someone realised that Commonwealth Intelligence had been quietly reading their mail *anyway*, it would cause a major scandal. And yet, Kitty was right. There were almost certainly spies on the planet's surface and those spies would have to send their messages back to Wolfbane *somehow*.

"I know," he said, finally. "Carry on."

Kitty's eyes never left his. "We were watching for signs of data being beamed into space that might be aimed at a spy ship somewhere within the system," she said. "Four days ago, we intercepted a communications packet that was heavily encrypted, so tightly bound that it took three days to unlock the encryption and scan the contents. It consisted of political intelligence from Avalon."

Ed smiled. "It took *that* long?"

"The encryption program was unfamiliar to us," Kitty said. "We've been checking message buffers to see if there were other encrypted messages, but if there were they were purged long ago."

She reached into her pocket and produced a datapad, which she passed to Ed. "As you can see, sir," she said, "most of the data is political in nature."

Ed studied the datapad for a long moment, skimming through the paragraphs one by one. It read more like a detailed letter than a spy report, but that wouldn't stop it being dangerous. Whoever had written the message had access to the council, or at least to a number of councillors...he shook his head, then passed the datapad back to her. It was sheer luck they'd stumbled across evidence the spy existed before something far more sensitive was discussed in council.

And we thought the council was above suspicion, he thought, numbly. *Why did we choose to believe that again?*

"Very well," he said. "Do you have a suspect?"

"We've narrowed it down to several hundred possible suspects," Kitty said. "However, that list would include nearly every councillor on the planet, as well as their aides and perhaps even their families."

Ed swore. "If we started investigating them all, Colonel," he said, "we might well rip the Commonwealth apart."

"Yes, sir," Kitty said. "I attempted to trace each individual piece of information, but I wasn't able to narrow the suspect list further."

"There was too much in the message," Ed said. There had been no tactical data, which was *something*, but it was still worrying. Political intelligence - which councillors might consider surrender, which councillors wanted to fight to the bitter end - might be helpful to Wolfbane, particularly if Governor Brown started making peace offers. "Can you track where the message *went?*"

"To one of the asteroid mining facilities," Kitty said. "I suspect it was probably rerouted from there to a hidden monitoring station. Past then, we don't know."

"I see," Ed said.

He cursed under his breath. It would probably be impossible to track down the final destination. Five years ago, Avalon had had a RockRat colony and a cloudscoop...and little else. Now, the entire system swarmed with mining stations and industrial production nodes. It would be easy for the enemy to hide a monitoring platform within the system, ready to intercept messages from Avalon and hold them until a starship arrived to take them home. As long as they took a few basic precautions, it would be impossible to detect the platform.

"A spy in the council," he mused. "Who?"

"Unknown," Kitty said. "It was sheer luck we stumbled across the message, sir."

Ed would have liked to believe it was Gordon Travis. The man had been nothing more than a headache since he'd been elected to the council, even though he had a respectable record as a businessman before and after the Cracker War. It was hard to blame him for being angry about the death of his son, but it didn't excuse outright treason...

He shook his head. Travis might have disagreed with both Ed and Gaby, but that didn't make him a traitor. There was no *proof*, apart from personal dislike, and that wasn't enough to condemn a man to death.

"We have to find the spy," he mused. "Do you have a plan?"

"Yes, sir," Kitty said. "Now we have a handle on the encryption program, I have reconfigured the monitors to watch for more encoded messages. I intend to start distributing pieces of false or compartmented information around the list of suspects, then see which pieces of intelligence are passed to the enemy. Once we know what the enemy knows, we can narrow down our list of suspects considerably."

"It seems workable," Ed said. He sighed. The last thing the Commonwealth needed was a witch-hunt for a highly-placed spy. "Is there no way to cut down the number of suspects now?"

"No, sir," Kitty said. "I don't think it can be done, short of introducing arbitrary standards to the mix - like, for example, excluding everyone from Avalon. That would cause another political headache if it got out."

Ed nodded. "Yes, it would," he agreed. "The other worlds would be understandably furious."

"Yes, sir," Kitty agreed.

She shrugged. "I could also dispatch a team of investigators to the asteroid mining colony, but it would tip off the spy...assuming, of course, the spy knows which route the messages take to leave Avalon," she added. "There might be an entire ring of spies on the planet's surface, like the agents who helped poor Mathew Polk get down to the ground."

"Wonderful," Ed muttered.

"But whoever put that report together is very highly placed," Kitty added. "I'd put money on it being someone from Avalon."

"But why?" Ed asked. "Why betray the Commonwealth?"

Kitty shrugged. "Money, power, revenge...there is no shortage of possible motives," she said. "A councillor might believe that he'd be promoted to local ruler when Wolfbane wins the war, assuming he serves them well beforehand. Lots of people dream of power and probably shouldn't be allowed to claim it. Or he may believe that Wolfbane is going to win and he's doing what he can to make himself useful, just to save himself from the purge at the end of the war."

Her eyes darkened. "Or his child might be a prisoner, held hostage to guarantee his compliance, sir," she added. "I'm going to start looking into their families too, Colonel, but I am frighteningly short of manpower."

"I know," Ed admitted.

He'd never had much use for Imperial Intelligence, not as a Marine. Intelligence estimates had often been massaged to produce the answers the Grand Senate had wanted, not answers that happened to bear more than a passing resemblance to the truth. And there had been far too many intelligence officers ready to alter their reports...which had ensured that military units had dropped into maelstroms because they'd been assured the enemy would break at the first sign the Grand Senate was prepared to use force. Han wouldn't have been such a disaster, he was sure, if the intelligence officers on the spot hadn't kept assuring everyone that there was no risk of an uprising.

And it had coloured his attitude towards Commonwealth Intelligence. The spooks could not be allowed to run amuck, develop their own agenda or start altering data to suit their political masters. But, at the same time, it had ensured that Commonwealth Intelligence was just too small to handle all of its responsibilities...

"Hire more manpower, if you can," he said. It wouldn't be easy. Even now, five years after the war, there was still a shortage of trained manpower. The people Kitty would need were in high demand, while unskilled immigrants couldn't hope to work for Commonwealth Intelligence, even if they could be trusted. "But keep this as quiet as possible. I don't want to spook the spy before it's too late."

"Understood," Kitty said.

Ed glanced at his wristcom. "I have a meeting with Emmanuel Alves in an hour," he said, shortly. It wouldn't be a pleasant meeting. The reporter had been dating Jasmine Yamane before she'd been captured on Thule and he'd asked, every time, if there was word of his girlfriend. "This evening, I want a comprehensive plan for showing false information to part of the council. Let's see what the spy hears, shall we?"

"Yes, sir," Kitty said.

"I want this person identified," Ed added, "but you are not to attempt to arrest him without my permission. We might be able to use this spy to our advantage."

Kitty nodded, doubtfully. "It will be at least six weeks before his intelligence reaches Wolfbane," she said. "The situation will have changed by then."

"I know," Ed said. He smiled, openly. "But I think I have the bare bones of an idea."

ABOUT THE AUTHOR

Christopher Nuttall is the author of 50 books on kindle and 27 books through small presses. He currently moves between Britain and Malaysia with his wife Aisha, his son Eric and a colossal collection of books. Follow his blog or facebook page for updates, special offers, snippets and more.

Website: http://www.chrishanger.net/
Blog: http://chrishanger.wordpress.com/
Facebook Fan Page: https://www.facebook.com/ChristopherGNuttall